THE
BONESHAKER

In her cupped hand she held a model of a bicycle and rider. She could see tiny gears. . . . But try as she might, she could see no place to wind it.

THE BONESHAKER

KATE MILFORD

with illustrations by

ANDREA OFFERMANN

CLARION BOOKS

Houghton Mifflin Harcourt
Boston   New York   2010

CLARION BOOKS
215 Park Avenue South
New York, New York 10003

The illustrations were executed in pen and ink.
The text was set in 11-point Letterpress.
Book designed by Sharismar Rodriguez

The sibyl's dialogue on pp. 142–47 and 304 is taken from
"Mesmeric Revelation" by Edgar Allan Poe.

For information about permission to reproduce selections from this book,
write to Permissions, Houghton Mifflin Harcourt Publishing Company,
215 Park Avenue South, New York, New York 10003.

Clarion Books is an imprint of
Houghton Mifflin Harcourt Publishing Company.

www.hmhbooks.com

Library of Congress Cataloging-in-Publication Data

Milford, Kate.
The Boneshaker / by Kate Milford ; [illustrations by Andrea Offermann].
p. cm.
Summary: When Jake Limberleg brings his traveling medicine show to a small
Missouri town in 1913, thirteen-year-old Natalie senses that something is wrong and,
after investigating, learns that her love of automata and other machines make
her the only one who can set things right.
ISBN 978-0-547-24187-6
[1. Supernatural—Fiction. 2. Automata—Fiction. 3. Bicycles and bicycling—Fiction.
4. Medicine shows—Fiction. 5. Demonology—Fiction. 6. Missouri—History—20th
century—Fiction.] I. Offermann, Andrea, ill. II. Title.

PZ7.M594845Bon 2010
[Fic]—dc22   2009045350

Manufactured in the United States of America
DOC 10 9 8 7 6 5 4 3 2
4500251424

This book is for Mom, Dad, Phil, Buddy, Stephanie,
Tom, Alexa, Jason, Amy, Susie, Walt,
and most of all, for Nathan

CONTENTS

ONE

The Town at the Crossroads

Missouri, 1913

STRANGE THINGS can happen at a crossroads.

It might look like nothing but a place where two dusty roads meet, but a crossroads can be something more. A crossroads can be something special, a compass with arms reaching to places you might never find the way to again; places that might exist, or might have existed once, or might exist someday, depending on whether or not you decide to look for them.

But whatever else it might be, a crossroads is a place where you choose.

The town of Arcane sat very near one such place, a shallow bowl of waving grass and scrubby trees where two highways met alongside the remnants of a dried-up river. On one of those highways you could go all the way from Los Angeles, California, to Washington, D.C. A fellow could leave his home in Baton Rouge, Louisiana, and visit family all the way north in Canada by way of the other. They were well-traveled roads, but there were great stretches of America along them where nothing much had yet been built, so Arcane and the other little towns that had sprung up here and there had hotels and saloons, dry-goods general stores, and water pumps and stables for the travelers passing through.

A hundred years ago, there had been a town there where the roads met, but now it was only a deserted shell of bare foundations and uneasy walls that leaned at odd angles under collapsing roofs. The founders of Arcane had started from scratch a little ways down the east–west road, and the new town had grown up stronger and bigger than the husk they now called the Old Village. But (maybe because of the nearness to that eerie, half-crumbled ghost town) travelers didn't stop off in Arcane for long. Folks bought their cans of gasoline or shoes for their horses or had a wheel replaced, but if they thought they could make it to the *next* town, even if the wheel bumped or the horse limped a little, they would try. People didn't like to stop in Arcane if they could help it, even if they weren't sure why. Even the drifter with the carpetbag and the old tin lantern slung on a pole over his shoulder wasn't likely to linger for more than a meal and a night's rest before starting another long march. Although, with this particular drifter, it would be hard to say for certain.

"My kind of town," he muttered to no one in particular

as he paused where the two roads met to survey the tumble-down remains of a general store. Despite the glaring sun overhead, the lantern glowed dimly through a pattern of holes punched in the sides. It gave a quiet jangle as he turned to watch the progress of a little twist of swirling dust crossing his path.

With his free hand he yanked the felt hat off his head and wiped sweat from his forehead before shucking out of his long leather coat. He pulled a watch from his pocket—a rather nicer watch than one would expect a drifter to carry—and flipped it open. He glanced down the eastbound road, away from the town of Arcane, and made a noise of impatience before adjusting the carpetbag and the lantern and continuing on. He had a roustabout's lean muscle, and although life on the road usually put years on a man quicker than life in town, under the sweat and smudges of dirt his face looked young. Only his eyes, light green like old glass and lined with wrinkles from squinting against the sun, gave any impression of age.

The drifter smiled as he strode toward Arcane, but the smile was odd and awkward, and even he walked a little faster on his way out of the Old Village than he had on the way in.

The people who lived in Arcane were just like anyone else. They went to work, kept kitchen gardens and cats and dogs, and had jobs and children and houses with broken screen doors or squeaky porch steps. The children waited all year for summer holidays, then for winter holidays and presents, then for summer again. There were bullies and victims, rich kids and poor ones, like there are anywhere.

But strange things can happen at a crossroads, and even if you were a perfectly normal child in a crossroads town you'd grow up hearing stories, maybe even see one of those odd happenings yourself. For instance, by the time she was thirteen years old Natalie Minks knew all those strange stories by heart. She knew the one about how the Old Village became an abandoned shell, and all the tales of that ancient forest to the southwest of Arcane, in which strange things had walked long ago. She even knew why Mrs. Corusk, who kept a little farm at the north edge of town, insisted on living by candlelight when most everybody else had had electricity since before Natalie was born.

It was hard sometimes to tell which stories were true and which ones weren't, but if Natalie was sure of anything, it was that in Arcane, you couldn't be sure of anything at all.

Except maybe my family, Natalie thought as her father slammed his finger in the big barn doors the way he always did when he came into his shop. Her family never seemed to change.

"Found it," he announced, waving a wrench over his head with his uninjured hand.

Natalie reached for a bicycle tire hanging on the wall and used it to pull herself up onto one of his workbenches. "How far's the trip?"

"About a hundred and ten miles." Her father sucked in a breath. "Natalie, be—"

A socket wrench on the bench launched itself from under her foot and skittered across the floor—no wonder her dad was always tripping over things in here. Natalie grabbed the tire again to keep from stepping on her father's collection of radio parts, only to have it spring away from the wall in her hand. Her arms windmilled.

Her father sprinted to catch her and took the most obstacle-laden route to do it, filling the shop with unmistakable sounds of destruction. Natalie caught her balance just in time to keep from landing on her backside on the shop floor, trampling any radio tubes, or, worse, stepping on the little clockwork flyer she and her father were building together.

"Careful," she said as her father skidded uselessly to a halt beside where she stood on the workbench. "I know."

He gave her a severe look and picked his way back across the shop to return to what he'd been working on.

She wouldn't have cared much about a bruise, but the flyer, which she and her dad called the *Wilbur* after the Wright brother who'd died only last year, was a mechanical labor of love. It was an automaton (the word itself was one of Natalie's newest and most favorite acquisitions), a small machine that would eventually move on its own when wound with a key. She set it aside gently, careful not to upset the gears inside it that controlled the tiny propellers and wings.

On tiptoe she could just see out the little window high on the wall above the workbench. She wiped a few years' worth of grime off the glass and stared at the crowd on the street. Of course, they were trying not to look like a crowd, but on any other Wednesday morning, half the town of

Arcane would've had better things to do than try to look busy outside Minks's Bicycle Shop.

"You got an audience." Natalie stretched a little farther and saw a clutch of boys from school playing half-heartedly with a board balanced on a big tin can. A few girls nearby pretended to watch them. It was the first day of the summer holiday. For sure the kids had better things to do. "A big audience," Natalie said smugly.

A noise like a circus animal passing gas erupted from the hulk of machinery crouching at the center of the shop. It didn't sound healthy.

"Dad?"

Only her dad's lower half was visible; the top half was hidden in the boxy front of the machine. Natalie waited patiently until the thing was puttering rhythmically and asked again, louder, "*Dad*. It's going to run, *right?*"

"Sure." His voice sounded like it was coming from inside a tin can. When he emerged he gave her a sooty smile. "It'll work. I promise."

When Natalie ventured outside an hour later, the crowd on the street had doubled in size. No point in trying to melt into it; they were all watching her. She climbed up to sit on the edge of a rain barrel and nonchalantly shined an apple on her overalls.

The first person to give up pretending he wasn't waiting for the big barn doors of Ted Minks's shop to open was a kid called George Sills. He sauntered over and gave Natalie a gap-toothed sneer. "My dad says Doc Fitzwater's motorcar couldn't make it across town, let alone all the way to Pinnacle."

Natalie chewed her apple and made a point of watching Old Tom Guyot shuffle across the street with his crutch and tin guitar instead of acknowledging George Sills. Tom was more interesting anyway.

George was fourteen and didn't like being ignored. He kicked the barrel she was sitting on hard enough to make Natalie grab the rim for balance. She gave him a withering glare.

"It's not just a *motorcar*, it's a *Winton*." A lot of motorcars came through Arcane, and they weren't all the same. There were little runabouts and bigger touring cars, Stanhope-style and high-wheeler-style autos. Some of the older ones had tillers to steer with; the newer ones had steering wheels. Most had radiators to keep their engines cooled with water (although Natalie had seen a Franklin once that was air-cooled and looked a little odd without a big radiator sticking up in front). Doc's car, like most of them, had to be wound with a crank to start up, but the new Cadillacs started electrically, and they came with electric lamps.

Natalie had seen nearly all the Fords, except the Model A, and could even tell the difference between the N, S, and T models. She had seen a few kinds of Bakers, a Moon, and a Speedwell—even a Fiat from Italy and an Oldsmobile Limited limousine earlier this year. *That* was a pretty motorcar. The Winton, though . . . the Winton was *beautiful*.

But explaining the difference to George Sills would be like trying to teach the alphabet to a puppy.

"Who cares what kind it is? It's ten years old! Dad says Doc could drive it over to the soda fountain, maybe, but only 'cause it's downhill all the way."

"Sure, if it was up to your dad. If it was up to *your* dad, Doc's motorcar wouldn't make it ten feet." Natalie spat a seed to the ground. "*Your* dad couldn't change a bicycle tire."

George's hands curled instantly into fists. Natalie jumped down, shoved her bangs out of her face, and brought up her knuckles the way Jack Johnson did in boxing pictures. If George was stupid enough to try anything in front of the whole town, she'd abandon all scruples and go straight for the knee he was still favoring after their last fight, her third—no, fourth—thrashing from George this month.

But before either of them could make a move at the other, the lumpy head of an alligator landed on George Sills's shoulder. He took one look, made a sound like a creaky window being shoved up, and jumped back about four feet.

The leathery shrunken head was little, brown, and attached to the end of a cane in the hand of a man as tall and thin and pale as a birch tree. His white hair stood up in windblown shocks all over his head, and his face had more lines than space between. "I'll have you know a fellow drove a motorcar like mine all the way from California to New York before there were proper roads across the country, Master Sills."

"Hi, Dr. Fitzwater." George tried to look as though he hadn't just screamed like a little girl.

Doc wore a monocle in one eye. The look he gave George through the little gold-rimmed lens made the boy turn tail and flee across the street. Then he took the monocle out and began to shine it with his handkerchief. The look he gave Natalie without it was much kinder.

"I understand you were in charge of polishing, Miss Minks. I expect the old beast will blind us all when it comes into the sun." His voice didn't match his creased and pitted face. It was more like the way new tires ran over smooth dirt roads: a steady, low sound like a purr. She opened her mouth to tell Doc how pretty the motorcar looked now, but the metallic whine of rusty hinges interrupted her. Every head in the street turned.

The shop doors were opening.

Ted Minks, sooty-faced and grinning, appeared in the dark gap between the big barn doors. He pushed one wide, then the other, and disappeared back into the shadows. A moment later, the broad nose of the Winton emerged.

It was a dark red motorcar with two high, tufted leather seats open to the air, and wheels with spokes, just like bicycle tires. Two of its headlamps were like eyes set back on either side, wide like a frog's, and the third was a single, Cyclopean eyeball in a brass casing, fixed right to the middle of the radiator. It had a steering wheel stuck up in front of the seat on the right-hand side. The brass fittings and trim that Natalie had polished so obsessively glowed.

She caught George Sills's eye across the street and stuck out her tongue.

"Hey, Doc!" her father called, wiping the sweat off his forehead and leaving broad, grimy fingerprints there instead. "How about a drive?"

Doc made a show of considering. "Wouldn't want to disappoint all the good folks who happened by to see me off."

"Guess we'd better see if your car works after all." Mr. Minks spotted Natalie leaning on her barrel. "Mind giving me a little help, Nattie?"

Mind? She was in the driver's seat almost before he finished talking, fingers wrapped securely around the wheel, just in case.

Her father turned the crank with both hands. "Ready?"

"Ready!"

It sputtered to life, just as he promised it would, and the street around them erupted into applause.

"Listen to the old beast growl." Doc Fitzwater put a gnarled palm on the steering wheel. "I can't believe you did all this in just three days." Natalie resisted the urge to smirk at George again. Anyway, her dad could've fixed the Winton up even faster if he'd wanted to. She had spent more time pestering him to let her help than he'd spent on the motorcar itself, until the three of them—Natalie, her brother, Charlie, and her father—had had to work through the night to get it ready for today.

Now Doc turned to Mr. Minks and spoke quietly, his back to the crowd. "I'm going as far as the Pearys' farm today, then by tomorrow afternoon I'll be in Pinnacle and you can ring the central exchange if you need me. Maybe sooner, if Maggie Peary doesn't insist on having a giant brunch before I leave." Natalie's father nodded, smiled tightly, and held out his hand to shake Doc's. "Nothing to worry about," Doc said.

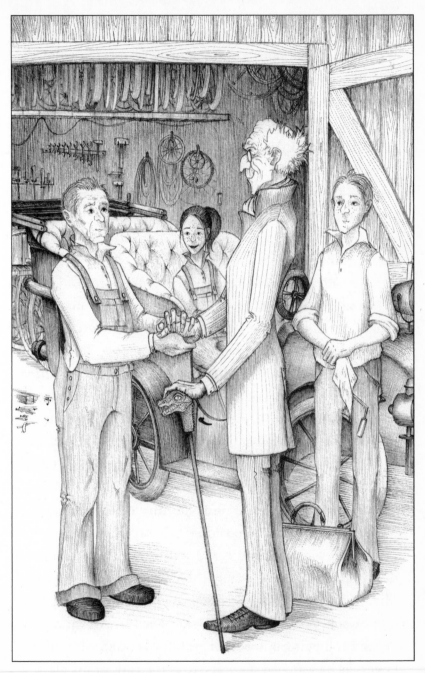

It was a dark red motorcar with two high, tufted leather seats open
to the air, and wheels with spokes, just like bicycle tires.

Natalie climbed reluctantly out of the driver's seat while Charlie put Doc's old Gladstone medical bag and his pebbly leather suitcase in the back of the motorcar. Doc turned to face the people on the street and shouted over the puttering engine.

"If I didn't know better, I'd think you all came out for the old Winton, not for me." He climbed into the seat and propped up his alligator-head cane beside him. "As soon as the epidemic in Pinnacle's under control, I'll chug straight back. In the meantime, Lester's ready to step in if anyone gets a headache while I'm gone."

Actually, red-faced Lester Finch looked pretty nervous to Natalie as he waved from the doorway of the pharmacy a little ways down the street. Then again, when had she seen him looking any other way?

Natalie looked around at the assembled town. There was her little gang of friends, a pair of boys and one prissy-looking girl; there was George Sills, giving them all the evil eye; her teacher, Miss Tillerman; Mr. Maliverny, who ran the saloon; and a drifter with a carpetbag and an old lantern at his feet. The drifter had the delighted look of a kid who'd stumbled on a sporting event. He caught Natalie's glance and winked one pale green eye.

There was Mr. Swifte, the smith from Ogle's stables; the woman Natalie privately thought of as the town hag, Mrs. Byron, who was (as usual) scowling disapprovingly at her; Simon Coffrett, the man who lived in Arcane's only mansion, flipping his pocket watch over and over in his fingers as he watched the scene over the rims of his glasses;

and tiny, bent, old Chester Teufels in his shabby, thread-bare suit being studiously ignored by everyone around him as he stood in an unobtrusive corner chewing on a finger-nail. Nothing out of the ordinary here.

Her gaze passed over all the excited or doubtful or curious folks watching Doc and his motorcar until her eyes fell on Old Tom Guyot's face, black and craggy and sharp-planed as a nugget of coal, and his ancient tin guitar slung over one shoulder.

Old Tom was watching her.

Natalie tilted her head. Was that so odd? After all, a minute ago she'd been the center of attention, sitting up in the driver's seat. But Tom wasn't just looking at her, he was *watching* her. All the while his head nodded slightly, as if to say *Yes, you're right; yes* . . .

She looked away quickly, blushing a little as if she'd been the one caught staring. Her gaze landed on Simon Coffrett, and she flinched. There was no mistaking it.

Mr. Coffrett was watching her, too.

It came out of nowhere—one minute she was just another part of the excitement of Doc's departure, the next she was part of something else entirely. Something was happening here that had nothing to do with Doc's motorcar. Something was happening here that she didn't understand.

Or something was *going to happen* . . .

A grinding pop drew her attention: Doc releasing the brake. Once again Natalie was just a thirteen-year-old girl standing with her curious neighbors, watching an old man drive an old motorcar out of town on an ordinary June morning.

They followed him down Bard Street, the main road through Arcane, then watched him go as far as the crossroads, where he became a dark little speck heading east. Soon he was out of sight.

"What's an epidemic?"

The moment it was out, Natalie wished she hadn't asked. Annie Minks always took questions seriously, which meant you had to be careful what you asked, and when. The kitchen was smoky already, and her mother didn't need anybody's help to burn another batch of pancakes. She turned away from the stovetop with the eager look she got when she was about to explain something. Natalie sighed.

"It's when a lot of people get sick with the same thing at the same time. Like the black plague, or smallpox, or influenza." Behind her, a plume of gray collected over the griddle.

"Like what's happening in Pinnacle?" Natalie asked, staring at the stovetop. The pancakes had smelled good for a minute, too. "Mama . . . ?"

Her mother opened her mouth to answer, then sniffed the air and remembered she was cooking. Natalie propped her chin up with her fist, elbow resting on the table, and watched Mrs. Minks turn the pancakes one by one to reveal their burned black bellies.

People said Natalie and her mother looked alike. It was hard to tell at thirteen, though; her mother was tall and liked brightly colored lawn dresses and shoes with heels, and her hair seemed perfectly happy all twisted up at the back of her head the way she had it right now. She had a compact of face powder that smelled like sunlight and a string of pearls that had belonged to Natalie's grandmother, which Natalie had worn exactly once, in a school play. She was, Natalie thought it was fair to say, beautiful.

Natalie wore dresses under protest. Overalls were much more convenient, and her favorite shoes were a pair long outgrown by her brother. Her hair mostly stayed in a ponytail nowadays, but a few pieces still insisted on coming loose (although those bits were growing out pretty well, considering how short she'd had to cut them a few months back—there had been an incident at school with some glue that she was pretty sure was George Sills's doing).

On the other hand, Natalie's disorderly hair was just about the same shade of nearly-black as her mother's, and her eyes were almost the same color, too: light brown, the color of coffee made just the way her mother liked, with a slosh of cream and a homemade sugar cube and a tablespoon of rum. Usually, starting about May, they even got the same wildly multiplying batch of freckles across their noses, which they would compare at the end of each sunny day, looking for any new matching spots. This year, though, Natalie's freckles were even more profuse than usual—lately her mother's face looked downright pale by comparison.

Mrs. Minks scraped the blackened pancakes into a pail with the rest of the spoiled ones and poured fresh batter on the griddle. "In Pinnacle they just have a persistent sort of flu, but it's got a lot of people sick."

Natalie decided to keep quiet until at least one batch

made it safely onto a plate; her stomach was grumbling and the kitchen was getting hot. Then she remembered something. "Mr. Finch looked worried when Doc left."

Her mother's shoulders did something funny, as if she'd felt a sudden draft.

"Well . . . people will be expecting Mr. Finch to fill Doc's shoes while he's gone. I'm sure that's upsetting . . . to him."

"But Mr. Finch knows how to give out medicines and take care of people, doesn't he?"

"Yes, but it's not the same as having Doc." Her voice did something chilly, similar to what her shoulders had done a moment before. "It's . . . not the same."

Not the same? Not much of an answer by anybody's standards, let alone her mother's. Still, it looked like this might be the one: the batch that survived. Natalie bit her lips to keep quiet while the edges of the pancakes set. Two more minutes. Maybe less . . .

Then her father and Charlie came in, smelling like the rough soap they used to get the oil and grime of the bicycle shop off.

"You didn't need to cook," Natalie's father said. Mrs. Minks turned and hugged her husband tightly. It looked like the end of the pancakes' last chance for survival, until Charlie took the spatula out of her thin hand and removed them from the skillet himself.

"What happens," Natalie asked when all four of them were seated with breakfast safely on the table, "if people start getting sick here?"

"Mr. Finch will take care of it," Charlie said.

"Mama says it's not the same."

Their mother looked at her plate. "Mr. Finch is fine."

"But that's not what you *said*."

For a moment there was quiet around the table. "I'm sure Lester Finch won't think twice about wiring a message to Doc in Pinnacle," Natalie's father said, looking at his wife.

"Just send a *wire?*" Natalie demanded. "That's *all?* But what if it's the Pinnacle flu? How would we *know?*"

"Mr. Finch could tell if the flu from Pinnacle showed up here," Charlie put in. Natalie shot him a *Shut up, will you?* look. Since when did her brother know anything about flus?

Flus, epidemics, persistent strange ailments, and know-it-all big brothers . . . she emerged from her thoughts just in time to hear her father say, "I bet I know how Natalie's going to spend the first day of the summer."

"Can we work on my automaton? I found a piece that only fits when it's backwards, so the, the *cam* doesn't—"

"I think I need a day away from gears, Nattie. Besides," he said with a smile, "don't you have something to show off to Miranda and the rest of your gang?"

He looked so proud.

"Oh, yeah. I guess I forgot." She dropped her chin back onto her fist and drew circles in the maple syrup on her plate with her fork.

While Natalie fidgeted at her kitchen table and Doc Fitzwater made his steady, chugging way out of town, another crowd in another dusty village watched a little caravan prepare for a different departure.

At the reins of the wagon in front, a tall man in blue-lensed spectacles stood and waved, smiling a showman's smile that did not reach his eyes. The hands that held the reins wore expensive leather gloves in a pearly pale ivory shade. A silk top hat sat on the seat beside him, and his mane of red hair shot through with gray shone in the sun. It waved about a touch more than it seemed it ought to in the soft breeze.

He sat with a whirl of dark cloak and flicked his wrists. The wagon lurched into motion, the first in a train of more old and peeling wagons drawn by mottled mules. The procession left a rattle of glass and the faint carnival smell of fresh hay, frying grease, and spun candy in its wake.

The caravan turned westward, toward Arcane.

TWO

The World's Fastest Bicycle

NATALIE'S LIFE was a mess of gears and yarns. If you looked closely, however (the way she loved to look at a mechanical device or a story), the tangle resolved itself into a perfectly crafted mechanism. All the parts were made to work together. In the same way that Natalie could tell when she was looking at a well-built machine, she knew her life was pretty good. Everything just fit.

Arcane, however, was different. The more complex a machine got and the more parts it contained, the more places there were where gears could fail to mesh. A town was like that. Sometimes it just didn't seem to work quite as smoothly as it did at other times, especially when the oil that eased the cogs' meshing ran out.

Like now, for instance. It was barely past suppertime; Doc hadn't even been gone a whole day, and already the town's cogs were starting to stick. It was in the air—something strange and hard to pin down. Natalie paused outside Lester Finch's pharmacy. Inside, despite the late hour, Mr. Finch still had customers lined up at the counter. She leaned her bright red enameled bicycle against her side and considered the shopfront.

"Don't you think there's got to be something odd going on out there in Pinnacle if Doc has to go and clean house for them?" Natalie wondered. "What's the matter with their doctor?"

"I don't know." Miranda Porter twisted a finger disinterestedly in one blond curl and half-shrugged. Then she put her hands on her hips and gave Natalie a critical look. "You're wearing that silly thing *again?*"

Natalie frowned and made an effort not to feel for the tiny brass sprocket she wore like a charm on a string around her neck. Just because Miranda couldn't think of anything better to talk about than necklaces didn't mean Natalie was going to sink to that level.

"Pay attention." Natalie jerked her head toward the pharmacy. "It's probably some awful kind of deadly sickness, like the Black Plague."

Anybody else would've picked up the cue, hissed in horror, and joined the game with another ghastly suggestion as to what was going on in the next town over, as gruesome and vile as possible. It would've made Natalie feel better, for sure—just a little bit of normal behavior, for goodness' sake; was that too much to ask? Miranda had been really good at those kinds of games once, but lately she seemed to find them beneath her. Natalie had given up trying to figure it out.

Now, predictably, Miranda just shrugged again. "Who cares? Pinnacle's practically in another state."

Hopeless *and* lacking factual information: an unforgivable combination. "It isn't. It's a hundred and ten miles," Natalie snapped.

"Who *cares?*" Miranda folded her arms bossily over her chest. Her eyes flicked around—looking to see if anybody was watching, probably. "When are you going to let me ride your bicycle?"

Natalie stopped dead in her tracks, strange ailments forgotten. "Why would you want to ride my bicycle?" she demanded. "Who are you trying to impress?"

Miranda's mouth squeezed itself into a tight little line. "Nobody."

"I bet it's Alfred Tate." Amazing. Miranda turned the same pink as her dress.

"*Shut your*—"

"Thought so." Natalie laughed. "Miranda, you can't ride it. You'll get your dress caught in the springs."

Miranda plunked her hands on her hips. "I will not."

Natalie propped the item in question carefully against a hitching post and regarded Miranda's pink calico dress so skeptically that her friend looked down to see if she had put on something absurd like an old-fashioned hoop skirt without noticing it. "I'm looking out for you, Miranda, that's all. Don't want Alfred Tate to see your dress tear straight off 'cause it's caught up, do you?"

Miranda glanced around before she could help herself. *"He's not here!"*

"So it's okay for everybody else to see your bloomers?"

"All right, then, *you* ride it."

Natalie's heart sank.

"If it's really the fastest bicycle in the world, show me." Pink hands on her pink hips, pink face draining to an angry white, Miranda tapped her foot, raising little puffs of dry dirt around her ankles.

Natalie decided to tough it out. "No."

"Because it probably isn't, and you don't want anyone to find out."

"Because it's late. Because you're pestering me, and I don't feel like it." *Anything* to stop this conversation . . . Natalie grabbed the bicycle's handlebars and stalked away. Miranda got the point—for once—and didn't try to keep up.

"How do you *know* it's the fastest bicycle in the world? You don't know that."

"I helped my dad build it! I know what it's made of!"

"Yeah," Miranda yelled after her, "it's made of bicycle parts, like any other bicycle! That's all!"

Natalie stopped again and whirled on Miranda. "Like any other . . . ?" People were so stupid. You only had to *look* at the bicycle to see that it was special. The frame alone was a work of art, and the rest of it was made of parts from the best bicycles there were, each piece picked out specially by her father to build Natalie the fastest, most perfect, most beautiful bicycle in all of Missouri, if not the entire world. It was unquestionably one of a kind.

It was just Natalie's size, and the whole frame, enameled in her favorite shade of red, was etched with a pattern of whorls and curlicues. It had a varnished wicker basket attached to the back (instead of the front, where it might've slowed the bicycle down), and the basket had a leather strap with a new brass buckle so that no matter how fast she rode and no matter how bumpy the street, Natalie's belongings would stay safely inside. Best of all, her father had sent away to Dayton, Ohio, for an actual Wright Cycle Company nameplate from back when the Wright brothers were still building bicycles, a little oval badge with a pointy top and bottom that now gleamed at the front of the handlebar stem.

If Miranda Porter in her *ignorance* couldn't see that it was the best bicycle in the country, well then, after thirteen years of life she at least ought to understand it was better than anything she, Miranda, had ever seen. Or probably ever would.

As for fast . . . Natalie had asked her father for the fastest bicycle he could build, and he had built her this one. Nobody, but *nobody*, was better at bicycles than Ted Minks, so the fastest bicycle from Natalie's father clearly had to be the fastest there was.

In the world. Ever. It was just good logic.

Maybe Miranda was just that big an idiot, and she simply tried harder to hide it when the boys were around. You couldn't talk to an idiot about all the extra springs in the frame that would let Natalie fly over rough roads, the beveled gears or the very special tires that wouldn't skid, the motorcycle pedals or the chrome-plated electric light between the handlebars that had been ordered from Chicago. It would be like trying to explain the Winton motorcar to George Sills.

"It's *old*," Miranda protested. "How could anything so old be fast? That just doesn't make any *sense*."

Natalie glared. "If you're talking about the frame, Miranda, it's not old."

"Well, antique, I guess I should've said, but that just means old, Natalie," Miranda said with a meanly sympathetic smile. "Why couldn't your dad find you something newer? I mean, if he was going to build you a bicycle in the first place?"

This was hopeless—an absolutely hopeless endeavor. Natalie settled for yelling, "You don't know anything!" and breaking into a run alongside the bicycle.

"You can't prove it!" Miranda's voice dripped victory. Natalie's face burned. "I bet it's *slo-ow*," Miranda bawled, "the slowest, oldest, most rickety thing there is! You won't ride it because then everyone would see and *know!*"

The world took on the same red as the bicycle, and the guilt that had been eating away at Natalie's stomach since breakfast started to boil. Tears hit her cheeks and dripped down into the dust under the tires. She kept running until she could turn a corner and get off Bard Street. When she was safely out of sight, she propped the bicycle carefully, lovingly against a wall. Then she sat hard, dropped her head onto her knees, and sobbed.

"I'm sorry, Dad," she said into her tear-wet overalls. She couldn't prove Miranda wrong, not even to defend her father, the most brilliant mechanic in Arcane (and Missouri, and America, and the world). If she had been able to hop on and pedal with every ounce of energy she had, Miranda would have had to take back all those awful things she'd just said. But that was impossible.

Natalie Minks, the girl with the world's fastest bicycle, couldn't ride it.

After a few minutes, she wiped her face dry on her shirt and got up. If Miranda saw this display, she'd think she was right.

Parallel to Bard Street, between the livery stable where Doc had kept his motorcar for years and the smithy behind it where Mr. Swifte, the blacksmith, lived and worked, a little alley called Smith Lane stretched, just wide enough for three people to walk side by side. Now Natalie walked the bicycle with as much poise as she could muster around the livery stable to the alley, swung her leg over the crossbar, and put a foot on one pedal.

The particularly marvelous thing about a bicycle (or an automaton, or a Winton motorcar, or any mechanical thing at all, really), was the way that it was made up of lots of pieces doing specific jobs. The insides of Natalie's flyer, for instance, were a beautiful puzzle, a jumble of parts. Once she put the puzzle together, those parts would work together at last and the flyer would do what she had built it to do.

Once you could see how all the pieces fit together and understand what their special jobs were, you could understand the machine. For Natalie, that was enough to make mechanical things beautiful, especially in the moment when suddenly, after staring at a puzzle of cams and cogs and wheels, it all came together and made sense.

Except for this exceedingly simple machine in her hands.

"Just like riding any other bicycle," she said softly, and kicked off.

One foot off the ground, and then the other . . . but the bicycle was already tilting . . . She flung her body the other way—too hard!—and put out her hand to keep from falling into the stable wall. Her palm whacked the rough boards and slid down along with the rest of her as the wheels shot out sideways.

She bit down to keep from crying out as her leg twisted painfully under the frame. Her palm burned; there would be splinters to soak out later. She shook her hand a few times and hopped to her feet, then got back on the bicycle. This time she kicked off too hard, so the pedals spun and she couldn't get her feet on them. After a minute she lost her balance and fell again.

The third time, she glanced down to put her feet squarely on the spinning pedals, leaned too far to the right, and steered straight into the stable wall. Unbelievable. The thing had a mind of its own.

The problem, of course, was that riding the red bicycle wasn't like riding any other bicycle. Not by a long shot.

Mr. Minks had bought it in Kansas City the year before from a shop that was going out of business, along with a whole tangle of frames and tires and pedals and gears. The second Natalie saw it, she had begged him to fix it up for her. Even filthy from sitting for decades in someone's shop, its heavy old metal wheels rusting and bent out of true and all its crimson enamel and etchings coated in grime, it was beautiful. And different.

It had a down-turned set of handlebars with rosewood grips. Its wheels were bigger than Natalie was used to, and they were less than six inches apart, which was a lot closer together than was normal on newer cycles. The one in the front was bigger by a little bit than the one in the back, too. Instead of a seat on a vertical saddle post, this bicycle's seat was positioned on a nearly horizontal bar that sloped from the steering column to a spring over the rear tire (just one of a collection of springs supporting it in various odd places). It had a longer front fender than any other bicycle she'd seen, and the fender had two little hooks on either side of it that were meant to hold the rider's feet when he or she wanted to coast without pedaling. That should've been the big tip-off that this was going to be a difficult bicycle, but even that wasn't its weirdest (and most interesting) feature.

Below the triangle that held the seat and connected the steering column to the fork of the rear wheel, another set of tubes completed the frame: a diamond cut in half by a vertical piece that formed a hinge between the front part and the back. The red enameled frame was built so that it could actually *pivot* at the middle.

"I don't know, Nattie," her father had said, looking critically at it. "I don't think this is the best choice for you. I have a feeling whatever I do to it, any bicycle built on this frame is going to ride like a boneshaker."

Natalie groaned. She'd ridden a boneshaker before, or at least she'd *tried* to ride it: Mr. Minks still had his father's Michaux velocipede somewhere in the shop, and if you could get going on it (which was a very big if), it rattled and shook you even on the smoothest roads till your teeth fairly chattered in your skull. Instead of tires with air in them, boneshakers had wooden or metal wheels, so every bump on the road went straight from the wheels to the frame to the rider.

"But what if we put better tires on it?" she protested, looking wistfully at the upward curl of the front fender. It would be such a pretty machine if it was fixed up. "And what about all the springs? Won't the springs help it ride better?"

"I think they're there to compensate for a bad design," Mr. Minks said, scowling at the springs in question. "In fact, I don't remember ever seeing a frame so over-designed before."

"What about the hinge in the middle? Didn't you say that was to help it steer and turn better?"

"Well, that's the idea, but . . . but I'll tell you what. We'll fix it up with the best parts we can find. I'll do my best to make it smooth and fast. Then you can decide how you like it."

He'd finished the red bicycle when he was supposed to

be working on Doc Fitzwater's car, and it was everything Natalie had believed it would be. But sure enough, despite its supporting springs and brand-new tires, it bounced along like a century-old boneshaker. And the pedals were in a weird place. *And* it was geared funny, so that each cycle of the pedals turned the front wheel, the one that drove the bicycle, in two complete revolutions. This was one of the tricks her father had used to make it faster, but it was messing up Natalie's best running starts. And worst of all, it turned out, was that pivoting hinge in the middle. It meant the bicycle responded to the slightest angle, the slightest lean. It meant Natalie had to totally relearn how to balance and steer, and it meant she ran into things a lot.

She loved it, nonetheless—all she had to do was figure out how to ride it before her father found out how much trouble it was giving her. But something about this bicycle—this weirdly perfect, beautiful bicycle—was impossible to control. It seemed to *want* to fight her, and for some reason, it always won.

After attempt number ten (in which, during a particularly fast running start, her pant leg got caught on one of those hooks on the front wheel as she was trying to hold her feet out of the way of the whirling pedals), Natalie decided she'd had enough. No way was Ted Minks's daughter going to fail to ride any bicycle, not with nearly a decade of prime bicycle-riding experience under her belt. Today, however, the bicycle won. Again.

She heard the music as she limped out of the alley. Back on Bard Street, Old Tom Guyot sat on the ground

Something about this bicycle—this weirdly perfect,
beautiful bicycle—was impossible to control.

with his back against the front of the livery stable, legs stretched out in front of him and his tin guitar on his lap. The round brass resonator set into the middle of the instrument caught the reddening light and shone like a setting sun all by itself.

Old Tom spoke without looking at her. "Y'all right there, darlin'?" His words came out just a little muffled by the flattened crown cap he held between his teeth.

Natalie felt a flush hot as a midsummer sunburn sweep over her face, but she was too tired and sore to run away from him the way she'd fled Miranda.

"Did . . . you see?" Was her voice always that small?

"Can't see much of anything with that old sun comin' down right in my eyes. I heard something like a . . ."

Natalie held her breath. *Don't say fall. . . .*

Instead, the long-nailed fingers of his right hand halted their nimble plucking and scrabbled in the guitar strings, fumbling a little as her feet had fumbled for the pedals, and then he struck the flat front of the guitar with his palm. The noise was exactly like Natalie falling elaborately off her bicycle, kicking a few spokes on the way down, and finishing with a swinging handlebar whacking the ground before bouncing back to hit her in the head. The sounds he made were so strange and improbable and fascinating that she hardly minded that they were mimicking one of her humiliating spills.

"How do you . . . do that?"

Tom slid his left hand up the neck of the guitar. On that hand, the fingernails were short and neatly trimmed, and on one finger he wore a piece of brown glass like a finger-length ring that he slid along the strings. The instrument wailed like an opera singer on a Victrola record.

"Lots of voices in a guitar." He let the operatic note hold for a moment, then started back into the song he'd been playing when she'd first come out of the alley, pausing only to take the flattened cap from between his teeth to use for a guitar pick. After a little while, he closed his eyes and started humming along.

The memory of her battles with her bicycle faded; the sounds of horses in the stable and buggies in the street dissolved. Tom's humming turned into strange syllables, sounds that weren't words but sort of *broken pieces* of words, bits and bobs of song dodging and darting over and around and under the music of the guitar, rising and falling and ducking, and every once in a while climbing sharp and clear and plaintive. . . .

Tom's teeth flashed bright against his dark skin. Lines came and went between his eyes and on his forehead, and the corners of his mouth twisted into smiles and scowls to make room for those pieces of words to escape. Sometimes he would stop singing and slap the side of his hand against the strings or his palm against the tin front of the guitar as if it were a drum, nodding his head along and then picking right up where he'd left off.

It made a strange tableau, and plenty of people paused to look: the old black man singing blissfully with the guitar flashing sunset colors on his knees; and the sweaty, bruised, and scraped girl, unmoving and rapt, absently holding on to a bizarre bicycle with her head cocked like a bird's. Neither of them noticed anyone else's stares.

I know something about Old Tom. The thought had barely taken shape in Natalie's consciousness when his voice launched into a string of syllables bursting with *Z*s and *B*s and she forgot to think about what that something was.

Inevitably, the song came to an end. Tom's eyes opened at last, and he smiled at Natalie. What was it, that extraordinary thing about Old Tom Guyot?

As she stood there thinking, trying to remember something just out of reach, it hit her again, harder this time: the sense of something happening, or something poised to happen, perhaps; something she could sense but not put a finger on. Something strange in her already odd little town that she could feel to the marrow of her bones, and that made goose bumps come springing up on her arms.

A sudden motion of Tom's hands made a piece of metal near the top of the neck of the guitar catch a flare of sunlight. And then, with a dizzy, lurching sensation that started at the back of her throat and flowed upward so that for just the briefest second her whole head spun, two things popped into Natalie's head. The first was a crystal-clear image of Old Tom Guyot, sitting beside a fire at the crossroads outside of town, hammering something round and gold-colored into the folded piece of metal that now held up the strings of his guitar. The second thing was what she had been trying to remember while Tom and his guitar sang with their peculiar voices. Two words: *the Devil*.

Natalie muttered something about home and dinner,

grabbed the bicycle's handlebars, and ran, so hard and so blindly that she almost sprinted straight into the side of a passing carriage. The carriage horse shied sideways, stamping in annoyance, and Natalie turned to call out an apology to the driver. As she glanced back, she noticed something strange.

Tom had tucked his crown cap pick between his teeth and begun playing again, only this song was sadder, softer, remorseful. Or reproachful, perhaps. He wasn't looking at Natalie anymore. She followed his eyes to the saloon across the street at the corner of Bard and Sanctuary. On the porch, Mr. Maliverny the saloonkeeper was pouring tea from a cracked pot into a china cup on the table in front of Simon Coffrett. Behind the lenses of his spectacles, Mr. Coffrett's eyes were on Tom. Then, when Mr. Maliverny didn't move away after he had finished pouring, Simon looked at the saloonkeeper.

There it was again. Natalie, frozen over her bicycle, felt something tighten in her throat, a moment of dizziness at the root of her tongue. Once, her mother had told her of how, as a little girl, she'd suffered from vertigo, which had sounded a lot like the way this felt. The world twitched, and instead of one Simon Coffrett she saw him separate into multiple specters that danced neatly around the first, like photographic negatives without shadows. Natalie shut her eyes and pressed on her eyelids. Only once before, when she'd been hit by a baseball, had Natalie's vision ever done anything like that.

Thud.

When she opened her eyes, she was flat in the street, the bicycle lying in the dirt beside her. Natalie pushed herself up, rubbing her head. Puffs of dust settled around her. It felt as if she'd fallen straight back onto her tailbone, hard.

From opposite sides of the street, Tom Guyot and Simon Coffrett were coming toward her, concern on both their faces. The specters that had moved around Simon were gone.

Face burning, Natalie scrambled to her feet on her own, righted the bicycle, and ran away without looking back.

The last of the sun cast long purple shadows, painting a stretched-out, abnormally tall skeleton of wheels and frame on the road as Natalie arrived home. The bicycle, of course, was perfectly fine; she herself was a mess, and she could not get those two words out of her head. *The Devil.*

She found her mother already in bed upstairs, reading *Harper's Magazine* and listening to Enrico Caruso on the Victrola.

"What on earth were you up to?" Mrs. Minks demanded. Natalie submitted to a thorough examination of barked elbows and shins. "Not another fight?"

"No. Just had a bumpy ride. Is it that late?"

"Not since there's no school tomorrow. Natalie, these scrapes are filthy!" She pushed back the covers with a sigh. "Go get some water."

Natalie scrambled down the stairs ahead of her mother, grabbed a pitcher from the kitchen, and walked outside to the pump by the vegetable garden.

Inside, her mother chipped ice from the block in the icebox into a bowl. "You're sure this wasn't a fight, Nattie?" she demanded when Natalie returned with the pitcher. Mrs. Minks carried the bowl to the table, dropped into the nearest chair, and wiped her forehead with the back of her hand. "I mean to say, *absolutely* sure?"

"Positive." Which wasn't entirely true, but Natalie was fairly certain her mother wasn't talking about fights with inanimate objects. She dunked a towel in the water and scrubbed at the scrapes until she thought they might pass for clean. "How's that?"

"Passable." Mrs. Minks twisted the ice up in another towel and handed it across the table. "That goes on your leg before that goose egg gets any bigger." She rose and rummaged in a cabinet for a tube of ointment.

"Are you going back to bed, Mama? You look tired."

"I am, sunshine. You can stay up, though. Not too late, but a little longer is fine."

"If I wanted a bedtime story, though, are you going to sleep right now?"

Mrs. Minks paused in her search and regarded Natalie cautiously. "*You* can't be tired." Natalie faked a yawn. Her mother, ointment in hand, gave an exaggerated sigh and started up the stairs. Natalie followed, grinning, up to her own little bedroom, shucked off her clothes, yanked her night-gown on backwards, and sat primly at the edge of her bed.

"So you're telling me you're ready for bed before it's even dark out?" Mrs. Minks's eyes were suspicious. "Which story did you want?"

There. She was hooked. There was nothing, *nothing* Natalie's mother liked better than telling stories or explaining things, except maybe questions that prompted stories or explanations. Natalie pretended to mull over the choices.

"Paul Bunyan?" Mrs. Minks suggested. "One of the Clever Jack stories, maybe?" Natalie rolled her eyes. Her mother loved Clever Jack stories, and there were about a million of them where he was always getting the best of some arrogant king or stupid giant or somebody. He never lost, so the stories got boring after a while. "How about the one where Jack wins three wishes from the angel Saint Peter and uses them to fool the Devil?" Natalie's mother asked. "That's the one where everyone thinks he's a pretty nice fellow, and then he starts using his wishes for terrible things, remember?"

Natalie shook her head. "Tell me about Old Tom Guyot and the Devil," she said.

And there it was: the look that, in the kitchen, always meant burned pancakes.

"Aaahh."

As Arcane settled down for the evening amid the sounds of katydids and chattering crickets and Annie Minks paused to remember a story, a little train of wagons sped along the east–west road toward the town. The creaky sounds of wood and metal and old wheels and the crystalline tones of bottles clinking gently together in warped and knotted crates accompanied the rougher noises of the ragged mules exhaling great, steaming gusts of smoky vapor into the summer night with each stamp of their hooves.

The wagons were moving faster now, had been ever since the caravan had gone out of view of the town it had left. You would still call what the mules were doing *walking*, but only because they all had at least one foot on the ground at all times. The gait wasn't graceful, but it was shockingly swift—any observer would have to spur his horse to a canter at least to keep up. There were no observers, of course. If there had been, the mules would still be clopping along at a perfectly ordinary pace rather than speeding on, smoking like chimneys with every breath.

The last irregular shape in the train was covered by a giant piece of dark oilcloth and, except for the furious treads of the creatures towing it, made no sound at all.

The tall man driving the lead wagon who had waved so jovially to the folk of the last town now sat hunched under his long, dark traveling cloak, even though it was a warm evening. The expression on his face might've been a grin or a particularly toothy scowl. If it was a smile, there was no humor in it.

Through the smoky exhalations of the mules, he kept his eyes on the twinkling lights far off on the horizon. At the speed they were moving now, they would pass through them around midnight.

THREE

The Devil and Tom Guyot

Back in the bedroom at the top of the stairs, Mrs. Minks considered her daughter seriously. "Are you sure you want this story right before bed? You won't have nightmares, will you?"

"No," Natalie scoffed. She didn't get scared by much anymore, but they always pretended she did. It helped set the mood. "You've told it to me before. Anyway, it's just a story."

Her mother sat very still for a moment before answering. "I also didn't tell you the whole thing last time. You were too young."

"I *like* scary stories, and you tell them best of all. Go on."

Annie Minks thought about it for a moment, tapping a foot on the floor. "What about something else for tonight?" she said. "The one about Jack and Saint Peter has the Devil in it, too. Remember? It's the one where Jack's so awful even the Devil's a little scared of him and won't let him into Hell? So he has to wander the earth with a coal of hellfire, looking for his own place?"

"Mama," Natalie said, exasperated, "no, I don't want that one. You just spoiled the ending."

Her mother hesitated. "It's just that the one about Tom and the Devil's a long one."

Was this still part of the game? Something in her tone, so light it wasn't light at all, gave Natalie goose bumps.

"No, it isn't. Unless it's a lot longer than I remember." Natalie decided not to mention that really she didn't remember much of it at all.

"It is longer."

"I'm awake!"

"And furthermore—and this is very important, Natalie —*nothing* is just a story."

This was definitely not part of the game. "Please?" was all she could think to say.

It took a few long moments, but slowly, slowly, the night went back to normal in the little bedroom. "I'm not too tired," Natalie's mother said quietly, as if trying to make up her mind. Natalie waited, breathless. "All right."

Natalie scooted back against the pillows.

"Well, this story takes place . . . oh, I don't know, forty or fifty years ago. Before Arcane was anything more than a saloon and a stable, but after the Old Village at the crossroads had died. Tom Guyot, I think, had lived a long life already. He had been a slave on a plantation, and he had escaped. He had been a soldier in the War Between the States, and he had survived."

A medal, Natalie thought as her mother paused for a sip of water. It had been some kind of war medal, that bronze piece he had been hammering into shape for his guitar in the brief image she saw before she passed out in the street. Then, just as she was wondering how she could possibly be so sure the vision had meant anything at all, Mrs. Minks set down her water glass and continued.

"Sometime after that, Tom was on his way home, some-where in Nebraska, I think, and the way I heard it, he walked most of the way from North Carolina. He didn't have much, but he had his guitar, the same one he plays now, and he would play wherever he stopped for the night.

"Now, supposedly he made that guitar himself when he was a boy, and whether he taught himself to play it or whether someone showed him the way to do it I don't know. But it might as well have been a part of his body, and he could play any song on it as beautifully as you'd ever hope to hear. If you've ever seen Tom Guyot play, really *seen* him, not just half noticed and kept on walking, you've seen what happiness looks like."

It was fresh in Natalie's mind, the way Tom's face had moved along with his voice, how he seemed to forget the rest of the world was there. She nodded.

"Now, I'm not saying he was happy the rest of the time," Annie explained, "or that having that guitar and playing it the way he did made the bad things in his life right somehow; that would be silly. Tom had been a slave, and he'd been a soldier. He probably saw things he'll never be able to forget until the day he dies."

"Like what kinds of things?"

"Things that aren't for putting in bedtime stories. Things you'd have nightmares about. Don't make that face; *I'd* have nightmares about them, too. The point is, Tom was one of the best guitar players there ever was, and once he was camping out in what was left of the Old Village on a summer night just like this one, and suddenly the crickets stopped singing and a man came and sat down by the fire and Tom knew right away that it was the Devil."

"*How* did he know?"

"Because the man who sat down on the other side of the fire made him feel the same way in his belly as all those awful, horrible, miserable things he'd seen and could never forget, only worse. Tom knew what real evil looked like, and he figured the only thing that could be worse than real evil was the Devil himself."

To see the Devil . . . what on earth would he look like? Red skin like badly dyed leather, probably some horns and fangs. And of course everyone knew about the Devil's feet in the shape of goats' hooves, and his tail, which had a little spade at the end and probably a stinger, too.

It wasn't hard to picture the Devil like that. It also wasn't very scary. Natalie tried again.

His eyes . . . his eyes would be thin and squinty, like the eyes of a thief, so that you didn't know quite where he was looking. Or . . . or wide open and staring, and *empty*. They would be dark like pits, with no whites at all, just holes in his head . . . or all white with no pupils, or an ugly gray the color of hot ash.

His teeth would be sharp, of course, like knives or fangs meant to tear meat away from the bone. Or like ogres' teeth, dull and cracked and broken from chewing the bones themselves, perhaps. Or maybe he didn't show his teeth at all, only gave you flashes when he smiled, so that you never knew what they looked like until he finally leaped across the fire and bared them at you a moment before he tore you to pieces.

Or he might have looked just like anyone else in the world. He might have looked perfectly normal, and unless you had seen real evil the way Old Tom had, you might not recognize him at all.

Which was a horrifying thought.

"So Tom knew he was in some trouble. The Devil was sitting no farther away than that chair is from you, and the fire was casting strange shadows on his face, and he was looking at Tom's tin guitar.

"'That's a fine instrument,' the Devil said. Tom didn't answer, just kept on playing. 'That's a fine song you're playing, too.' Tom didn't answer then, either, just played on and ignored him.

"Well, the Devil doesn't like to be ignored. When Tom didn't hear him speak again, he looked up and saw that there was no one on the other side of the fire. Then he turned his head and found the Devil sitting . . . right . . . by . . . his . . . *side!*

"'I paid you a compliment,' he said. 'Perhaps you didn't hear.'

"Then Tom spoke his first words to the Devil. 'I heard you.'

"The Devil looked Tom over. He saw a poor man, and he saw the only thing that man had in the world to hold on to: a guitar. He also thought he knew what a poor man with nothing but a guitar would want more than anything in the world.

"The Devil said his next words very quietly. 'Do you know who I am, Tom Guyot?'

"It probably scared Tom, and scared him a lot, to hear that creature say his own name. He stopped playing and said, 'I know who you are.'

"'Then you know I can help you. Let me have a turn on that guitar.'

"If there was one thing Tom *wasn't* going to do, it was hand that guitar over to the Devil. He shook his head and kept on playing.

"The Devil leaned in closer and whispered, 'Let me have a turn on that guitar, Tom, and when I give it back it'll surprise you.'"

"How can a guitar surprise you?" Natalie asked. That very afternoon, that same guitar had made noises she had never thought a musical instrument could make . . . but no, he couldn't have agreed to it, could he?

"I don't know, and neither did Old Tom, but he didn't ask for an explanation just then. The Devil spoke again. 'Let me have a turn on that guitar, Tom, and I'll give it a *voice*.'"

A voice? She *had* heard the guitar sing just like a real

voice on a record. She had heard it with her own ears! Tom couldn't have really given the Devil his guitar, could he? Those amazing sounds couldn't have been because the Devil gave the guitar a voice . . . could they?

Natalie bit her lip. She'd heard the story before, so she should've known the ending. But it was like a whole different tale this time. After all, she'd already heard the guitar do all the Devil had promised. . . . Her mother, however, was in full swing. The tale hurtled on like a boulder down a hill.

"Tom stopped playing, and the Devil knew at last that he was listening. 'All I have to do is tune it, Tom. Let me tune it, and then let me play one song on that guitar, *just one song,* and afterward it will play anything at all. Anything. Songs you don't know, songs no one's ever heard before. And with it, you will play them better than anyone else in the world.' The Devil smiled and said the words that had never failed him before. 'You'll be famous, Tom. You'll be the most famous guitar player in the world, the most famous there ever was or ever will be.'

"For a long, long moment, the only sound was the crackle of the fire. The Devil waited. His fingers itched to take that guitar, because the Devil knew that guitar was like Tom's soul, and if Tom gave one up it would be the same as giving up the other.

"Then a strange thing happened there at the crossroads. Tom turned his head and, for the first time, looked the Devil straight in the eye.

"'My guitar already has a voice,' he said."

Natalie's breath escaped in a rush of relief.

"The Devil was surprised, but only for a minute. 'I'll give it a better one,' he said.

"'I like the one I gave it.'

"Well, the Devil was *astounded*, but only for a minute more. Then he got angry. Who was this man, this poor man with nothing but a guitar, who dared look the Devil in the eye?

"'Give me the guitar or I'll take it from you.' His voice was deadly and cold, and so quiet Tom heard the words in his heart instead of his ears.

"But Tom didn't flinch. He said, very clearly and calmly, '*No.*'

"Well, that made the Devil so furious he had to work hard not to let it show. When the Devil gets angry, he loses control of his disguise, and no one, not even the bravest man or woman in the world, can see the Devil in his true form and live. If Tom died of shock or terror before the Devil got hold of his guitar, then his soul would escape, so the Devil had to keep calm. He made fists with his hands, clenching and unclenching them over and over. They didn't look like human hands anymore, but it was taking so much effort to keep the disguise on his face, the Devil couldn't worry about that.

"'I'll tear your head off and take that guitar out of your dead, stiff fingers,' he said as quietly and coldly as before.

"Those words felt like icicles growing between Tom's ribs. He didn't know what the Devil knew, that if he died before handing over the guitar the Devil wouldn't get a thing out of it, and the truth was it didn't matter, because the Devil was so enraged and insulted that he almost didn't *care* about Tom's soul anymore. What Tom did know was that he was in terrible danger, body and soul.

"But in the same way that the Devil thought he understood the poor man with the guitar, Tom had some ideas about the Devil, and he decided to take a chance.

"'I'll make you a bet,' Tom said finally. 'I bet with the voice I gave this guitar myself I can beat any song you can play on any other guitar you can find on the earth or in Hell.'

"The Devil looked at Tom for a long time. He looked at Tom's hands, and he looked at the guitar, patched together from coffee tins and milk cans. He looked at the old, yellowed gut strings, the finger slide made from a broken bottle. *Humans are so arrogant*, he thought. All that anger, and this would be easy after all.

"He unclenched his fists, and the sight of his hands uncurling made Tom sick to his stomach. Each finger was thin and had so many joints that they looked more like spiders' legs than human fingers, and there was no skin at all, only a horny covering like an insect's shell. Worst of all, at the end of each finger was a tiny, perfectly formed human face where there should have been a fingernail."

Natalie clenched her own fists. Her knuckles showed white through her skin.

"The Devil reached those hideous claws into the fire and pulled out his own guitar. It was metal, like Tom's, only this one was the deep red of hot steel, smoldering

He unclenched his fists, and the sight of his hands
uncurling made Tom sick to his stomach.

as though it had been forged for this very purpose only moments before. Smoke rose in little columns where his dreadful fingers touched it, as if it was blistering enough to burn even the Devil.

"Tom felt a change in the atmosphere. Spirits filled the air around them: an audience to decide the winner of the bet. He could hear their whispers, like he had heard the Devil's cold, deadly threats, in his own heart.

"The Devil strummed an experimental chord. The faces on his fingertips made a keening sound, a thin, weeping wail that raised goose flesh on Old Tom's back. He couldn't tell if they were singing . . . or screaming. The Devil looked at Tom and smiled."

Natalie's mother hesitated just a bit longer than was necessary for dramatic effect.

"'Now we begin.'"

FOUR

Some Kind of Grace

WHILE ANNIE MINKS did what she did best (talking while *not* cooking), night fell all around the town of Arcane. Inside the livery stable Tom Ogle's pack of horses and mules were tucked in for the night, and the forges were cooling at the blacksmith's behind it. All the kids had been chased home from the soda fountain at the general store, and the adults had retired to porches and parlors and kitchens for cups of coffee or pipes of tobacco.

The little procession out on the east–west road stopped so the drivers could light the oil lamps hanging from the front corners of each wagon and adjust the harnesses of the steaming mules. Then they lurched into motion again and continued on toward the Old Village and Arcane beyond.

Just as the first wagon reached the crossroads at the

center of the deserted village, the front left wheel sprang off its shaft. The wagon lurched sideways with a clattering of glass from inside.

The wheel rolled out of the lantern light into the darkness by the side of the road. The man holding the reins of the front wagon raised an eyebrow in annoyance, hauled the mules to a standstill, and jumped lightly down to inspect the damage. There was none.

Now the other four drivers approached, lanterns in hand, to see what the holdup was. The man with the red and gray hair spoke softly.

"Find the wheel."

He watched grimly as the others plunged into the darkness with their lanterns, then turned slowly to examine the dead town around him.

"This place," he murmured, "is a little worse for the wear these days." He squatted to examine a fresh set of footprints and allowed himself the slightest twist of a smile. "But the traffic appears to be about the same."

At length the other four drifted back to the wagons, empty-handed.

"It's gone." The man who spoke had spiky gray hair. "Not going to find anything you lose in this spot, Jake."

"We've driven through this way before without trouble."

The spike-haired man looked around as if to say, *A lot has changed around here.*

"So there should be even less trouble this time." The driver with the red and gray hair flexed his fingers on the handle of his whip. It was a gesture of annoyance, although none showed on his face. "It's a *wheel*. It moves, then it stops. Look again."

The spike-haired man looked at him for a moment, then turned wordlessly and was swallowed up by the darkness that lay beyond the road. "The man says it's here, lads."

Another of the four made a sound like a short laugh. They disappeared into the dark again.

Up in Natalie's bedroom, the battle between the Devil and Old Tom Guyot was about to begin.

"Now, when two people make a bet, they have to agree on the stakes," her mother explained, "and what they agreed on that night at the crossroads was that if the Devil won, Tom had to give up his soul when he died, and until then the Devil would get Tom's hands as a down payment."

"His *hands?*" Natalie squeaked.

"In place of his own, Tom would have to wear a pair of demon hands for the rest of his life, hands that answered to the Devil. If Tom won—and here the Devil actually laughed out loud, and you can imagine how awful a sound that was—the Devil would owe Tom a favor, with no strings attached."

It didn't sound like a very good deal, and Natalie said so.

"You forget," her mother reminded her, "that he would also get to keep his soul and his life."

Neither of which seemed like things he should have to fight the Devil for, Natalie thought.

"The air was heavy, thick with smoke from the fire

and spirits from every realm of the cosmos. The terms were set. The contest began.

"The Devil went first, and he could indeed make a guitar sing in ways Tom had never imagined. But you couldn't really call it *music*. It was something between rhythm and misery, and it made Tom's bones scratch and scrape against each other as if his skeleton was fighting to crawl out of his skin and escape without the rest of him. There was no question, though: the Devil could play that guitar like no man on earth.

"Then the singing started, and Tom thought he would go mad with terror. Those tiny human faces at the end of the many-jointed fingers on the Devil's hands twisted in agony as they crooned and chanted to the sounds from the hellish guitar.

"It seemed to go on for a century, each measure more haunting and dreadful than the last, until even the spirits in the air wept in hopelessness. Tom looked at his hands, the hands he thought he would never see again. The Devil saw and laughed as he picked the strings on his smoldering, smoking guitar.

"Finally, with a last moan, the song came to a sudden end like death striking in the middle of a sentence, and then . . . silence.

"Tom's heart shuddered against his ribs. It would be a blessing, he thought, to have already lost and not have to suffer through the act of failing. Still, he positioned his own guitar on his knees and whispered to his shaking hands that if this was the last song they would all play together, they'd better make it a song worth dying for."

In the little bedroom, the weight of an entire world holding its breath descended onto Natalie as she sat, still as a statue, and listened.

"And then," her mother said at last, "Tom began to play."

Out at the crossroads, the man with the red and gray hair smoked a thin cigarette and waited. One by one, the drivers trudged back to the road. The wheel, they insisted, had vanished. Just vanished, like . . . magic.

The man rolled his eyes and crushed out his cigarette. "Magic has better things to do with itself than pop wheels off a wagon." He pulled the cloak around his body and exhaled one last mouthful of smoke up at the stars.

The drivers glanced sideways at one another.

"So we shall roll on like a bunch of half-shod idiots who can't find their wheels with four pairs of eyes," he said coldly. "Rig what you can. We'll have to stop in that town for repairs tomorrow."

"Only for repairs?" This from a man who wore mirrored spectacles, despite the dark.

"Less than two days out of that last village, what do you suggest?" He shook his head. "There are reasons we have rules."

"You said yourself there shouldn't be any trouble here. If we don't set up, it'll look strange."

The man in the cloak gave a harsh bark of a laugh. "Strange? I can't imagine how we could ever look *strange*."

But his hauteur diminished a little. "I'll give it some thought. See to the wagon."

Natalie's fingernails cut little moons into her palms as she sat without breathing.

"Tom couldn't remember afterward what song he thought he was playing, or what notes his fingers plucked out or what words he sang. He only knew he put his hands to the guitar and gave himself up to it. Perhaps he lost consciousness, or perhaps his hands were even more desperate to beat that Devil than Tom was, or perhaps the guitar itself came a little to life. All he knew was that when he became aware of what he was doing, it was because he sensed the atmosphere changing again.

"All around him, the spirits, dark ones and light, were moving like winds, and for a moment he thought he could actually see them, as if in order to glimpse Tom better they were venturing into his own world, poking their deathly faces through the fabric of Hell into the light of Tom's smoldering fire.

"They were whispering. It was like the chant of the Devil's fingers, just as haunting and fearsome, and Tom knew the spirits were passing their judgment.

"All the while he kept on playing, but to his horror, although he could feel the guitar vibrating against his palms and knees, *he couldn't hear the music.* He couldn't hear his own voice, although he could feel it resonating in his chest and thrumming in his vocal cords.

"If he had looked up, Tom would have seen the smile fading from the Devil's face. He would have noticed those spidery hands clenching and unclenching again. Tom might not have been able to hear the song, but the Devil could, and he wasn't happy about it.

"But Tom didn't look up. He kept on playing, and since he couldn't hear the music, he listened to the murmurs in the night and slowly realized what they were saying. It was one single word, chanted over and over. That one word echoing in the thickened air . . . was *grace*.

"The Devil knew before Tom did that the contest had been decided. He leaped to his feet and roared, his human disguise peeling away like the old skin of a snake so that his true shape, the shape that matched his hands, caught the last light of the fire.

"Tom saw none of this, nor did he hear it.

"The Devil leaped at him, baring his fangs in jaws that opened sideways, and just a second before those jaws tore into Old Tom Guyot, the spirits rushed into the space between them. They spun into a whirling gust around the furious Devil and picked him up as easily as a twister takes a house into the air. Then spirits, Devil, and all spun together faster and faster into a tighter and tighter spiral, until only a thin bright line remained, stretching from the sky to the earth and beyond into the deeps. Then it blinked out.

"That's when Tom suddenly heard the music he was playing. It was as if someone's hands had covered his ears and then had uncovered them again, and as soon as he heard the song, he knew he had beaten the Devil. He raised his head slowly.

"The Devil was gone. Only Tom and his guitar and the dying fire remained." Natalie's mother paused, as if there might be more . . . and then: "That's the story of Tom Guyot at the crossroads."

Slowly Natalie uncurled her stiff fingers. "That's not . . . true, is it?"

Her mother shrugged. "It's a story that's been part of this town since before I was born. I don't know if it's true or not. Maybe it's a little bit true and a little bit false."

"It has to be one or the other." Natalie did some calculations in her head. "Anyway, if Tom was old fifty years ago, how could he possibly still be alive today?"

"There are a lot of things I don't know how to explain." It was an odd thing for Natalie's mother, who loved to explain things, to say. "All I know is that it takes some kind of grace to beat the Devil at anything."

Which made even less sense than Tom Guyot's age—Tom walked with a crutch, and badly. If there was anything he *wasn't*, it was graceful.

"It has to be one or the other," Natalie insisted.

"The only person who knows for sure is Old Tom." Again that hesitation, so unlike her mother. "You could ask him what happened that night at the crossroads."

Outside the window beside the bed, Bard Street stretched away into the dark straight through Arcane and all the way to that very spot. Natalie knew exactly where the two roads intersected amid the ruins of the Old Village. She imagined Old Tom's campfire on that night long ago, and for a moment she thought she could even see lights out there in the distance—tiny sparks like the pinprick lights of fireflies, or stars.

FIVE

The Snake Oil Salesmen

I SEE YOU DIDN'T BRING your bicycle out today."

Natalie rolled her eyes and kept walking. "We have other things to do today."

"And what, exactly, are you planning to do with *that?*"

Miranda, pink and prissy, jabbed a finger at the jar Natalie held. Natalie sighed. Barely lunchtime, and already Miranda was getting on her nerves. On the other hand, Natalie had two more friends along today. There were great benefits to these particular friends. One: Miranda was sweet on Alfred Tate, so she tended to tone down her more annoying qualities if he was there, and two: when she didn't tone down far enough, Ryan Wilder was even quicker to point out when she was being annoying than Natalie was.

"It's a *bee*. You can do *plenty* with it," Ryan said, without bothering to look at Miranda.

"Like what." She didn't even bother to make it sound like a question.

Natalie handed the jar to Alfred and held up a hand, ticking off answers on her fingers. "Bees make honey. Bees make wax. Bees sting people who annoy them."

Ryan snorted and Alfred bit his lips to keep from grinning. Natalie took back the jar and started walking again.

"You can't do any of that with only one bee!"

It just went to show how little regard Miranda had for accuracy. At least one of those things you could do with one bee—and very effectively, if you took off the punctured lid and upended the jar on Miranda's head.

But that would be a waste of a perfectly good bee.

"We're going to sell it."

"*Sell it?*"

Natalie ignored the dripping disbelief in Miranda's voice and marched up the stairs of the general store with Ryan and Alfred in tow.

The key to this sort of thing was to look businesslike. Back straight, shoulders squared, Natalie strolled past the bigger kids at the soda fountain with the jar in both hands and the boys following like lieutenants. Miranda trailed along behind them.

Arcane's general store had always felt a little bit like the center of the town to Natalie. At the front on the left when you walked in there was the soda fountain, where you could sit on a high leather stool and have ice cream or root beer, or Mr. Tilden, who ran the store, could mix you up something made of soda and syrup (Mr. Tilden was an artist with flavored syrups). On the right-hand side, across from the fountain with its high stools, sat two wrought iron tables, each with four little chairs. The space in between the tables and the fountain formed a sort of aisle you could follow all the way through the store.

Past the soda fountain on the left was the cracker barrel, where all the broken cracker pieces lived. For a penny you could scoop as many cracker bits as would fit into a little paper bag, and every once in a while, like a buried treasure, you found a perfect, whole, unbroken cracker somewhere in the mix. On the right, opposite the barrel, were two spinning display racks: one held dozens of picture postcards and the other packets of flower and vegetable seeds.

Beyond the cracker barrel, the aisle passed between two big, curvy glass cases full of five- and ten-cent goodies: tiny perfume bottles, fans, hatpins, artificial flowers, celluloid collars, and chewing gum. Behind the five-and-ten cases stretched two mahogany counters, one on either side of the room. Mr. Tilden kept all sorts of goods on shelves behind the counters, from Chinese firecrackers (Natalie had been allowed to pick out a whole dollar's worth of explosives to set off for her birthday last year) to medicines to flour and sugar and fabric. Small glass displays and racks stood here and there up and down the lengths of the two counters. At the very back of the store was Arcane's central switchboard, where every now and then telephone calls and telegraph messages came in. Mr. Tilden's wife usually ran "Central."

Mr. Tilden himself was busy with a customer at the left-hand counter, and there was no mistaking who. Only Mrs. Byron wore dresses like that, with old pearl buttons down her rigid back.

But businesspeople didn't let old widows get under their skin. Natalie reached up to set the bee on the counter and waited for Mr. Tilden to finish, studiously refusing to look up at Mrs. Byron, who smelled of disapproval the way some ladies smelled of too much perfume.

Mrs. Byron sniffed. "Miss Minks."

"Hello, Mrs. Byron." Businesspeople were polite, even to hags. Even a hag could become a customer. You never knew.

Across the counter, Mr. Tilden looked up from the parcel he was wrapping and glanced from Mrs. Byron to Natalie to the bee in its jar. A very slight smile crossed his face as he turned and disappeared momentarily into the back room.

Mrs. Byron sniffed again, loudly enough to make Natalie glance up. It was a mistake. The look Mrs. Byron gave her was so full of dislike that Natalie had to look away. But businesspeople didn't lose their poise. She shoved her hands in her pockets and stared hard at the bee zooming around in the jar. *I'm a businesslady, I'm a businesslady.*

"There were tire treads in my rose garden this morning, Miss Minks."

Not again. Natalie took a breath and said as calmly as she could manage, "Mrs. Byron, I never—"

"Nonetheless they are there, Miss Minks. I shall have to speak to your father, I suppose," Mrs. Byron said crisply. Her eyes glittered meanly behind the little pince-nez glasses perched on her thin nose.

Behind Natalie, Ryan and Alfred shouted in protest. "I never!" Natalie snapped. To heck with business, a false accusation was a false accusation. "I never did that! You can't go and tell my dad—"

"Do take care not to shout, Miss Minks. It's unbecoming in a young lady." Her gaze flickered over Natalie, taking in her overalls, bee, and companions. Clearly, she thought *shouting* was just one item on a lengthy list of unbecoming attributes Natalie had collected.

Natalie willed the red flush off her face (*Businesslady, businesslady!*) as Mrs. Byron swept past in a cloud of musty violet scent. "That old lady's a bat," Ryan muttered when the door had clattered safely shut behind her.

Alfred whistled. "How come she hates you so much, Natalie?"

"'Cause she's a *bat*," Ryan insisted.

Natalie found herself staring through the jar at Mr. Tilden and swallowed down the last of her indignation with effort. "I notice, Mr. Tilden, that you don't have much in the way of bees for sale in your fine shop."

As she spoke, a light bulb over the switchboard built into Mrs. Tilden's exchange desk began buzzing. Natalie had asked about the exchange desk with its board full of cords and plugs often enough to know that this light meant someone wanted to complete a telephone call. Mrs. Tilden put down the novel she was reading, chose one of the score or so of cloth-covered patch cords from the rows set into the back of the desk, and plugged it in. She lifted a bell-shaped earpiece from a hook set into the wooden side panel, then leaned in close to speak into a small silvery horn on a candlestick-shaped stand near her elbow. "Central," she said crisply. She listened to a voice in the earpiece for a moment, then reached for a pad of paper and began to jot something down.

Meanwhile, Mr. Tilden wasn't quite sold. "Er. No bees. How right you are." Natalie followed his glance to a rough sort of rack by the register where five or six interesting gears and sprockets hung from braided strings like the one around Natalie's neck. A hand-printed sign on the rack read: NECKLACES TEN CENTS.

"You're . . . ah . . . expanding your business?" Mr. Tilden gave the jar a wary look.

"Yes. To include a bee business," Natalie confirmed.

"I see. And this would be . . . one such bee."

"Yes."

"A . . . a home-caught bee, naturally?" Mr. Tilden hazarded.

"Exactly."

The light tinkling sound of the bell over the door and the quick tread of feet reminded Natalie to hurry along. "And for twenty—no, fifteen cents—"

Mr. Tilden handed Natalie four nickel packs of Tootsie Rolls as he glanced at the newcomer striding up behind her. Natalie sighed, pocketed the candy, and lifted the jar again. Businesspeople knew when to cut their losses.

The three of them had just about reached where Miranda stood by the soda fountain when Ryan stopped. "Natalie." She followed his nod to where the new customer stood at the counter with Mr. Tilden. They were speaking quietly, but Natalie listened hard and heard the newcomer pronounce the word *mechanic*.

Something about this man seemed . . . out of place in the general store. It was hard to say where a man like that might belong, but he surely didn't belong *here*.

He was taller than anyone she knew, and he wore an old-fashioned frock coat like her grandfather wore in old pictures: long and flared at the bottom and too heavy for a summer noon. He carried a tall silk hat under one arm, and there was something odd about his hair, too; the way it stood off his scalp was like the way her hair billowed when she dunked her head underwater.

Mr. Tilden waved her over. "Natalie, want to show this fellow over to your dad's shop?"

The stranger turned.

He was even odder face-to-face. Under that mop of red hair so full of gray, his face was young; older than Charlie's, who was sixteen, but younger than her parents'. His eyes regarded her from behind blue-lensed glasses. He held out a hand.

Natalie handed the jar to Alfred and shook the fellow's hand. Her small fingers disappeared into a pale leather-gloved palm. Whether it was because of the curiousness of gloves in June, or something about the feel of the glove itself, Natalie took her hand back a little faster than was probably polite.

"Your father is a mechanic?" the newcomer asked.

"A *bicycle* mechanic," Natalie corrected, wondering for reasons she couldn't put a finger on whether there was a courteous way to get out of going anywhere with this fellow. "But he can fix anything."

The stranger paused, considering something, then conjured a business card from his waistcoat, handed it to Mr. Tilden, and put the silk hat on his head. "Lead on."

The kids from the soda fountain had all clustered out on the porch. They were whispering among themselves and staring at a procession of boxy mule wagons painted in fading jewel tones and draped with bunting, lined up out on Bard Street. Some of those wagons might once have been beautiful; carved figures stood out from the corners, rising suns and linked rings circled the sides, and giant medallions like big round shields glimmered feebly with old gilt and silver flake.

The little knot of kids parted for the man in the silk hat. Natalie straightened as she strode along behind him so she would look a little taller.

"Go on ahead," he barked to the man holding the reins of the head wagon, then looked down at her sharply. "Well?" he said. "Which direction is it?"

"This way." She pointed to the right and stumbled into motion; he was already out in front as if he knew the way, long legs carrying him twice as fast as hers could.

Natalie sprinted to catch up. "Is that a circus?"

"Does it look like a circus?"

"A carnival?

He didn't answer. It was a really aggravating adult habit.

"Well, what *is* it?"

"It is a medicine show."

"What's a medicine show?" Natalie turned to look at the wagons, slowing down just to annoy him. "I've never heard of one of those."

"There's likely a great deal you've never heard of," the stranger said, pausing to glare at little old Chester Teufels, who was leaning against one of the legs of Arcane's big old water tower and laughing hysterically for no apparent reason as they passed. "How far is the shop?"

"You don't know?" she mumbled, jogging a few steps to keep pace. He glanced at her sharply without breaking stride, and she smiled cheerfully. "We'll get there when we get there." And then, under her breath, as she fell behind once again, "Sorry if I'm holding you up."

The big barn doors of Minks's Bicycle Shop were half-open. Natalie sprinted in just ahead of the man in the frock coat. He swept his hat off his head, glanced around appraisingly, and stepped carefully inside.

"Mr. Minks?" Natalie's father straightened at his workbench. The stranger offered his gloved hand. "My name is Dr. Jake Limberleg."

Jake Limberleg? What kind of a name was Limberleg?

"The grocer recommended you to replace a wagon wheel," Dr. Limberleg continued. He stopped in front of the workbench under the window and stared at Natalie's automaton, the little clockwork flyer with the name *Wilbur* painted across its side, lying unfinished in the dusty light. "Your daughter"—he glanced at Natalie mildly—"says you can fix anything."

"Well, I'm pretty good with wheels, anyhow," her father said. "Let me guess. The left one in front."

The doctor tapped his fingers on the brim of his hat. "How astonishing."

"Not really. Happens all the time. Popped off where the roads meet, did it?" Mr. Minks collected a few tools into a satchel. "Where's the wagon? Did you find the wheel?"

"We did not." Dr. Limberleg lifted the *Wilbur*. Natalie bit her cheek to keep from telling him to put it back down, that it didn't work but only because it wasn't finished, that the clockwork wasn't tightened up inside and it would all come apart . . .

Dr. Limberleg's eyes slipped sideways at her as if he could hear her silent protests.

"I happen to collect automata." He smiled faintly.

In his fingers the automaton lurched into jerking motion for a second, propellers spinning like the blades of a fan.

How on earth . . . ?

The key to wind the mechanism lay three feet away on the bench, right where she'd left it. The *Wilbur* couldn't possibly have done what she had just seen it do without being wound at all . . . could it?

Dr. Limberleg smiled lazily at her shock. He put the

Wilbur down and disappeared back through the workshop door into the sun.

Natalie snapped her head around to look at her father, but Mr. Minks was still sifting through his tools and hadn't seen a thing.

How did he do that?

When they joined the strange man outside the shop, he was eyeing Natalie's red enameled bicycle, which leaned against the side of the barn where she'd left it the night before. "A Chesterlane Eidolon," he said in a tone of vague surprise. "I haven't seen another one of those in some time indeed."

Natalie stared at him, then at her father. The idea that Mr. Minks hadn't been able to identify the bicycle, but this aggravating stranger had, was shocking. And . . . what had he meant by *another one?*

"A Chesterlane!" Mr. Minks was looking at the bicycle as if through new eyes. "Darned if it isn't! Do you know, I've been trying to figure out what that frame was for near a year now."

"Lovely restoration," Jake Limberleg said. "With some rather inventive adjustments."

"Well, I was pretty sure it would be a tough cycle to use," Mr. Minks said, "but Natalie seems to be doing fine with it. Isn't that right, Natalie?"

"Fine," Natalie said coolly. Jake Limberleg fixed her with a look that made it plain he somehow knew she wasn't telling the truth.

As Limberleg stalked off, his customary three strides

ahead, Natalie tugged on her father's sleeve. "Wait for me. I'm going to see if Mama wants to come for the walk."

"Natalie." Her father grabbed the strap of her overalls as she turned toward the house. "I think she's taking a nap. No need to wake her up."

They followed Jake Limberleg through Arcane in the noonday heat to an empty lot at the end of Heartwood Street, a flat, dusty space bordered on three sides by green fields of early summer corn. A couple of men were busy unhitching the mules from the wagons, and near the front of the lot another was working with a loud hammer on a skeleton of wood that looked as if it might turn into a stage. That man, spiky-haired and scowling, looked up as they approached.

Her father whistled. "What's this?"

"A medicine show," Natalie said immediately.

Dr. Limberleg glanced at her through half-lowered eyelids. "It is Dr. Limberleg's Nostrum Fair and Techno-logical Medicine Show, in point of fact."

Natalie put her hands on her hips. He wouldn't have had to correct her if he'd answered the question properly when *she'd* asked it. Dr. Limberleg returned her gaze, but Natalie found she couldn't look at him for long without wanting to look somewhere else.

Where the lot met Heartwood Street, a man in a bowler hat was deep in conversation with Simon Coffrett. "Jake," the man in the bowler called. "Look who's come to see us!" The stand of trees that surrounded Mr. Coffrett's mansion was visible past the wagons, just a bit farther out of town to the southwest on the edge of the forest. Natalie supposed he must own the lot. According to her mother, Simon Coffrett's family had lived on the estate called Coffretfonce since the days of the Old Village. Maybe longer.

"On the left," Dr. Limberleg said to Mr. Minks, then strode off to join Mr. Coffrett and the man in the bowler.

"Dad? Can I look around?" She made sure that Dr. Limberleg was out of earshot before she asked. If he didn't like her questions, he sure as anything wouldn't like her poking around.

"I don't see why not."

What she wanted to see most sat a little ways behind the stage the man was working on: a gigantic wheeled object covered in a huge piece of dark fabric. The top was pointed, as if what was underneath had a spire like a church, and the wheels didn't look like a wagon's at all. They were brass-rimmed, with spokes like those on a bicycle or a motorcar—but the thing sitting on those tires was too tall and too wide, too huge altogether to be any sort of motorcar Natalie had ever seen. Plus the wheels were mismatched: two were very, very large, and two were very, very small.

She crept closer, sure that she could see a pedal peeking from under the forward edge of the cover. The cloth was heavy and a little slick, the kind that kept rain from soaking through. She took hold of the edge and bent to peer under it.

"*You!*"

Natalie dropped the cloth and stumbled back so fast

she tripped and sprawled and had to pick herself up off the ground in order to put some distance between herself and the man with the spiky gray hair. He strode at her like an angry bull, head lowered and shoulders hunched . . . and with a claw hammer in one hand. Natalie scrambled away until she felt one of the other wagons come up against her back, and prepared to scream.

But he stopped in front of her and pointed the hammer at the thing under the cloth behind him. "That's dangerous, what's under there. A lot of electricity. You want to keep clear."

"Got it." Even Natalie could see that there wasn't any electricity in evidence at the moment, but between the hammer and the man's glowering stare, arguing didn't seem like a particularly good idea. She sprinted, red-faced, back across the lot and crouched beside her father, who was making notes in a little book.

"Caught you, did they?"

"I wasn't going to touch anything," she grumbled. "I just wanted a look. There's something huge over there, under that cloth. Is that the . . . nostrum? What's a nostrum, anyway?"

"A nostrum's just another word for a medicine, or a remedy."

Natalie considered the oilcloth-covered thing, then turned her head to glance at Dr. Limberleg with his funny hair and pale blue lenses. "So who are they, Dad?"

"Snake oil salesmen. Too bad Doc's out of town. He'd have a ball with this . . . what did he call it?"

"Dr. Limberleg's Nostrum Fair and Technological Medicine Show," Natalie recited. "What's a snake oil salesman?"

"It's a not very nice term for somebody who travels around selling patent medicines. Nostrums."

"What's wrong with selling medicines? Mr. Finch sells medicines, and so does Mr. Tilden."

"Mr. Finch is a pharmacist. He sells prescription medicines when Doc Fitzwater thinks someone needs them. Patent medicines are different. Anyone can make up a patent medicine, so it's hard to know if you're getting a remedy that works or just something weird in a jar."

"So is Mr. Tilden a snake oil salesman?" Mr. Tilden kept rows of oddly shaped bottles behind the left-hand counter in the general store. They had fantastic names like Vegetable Compound or Kickapoo Indian Sagwa and Natalie's favorite of all, Dr. Henrik Vermola's Worm Confections.

"I'll explain later." Mr. Minks shouldered the satchel and rose as Dr. Limberleg crossed the lot toward them. "How long is the show in town, Doctor?"

"I suppose that depends on you, sir. We had not planned to stop here at all, but . . ." He waved a hand at the damaged wagon. "Two days at least."

"I'll see what I can do."

Natalie barely registered the conversation. A few yards away from the brass-wheeled contraption, a man wearing silvery spectacles was unloading another wagon. Half of it was piled with ominously coffin-sized crates. The rest was full of old bicycles. Some of them were true boneshakers, older even than her grandfather's antique Michaux.

Dr. Limberleg followed her gaze. "We appear to have similar interests, young lady. We use gaslight and oil for the most part, but certain elements of the fair require electricity. The bicycles power my generators, and a few other things." He raised an eyebrow and nodded at the wagon. "In fact, I believe one of them is a Chesterlane rather like your own."

Natalie craned her neck for a better look as the man in the silver glasses lifted two more cycles down to the ground, one in each hand. The Chesterlane was easy to spot, even without all the adjustments Mr. Minks had made to Natalie's. The tires were plain iron rims, but the front one was bigger than the back, and it had the same elaborate collection of springs, the same oddly placed pedals. It was blue, but just like hers it was etched with golden whorls that caught the sun.

"Shaky as it is," Limberleg said, taking off his spectacles to polish the lenses against his coat, "the Chesterlane Eidolon can be very, very fast. And it's one of the more powerful bicycles I know of. If you can keep it from behaving like some primitive boneshaker, that is." He gave her a pointed look. "Most can't."

Natalie nodded seriously, hoping she was wrong about how much Dr. Limberleg could tell about her shaky relationship with her own bicycle, and followed her father back down Heartwood to Bard Street. About midway down the road, she glanced back over her shoulder. Limberleg was talking to the man with the hammer, and they were both looking at her.

Simon Coffrett leaned against one of the painted wagons while Limberleg and the gray-haired man watched Natalie and Ted Minks until they were out of sight. "So what brings you back this way, Jake?" Simon asked.

"It's such a nice place to visit." Dr. Limberleg smiled thinly. "You all roll out the carpet so nicely. Makes it difficult to leave."

"Can't say that's ever been my intention before."

"Yes, and to what do I owe this unexpectedly pleasant reception?"

"Learned my lesson," Simon replied, hands in his pockets.

Limberleg gave him a look that plainly said he didn't believe a word.

"All right," Simon said with a little smile. "Evidently I have a price and you can afford it."

The gray-hair and the bowler hat wandered closer to hear Simon's next words, but before he could continue, someone laughed.

Silhouetted by the sun, the drifter with the carpetbag and the lantern stood in the road, doubled over in hilarity. The man in the bowler hat took a step toward him. Simon looked mildly at his fingernails.

"Well, fancy that," Limberleg muttered, glancing from Simon Coffrett to the drifter and back. "Something funny, friend?"

"Just can't believe my lucky timing's all," the drifter said. "A medicine show! Might have to stick around and have a look. You know, 'fore I get on my way."

Limberleg exchanged a glance with the gray-haired man. "It's a welcoming kind of town," he said at last, turning his gaze to Simon Coffrett. Simon looked at his fingernails again.

"Yep, seems that way." All the humor melted off the drifter's face. He twirled the lantern pole in his fingers. "Can't wait to get to know it better." Even in daylight, the little lantern glowed behind him as he strolled away down Heartwood Street back toward the center of town.

Limberleg smiled his thin smile again and spoke to Simon Coffrett. "Learned your lesson."

"A man can only make so many mistakes before he starts doing things right," Simon said placidly. "Welcome to Arcane."

SIX

Vitamins

WATCHING HER FATHER climb a ladder was enough to give Natalie a heart attack. Clumsy at the best of times in a workshop that, at its cleanest and most organized, was still an obstacle course, he usually took the rungs as if he were nimble as a monkey and generally missed the first three and tripped over whatever was at the bottom of the ladder before he made any vertical headway. If he managed to survive the ascent, he still had to navigate the loft of the old barn, which was chock-a-block with scores of spare wheels and tires designed by vengeful gods to entrap feet and imitate alpine landslides at the slightest touch. Sometimes it was better not to look. Certainly it was better not to talk, or breathe.

Natalie turned the flyer's wind-up key over and over in one hand and waited until her father was safe in the loft and the first round of torture, with its attendant banging and bruising, was over. "So if Mr. Tilden sells patent medicines," she asked at last, "and Dr. Limberleg sells patent medicines, how are they different?"

Mr. Minks rolled aside a dusty antique wheel from an old covered wagon and measured the one underneath. "If you bought medicine from Mr. Tilden and got home and discovered it didn't work at all, what would you do?"

"Take it back and ask Mr. Tilden for something else." Natalie covered her eyes with one hand as she spoke. He was uncomfortably close to the edge of the loft.

"But what if you'd bought a medicine from a traveling salesman, some elixir nobody'd ever heard of, and forgot how to use it? Maybe you couldn't go back and ask, because he'd already left town. Suppose you accidentally took too much and instead of curing your toothache, it made you sick?" He paused to measure another wheel. "And then sometimes the medicines are harmless but they don't do anything. Some people try and sell you sugar syrup in a fancy bottle or pass off mints as wonder pills."

"So why does anyone buy anything from a snake oil salesman?"

"Not all of them are frauds. You just never know. Dr. Limberleg's medicines could be real. I guess we'll have to go to the medicine show when it opens and find out for ourselves." Her father grinned at her through cobwebby spokes. "Who knows? He may even be a real doctor."

"Hmm." Natalie turned to the workbench under the window and planted her chin in her palm. Between her elbows lay the machinery that made up the mechanical flyer. With the fingers of one hand she tapped the key thoughtfully against her cheek.

How had Dr. Limberleg made it go without winding it?

It was a simple enough machine, really. Her brother Charlie had carved the pieces with his whittling knife and their father had designed the mechanism using gears and wooden dowels. It was made of spruce, just like the real *Flyer I* that Wilbur, and then Orville, had tested at Kitty Hawk when Natalie was just a tiny little girl.

Natalie had finished building the flyer a couple days earlier and had tried to wind it, but it hadn't moved a twitch, so she'd taken the key out (and one or two other parts) to try to fix it. Something was wrong inside. Even *with* the key, the *Wilbur* shouldn't have worked. But somehow, Dr. Limberleg had made it move, and without winding it at all.

She picked up the automaton and turned it over and over, following the uncomplicated chain of moving parts inside. No answers there. At last Natalie slotted the little brass key into its port, turned it once, and set the flyer on the workbench. Slowly she lifted her hands away.

It didn't move.

Maybe the mechanism just needed coaxing. She nudged the key with one finger. It stayed stuck firm. She wiggled it. Nothing. Natalie glanced up to be sure her father was safely out of sight among the spare wheels, then picked the flyer up and shook it.

Nothing.

"Natalie!"

She turned, holding the automaton behind her back as she looked up into the loft.

"I meant to stop by the pharmacy and it slipped my mind. Would you mind riding over there and asking Mr. Finch for Mom's vitamins?"

Natalie tilted her head. "Umm, sure." This was new. "What vitamins?"

"Just ask him exactly that. Annie Minks's vitamins. I'd go myself, but this'll take me a while. Those wagons Limberleg has are ancient." He smiled down at her, dusty and covered in cobwebs, from the edge of the loft. "You can do it in no time on that Chesterlane, I bet."

Natalie walked. It was such a short distance anyway, practically across the street . . . silly to ride a bicycle, really. Still, she continued to mutter "Chesterlane Eidolon, Chesterlane Eidolon" to herself as she walked down Bard toward Mr. Finch's shop.

Mr. Tilden from the general store was walking up the pharmacy steps when Natalie crossed the street. She caught the door just before it banged shut and slipped through behind him.

"Lester. Got a telephone call from Pinnacle. Some good news, finally."

The pharmacist stood behind the counter with his back turned, singing along to a ragtime record, but the tone of Mr. Tilden's voice would've made anyone stop and pay attention. Mr. Tilden clearly hadn't noticed Natalie come in after him. She could have turned politely away or even stepped back onto the porch, but something made her slip out of sight around the far side of a huge dispensing cabinet full of boxes and jars.

At the counter Mr. Finch chuckled as he turned down the music and clapped Mr. Tilden on the back. "Well, at least Doc got to take the old Winton out for another trip. He won't mind so much if there's nothing for him to do."

If there was nothing for Doc to do in Pinnacle, the flu must have stopped spreading. She leaned a little closer. The pharmacist was still talking.

". . . take a lot off of everyone's minds. Shall we put up signs?"

"Not yet." Mr. Tilden's voice was so sharp that Natalie jumped back. "Not until the hucksters leave town. Can you imagine if we announce that the flu's burned itself out the day before they open up shop? Whether they even came through Pinnacle or not, they'll take credit for it."

"I guess it can't hurt to wait until they're gone to make an announcement." A momentary pause. When Mr. Finch spoke again, his voice was quieter. "I met them on their way into town. Something about those folks puts me on edge, Ed. They put hairs up on my neck."

Hidden in her corner, Natalie nodded in agreement. Mr. Tilden must've been doing the same, because the next words he said were, "I hate to say this, because I never like the way other people mean it when they say it, but I have to tell you, Lester, I just don't like the looks of them. I don't like the way they *seem*."

Which made perfect sense. Miranda, for instance, said once that she didn't like Old Tom's looks, but that was just snobbishness because he was old and poor and threadbare. Even Doc Fitzwater, with his monocle and alligator cane and his face like cracked desert earth, *looked* strange, but nothing about Doc put hairs up on your neck.

Something about Dr. Limberleg and his crew wasn't quite right.

The door jangled open, and Natalie flattened herself against the cabinet. Skirts swished.

"Afternoon, Miss Albert," Mr. Finch called to the swishing lady.

Natalie peeked around the cabinet. No one was facing the door. She crept out of her corner into plain view and pretended to read a big framed document on the wall by the door while she waited to be noticed.

The words printed on the old-fashioned brown paper looked official, like a university diploma. HIPPOCRATIC OATH, it said at the top. For a moment Natalie forgot the discussion she had overheard and tried to work out what *Hippocratic* meant, and whether it had anything to do with hippopotamuses, and why on earth anyone would involve them in any sort of oath. The beginning line didn't help much: *First, do no harm.*

"Natalie!" Mr. Finch's voice brought her back to attention. "When did you come in?"

"Right after Miss Albert," she lied.

The two men exchanged a look. Natalie could tell that they were disturbed to see her appear out of nowhere. She thought hard, and then, for lack of anything better to do, pointed to the wall.

"What's *Hippocratic* mean?"

It worked. Miss Albert laughed, and the two men exchanged another look, this time one of relief.

"What can I do for you, Natalie?" Mr. Finch asked, dropping a box into a bag for Miss Albert.

"Dad sent me for vitamins."

Mr. Finch frowned. "Vitamins?"

"I don't know what he's talking about either," Natalie said with a shrug, "but he said to come here and ask for Annie Minks's vitamins. He's working on a wheel for Dr. Limberleg or he would've come himself."

Mr. Finch tapped his fingers on the counter and eyed the dispensing cabinet. Natalie folded her hands together to keep from fidgeting. Had he guessed she had been hiding behind it?

"Did your father say why he thought your mother needed vitamins today?"

Natalie shook her head. Mr. Finch came around the counter and strode to the cabinet. She peered into it along with him when he opened it, trying to guess what kind of vitamins her mother took that she'd never noticed before.

Mr. Finch hesitated. He looked down at her, then over at Mr. Tilden. "I think I know which ones he means," the pharmacist said at last. "I'd better take them over myself to be sure."

"If Mr. Finch is going to go see your dad himself, how about coming back to the general store with me, Natalie?" Mr. Tilden asked. "You left something there this afternoon, remember?"

Reluctantly, Natalie followed Mr. Tilden out of the pharmacy and down the porch steps. "Hippocrates was a doctor in ancient Greece," the grocer said after a moment's silence. "He had very high expectations for anyone who learned how to heal people, and the Hippocratic oath is a promise doctors make to behave according to his ideals, and to always use what they know to do good rather than harm."

"That's what it said, right at the top. 'First, do no harm.'"

Nearly everyone they passed on their way to the center of town was talking about the medicine show. Even the drifter with the pale eyes and the tin lantern turned one of Dr. Limberleg's cards over in his dusty fingers.

"I hear their last stop was in Pinnacle," a woman sweeping her porch said to a neighbor.

"Did he say anything about the flu?" the neighbor asked. Mr. Tilden tensed. He paused to re-tie his shoe, which looked secure enough to Natalie.

"He said they'll give a whole presentation on it. Tomorrow morning, when the fair opens."

"Can you imagine if Doc was here?" Both women laughed. The grocer stopped fiddling with his shoelaces. When he stood up he seemed to have relaxed a little.

Out in front of the general store the kids were talking, too.

"Natalie!" Ryan balanced on one side of a watering trough and waved a scrap of paper at her: another one of Dr. Limberleg's calling cards. "They're going to have films, too," he shouted, "real moving-picture films!"

"Who said?" Natalie jogged ahead of Mr. Tilden to where her friends clustered in the shade of the porch. "Dr. Limberleg?"

"No, another fellow. One with a funny walking stick."

"So?" Miranda said. "It isn't as though nobody's ever seen a film before."

The boys paused to give Miranda twin looks of shock and disgust, then burst into loud protestations.

"It isn't as though we get them every day, either—"

"It's been *a year at least*, Miranda!"

"—in the cities they have *four a week* sometimes, and all we got last year was—"

"Four a week! Four a week, *do you know how many that means we missed?*"

"—was that Keystone Kops one—"

"Yeah, and I only got to see it four times before—"

"All right, all right, FINE!" Miranda bellowed. Ryan and Alfred glowered and wandered a few paces away to discuss her lack of culture in lowered voices. "But what about the rest of it? You don't have a carnival with just films."

"Well, it's not a carnival, for one thing," Natalie informed her. "It's Dr. Limberleg's Nostrum Fair and Technological Medicine Show."

"She's right. Says so right here." Miranda deflated as Ryan held up the card (directly in front of Miranda's nose and with maybe a little more flourish than was strictly necessary) to show her that Natalie knew what she was talking about. Natalie, who hadn't had a good look at one yet, plucked it out of his fingers and squinted to read.

DOCTOR LIMBERLEG'S NOSTRUM FAIR
AND
TECHNOLOGICAL MEDICINE SHOW

Jake Epiphemius Limberleg,

DOCTOR OF MEDICAL SCIENCES, EMERITUS
PROPRIETOR AND DIRECTOR OF
RESEARCH AND DEVELOPMENT

Welcome to your very good health

"So I guess they'll have medicine stuff." He shrugged and turned to Natalie. "What about when you took him to your dad's shop? Did you find anything out?"

"They're snake oil salesmen," Natalie said authoritatively. It merited a hiss of breath from the kids around her, although probably only because it sounded so sinister. "Dad says they might be frauds. We have to wait and see."

Before anyone could respond, Mr. Tilden called from the porch, "Come inside a minute, Natalie."

She trotted up the stairs after the grocer, who went straight to the side with the patent medicines to retrieve something from behind the counter. While Natalie waited, she studied the collection of oddly shaped bottles on the wall and read again their even odder names: Cathartic Nerve Food, Spartan Vegetable Panacea, Wintergreen Catholicon . . .

Then she was staring at a frenzied bee in a jar. "Your . . . *associate* Alfred left this behind. The bee was concerned, but I explained to it that some business had called you away temporarily," Mr. Tilden said. He followed Natalie's eyes to the medicines on the wall and looked back at her again, eyebrow raised.

Natalie pointed past him at the patent medicine wall. "That sign wasn't there before, was it?"

Mr. Tilden glanced at the sign over his shoulder: WE SELL PATENT MEDICINES BUT DO NOT ENDORSE THEM. "No, it wasn't."

"Snake oil salesmen." She shook her head knowingly. "Anyhow, thanks for watching the bee for me." Natalie wrapped her arms around the jar and headed for the door. Then she heard the twang of guitar strings on the porch. Her heart sped up. It was Old Tom Guyot.

SEVEN

The Prankster Demon

SHE SHOVED OUT THE DOOR with the jar in her arms. Old Tom sat on the steps with his guitar on his knees. Before she could figure whether or not she ought to be a little afraid of him, Tom turned and spotted her staring.

"What's that you got?"

She tried to look as if she hadn't just been deciding whether or not to scoot closer for a better look at the man who'd met the Devil. "Got a bee."

"Lessee." She took a step closer and held the jar out at arms' length. He peered through the glass. "Sure wish I had a bee," Tom said at last.

"Well . . . it's for sale."

"No foolin'!" Tom leaned forward for a better look and rubbed his lined cheeks with his fingers. "What's a bee like that one cost?"

"Fifteen cents."

Tom looked from Natalie to the bee and back again. "Well, that's fair."

"*Really?*"

"Well, sure. It's got six legs. Five cents a pair." Then Tom sighed. That kind of sigh always meant: *I can't*, or *Not today*, or *Sure wish I could*. Natalie's shoulders slumped a little.

"I'd certainly like to have that bee, but I haven't got much folding money these days." Tom looked sadly at the jar. "That your *last* bee?"

"Yessir." It was her *only* one, so it wasn't exactly a lie.

"Well, then I guess . . ." He gave Natalie a thoughtful look. "What do you think about a trade?"

A trade? "What kind?" Out of the corner of her eye she could see Ryan and Alfred watching curiously.

"Instead of three nickels, how about three questions?"

"I can ask you? What kind of questions? Any I want?"

"Sure. That's the only way it's fair."

"Okay, I'll trade." She sat on the step, plunked the jar down between them, and pretended to think.

There was, of course, only one subject she wanted to question him about, but it didn't seem right to ask, not just like that, not a man who was (almost) a total stranger. Maybe she could start with a harmless question—like maybe what his favorite color was—and work up to the big one. . . . And then she saw, hanging from Tom's wrist, a braided string with a shiny steel gear tied to it.

"That's one of the charms I made, isn't it?"

Tom laughed. "You know anybody else who makes decorations out of gears in these parts, Miss Minks?"

And with that, Natalie knew she could ask Tom Guyot anything. She took a deep breath.

"I heard you met the Devil at the crossroads." She said it fast, in case she lost her nerve, and tensed in case she was wrong and had to run.

But Tom didn't get angry. "Ahh," he said, the same way Natalie's mother had the night before. "I thought you might ask about that."

"My mother told me. Is it true?"

Tom smiled a little sadly. "You don't think your mama would lie to you, do you?"

"She would *never* lie to me, but . . . well, the *Devil?* So it really happened?"

Old Tom nodded soberly.

"What did he look like? No, wait." It wouldn't do to waste her second question on something she wasn't sure she really wanted to know. "When you beat him, he owed you a favor, right? What did you ask?"

He grinned. "Now, that's a good question, and the answer is: I haven't collected the favor yet." He reached into the watch pocket of his old waistcoat with his long-fingernailed right hand. At the end of the chain fob, hanging just beside his old pocket watch, was a coin with a hole in the center. It was an odd green, like what happens to copper when you don't polish it, and the edges were raggedy, as if little bits of it had been snipped off with metal-cutting shears.

"What's that?"

"Don't rightly know, but I think it's the favor. Just showed up there on that old chain the next day."

Natalie looked at it mistrustfully. "Do you . . . doesn't it bother you to carry it around all the time?"

"Can't help it. If I throw it away, I find it later in a pocket. Try to lock it in a box, it winds up inside my shoe. Figure I'm stuck with it until I trade it in."

"Well, why haven't you used it? It's been ages, hasn't it?"

"Just hasn't been anything worth using that favor up for. Hasn't been anything I've needed or wanted I couldn't get myself with a little hard work." He put the watch back in his pocket. Absently his fingers picked over the strings of the guitar, the long nails plucking them as neatly as the crown cap he'd used the day before. Natalie was so transfixed that she didn't even notice Mrs. Byron walk past and shoot her a look that suggested the old lady had a bad smell in her nose.

"Your dad does a lot of business from travelers losing wheels and tires out there in the Old Village, doesn't he?" Old Tom continued.

"Yes. . . ." Only that afternoon, her father had correctly guessed which wheel Doctor Limberleg's wagon had lost, and that it hadn't been found. "And it's . . . always the same one, isn't it? The front left wheel, and then it goes missing."

"Wonder why, ever?"

"I just figured it was a big stone or something that people kept on hitting."

Old Tom shook his head. "That'd make good sense, but the truth's something else again." He chuckled. "In fact, you might say I'm responsible for all those wheels and tires and even a mess of horseshoes coming off just there."

"How?" She didn't know if she had any questions left and waited to see if he would answer.

"The night I won my bet, that old Devil got so mad he off and left without speaking to me again. Just fine so far as I cared. I was pleased as punch to have kept life and soul, but the Devil's promise is binding, on you and on him just the same. So a year or so later, there I was, and a demon comes up to me in the street, polite as you please."

"In the street? In *Arcane?*"

"Right at the edge of town there, in fact, 'neath the water tower." Tom pointed down the lane to where the big wooden tower stood at the corner of Bard Street and Heartwood. "Walked right up and started talking. Well, he looked real enough to me, but people started staring pretty soon. Guess I looked like I was talking to myself, but what could I do?"

"He was invisible, but you could see him anyway?"

"Well," Tom said thoughtfully, "that's hard to say. Invisible doesn't always mean what you think it does."

"I know what it means," Natalie protested. "It means you can't see something."

"Sure, but there's what you *can't* see, and what you *don't* see. Sometimes there's a difference. I suspect there's more than one way to keep folks from seeing you if you don't want 'em to."

He slid the short-nailed hand that wore the brown glass bottleneck up the neck of the guitar, picking the strings with his long-nailed right hand, while Natalie gave his words a little thought.

"Now this fellow, the one I met here in town, he wasn't *the* Devil," Tom went on, "just a mid-grade demon sent to tie up loose ends, 'cause the Devil himself was so mad he'd just as soon have killed me as looked at me.

"'Tom Guyot, I presume,' he said, all prissy like some Philadelphia lawyer. I told him I was, and he said, 'I believe something is owed to you. Kindly tell me what it is and I will settle the debt.'

"Well, it took me a minute to figure out he was asking what I wanted from the Devil to pay off the bet. 'Don't know,' I said. 'I'll think on it.' And I went on my way.

"Next day, same corner, there he is again, glancing around this town like he'd had to track me down in a slum not once but twice. 'Have you thought of anything?'

"'Nope, can't say's I have,' I said. 'I'll think on it a little more.' And off I went again. It was kind of funny, telling a demon all duded up like a lawyer *I'll think on it*. 'Spect I laughed.

"Next day after that. Same corner. Same suit, bigger scowl. Lookin' like he'd sat up all night waiting for a train. 'Have you thought of anything, Mr. Guyot?'

"I laughed again at the lawyer-demon calling me 'Mr.'

That must've stuck in his craw. 'No, sir,' says I, 'but I'll gladly tell you when I do.'

"This time when I walked away he followed me. 'What about money? Wouldn't you like to have a proper house instead of a cabin, or even a whole town to be mayor of? I can snap my fingers and make you rich.'" Tom paused and chuckled. "Why *money*, always?"

"Probably because you don't look like you have any," Natalie said reasonably.

"I suppose. I told him no, I didn't want money from snapping fingers. 'What about fame? I can make you the most famous guitar player in the world. Just like that.' And he made a puff of smoke rise out of his palm, like some sort of vaudeville magician. I probably laughed at that, too.

"Now he was frantic. 'Surely there must be something.' What didn't figure for me was, why'd he care if I collected now or in another year or six or twenty?

"Well, he kept stopping me in the street with suggestions, and they got pretty strange pretty quick. He thought I'd like a career on the stage. Would I like an ocean named after me? Perhaps to discover a silver mine, or marry the most beautiful girl there was, or be fifty years younger, or live forever, or be able to fly. Every day he was a little less polished. He didn't bother looking like he'd shaved anymore, and finally he stopped knotting his tie and even tucking in his shirt.

"Then days would go by before he could think of anything new to suggest. He wouldn't talk to me for a week, or a month, or finally, for a year at a time. Other times he'd walk along behind me for hours, chewing his fingernails and lookin' like he was trying to do higher math in his head. Then he stopped showing up altogether.

"That's when wheels started falling off wagons out there at the crossroads, and I put twos together and got a number that made sense. *That old demon couldn't leave.* He was stuck there until I chose my favor!" Old Tom paused for a long, hooting laugh.

"And he's still there?"

"He's still out there in the Old Village, just a prankster demon who pulls wheels off of carts and shoes off of horses for the lack of anything better to do with his time. 'Course, he used to play proper tricks, but now he don't seem to have the heart for it anymore. He does come back into town from time to time, but I think he's 'bout given up on me."

"Why can't he do anything else? He's a demon, after all."

"'Cause he was given a job by Old Scratch, and since that job's a matter of the Devil's debt, he's bound to that task till he completes it. That's what I think. So it's sort of my fault about the lost wheels, but I can't help it. And yes, I think it's funny, if you want to know."

After her mother's story about awful hands and tearing-sideways jaws, it was funny, terribly funny to think of some mid-level demon stuck at the crossroads forever, getting messier and crankier day by day and thinking of more and more elaborate and outlandish wishes to convince Tom to make. They laughed together for a while.

"So how did you beat him?" Natalie asked at last. "The real Devil, not the prankster demon."

Tom strummed the guitar with his eyes closed. The bottleneck on his left ring finger squeaked gently as it slid over the strings. "How do you think?"

"Because you're the best musician in the world?"

The guitar in his hands made a sound like laughter. "That's what everyone thinks."

Natalie frowned at the tin guitar with its round brass resonator in the middle shining in the sunlight. "Because your guitar was special."

"Nope."

"Because the Devil wasn't much good at music?" she hazarded. It would spoil the story if that was all there was to it.

But Tom shook his head again. "Devil's good at whatever he needs to be good at."

"Mama says it's because you have some kind of . . ." Natalie tried not to look at his crutch, propped against the stair beside him. Would he think she was making fun of him? "Some kind of *grace*."

"Doesn't sound right, does it?"

"Not really," she said before she could stop herself, then turned a deep pink. "I didn't mean—"

Tom hooted again. "Not that kind of grace!" He laughed until he had to set the guitar down and wipe his eyes. "The other kind."

"I don't know any other kind," Natalie said a little defensively.

Tom didn't answer, but the guitar did something very graceful instead, and for a few minutes she just sat and listened.

"Weren't you very afraid?"

The music stopped. He looked up, and for a moment he looked just exactly as ancient as he must've been if he was already an old man fifty years ago. "I thought I would die of the fear."

"How did you survive?"

"I looked him in the face, the way you're looking me in the face this very minute. It was a very hard thing to do, but not doing it would've been worse."

How could looking at a terrifying thing be better than not looking at it? Natalie scratched her head. Looking straight at the Devil seemed like the kind of dangerous thing that would invite trouble no matter what.

Tom spoke as if he could read her mind. "When there's evil standing in your way, you got to get around it however you can, Natalie. You got to look it in the eye, let it know you see it and that it can't creep up on you. What's dangerous is pretending it isn't there at all and letting it get closer and closer while you're looking someplace else, until suddenly evil's walking alongside you like you were two friends out for a stroll on Sunday. So you *look it in the face*. You tell it with your eyes that you know what it is, that it don't have you fooled. You tell it you know what *good* looks like. That might be something like your ma's idea of grace. I don't know; I never got much Sunday school. I call it confidence, that's all."

"Like this?" Natalie gave Old Tom a severe, narrow-eyed stare.

"That looks like a pirate." She tried again, more fearsome and less squinty. "All right, well, that's better, only it's no good trying to be scary. You just want to look . . . *sure* . . . know how I mean?"

This time she succeeded in getting a mote of dust in her left eye. "I'll work on it." Natalie jammed a pair of knuckles in her eye to work the dust speck loose. When she looked up again, she and Tom were not alone on the steps.

Dr. Jake Limberleg stood before them in his frock coat and top hat, a sheaf of printed pages in one bone-pale gloved hand. He towered over them, his hair bright red in the sun.

Natalie scooted aside in case the doctor wanted to pass, but he didn't move, just stared down the bridge of his nose at Old Tom. Out in the heat somewhere the rising-falling rattle of a cicada song swelled and sank away. Still the two men regarded each other silently.

In the long, awkward quiet, nobody paid any attention to Natalie. Normally that would have infuriated her, but just now, caught between these two, she would happily have sunk straight through the steps.

"Those are mighty nice gloves," Tom said.

Dr. Limberleg smiled thinly. "I find them quite comfortable."

Natalie was just beginning to consider slinking off when she noticed the way Tom was looking at the snake oil salesman. Confident, fixed, *sure*.

Dr. Limberleg's smile thinned even further. Another awkward moment passed . . . then Limberleg turned away.

"It worked," Natalie whispered. "Even on a snake oil salesman!"

The doctor looked back and gave her a slit-eyed stare. Natalie squirmed and glanced about, desperate to look somewhere else, anyplace, across the street to where, suddenly, things were happening.

EIGHT

To Your Very Good Health

FOLKS ON THEIR PORCHES and in the street turned, carts and buggies lurched as horses shied in their traces. After a moment's confusion, the drivers in the street reined their carriages and wagons aside and turned to see what had startled all the animals.

Music, odd and clanking and full of strange syncopation, erupted from a little line of figures and vehicles that seemed to have come from somewhere in the direction of the water tower. Natalie moved to the edge of the step and looked around the wide skirt of Dr. Limberleg's frock coat and saw—she squinted and rubbed her eyes. Maybe it was the dust.

The thing at the front of the procession in the street looked mechanical, with shining edges and bright moving parts that caught the light in time with the bizarre tune it was clinking out. All its parts moved in opposition like

Natalie's little flyer in the workshop . . . but it was far too big to be made of clockwork.

Then: *"Ladies and gentlemen!"* Faces turned. The doctor whirled to address the citizens of Arcane, making the bottom of his coat billow out and forcing Natalie to duck to avoid being hit in the face with it. He flung an arm toward the clunking musical thing. "May I introduce *the One-Man Band!"*

The One-Man Band bowed, grinding out its song without cease. At last it drew close enough for Natalie to see that it was nothing more exotic than a man packed into an armorlike apparatus hung with instruments, some of which Natalie recognized and others she did not. With each step a pair of cymbals like brass wings on his back clashed together. His left fingers depressed valves that must've connected to some of the horns seeming to protrude straight out of his chest; his right hand worked buttons that might've had something to do with the accordion-thing that bellowed from under one arm. His face was mostly covered by various harmonicas and mouthpieces.

"The One-Man Band!" Limberleg announced again. More people were emerging now, and scattered applause peppered the street. Beside Natalie, Old Tom made a noise that sounded like "huh." His fingers made vague drumming sounds on his guitar.

It wasn't much of a parade, really. Just a shabby, strange sort of procession: after the One-Man Band came a string of four little chariots. Rather than being drawn by gleaming stallions the way chariots ought, these were pulled by the same piebald mules that had pulled the big wagons through town.

"The Paragons of Science!" Dr. Limberleg announced with another flourish.

She had seen two of the men at the reins before: the spiky gray-haired man, dressed not in work chambray anymore but in a costume with big floppy boots and a velvet cape stitched all over with dull gold embroidery. In the hand that wasn't clutching reins he held a huge hat with an even bigger feather curling off the brim. Faded bunting on the side of the chariot proclaimed AMBER THERAPY in old-fashioned script.

The other three were dressed just as oddly: the one whose chariot read PHRENOLOGY wore an outfit that looked like something made for Aladdin. A turban hung with dark gems swaddled his head. Next was HYDROTHERAPY. The driver of that chariot wore a dusty toga and a green wreath on his brow. Last of all came MAGNETISM. Natalie didn't notice what the driver wore because he turned his head, took off his silvery spectacles, and caught her in his gaze, and when that happened Natalie couldn't look away.

It was as if someone had tied strings around her eyeballs and now the man in the Magnetism chariot had both strings in his hand. She leaned forward, drawn by the pull on the invisible strings around her eyes. She tried to haul herself back to the step she sat on, but the pull, the *pull* . . .

Tom's fingers drummed just a bit louder on the guitar. Natalie shook her head and squeezed her eyes closed. When she opened them, the Magnetism chariot had moved on and a contraption even more outlandish than the One-Man Band was passing in its place.

Tunes vaguely reminiscent of ragtime music tinkled from an upright piano weaving back and forth across the street. The piano tilted crazily from side to side thanks to its being mounted on, of all things, a *bicycle*—and not just any bicycle, but a high-wheeler with one giant, spindly wheel as tall as a man in front and a tiny one in back. A couple of folks in Arcane still rode high-wheelers, even though they were very old-fashioned. Her father had worked on a few of them . . . all without pianos, of course.

How on earth a piano had managed to get stuck somewhere in the middle and how the spindly high-wheeler could support it was anybody's guess. But the cyclist's seat over the front wheel put him at just the right level both to play and to be able to see over the top. In place of proper pedals going around in circles, the high-wheeler's went up and down like a pair of bellows, changing the timbre and the resonance of the piano. The rider played with frantic, alien motions of his arms that made absolutely no sense until Natalie spotted the leather belts wrapped around his elbows. The belts were looped at their other ends through a pair of brass rings in the wooden panel just below the keyboard, which seemed to be the closest thing to handlebars the contraption had.

Not much of the One-Man Band's face had been visible behind his grid of wire and instruments, but Natalie would have sworn he and the piano player were twins.

The smallest member of the parade sat precariously

"The Paragons of Science!"

Dr. Limberleg announced with another flourish.

on top of the wobbling piano, legs dangling off the front as if he were riding between the handlebars of an ordinary bicycle: a small child dressed in a jester's costume. The balding velvet triangles of the costume ended in tarnished bells that jingled as the child wiggled in time to the music. After a few minutes' watching, Natalie still couldn't tell if it was a real kid or a wind-up doll.

The procession ground to a halt, and the four men Dr. Limberleg had called the Paragons of Science stepped down from their chariots. The child on the piano climbed off with the ease of a squirrel and somersaulted the last few feet to the surface of the dirt road. Each of them clutched a sheaf of handbills.

The doctor strode forward into the street, stepped up into the vacant Amber Therapy chariot as if it were a pulpit, and swept his tall hat from his head with a deep bow. His red hair swirled in the air as if caught in a current, and in the bright afternoon sun the gray streaks flashed like silver.

"Ladies and gentlemen," he announced grandly, "I invite each of you to tomorrow's official opening of Dr. Jake Limberleg's Nostrum Fair and Technological Medicine Show! Yes, friends, tomorrow, thanks to the generosity of the good Mr. Simon Coffrett, who has graciously allowed us use of his lot"—here Dr. Limberleg bowed toward where Mr. Coffrett leaned against the porch of Mr. Maliverny's saloon, teacup in hand and looking mildly amused—"where we will open our doors and our cabinets to you!"

A fist ringed with bells shoved a creased handbill into Natalie's lap. Under the frayed hat she glimpsed a small face that wasn't like a child's at all. The sight of it close up was so unexpected that she actually recoiled before she realized it had to be a mask: the harlequin's face was the pale white of birch bark, but smooth as porcelain, with round, faded rosy spots high on its cheeks and glossy lips painted around a perfectly curved smile. It had glittering human eyes, but Natalie thought she heard something click as it blinked, its pale eyelids dropping and snapping open again like a fancy doll's. Then it was gone in a string of somersaults.

Natalie frowned at the handbill.

☞ COMING! ☜

JAKE EPIPHEMIUS LIMBERLEG,

DOCTOR OF MEDICAL SCIENCES, EMERITUS, WELCOMES YOU!

WONDERS
OF SCIENCE,

MIRACLES
OF MEDICINE!

ALL YOUR AILMENTS CURED WITH THE LATEST ADVANCES

ACCOMPANIED BY

CARNIVAL ENTERTAINMENT IN HIGH CLASS!

SPECIAL PROGRAMME OF
NEW AMUSEMENTS!

UNRIVALED EDUCATIONAL OPPORTUNITY—A WINDOW INTO THE MEDICINE OF THE NEW MILLENNIUM! NO QUACKERY OR SPIELING—ONLY THE

NEWEST TREATMENTS
AND
PATENTED PANACEAS!

NOTHING LIKE IT EVER PRESENTED IN YOUR TOWN!

Welcome to your very good health!

"Simon rented 'em the lot?" Tom mumbled, reading over her shoulder. "Wonder what made him do that."

"Forget what you know about medicine! Forget what you think you know about the mysterious machine that is your own body! Forget what you thought you had to live with: the aches you could not cure, the hurts that would not fade! Forget what you know about medicine, and allow me to introduce you to new horizons, new hopes, new health!"

Old Tom looked up from the handbill and made that "huh" sound again.

"Come with your questions and doubts, friends," Dr. Limberleg continued, his lips stretching wide as the four Paragons and the child-sized harlequin passed among the townspeople handing out printed pages and tacking others to porches and pillars. "Come for news. Come for entertainment, if not for a cure. Moving pictures! Cabinets of curiosities! Exotic restoratives, including that time-honored and celebrated treatment for anxiety, the ducking booth!"

Dr. Limberleg pantomimed throwing a baseball across the street, and the harlequin fell neatly to its backside as if it had been dropped by the invisible ball.

The doctor waited for the laughter, still a little hesitant, to die down before adding, "And of course, complimentary trials for any soul bold enough to experiment with the marvels we will exhibit. All clinically verified, all guaranteed. Yes, friends, *guaranteed*, thanks to the wisdom of science and its miracles that my colleagues and I have brought to your front door!"

He hopped nimbly down from the chariot and turned to face Natalie and Tom, his smile diminishing to that narrow line again.

"Until tomorrow," he said.

NINE

The Old Village

TELL ME AGAIN why we're going all the way out there?" Miranda whined.

"So Natalie can tell the story right, Miranda," Ryan snapped, his voice so thick with irritation he didn't even have to add *geez*.

"And *why* didn't we ride our bicycles and save some time?" She looked impishly at Natalie.

"I *told* you, anything that goes through the crossroads loses a wheel." Which was so perfect an excuse to have left the red bicycle at home that even Natalie's guilty conscience let her off the hook. "Everyone knows it. That's how the medicine show wound up here. They weren't even going to stop in Arcane, Dr. Limberleg said."

They were halfway to the Old Village, kicking stones through the dust as they hiked toward the ruins. Alfred had saved Natalie the trouble of trying to convince her

gang to make the hike; after the procession he and Ryan
had descended on Natalie, wanting to know what on earth
she and Old Tom were talking about for so long.

"I'll tell you, but you have to swear to the secret," she
had said. "And we have to go out to the Old Village so I can
tell the story properly." That was all it took. Five of them
set out late that afternoon: Natalie, Alfred, Ryan, Ryan's
brother Jason, who had been allowed to come on condition
that he brought his Scout knife with all the attachments
(just in case), and, of course, Miranda, who was beginning
to have second thoughts.

It wasn't hard to get to the Old Village; you just walked
east out of Arcane on Bard Street until you got there. It was
the fact that none of them had ever gone there just for the
sake of going that made it such an adventure. Now, loaded up
with a canteen borrowed from Mr. Tilden and a bag of cookies donated by Alfred's mother in exchange for a promise to
be back before sundown, they were three-quarters of a mile
from the crumbling center of the Old Village and beginning
to pass the remains of the outlying houses.

"I don't know why you couldn't just tell the story
where we were," Miranda huffed, looking uncomfortably
at a pile of crumbled stone steps leading up to a collapsed
porch with no house attached. From hidden, shady nooks
the cicadas chattered, tides of sound swelling and receding.
Everything shimmered, hazy in the heat.

"Anyone know what this town was called, anyway?"
Ryan asked, stopping to lift a battered sign with ancient,
flaking paint that had nothing coherent to say.

"Old Village," Jason said.

"That's what we call it," Ryan said patiently. "What did it *used* to be called? Was it called Arcane, too, before it . . . before it . . . got deserted?"

"I know," Natalie said from the front of the caravan, walking between the parallel tracks from Doc Fitzwater's Winton. "Mama told me all about it once. Want me to tell you?" she asked innocently, glancing over her shoulder.

Of course they did. Annie Minks's stories were legend, and Natalie loved telling them.

"It was a French trading post at first. I forget what they called it, or maybe Mama didn't know. Then later the Americans built a mill on the river"—Natalie nodded at a mass of stone bricks a short distance away on what must once have been a riverbed but had long since gone dry—"and it grew up into a town: Trader's Mill, after the old trading post and the new mill."

They stopped amid the wrecked foundations and half-fallen porches on either side of the road to rest in the shade of a slender maple tree that had climbed over long years through a little stretch of stone wall. A quiet wind rustled past, turning the leaves belly-up and silver. Natalie and her friends listened to the noises of bugs and breeze as they passed around the canteen and ate a handful of broken cookies each.

"So what happened to it?" Alfred asked, passing Natalie the cookie bag.

"Mama said it was sometime before the War Between the States." Tall things, parts of old buildings, cast lengthening shadows up ahead. "She said it's an old mystery that was never solved. Nobody really knows exactly what happened."

"What do you mean, nobody knows?" Miranda demanded, swatting at a pair of big buffalo gnats buzzing around her head.

"I mean, nobody knows," Natalie snapped. "Do *you* know? Go ask your dad if you don't believe me; see what he says. Ask Mr. Tilden. Ask anybody."

"So how does your mother know?"

This won some raised eyebrows and glancing back and forth from Ryan and Alfred and Jason. Natalie's mother's knowledge of Arcane and the strange things that went on in it was not to be questioned, least of all by Miranda Porter.

"A diary," Natalie retorted. "The man who wrote it was my mother's great-grandfather or something. She still has it. He was a judge."

The boys sat back on their heels with looks of awe. It even shut Miranda up, but only for a minute out of respect for the undeniable niftiness of an ancient diary. "It's a whole town," she argued after a decent pause. "Whole towns don't just go empty and fall off the map!"

"Sure they do," said Natalie. "Didn't you ever hear about Roanoke?"

"Yes, in school, just like you did," Miranda replied, swatting spastically at the flies again, "but that was hundreds of years ago. Who cares?"

"It doesn't matter how long ago. That's not the point," Natalie said patiently as she rolled the cookie bag closed and dusted off her hands. "An entire *settlement* disappeared in Roanoke, and all they left was one word carved on a tree, so I guess you're wrong and sometimes towns do fall off the map. Now do you want to hear the rest or not?"

Miranda sighed and rolled her eyes as the group started moving again.

"Anyhow, it was back before the war, and there were no telephones and not many telegraphs either, and the only people who really traveled much were doctors and judges and folks like that. My great-great-whatever was a traveling judge, and he was the one who came into Trader's Mill and found out that something was wrong."

They passed a little strip of storefronts with nothing behind them but vacant land. Through the empty doorways, they could see a stand of cottonwood trees and sassafras overhanging the dry riverbed.

"The judge and his assistant were on the road outside Trader's Mill, and they saw someone running toward them out of the town. It was a lady, and she was crying, and she would only say over and over, 'They're falling, they're falling.'"

Bang! All five of them jumped. On the wide porch of a caved-in house, a door, miraculously still on its hinges, swung a little and snapped against its useless frame with a loud bark. Natalie grinned. You couldn't *pick* a better place for this story.

"So they rode into town with the lady," she continued, lowering her voice the way her mother always did when something was about to happen. "The whole village was very quiet. For a while he didn't see anyone. And then . . ."

She paused, partly for effect but also because ahead of them she could see where another road met theirs. The crossroads.

The boys were hanging on every word but trying to look nonchalant about it. "Then what?" Ryan asked at last.

"In the diary, the judge only said that the ones who could still move . . ." What words exactly had her mother used?

Suddenly, there it was again—a dizzy, vaguely sick feeling, like the one she'd had yesterday . . . something in her throat felt like it was spinning the way you could start a globe spinning with a good smack of your palm. Natalie squeezed her eyes shut and hoped it looked as if she was just thinking hard, and abruptly remembered what the diary had said.

"The ones who could still move . . . *flung themselves about like the clumsiest of machines.*" She opened her eyes carefully. The dizziness faded.

"What does that mean?"

Natalie shrugged. "That's why no one knows what happened. The judge didn't say anything else. He and the lady and the men who'd come with him rode as fast as they could out of town to find help. They rode straight through to Pinnacle without stopping even once, and the horses were half-dead by the time they got there."

"And then what?" Jason asked, wide-eyed.

"Well, then the doctor in Pinnacle rode back with the judge. By the time they got to Trader's Mill, days had gone by . . . and the whole town was empty. Everyone was gone, without any clues. And you want to know the really creepy part?" The boys had the good grace to go bug-eyed in proper *It gets worse?* fashion. "The judge married the lady who came running out of the town, and until the day she died she refused to talk about what she'd seen ever again. Even the judge wouldn't talk about it, not even with his own children, because it upset her so much."

Natalie stopped twenty yards from the crossroads and looked around. She could almost taste the dust in the late afternoon haze. The cicadas buzzed to a rattling crescendo, then the sound dimmed to a low murmur. Beyond the ruins, tall grasses and old, overgrown hedges of Osage orange brambles hinted at buried gardens, lost yards, and vegetable patches gone feral and wild. Off to the southwest, the old forest crouched near the horizon.

"So they all left," Miranda said, as if it couldn't be more obvious. "Something . . . something happened and they all left."

"Maybe. Except that what the judge wrote sounds like nobody in the town could walk anymore. And where could they have gone? The closest town is Pinnacle, and the judge would've met them on the way back. Anyhow . . . here we are."

They stood at the crossroads. Four straight lanes stretched away in four different directions. Around them some of the ruins of the Old Village were still recognizable: the wide front and side of a livery stable, the eroding skeleton of a church, an overturned watering trough by an iron pump.

While the boys poked around and Miranda glanced about nervously, Natalie studied the crossroads and tried to guess where Old Tom would have built his fire.

This time, when the buzzing started, Natalie sat down just to be sure she wouldn't fall over in front of her friends the way she had fallen in the middle of Bard Street. *Again?* She drew her knees up against her chest as the sparks started flicking across her vision and waited for them to clear.

The image that began to form behind her closed eyes had the detail of a memory, and yet it came in pictures, like a dream. It had a *feeling*, too—in the way that remembering a moment of humiliation sometimes makes your stomach twist, even though the moment itself is long over.

Instead of early evening, it was early morning, and a man was walking toward the crossroads. Natalie's friends were nowhere to be seen; only the man coming toward the place where the two roads met. He stared ahead, not looking left or right, and Natalie understood without quite knowing how that the man on his way to the crossroads saw things that weren't there. More than that, he was *used* to it; it happened every moment of his life, waking and sleeping.

As Natalie waited for the odd string of what felt like memories—although they certainly weren't her memories—to unfold, the man drew close to the crossroads. Shimmering like mirages or trick photography, the tumbledown houses and disintegrating façades of the village around him painted themselves over with different buildings, whole buildings. The Old Village became Trader's

Mill, as it had been decades before. And just as suddenly, the man wasn't alone.

The streets were thick with people—but there was something terribly, terribly wrong with them. They lurched like poorly handled puppets, pitching and reeling as they staggered through the town. Some fell and did not get up, pulling themselves along on stiff arms and legs until they could no longer even crawl.

Like the clumsiest of machines, Natalie thought dimly, horror curling up from her stomach. Dimly she shoved herself to her feet, desperate to run, to hide somewhere from the terrifying scenes.

At the center of the town, the man who had walked to the crossroads took his spectacles from his eyes and wiped the dust from the lenses one by one. When he put them back on, the streets emptied. The awful figures winked out of existence, and the pristine façades of Trader's Mill shimmered away, leaving the dilapidated Old Village in its place. Nothing but abandoned, derelict wrecks: caved-in porches, crumbling brick walls, and collapsed roofs. Nothing in the streets but dust and raggedy weeds. No puppetlike people falling and creeping like mechanical toys winding down. No one at all but the man who saw things that weren't there: Simon Coffrett, who Natalie now somehow knew had walked with visions since he had first opened his eyes in this world.

"Hey, Natalie!" Ryan shouted. Natalie jerked out of her reverie to find that she had, in fact, climbed back to her feet and staggered several yards away from the crossroads. It was late afternoon again. Behind her, Ryan stood on tiptoe and peered through a broken window into what had probably been the general store, just on the other side of the crossroads. "Look at this!"

Natalie shuddered one last time at the memory of the grim figures she had seen flooding these streets and sprinted to where Ryan stood. She was not as tall and had to climb on a piece of broken stone before she could see over the windowsill.

"Oh," she breathed.

Inside, the general store was mostly intact. Wheels of every size and description hung on the walls and from the ceiling. They were propped up three and four deep on the floor, too; some new-looking and made of metal and rubber, and others ancient, made from wood. There wasn't a speck of dust to be seen on any of them. Between the wheels here and there hung horseshoes, which gleamed as if they had actually been polished.

The whole room looked oddly well kept for being in a town that had been abandoned for more than half a century. It looked, on the whole, as if someone was tending to it. Like, for instance, a very bored and frustrated demon who had nothing else to do but polish the wood and metal until an old guitar player finally decided on a wish. Natalie laughed.

"I know why those are there! Old Tom told me about them."

"Old Tom is weird," Miranda sniffed from where she stood in the shade a few yards away. "And why doesn't he cut his fingernails?"

"He is not weird." Natalie jammed her hands on her hips. "He's a lot more interesting than *some* people I can think of, but that's not the same. And since you asked, his fingernails are long on one hand so he can play his guitar without a pick if he wants to, which you could've figured out for yourself if you paid any attention. In *fact*," she continued loudly as Miranda opened her mouth to make some retort, "if you weren't a coward, you could have asked him and I bet he would've told you this story himself!"

"So, tell," said Alfred, tossing aside a round green bottle from which he had been idly peeling a yellowed label. "We're supposed to be back before sundown," he added with a look at the sinking sun.

"All right." Natalie jumped down from the stone she stood on, nearly landing on her backside as her foot came down on another fat, round bottle. She kicked it aside and walked to where the roads converged. The sky was still a deep, bright blue, but the shadows were inching eastward.

"It starts with Old Tom, hiking home from the war."

She told the story about Old Tom and the Devil, and then went on to tell about the prankster demon and how he kept busy by pulling wheels off wagons until Tom decided on a favor. They were nervous at first, sitting right where the thing was supposed to have happened; fearful as Natalie described the Devil's horrible hands and deadly challenge; then riveted as the great contest took place and

Tom was declared the winner by a ghost town full of the spirits of all the ages. The bit about the prankster demon made them laugh until Ryan remembered that there was a roomful of wheels only a few yards away from where they sat.

"It can't be true," he muttered, staring over his shoulder at the broken window.

"Wheels come off for lots of reasons," Natalie said reasonably, "but nobody's lived here for . . . well, since before the war. Don't you think they'd at least be a little dusty?"

"Um—"

Then they nearly jumped out of their skins.

A long shadow fell across the crossroads, and not a shadow that belonged to any of them. Five kids prepared to scream. Someone, not a child, cleared his throat only a few feet away.

"Excuse me," said tiny old Chester Teufels.

Five screams fizzled out in relief.

"We didn't see you," Natalie managed when her heart started beating again.

"I know," Mr. Teufels said in his weak, tired voice. He looked even more shabby and threadbare than usual. "And I didn't mean to scare you. I was taking my evening constitutional and I saw you heading this way. I didn't see you at the end of my walk, so I came to see you got safely on your way home."

The kids nodded a little frantically and half walked, half sprinted down the road back to Arcane.

"Thanks," Natalie called over her shoulder. "We'll go straight home!"

"It's just that you never know," Mr. Teufels's weak voice called after them, "whether these old places are safe or not."

By the time Natalie had trudged back to Arcane, parted ways with Miranda, Ryan, Jason, and Alfred, and ran through town to her house at the far end of Bard Street, she figured she had to be very, very late for supper. She ran around the side of the porch and got the old iron pump working long enough to wash her hands and face, then raced inside.

Instead of walking in to the stern looks that she was accustomed to getting when she scrambled in late for a meal, Natalie found Charlie alone in the kitchen, stirring a pot on the stove.

She stopped on the kitchen threshold. "What's that?"

"Tomato soup."

Natalie looked around suspiciously. "Tomato soup?"

Charlie looked at the contents of the pot and then back at Natalie. "Yeah, tomato soup!" He lifted the spoon he was stirring with and examined the orange liquid dripping from it before plunking it back into the pot. "Supper, Nattie," he said defensively. "What do you think?"

"Okay, but why are *you* cooking it?"

"What's wrong with me cooking?" Charlie demanded.

"You burn things worse than Mama does!"

"I do not," he snapped. He yanked the pot off the burner, completely forgetting to use a potholder. "*Ow!*"

"*And* you're supposed to make cheese sandwiches when you make tomato soup! Everybody knows that." Natalie folded her arms and looked around. "Where's Mama, anyway?"

"I'm here," came a voice from the top of the stairs. "I'm right here."

Natalie peeked out of the kitchen and up the stairs. Mrs. Minks yawned and rubbed her eyes as she made her way down.

"Mama," Charlie said, peering over Natalie's shoulder and hiding his burned hand behind his back, "go back to bed. I can handle supper."

"Where's your father?" Mrs. Minks asked peevishly. "Whose brilliant plan was this? Not waking me up to fix supper. Honestly."

"Mama, I'm sixteen. I can open a can of soup without—"

"He forgot the sandwiches, Mama. You can't have tomato soup unless—"

Abruptly, they both stopped talking as Mrs. Minks swayed on the stairs and stumbled down the last five steps. Natalie and her brother leaped forward, catching their mother just in time to keep her from sprawling headlong into the kitchen.

"Nattie, get Dad," Charlie said quickly. "He's in the shop."

"I'm fine, Charlie," Mrs. Minks snapped, leaning on his shoulder as she flexed the foot she'd twisted on the way down. "I just lost my balance. Nothing a little tomato soup won't fix."

Natalie hesitated in the doorway while Charlie helped Mrs. Minks to a chair at the table. She glanced from her mother to her older brother, frowning.

"Mama, maybe Dad'll want some soup, too," Charlie said. "Don't you think we ought to call him?"

Mrs. Minks laughed tiredly and coughed into a handkerchief. "All right, all right. Natalie, go call your father and tell him supper's ready, will you? And if your brother has no objections, I'll see about some sandwiches."

Over their mother's bent head, Charlie shot Natalie a sharp look, its meaning perfectly clear. "Um. I'm not really that hungry, actually," Natalie said, staring back at her glaring brother. Then she slipped out the door.

On her way across the porch, Natalie turned to peer back in through the kitchen window. Charlie was pacing. Her mother was resting at the table, head in her arms.

Natalie decided she really wasn't in the mood for sandwiches after all.

TEN

Dr. Limberleg's Nostrum Fair and Technological Medicine Show

WHY ISN'T MAMA COMING?" Natalie asked as she followed Charlie down the street toward the lot on the first day of the medicine show.

"She's tired."

Natalie scowled. That wasn't a reason.

"She's *tired*," Charlie repeated before she could demand a better one. "And her foot's still sore from last night. That's why Dad went to Mr. Finch's shop."

"I know, I know. Vitamins. Mr. Finch won't even be up yet," Natalie grumbled, glancing over her shoulder toward the pharmacy. "And didn't he just bring vitamins over yesterday? Why on earth didn't he bring *more* if they were going to be gone after a day? And anyway, vitamins don't do anything for you if your foot's sore."

"Everyone's up," was all Charlie said.

He was right, of course. The whole town was out and about, and most everyone meandered toward the empty lot at the end of Heartwood Street, trying to look as if he or she was doing anything else *besides* going to the medicine show. Even Mr. and Mrs. Tilden had turned out. It was like the morning Doc had left; Arcane had taken to the street but didn't really want to be caught there.

At the end of Heartwood the ground rose sharply and the dirt road hooked left, and there it was, ringed on three sides by the swishing green cornfields.

A banner stretched over the entrance to the lot, welcoming them to DR. JAKE LIMBERLEG'S NOSTRUM FAIR AND TECHNOLOGICAL MEDICINE SHOW. The empty field was gone, and in its place was . . . well, it was still hard to say exactly what had moved in.

The five wagons and the cluster of tents had multiplied overnight to become a little village. Pavilions of all sizes filled the lot, draped with bunting and streamers that rippled halfheartedly in the breeze. Their faded colors had probably once been bright and festive, but in the sharp morning sun they looked a little worse for the wear. A high webwork of wires stretched overhead, supported here and there by narrow wooden poles; maybe they would string lights up there when it got dark.

Still, it felt like a carnival, with pitchmen calling and a delicious blend of fresh sawdust smells and the scents of different kinds of sugar and syrup and frying things mingling in the air. There was music, so the twinned One-Man Band and cycling pianist must have been around somewhere.

The giant thing on its mismatched, brass-rimmed tires had to be around someplace, too—and Dr. Limberleg's generators, the ones powered by his collection of old bicycles. Including at least one Chesterlane Eidolon, just like hers.

There was no way she was asking for Dr. Limberleg's help with her own bicycle . . . but maybe if Natalie could get a good look at his blue Chesterlane, she could figure something out herself.

At the front of the fair, a stage built on the center wagon slowly collected the citizens of Arcane to itself. A painted cloth hung as a backdrop, depicting scenes from the history of medicine throughout the ages. Four spindly chairs lined one side, and an angular black podium stood alone on the other.

"Natalie!" Ryan and Alfred jogged up. "Where do you think the picture show'll be?" Ryan demanded, scowling at the forest of tents as if willing them to part and show him the way straight to the one pavilion he cared about.

Before Natalie could answer, an unseen drum rolled, echoing hollowly through the fair. The small figure of the harlequin appeared on the stairs rising to the stage. On the topmost step it took hold of a rope hanging beside the backdrop, gave one-two-three swings of its arms, and jumped to the ground. The illustrated curtain parted, and a tall figure stepped through the gap to the center of the stage.

"My dear friends, welcome to your very good health!" proclaimed Dr. Jake Limberleg.

He swept his top hat from his head with one gloved hand and bowed, which made his wild hair and his frock coat billow spectacularly. The audience applauded politely. Natalie put her hands on her hips instead. If he wanted to impress her, he was going to have to work for it.

Dr. Limberleg's eyes roved the curious and doubtful faces of the audience from behind the pale blue lenses of his eyeglasses. "We come to you from the doorsteps of your neighbors in Pinnacle," he announced, "where I am pleased to announce we were present for the final days of the now-famous Pinnacle flu!"

All around Natalie people stiffened; hands waving paper fans hesitated just a second in their back-and-forth motion.

"I like to believe we had something to do with bringing about the flu's end." Dr. Limberleg grinned. "But"—had he just looked straight at Mr. Tilden?—"I'll save that story for your own Dr. Fitzwater to tell when he returns."

Murmurs whispered through the crowd. Mr. Tilden frowned slightly. This clearly wasn't what he had expected the snake oil salesman to say.

"Allow me to present my colleagues, the Paragons of Science!" The unseen drum rolled and the harlequin scrambled back up the stairs to perform its leap for the rope once more. When the curtain parted again, the four men who had driven the chariots through Arcane stepped, side by side, onto the stage.

"From New York City," Dr. Limberleg declared, "Dr. Paracelsus Vorticelt, specialist in the arts of Magnetism and Lodestone Healing!"

He swept his arm toward the Paragon at the end of the line, dressed in an angular suit with a high celluloid collar.

He swept his top hat from his head with one gloved hand and bowed,
which made his wild hair and his frock coat billow spectacularly.

His walking stick was narrow and white, and like Dr. Limberleg he wore wire spectacles, only his appeared to have mirrors for lenses . . . or perhaps it was just the way they caught the sun that made them seem too dark and reflective to see through. He made a short bow.

Then Paracelsus Vorticelt removed his spectacles. His eyes, unblinking and bottomless, seemed to be all dark pupil with only the faintest rim of white. People swayed like cattails as his gaze gripped them, released them, and moved on. Natalie looked at her shoes and watched him out of the corner of her eye until she heard Dr. Limberleg's voice again. Just the memory of looking at Vorticelt made her head hurt.

"From Edinburgh, Scotland: Sir Willoughby Acquetus, expert in the ancient Greco-Roman science of Hydrotherapy!"

The last time Natalie had seen Acquetus he had been wearing a toga. This time, he wore a waistcoat under a long black robe like a university professor's or a judge's. A short white powdered wig sat on his head. He smiled vacantly for exactly three seconds, then returned to examining the silver head of his walking stick.

"What's a paragon, anyhow?" Natalie asked, frowning up at Charlie.

"A paragon is a perfect example of something," Charlie said after a moment's thought.

"Like an eidolon," Natalie said. She'd looked up the word in the dictionary the day before. "*Eidolon* means an image of something, but it can also mean a phantom or an apparition."

"Kind of," Charlie said, grinning at Natalie's recitation. "Only a paragon is a little bit more than that. A paragon is something that shows you exactly how others like it should be."

"So they're the Paragons of Science? These folks are supposed to show us what science looks like?" Natalie glanced from Charlie to the wild figures on the stage. "Is it a joke?"

"They don't look like they're joking," Charlie muttered.

Onstage, Dr. Limberleg gave another flourish of his cape, eyes lighting on Natalie for a moment as if he had heard every word and didn't appreciate the interruption. "From Vienna, Austria," he snapped, "Herr Doktor Thaddeus Argonault, the greatest student of the great Dr. Spurzheim, is the modern world's leading authority in Phrenology!"

Argonault looked by far the most normal of the four Paragons—at least until he stepped forward and doffed his bowler hat, revealing an elaborate network of lines and numbers tattooed right onto his bald scalp.

"And from Paris, France: The Chevalier Alpheus Nervine, world-renowned pioneer in Amber Therapy!"

Natalie didn't need to know what Amber Therapy was to dislike Alpheus Nervine right off the bat; once someone's chased you with a claw hammer it takes a lot to change your opinion of him. He looked as if he'd gotten dressed that morning and then remembered he was supposed to have put on the costume he'd worn for the procession. The floppy boots on his feet and rapier buckled at his waist looked a little strange over rough work clothes.

The Paragons took seats on the spindly chairs while Dr. Limberleg continued his spiel. "No doubt there are those among you who look around this morning and see nothing but quacks. Hucksters." His blue-lensed eyes fell on Natalie again. "*Snake oil salesmen.*" She recoiled a little, and for a second Dr. Limberleg's smile widened. "But allow me to change your minds!"

Somewhere out of view, a collection of horns played a fanfare that ended in an out-of-tune squeak that made even Dr. Limberleg cringe before he could stop himself.

He prowled the stage, aiming his leather-clad finger at first one, then another person in the audience. "*You,* sir, are welcome to explore the sciences displayed before you today in the persons of Messieurs Vorticelt, Acquetus, Argonault, and Nervine! *You,* madam, are our guest on a tour of the arts of the healing and curative disciplines!"

A burst of what was probably supposed to be celebratory music erupted from behind the stage.

"You may notice," he added when the discordant tune stopped, "that there are no shills or spielers passing among you with boxes of tinctures and ointments. The reason is merely this: patent medicines and advanced treatments are dangerous! We do not believe in administering as if all ailments were the same, to be salved with a bit of wintergreen and snake oil!"

Natalie glanced at Mr. Tilden, trying to figure out what he might be thinking. The grocer's face was sharp-eyed but otherwise expressionless.

"We will indulge your curiosity and your skepticism for one day as the Technological Medicine Show to establish our credentials, and during this time we will offer no products and indeed no *services* except those that assist the advancement of knowledge. Tomorrow morning, we will reopen as Dr. Limberleg's Nostrum Fair, in which"—and here he stopped and knelt on one knee at the edge of the stage, bringing his too-tall form almost to eye-level with the taller men in the audience—"in which, if we have earned your trust, we will diagnose anyone who wishes to be healed and prescribe an appropriate course of treatment. And now . . ."

Dr. Limberleg stood swiftly, launching himself with weird grace back to his full height amid a sudden racket of horns and percussion that sounded like a Sousa march gone demented, the volume of which forced him to stop talking and wait for silence again.

He managed to look magisterial for another moment or two before it became clear the noise had gone on too long. The Chevalier Alpheus Nervine turned his head to look sharply in the direction of the painted curtain and whatever it concealed—presumably the One-Man Band. The racket stopped so suddenly that Natalie had an odd feeling of wind in her ears, as if the sound had been sucked not just out of the air but straight out of her head.

"Welcome!" Dr. Limberleg got the showman's smile back on his face and swept his arms high one last time. "Welcome, friends, to Dr. Limberleg's Technological Medicine Show!"

@ @ @

"We're going to do this right," Natalie began. Ryan and Alfred nodded. Miranda Porter tapped her foot impatiently. "There's four of us. We'll go in twos and see what we can find." Ryan opened his mouth. "I know, I know," Natalie sighed. "You just want to see the films. Fine. After that—"

"Hang on." An alarmed Alfred glanced at Miranda, edging closer. "I get Natalie."

Miranda shot a venomous look at Natalie through slitted eyes. Ryan shot the same look at Alfred before he struck off to the left with Miranda flouncing along behind him.

Natalie and Alfred went right. "What are we looking for?" Alfred asked.

"Anything interesting. Like that big wheeled thing, or the generators and the bicycles that power them up."

"Films are interesting," Alfred muttered.

Natalie sighed expansively. "We'll find the films. I just want to see what this place *is* first."

They passed the older boys at the ducking booth just in time to see George Sills hit the target dead center. The thin, pale man in the booth had time only to make a tired face before he splashed into the tub below. His joints creaked audibly as he climbed out, making Natalie think of rusty gears. At other concessions, people threw balls at bottles or fed coins into zoetropes that spun still pictures before the watcher's eyes until the images appeared to move.

They passed a clump of curious folks surrounding a harassed-looking Mr. Tilden. Natalie heard someone ask,

"Is it true?" Poor Mr. Tilden. It was exactly what he'd been trying to avoid; now everybody thought the hucksters knew something about the Pinnacle flu that the rest of Arcane didn't.

Every once in a while, blasts of disjointed music from the One-Man Band exploded somewhere deep in the maze of booths and pavilions and fluttering tents. Natalie and Alfred decided to look for the source of the clanging and see where that took them.

They wound through the concessions and past an open-fronted tent full of printed placards on easels, a few more spindly black chairs, and a table piled with books and pamphlets. The bunting across the front of the tent read MAGNETISM.

After the experience of eye contact with Vorticelt, nothing could have prevented her from having a closer look at whatever there was to read about Magnetism—as long as Vorticelt himself didn't show up. She nudged Alfred, took a few steps toward the tent, and stopped. Alfred stood unmoving behind her. "What?"

"I still have a headache from earlier is all," he mumbled.

Natalie peered inside the tent, but the only person there was a thin and pale man who sat very still on his chair as if he was asleep.

"The Paragon's not in there. I just want a look." She tiptoed inside, leaving Alfred fidgeting on the threshold.

CURE NERVOUS DISEASES WITHOUT DRUGS OR MEDICINES, the first placard proclaimed over a picture of a languid, tired-looking woman that reminded Natalie for a moment of her mother. PARACELSUS VORTICELT, THE PARAGON OF MAGNETISM, THE ONLY HEIR OF THE GREAT MESMERIST HIMSELF, announced the second card. Beneath the words an angular image of Vorticelt brandishing his narrow white cane like a wand stared out of an oval frame, facing a second image of someone in a long white wig and a costume from sometime hundreds of years before. Presumably the Great Mesmerist, whoever that was. The third placard read: PARACELSUS VORTICELT PERFORMS MIRACLE CURES USING ONLY THE FORCE OF ANIMAL MAGNETISM.

"What's animal magnetism?" Natalie said aloud.

The thin, pale man lifted his head and spoke quietly from his chair. Either he was the same man who had ridden the piano-bicycle in the procession, or Limberleg had hired a bunch of brothers with a really strong family resemblance.

"Animal magnetism restores balance to the body's magnetic fluids." His voice was soft and there was something grainy about it that reminded Natalie of a phonograph record. "It is called animal magnetism because instead of magnetic minerals, it requires only a highly magnetic human animal to achieve the same effect. A practitioner uses a rod to conduct the magnetic charge from himself to his patient, but Brother Paracelsus is so magnetic that his gaze alone is enough to achieve the necessary effects. A course of magnetized water taken externally, preferably Paracelsus Vorticelt's patented Aqua Magnetica, is recommended in chronic cases of magnetic disparity."

"So he just stares at you and you're cured?" Natalie asked, reaching for one of the pamphlets. *Disparity* she didn't understand, but Natalie knew what it meant to take a medicine externally. "And people are supposed to buy water to rub on afterward? Can't they just take a bath?"

Rather than answering, the thin man blinked slowly and his head dropped back to his chest as if he had gone to sleep again.

"This has got to be a joke," Natalie muttered, tossing the pamphlet back on the table.

The tent next door, proclaiming MAGNETISM TREATMENT on its frayed bunting, was tied up tight. Natalie tried to peek through the flaps, but Alfred grabbed the strap of her overalls to haul her away. He didn't relax until they'd turned a corner and all things Magnetism were out of sight.

"Hey, look at that." He jogged over to a glass case in front of the entrance to a large red pavilion. Something inside the case moved, catching the light. "What is this thing, Natalie?"

"Cabinet of Curiosities," she read from the draped banner over the doorway.

"I mean what's *this*?"

Natalie edged around two bigger kids and put her face up to the glass. A tinny, discordant music-box tune muffled by the brass-fitted glass panels accompanied a perfect replica of the One-Man Band as it strolled across a little moth-eaten velvet-covered dais inside the case, manipulating its tiny instruments.

"It's an automaton," Natalie said slowly. "A little machine. He—Dr. Limberleg—collects them."

"What makes it move?"

"Clockwork. They wind up." The little man executed a sharp turn and began pacing in the other direction, the brass cymbals clashing on his back.

"So it's like the one you're making with your dad, right?"

"Not really," Natalie said, swallowing uncomfortably. "Let's go." She remembered Mr. Tilden's words the day before: *I don't like the way they seem.*

Alfred hesitated at the glass case. "Hey, Natalie? If it's a wind-up, where's the key?"

The small figure, showing no signs of winding down, turned sharply again. The faint discordant music didn't seem to repeat at all. Natalie watched for a moment, until the automaton did another sharp turn.

"I don't know." She took a couple of determined steps away from the case, but Alfred darted the other way, right up to peer through the curtains into the tent. When she didn't follow him, he stared back at her, incredulous.

"You don't want to go in? You love mechanical stuff."

I love mechanical stuff because I understand it, Natalie thought, *but I don't understand this automaton at all, and it scares me.*

"Nah. I . . . I see enough of it at home."

"Sure looks swell in there," he said wistfully.

Natalie looked desperately around for something, anything else to distract Alfred from the curtained pavilion in front of them. To one side, the lane opened onto a row of concessions, and at the end of that row she spotted something lit up like a star, gleaming with a blinding light. "What's that?" she said, too eagerly, and shaded her eyes as she pulled him away from the Cabinet of Curiosities toward it.

As the two of them wandered closer, a group of older girls surrounded the shining thing for a moment, shading enough of the glare for Natalie to make out the shape of a box, brass below and glass on top, capped by a little canopy of faded red silk. The tallest of the girls turned a crank on one side and leaned in close to the box for a moment. Laughter, then squeals from the group as the girl who had turned the crank bent to retrieve something from a little door in the brass part. Whispers, giggles, and shrieks from six bent heads, then the girls strolled away, on to some other amusement.

When she and Alfred reached it and saw what was inside, Natalie's jaw dropped. She could tell immediately that she was looking at something mechanical, but she'd never imagined an automaton on this scale.

The box contained a woman—or at least the top half of one, visible from the waist up and leaning slightly to her left so that her ear rested against the small end of a tortoiseshell ear trumpet. Her face was young and smooth and beautiful, and looked like it might be made of wax. Her eyes were thick-lashed and closed. The graceful fingers of her long hands sat folded neatly atop a green jade box carved with swirls and flowers. She wore an embroidered silk gown of some vaguely Oriental style, and her shining black hair was done in a fancy updo of twisting rolled curls—and topped with a small gilded birdcage. Inside it, a little yellow canary chirped and fluttered. The bird, at least, looked like it might be the real thing.

"Say," Alfred said admiringly. Natalie gave him a sharp look, and he blushed. "Well, she *is* kind of pretty," he grumbled.

The squeamish feeling she'd gotten from the miniature One-Man Band was too fresh in her memory for Natalie to particularly like the looks of this thing. Warily, she read the white lettered card that stood inside the glass beside the jade box.

PHEMONOE

WHO FORETOLD THE RULE OF

Alexander the Great

ANSWERS YOUR EVERY QUESTION FOR A PENNY

BY MEANS OF

The Most Ancient Art of Gelomancy!

PAY A PENNY,

TURN THE CRANK,

SPEAK YOUR QUESTION CLEARLY INTO THE EAR TRUMPET,

THEN GIVE A GOOD HEARTY LAUGH

AND

Natalie examined what she could see of the mechanism connected to the ivory-handled crank on the side. Below the coin slot, a little weighing pan, like those on a set of scales, hung from a lever suspended from the ceiling of the box. The other side of the lever held the crankshaft connected to the ivory handle. Natalie smiled and relaxed. This was no weirdly inexplicable thing moving on its own. This she could understand.

"That lever keeps the crank from moving until the weight of the penny in the pan releases it," she explained. "When you turn the crank, it winds up Phemonoe here so she can do whatever it is she does."

"So what's *gelomancy?*"

"Dunno." Natalie rooted in her pockets and came up with a coin. "Here."

Alfred dropped the penny through onto the little metal weighing pan and gave the handle three good turns until it would go no farther.

In its cage among the piled black hair, the canary fluttered and chattered, but the sibyl herself didn't move.

The wide end of the ear trumpet, covered by a delicate brass grille, was set into the glass above the ivory handle. "Alfred," Natalie said, tapping the grille, "you have to ask your question first. And you have to laugh. I guess that's what gelomancy means." She grinned. "Ask it if you're going to marry Miranda Porter someday. That ought to be good for a chuckle. Plus you already know the answer, so it'll be a good test of the sibyl's accuracy."

Alfred gave her a dark look and leaned close to the ear trumpet to whisper something inaudible through the brass grille, then gave a loud laugh.

At the moment Alfred laughed into the trumpet, the woman inside the glass box moved. Her shoulders lifted, the way someone's will on a deep, deep inhalation, and her eyes popped open to reveal bright blue balls of painted glass. She straightened, leaning away from the trumpet, unfolded her long-fingered hands, and tapped on the surface of the box. Her glass eyes seemed to focus on Natalie, standing directly in front of the box. Then she blinked and turned to stare at Alfred, still standing to the side next to the ear trumpet. Her eyes narrowed as if she were thinking carefully.

The sibyl stopped tapping, lifted the lid of the green jade box, and withdrew a white card. A second later it made a soft sound as it landed in a compartment behind a little door in the lower, brass part of the box. The canary chirped a few notes and rustled its wings.

Alfred zipped around and extracted the card from its compartment. Natalie watched the sibyl swivel her head in order to follow him around the box, blue eyes unblinking.

"To be happy at any one point we must have suffered at the same." Alfred scowled at the card, turned it over, and frowned

at the sibyl. In response, the sibyl folded her hands neatly, leaned back toward the trumpet, and closed her eyes.

"Seems like maybe Phemonoe thinks you like being tortured by Miranda," Natalie said with a grin. Then she realized her friend was blushing. "Alfred," she said sharply, "do you secretly actually *like*—"

"Are you kidding?" Alfred hissed, shoving the card in his pocket. "I don't know what this so-called fortune means and neither do you! Here's a penny; *you* try. Ask her if you're going to marry George Sills, why don't you! See how you like it."

Natalie plucked the coin from his fingers. "I have a better question." She dropped in the penny, wound the crank, and leaned close. "Tell me something useful," she said into the tortoiseshell horn. "Tell me where the generators are. Tell me where to find Limberleg's Chesterlane Eidolon." She forced a riotous laugh into the ear trumpet, and the sibyl took another deep breath, as if inside the box she was inhaling Natalie's laughter straight into her lungs.

The wax woman raised her head, tapped her fingers, and turned to look straight at Natalie. She opened the jade box and selected a card.

Alfred plucked it from the compartment, glanced at it, and handed it airily across to Natalie. "*I am willing to do so, but it requires more effort than I feel able to make*," Natalie read aloud. She looked from the card to the sibyl, who had not yet closed her bright blue eyes again. "Give me another penny, Al."

"Tell me something useful," she said into the tortoiseshell horn.

He did. Natalie started up the sibyl again, laughed, and waited for the next card, which read, *You do not question me properly.*

"Is this a joke?" Natalie demanded.

"Natalie, they're already printed," Alfred protested. "It's like one of those tea cakes with fortunes in them. They don't really mean anything."

She held out a hand for another coin. Alfred sighed and handed one over. Natalie turned the crank and asked, "How would you prefer I question you, if you please?" She waited for a long minute, but the sibyl did nothing.

"You forgot to laugh," Alfred reminded her.

Natalie rolled her eyes. "I already wound it! The laugh can't possibly—"

"You're the one who's asking a wax lady in a box how she prefers to be spoken to, so you might as well follow the inst—"

"Okay, FINE!" Natalie bellowed her loudest, most obnoxious laugh into the tube. The sibyl opened her eyes, gave Natalie what almost seemed like a look of reproach, and dropped a card that read, *You must begin at the beginning.*

Natalie looked at the waxwork woman for a long moment. "That's really incredibly unhelpful." The sibyl replied by folding her hands and closing her eyes. The canary chirped a note and regarded Natalie with a beady gaze.

"Now, Phemonoe," spoke a voice from behind them. Dr. Limberleg stepped up between Natalie and Alfred and rapped on the glass with a gloved knuckle. "Don't be cryptic. The young lady has paid her penny. Answer her question."

Natalie gave him a sharp look, certain he was making fun of her. Before she could think of a suitably sharp comment to accompany the glance, however, the sibyl in the glass case raised one slender hand from the jade box and pointed to her right.

Natalie's jaw dropped open in shock.

"I presume that will be more helpful," Dr. Limberleg said. "Good morning." The look on his face as he strolled away reminded her of the day before, back in the bicycle shop, when he'd made the *Wilbur* go without the key. Now he'd done the same thing with the waxwork sibyl: no coin, no winding, only the sound of his knuckles on the glass and a spoken order. And Natalie was pretty sure he'd done it just to unnerve her.

When Limberleg had disappeared around the corner, the sibyl lowered her arm, folded her hands, and closed her eyes.

"Hang on, you," Natalie snapped. "I have one more question."

Alfred closed his eyes briefly, too, probably praying for patience, and gave Natalie his last penny. She fed it through the slot, turned the crank, leaned close to the grille.

"Dr. Limberleg," she said, trying to find a way to phrase the question she wanted to ask. "There's something strange about him, about this medicine show, something that doesn't feel right. Who is he?" She forced a chuckle and stepped back.

The card that Phemonoe returned this time read *It is a thing difficult to tell*. And then, without waiting for another penny, winding, question, or laughter, she dropped a second card into the compartment.

All things are either good or bad by comparison.

"If you want to ask it anything else," Alfred said pointedly, "could you try and find out where the films are, please?"

Clutching the cards with their cryptic answers in one hand, Natalie stared numbly at the woman in the box that had just moved without being wound. It was one thing if she could believe Dr. Limberleg had made it move through some perfectly normal means she hadn't spotted, like a magician producing a coin from your ear. It was another thing entirely if there was no magician and the coin turned up in your ear anyway, seemingly all on its own.

The sibyl closed her eyes as she leaned to the side, touching her wax ear to the end of the tortoiseshell trumpet. This time, however, her fingers continued to drum slowly on the green jade box. *Ta-ta-ta-tap. Ta-ta-ta-tap.* Natalie's skin began to crawl.

Before the creeping dread managed to get a complete hold on her, however, a familiar voice shouted her name. "Natalie! Alfred, over here! They're about to start a picture!" Miranda waved from a corner a little ways down the row of tents. Natalie took a deep, calming breath. Whoever thought she'd be so glad to see snotty, snippy Miranda?

They followed Miranda around a corner and into a darkened pavilion. Inside, they pushed through a heavy velvet curtain; on the other side a dozen wooden benches filled with people faced a taut white sheet that stretched from floor to ceiling. Ryan waved from a spot right in the middle.

"You hold our spot now, Al," Ryan called. "I want to have a look at the projector." An awkward scramble followed to get Alfred (glowering) and Miranda (beaming) to the middle bench and Ryan out.

"You have to see this," he said as he stumbled to the aisle and pulled Natalie back the way she'd come in. "Look at this thing."

Her jaw dropped for the second time. How had she walked right past it?

At the back of the tent, just this side of the heavy curtain, was the high-wheeled bicycle. It stood, piano and all, mounted on a platform so that the huge front wheel and tiny back wheel stood a few feet off the ground. Rather than tires, however, the bicycle was now fitted with circular film reels looped with celluloid. A projecting lamp and lens had been mounted to the middle and front.

Squinting in the dark, Natalie followed the mechanism with her eyes, staring at each part and trying to see where it connected to the next. With more than a touch of relief, she saw it all come together; outlandish, but understandable.

"The pedals turn the reels to put the film through the projector . . . so one person can run the projector and play the piano. . . ." Someone had to play music to accompany the film because moving pictures had no sound of their own. "It kind of makes sense," Natalie admitted.

The pianist was already up there, the one she had seen

the day before. Today he was dressed in the same sort of light brown suit as his twin in the Magnetism tent, and he also sat with his chin on his chest as if taking a nap. As Natalie and Ryan stared up at him, he blinked, raised his head, and began to pedal.

They crept back to their seats and clambered over Miranda and Alfred as the pianist played an opening fanfare, and a round white circle of light appeared on the sheet. The circle widened and darkened, and the first images flickered to life.

For a moment Natalie wondered uncomfortably what sort of uncanny films a fair like this one was likely to have. After the first one, a picture about a rocket trip to a big-eyed, grinning moon with a cratered human face, she decided there was quite enough oddity possible on film without the hucksters' needing to be involved, and sat back and enjoyed the next two without another thought.

ELEVEN

Phrenology

AFTER THE LAST FLICKERING LIGHT died away, Ryan had seen all he wanted of the fair. Alfred left, too, the better to avoid being stuck with Miranda following him around. And without any boys at all to spend the day with, Miranda had no reason to stay.

Natalie prowled alone between the tents and booths, following the clashing of the One-Man Band through the maze, until she heard Dr. Limberleg's sharp voice over the noise and picked out the word *phrenology*.

Thaddeus Argonault's strange tattooed head flashed through her memory. Argonault was the phrenologist; what on earth sort of medicine did a doctor like that practice?

She made her way through the people around the stage. Dr. Limberleg stood at the lectern with Thaddeus Argonault seated off to the side on one of the scrawny chairs. A huge, antique-looking picture of a man's head in profile hung behind them. The head was sectioned off into dozens of little compartments like Argonault's scalp, but in the picture, each compartment had another drawing inside instead of a number.

"In earlier years it was thought a man's character could be read on his head," Dr. Limberleg intoned, "that his kindness or goodness or genius or evils could be found out by examining the shape of his skull. By simply *feeling a person's head* and consulting a chart, phrenologists of the last century believed they could see who you were."

The fringe of red and gray hair poking out from under the top hat waved even more as Dr. Limberleg paused to laugh at the follies of the last century.

"We know now that this is absurd, because the surface of the scalp changes. Worry, sickness, sadness . . . these things cause pressure in the brain, which can be detected by the modern phrenologist. By feeling a fellow's scalp, I can diagnose his illness with the keenest accuracy. Tongues may lie, thoughts may mislead, but the brain, the *physical* brain, cannot!"

With a flick of his gloved fingers, the picture of the head fell to the floor, revealing another newer and fancier diagram behind it. The names of Dr. Limberleg and Thaddeus Argonault arched over this new illustrated head. The compartments on this one had labels like anxiety, exhaustion, consumption, weak blood, cancer.

"Phrenology allows us to put a finer point on illnesses,

and thus to remedy them with advanced treatments like Amber Therapy that, if used without the greatest care, may be dangerous rather than curative."

Dr. Limberleg took a wooden pointer from the lectern and gestured at one area of the diagram. "In this way, Dr. Argonault and I have personally restored cases of insomnia"—another box—"chronic ague"—a compartment near the temple—"and arthritis, to say nothing of nearly impossible-to-heal cases of malnoia, wandering spleen, and"—jab, jab, jab—"cancers of the brain, liver, and stomach. We even cured a fellow in New Orleans who had fallen afoul of some bad voodoo, and I don't mind telling you the effects of zombie poison are not a simple matter to make sense of." A murmur slid through the people surrounding the stage, and Dr. Limberleg permitted himself a dramatic pause.

Into the hush, another voice spoke. It was low and soft and bleak, ever-so-slightly accented, and cold. Natalie's skin stood up in goose bumps.

"Tell them about the case of asomatognosia," Thaddeus Argonault said.

For a moment Dr. Limberleg faltered. He glanced sideways at Argonault.

No one spoke. Was she the only person in the audience who didn't know what that meant? "What's asomatognosia?" Natalie asked loudly, pronouncing the strange, complex word with meticulous care.

Dr. Limberleg tore his eyes away from the impassive Thaddeus Argonault to glare at Natalie.

It was like a punch to the throat; such violent hate blazed forth from his eyes that she actually took a step closer to the pale-eyed drifter next to her. In fact, she nearly ducked behind the hem of his leather coat, so desperate was she to put something, anything, between herself and Limberleg's stare. Then it was gone.

"The gentleman to whom . . . Dr. Argonault refers . . . was convinced that . . . his hands were not his own." Dr. Limberleg forced a showman's smile. "But that's for another time, ladies and gentlemen, and if Dr. Argonault"— here he snapped a quick, unsettled look at the tattooed Paragon, who stared mildly back—"consults his otherwise flawless memory, I'm sure he will agree that the particulars of that . . . case . . . are not appropriate for a . . . a *family* presentation."

Argonault sat with one ankle on his knee and jiggled his foot idly, watching Limberleg with an expression that seemed to say, *Well, get on with it, then.*

"A volunteer!" Limberleg called, flourishing one hand. "Who among you wishes to challenge this Paragon? Who would dare Dr. Argonault to guess their afflictions? Be warned! From the hands of a phrenologist, no secret is secure!"

The crowd shuffled. Argonault looked expressionlessly from one face to the next, waiting. Natalie did the same. *Somebody* had to be curious enough to do it.

She was almost to the point of volunteering herself just to see what Dr. Limberleg would do when he called out in triumph, "You, sir!" A blur of velvet and bells shoved past her and a moment later the harlequin pushed through the crowd again, leading someone to the side of the stage. It was Mr. Finch, doing his part to expose the hucksters for the shams they were. His hands worried the brim of a straw hat as he walked to the center of the platform.

Argonault placed the spindly chair front and center. Mr. Finch lowered himself onto it, staring determinedly over the heads of the audience. Argonault stood behind him and lifted meaty hands over his scalp.

The pharmacist flinched slightly when Argonault's fingertips touched him, but the phrenologist didn't seem to notice. He pressed with his spread fingers on the surface of Mr. Finch's head, then picked his hands up and pressed them down again in a slightly different spot once, twice, three times. Then he put his hands in his pockets and turned to considered the diagram at the back of the platform. Mr. Finch stared doggedly into thin air, his face shining under the glaring sun.

"Ulcers." The word came out like a feral cat's satisfied growl.

Mr. Finch's eyebrows drew together over his nose, unimpressed. "Plenty of men in my profession have ulcers."

"What profession is that?" Argonault asked, in a voice that suggested he really didn't care that much.

"Medicine, sir! Plenty of medical men have—"

"I don't." Argonault spoke without turning, his voice rebounding off the diagram to drift back over the stage. "Though you're right, of course. Ulcers aren't uncommon.

But you've had yours since . . . since you were a child." His voice trailed up, thoughtful.

Mr. Finch paled.

"You must've been under considerable stress at a very young age," Argonault said pensively, still gazing at the diagram. "Something very specific, I think." The pharmacist flinched again. Why did he suddenly look so ill?

Then Natalie had it. Something awful must've happened to Mr. Finch when he was young, and he didn't want to tell the whole town about it. Or maybe he was afraid Argonault knew what it was and would tell everyone himself.

"The ulcers are worsening since the doctor's departure." Argonault turned at last and considered his volunteer. "You're in some pain, even now, aren't you?"

Mr. Finch nodded weakly. "Some."

So that was why he had come over so pale and strange. His ulcers hurt, even as he was sitting there. And of course it was absurd to think that Argonault could tell anything about Mr. Finch's childhood. That would be like reading someone's mind.

Which was, of course, impossible.

Still, Natalie thought maybe she wouldn't put her hand up, after all.

The town applauded Mr. Finch as he descended the stage. Limberleg shaded his eyes and scanned the crowd. "Who else? Who else would challenge Dr. Argonault's prowess? In fact," the doctor announced with a gleaming smile, "I, myself, shall perform the next diagnosis! Come along now, friends, step up!"

"Try me."

Natalie recognized that voice. So, somehow, did the hucksters. Argonault's eyes narrowed. The harlequin, having launched into motion in a symphony of bells, stopped dead on the last step, its painted smile looking oddly false as it blinked twice, turned, and cocked its head as if awaiting instructions from Dr. Limberleg.

The doctor stood frozen on the platform staring coldly through his blue-lensed spectacles at Old Tom Guyot.

"Old man," Dr. Limberleg said quietly, "you want us to put pins where your joints ache?"

Tom laughed and, since no one seemed inclined to invite him up on the stage, hiked himself up the stairs past the harlequin all on his own. "And don't say gout, or arthritis," Tom ordered, lowering himself into the chair. "Tell you right now I can't nearly ever get the stiff out of my left knee, so don't bother telling me nothin' about that." He leaned back, interlaced his knobby old hands over his belly, and waited.

Argonault looked steadily at Dr. Limberleg for a long minute. The snake oil salesman's pale-gloved hands hung at his sides, fingers moving absently. Finally he raised them up in the bright sun as if to show there was nothing hidden in his grip and strode forward with a flourish of his coat. Slowly, slowly, Limberleg brought his hands down on Tom's head. He touched it once, twice, three times with quick, light fingers as if he wanted the whole thing over and done with as quickly as possible.

"Well?" Tom said, swiveling awkwardly to look up at him.

"Besides gout."

"Sure, I know all 'bout that and so does everybody else in town. Tell 'em something else."

Limberleg gave him a thin-lipped scowl. "Well, all right. This man"—he flourished a hand at Old Tom—"this man who has such dreadful arthritis that to play a chord on that tin kettle of his makes him want to weep—"

"I said no arthritis," Tom reminded him pleasantly.

"This man has a bullet still floating about with the bits of the kneecap it shattered half a century ago—"

"And I already told about that knee."

"But other than that," Limberleg continued, speaking right over Tom's objections, his voice rising as if coming to the climax of a joke, "he's in such *perfect* physical condition that the poor bastard might just live forever!"

Old Tom let out a whooping laugh, slapping a palm on the knee that, according to Dr. Limberleg, had been smashed for fifty years. The townspeople in the audience burst into laughter and applause. Limberleg smiled coolly, clapped along as Tom ambled off the stage, and called for a final volunteer. This time, the harlequin descended in a whirl of bells and returned with Simon Coffrett, adjusting his glasses and smiling his mild smile.

He sat with the air of a man settling into a leather armchair. "Try not to muss the hair up too badly, will you?"

If it was a joke, the bald Paragon of Phrenology didn't laugh as he stepped forward again. Expressionless, he flexed his big hands over Mr. Coffrett's head, spread his fingers, and brought them down onto the rich man's scalp. After a moment he shifted them slightly, and again; then Argonault lifted his hands away.

His eyes narrowed a fraction. He flexed his hands and dropped them onto Mr. Coffrett's scalp once more. This time Mr. Coffrett winced a little.

"Everything all right, there?" he asked mildly.

Argonault smiled without any humor. "You have strange things going on in your head, Mr. Coffrett."

"Is that your expert opinion?"

Another slight narrowing of the eyes from Argonault, then: "Based on the particular pressure here"—he pointed at the diagram behind him carelessly, so that it was difficult for Natalie to tell what spot he meant—"you suffer from a sleep disorder. One that makes you act out the things you dream." Argonault shoved his hands in his pockets and considered the head before him. "I imagine your doctor has tried several drugs on you, chloral and so forth, but if I had to guess, the one thing that helps you get through the night is to sleep in a very small enclosure . . . or perhaps in restraints."

Natalie stared. *Restraints?* To sleep in?

"Well guessed," Mr. Coffrett said, smiling mildly. He rose, and the audience applauded, if a little awkwardly.

Argonault smiled back, a completely unfunny smile. "And something you didn't tell the good Dr. Fitzwater?" he said conversationally. Natalie edged closer to hear over the clapping.

"You think you're dead, Mr. Coffrett," the phrenologist

said. The applause on all sides stopped cold, but Natalie didn't notice.

The strange, thick buzzing rose suddenly in the back of her throat again. She swayed on her feet as dull sparks flickered across her eyes, the way they do if you look too long at the sun. Dizziness fought with mortification at the thought of falling down or worse, *fainting* in front of her whole town and (worse still) these two weird doctors.

She squeezed her eyes closed, willed the dizziness away, and waited for the sparks to stop so that she could open her eyes. Instead of dissipating they merged into larger shapes, brighter colors. Natalie felt herself pitch backward and prepared herself for the inevitable collapse onto the dirt under her feet.

It didn't happen.

The image that painted itself across Natalie's senses in the moment she felt herself tumble off-balance was the same odd blend of dream and memory as the vision of Trader's Mill she'd had the day before. But instead of the dusty tents of the medicine show, Natalie saw only the wide-open vastness of the heavens. The world sprawled far, far beneath—so far away that overhead, almost without transition, the blue day-sky became night, spattered with stars closer and larger than any Natalie had ever seen.

Arms outstretched as if reaching for something in the rushing air, knees drawn up in what Natalie recognized immediately as a *jump*, a tall figure plummeted through the sky. As the wind rushed past and it fell faster and faster, the figure curled into what was unmistakably a posture of pain . . . or maybe sadness so deep it was almost the same thing. Then, after long seconds, the figure uncurled and straightened to plunge head-downward, watching the earth rush upward with an expression Natalie didn't quite have a word for.

Even without the spectacles, it was unmistakably Simon Coffrett.

"*Jumper*," Natalie whispered, without knowing why she said it.

Unseen beside her, the drifter in his unseasonable leather coat, the one she'd almost hidden behind only moments ago, looked at Natalie sharply, green eyes glittering. Then he glanced up at Simon Coffrett sitting on the stage and gave a short chuckle. "Well, I'll be damned," he murmured.

Then, just as quickly as it had arisen, the apparition of wide sky and plummeting space dissolved into dull sparks that flickered and died, and Natalie opened her eyes to find herself exactly where she'd been all along. She was even—thank goodness—still on her feet.

The drifter glanced down at her, half a grin curling over his teeth. "Y'all right there, honey girl?"

"Fine, thanks," Natalie muttered. Everyone else was staring up at the stage, where Mr. Coffrett and Argonault still stood facing each other with humorless smiles on their faces. She shook her head to clear it of the last lingering cobwebs of dizziness. What had Argonault said before she'd blacked out?

You think you're dead, Mr. Coffrett.

"Good one," Simon Coffrett said at last.

"Who knew scientists had senses of humor, ladies and gentlemen?" Dr. Limberleg swept forward, white teeth agleam, to shake Mr. Coffrett's hand. "I myself once saw Dr. Argonault laugh, but it wasn't until three days later that I finally convinced myself I wasn't hallucinating."

Argonault, looking almost bored, turned to glance sharply at the curtain behind the platform, and a second later the frantic drums and horns of the One-Man Band burst into life. This seemed to signal the end of the demonstration.

"Questions are welcome at the Phrenology Pavilion," Dr. Limberleg shouted. "Join us at two sharp for our next presentation: the intricate Art and Science of Hydrotherapy in Medicine!" He strode off the stage and disappeared into the tent behind it. Thaddeus Argonault followed, his lips stretched into a shape that, on anyone else, might have passed for a smile.

Slowly the crowd around the stage began to disperse. Natalie watched them dissipate among the pavilions of the fair, trying to decide what to do next. She sat on the bottom step of the short staircase leading up to the platform and put her hands in her pockets. Her fingers immediately found the paper corners of the sibyl's cards. She took them out and flipped through them one by one until she got to the card that read: *You must begin at the beginning.* It was right after dispensing that card that the sibyl had pointed one of her wax hands toward the front of the fair.

"Well, I'm at the beginning." There were two things

she most wanted to find, of course: the giant contraption Alpheus Nervine had chased her away from, and the fair's power generators, so that she could examine Limberleg's blue Chesterlane. Natalie glanced around. The big-wheeled object was still nowhere to be found but maybe this was as good a place as any to look for the generators.

They were used to produce electricity, so Natalie turned a circle, eyes peeled for anything that might be electrified. High above the medicine show, Arcane's power lines ran between giant wooden poles much taller than the posts that held up the fair's overhead wires. Dr. Limberleg wasn't using Arcane's electricity, though; if he had used the town's power, he wouldn't need to generate his own.

It was far too early for the fair to have turned on any lights, but there were strings of dusty bulbs outlining the edges of the stage like footlights. Natalie followed them around to the side of the platform, where the bulbs ended and a twisted cord ran up to twine along the overhead wire.

The wire, in turn, led her off through the concessions to the left of the stage, between racks of candy-floss, past the ducking booth and past the zoetrope, until the rustling green of the cornfield on the eastern side of the fair showed through between the tents.

Natalie stopped at the edge of the lot and surveyed the waving stalks of corn gleaming in the noonday sun. From here the noises of the medicine show were mere murmurs drifting to her through flapping canvas. To the left, Natalie could see the water tower looming over the roofs of Arcane less than a half mile away. It was a little jarring, somehow; inside the maze of the fair, it was almost possible to forget that she was still in her own hometown.

To the right, the wire she'd followed twisted down at an angle, joined by other wires from other parts of the fair. They all met up at an apparatus that could only be a generator. It stood at about the height of a tall man, and most of that height came from a huge iron loop that sat on a short bank of machinery. A metal bar passed through the lower part of the loop, with a giant brass wheel attached to one side and a bicycle attached to the other: the blue Chesterlane Eidolon.

It stood up off the ground on a pair of brackets so that someone could pedal, rotating the big brass wheel to power the generator while the bicycle stayed still. More importantly, the bicycle would stay *upright*. It couldn't possibly fall over.

It was just too good an opportunity to pass up. Natalie looked around, but there was no one in view. Heart pounding in her chest, she tiptoed along the narrow strip of hay-strewn ground between the tents and the cornfield to where the blue Chesterlane stood. She reached out cautiously and ran her fingers along the enamel. Dr. Limberleg would be *furious* if he caught her touching it.

Which was reason enough to do it. Natalie grinned, grabbed the handlebars, put a foot on one pedal, and swung herself up onto the seat.

The Chesterlane stayed upright. Experimentally, she put both feet on the pedals—another thing she hadn't yet managed on hers. She pushed them around once, and immediately saw one reason for the trouble she'd been

Inside the maze of the fair, it was almost possible to

forget that she was still in her hometown.

having. The pedals were so far forward, she actually had to lean a little bit to either side to complete a rotation. That shouldn't have been a problem, except the hinge at the middle of the frame allowed the front half of her bicycle to lean with her, causing her to either run into walls or fall over sideways. The hinge on this one moved, too, but the bicycle was secure, so it didn't matter.

She took another look around. Still nobody in sight. She began to pedal.

Natalie sprinted down Bard Street, past the open doors of her father's shop and straight on to her house, pausing only to glance at the red Chesterlane where it leaned against the barn. Feeling better than she had in a long while, she took the stairs to the second floor two at a time.

Her mother's eyes slid open as Natalie burst through her bedroom door. "How was the medicine show, Nattie? You're home early."

"I'm going back." Natalie climbed up on the counterpane next to her mother. "I thought maybe you'd be less tired and would want to come back with me. They're doing another presentation at two o'clock. Hydrotherapy. What's that, do you think?"

"Something to do with water, I suppose." Her mother's lips stretched into a smile. "Maybe I can make it tomorrow."

For a moment they sat without saying anything. Natalie, who had been about to tell her mother about the strange dizziness and the odder thing that had felt like a memory of falling, decided not to mention them right now.

The recording that had been playing on the Victrola came to an end. The needle skipped rhythmically in the quiet room. Something strange and uncomfortable began to stir somewhere between Natalie's throat and her belly, dissolving all the happiness she'd felt after her experiment with Limberleg's blue bicycle.

"Aren't your vitamins working, Mama?" she asked at last.

Mrs. Minks's heavy-lidded eyes opened wider, a little bit at a time. She opened her mouth, too, but after a moment she closed it again without saying anything at all and put her arms around Natalie instead.

"Tell me about it before you go back," she said. "Tell me a story."

Something damp fell on Natalie's cheek. She brushed away a tear that wasn't hers. "I don't know any." There were tears starting in her own eyes and she didn't understand why.

"Make it up as you go along," her mother said gently, brushing Natalie's messy hair off her face. "It'll be a good one; I'm sure of it. Storytelling's in your blood."

Natalie thought about the tales she'd told the afternoon before out in the Old Village. Those had been good stories, even if they weren't hers alone. "I guess I could try."

Sometime later Natalie descended the stairs to find the kettle howling on the stove and her father staring at a telegram.

"Mama wants to know if you're making coffee."

"Sure am." His voice was just a little too bright and

casual as he shoved the paper into his pocket. "How about if I take it up?"

"I'll do it," Natalie said, making her voice sound non-chalant, too, as she took the kettle carefully off the stove.

"Don't you have a fair to get back to?"

"I don't mind."

Her father smiled. "Go on. I'll fix it just the way she likes. One sugar cube and one tablespoon of cream. Go on, Natalie."

She swallowed and looked at the stairs. "And a little rum, Dad." Then Natalie turned and sprinted out the door and down the porch stairs to find Mrs. Byron, of all people, standing in the lane, her gray hair shining like steel.

Natalie just managed to stop herself from colliding with the old lady. Mrs. Byron scowled and brushed non-existent dust from the lace front of her dress, releasing a whiff of stale lavender. Amazing: it didn't matter what kind of flowery scent she wore, it always smelled like something dried out and dead.

"Well, Miss Minks?" she said, staring down over her pince-nez glasses.

"Yes, Mrs. Byron?" Natalie said to the toes of her shoes.

"Someone, Miss Minks, has been riding through my roses again." She smiled coldly. "Is your father at home?"

Natalie didn't know whether it was the sense that bigger and more important things were going on in Arcane than some roses getting trampled by persons unknown or the certainty that her father had better things to do than hear about it that made her say what she said next. It just seemed silly to go on standing there taking abuse from a crabby old woman obsessed with the evils a bicycle could do.

She made herself look Mrs. Byron straight in the face. "I know for a fact you've never seen me ride through your garden, because I never have. Are you really going to lie and tell my dad I did?"

Mrs. Byron's cheeks pinkened. "I will not have you speak to me that way, young lady!"

"Because he's home, if you really think you can convince him I'd do something that babyish." It was easier to hold the stare now that Mrs. Byron was doing all the fidgeting. "But if it's just that you don't like me"—and here Natalie actually smiled, because Mrs. Byron's mouth was muttering silent, angry sounds that made her false teeth move around between her lips—"then go on, and I'm sorry I interrupted. I can take it, if it makes you happy."

For a moment they just stared at each other. Then Mrs. Byron's head pivoted on her thin, corded neck, and with a little snarl of fury, she continued on her way down the lane. The noise of cicadas swelled, as if the insects were applauding from their hidden shady places in the rustling trees.

"Look it in the face," Natalie murmured to herself. "I never realized it was that easy."

An hour ago nothing could've kept her from going back to the fair, but now something was begging Natalie to stay here, close to home. So instead of heading for the village of tents at the end of Heartwood Street, she slipped through the big barn doors of the bicycle shop. The *Wilbur* sat on the bench under the little window, right where she'd left it. She wound it carefully. Nothing.

It was as good a way as any to pass the time. Natalie began removing pieces until the flyer had been reduced to a neat pile of gears and cams, carved figures, and one big coiled spring. Then, glancing at the drawings tacked up over the bench and tracing the connections with her fingers, she started to put it all back together.

The barn door banged, and Natalie heard her father curse quietly. She looked up to see him shaking his hand as he stepped through the doorway.

"I thought I saw you come in here. Hi, Nattie." He glanced at the workbench full of pieces. "Not going back to the fair?"

She shook her head and scowled at a gear that didn't want to fit its shaft.

Her father turned the shaft around so the opposite end met the gear in question. "Other side."

Together they reassembled the little figure piece by piece until only the key was left. Natalie fitted it in place and wound the automaton carefully. Slowly, jerkily, the *Wilbur* began to move.

"Hey!" Her father clapped her on the back. "You did it! Look at him go."

Natalie set the little flyer on the workbench. The twin propellers spun and the double wings twisted back and forth in opposite directions, first one tipping its back edge downward, then the other. The *Wilbur* rolled forward hesitantly, whirling and warping jerkily for perhaps five seconds, each repetition a touch slower, until at last it lurched to a stop.

"It doesn't work very well." Natalie wound the key again and watched the automaton lurch along the workbench again only to slow down almost immediately.

"Sure it does. You did a great job."

"It just . . . it doesn't go for long," she said. It had seesawed maniacally in Dr. Limberleg's hands. Why was it poking along now?

"Everything stops eventually." He took the machine from her and wound it himself. "No machine that's ever been built or born can run forever."

"Born?"

"I was thinking of people." He watched the flyer scoot along to stillness. "And then, some things aren't built to run smooth and easy in the first place. It doesn't mean they aren't doing what they're supposed to do. Like your bicycle, for instance." He smiled at the *Wilbur* and handed it back. "This was just a simple mechanism, to show you how the parts worked. We'll build a more complicated one next time, one that will run a little longer. Or we can just keep working on this, maybe get it to go a little faster, maybe even go twelve seconds like the real *Flyer I*. How's that sound?"

"Okay." Natalie swallowed her disappointment and tried to look cheerful. "That sounds great."

Her father gave her a quick hug and left the workshop. She set the *Wilbur* carefully on the workbench and followed as far as the barn door. As he crossed the yard onto the front porch of the Minkses' house, he took a crumpled piece of paper from his pocket—the same telegram he'd been reading when Natalie had found him in the kitchen.

Beside the door, the red enameled bicycle leaned against the shop wall.

"Chesterlane Eidolon," Natalie said slowly, giving it a stern look. "All right. Let's give this another try." Her frown deepened at the thought of the unfinished flyer springing to life in Limberleg's hands, his smug reaction to Natalie's shock. He probably thought he could work the red bicycle just fine, too. Natalie snorted.

She grabbed the handlebars and stalked down the street toward the little alley between the stables and the smithy where she'd been practicing before, running through the things she'd figured out on the blue Chesterlane at the fair. "Let's go," she muttered to the bicycle. "And I don't want any trouble from you."

"It will have surfaced in Pinnacle by now."

"I am aware of what day it is," Jake Limberleg snapped.

The last citizens of Arcane wandered homeward, silhouetted by the final rays of shadowy summer light. Stars began to creep from the horizon toward the vault of the sky, mingling with fireflies and the songs of crickets in the cornfields.

"Dr. Acquetus is merely reminding you that we are on a schedule." This, dryly, from Alpheus Nervine, one hand tapping the handle of the rapier that hung from his work belt. "Since you elected to set up shop here, like a fool, less than two days out of that last sorry little burg."

"With the deal the dead man gave us on the lot, could I afford to pass it up?"

"Don't jest with me, Jake," Nervine said evenly.

"What choice was there?" Limberleg demanded. "If we hadn't, if we had left everything shut and silent but had to wait here for a wheel anyhow, don't you think it would've raised some eyebrows? Isn't that what you said?"

"It was your call to make," Nervine snarled, "and it's too close."

"I said that to you out there in that godforsaken ghost town! I said, *We have rules*," Limberleg spat.

"It will have surfaced in Pinnacle by now," Acquetus repeated, louder. "Assuredly, the flu that was going around before we got there bought us some time, but when they realize the gingerfoot is something different, they will draw the obvious conclusion, and they will contact Arcane by some means tomorrow night or the next morning with warnings—"

"We can stop the communications."

"—and we are not prepared to depart on schedule," the phrenologist continued as if Limberleg hadn't spoken. "If we start dispensing tomorrow, we *must* be able to depart on schedule, Jake. *Where is our wheel?*"

Thaddeus Argonault and Paracelsus Vorticelt, occupied with tying the flaps of the tents closed, stopped their work to listen to Limberleg's answer.

"Are you suggesting we creep away, crippled, dispense

nothing?" Limberleg asked. His tone came out much closer to relief than indignation.

Behind him Nervine laughed. It was not a happy sound. "That," he said, "is not an option at this point."

"I am *suggesting* that we find out what is holding up the bicycle man and remove the obstruction," Acquetus said slowly. "I *suggest* we give that the highest priority."

"I'll see to that," Limberleg muttered. "In the meantime, Willoughby, perhaps you and Alpheus could see to the wires." He smiled grimly. "We wouldn't want to spoil any surprises for anyone. Not before they get to see the gingerfoot for themselves."

"What about the old man?" Vorticelt removed his glasses and polished them slowly, looking carefully at the mercury-colored lenses in his fingers.

"What about him?"

Vorticelt looked up from his polishing, fixing Limberleg with his bottomless, all-pupil gaze. Argonault, Acquetus, and Nervine turned their eyes on Limberleg one by one.

"I needn't tell you *what about him*, Jake," Vorticelt said, deadly calm.

"He's one man, and he's outcast here." Limberleg stared back, trying to meet Vorticelt's dreadful stare with an equally awful one of his own and not quite succeeding.

"Don't be simple." Nervine folded his arms over his chest. "Nothing in this ridiculous town is simple, Jake, and we've known it since that damnable wheel disappeared. Wake up."

With that, the Paragon who called himself the

Chevalier of Amber Therapy turned on the heel of his floppy boot and stalked into the shadows.

"What about the other one?" Argonault asked, looking more at the other Paragons than at Limberleg.

Vorticelt answered. "The other one is past involving himself in matters like this. However"—he glanced at Argonault, and something like a smile flickered across his face—"there is, of course, the dead man."

"I'm not so sure you got a right read on this place, fellows."

Limberleg and his three remaining colleagues turned to face the new voice. The drifter in the long leather coat leaned on the pole of his lantern and regarded them with grim amusement, the old eyes glittering in the too-young face.

"'Course it looks like the, what'd you call him, the *dead man* is giving you the run of the place, so maybe the rest of it doesn't matter so much. Why's that? Why would a fellow like that deal with you?"

"I've been meaning to ask who the hell you are," Argonault said coldly.

"Surprised you got to ask," the drifter replied. "After all, I've been waiting for you lot to show up."

"He's a phrenologist," Limberleg said evenly. "Just let him get his hands on your head and there won't be a need for further questions."

"Yep, that's a good one." The drifter set down his carpetbag, perched his lean frame comfortably on it, and produced a cigarette from his pocket. The three remaining Paragons looked at one another and then at Limberleg as the new-comer lit his cigarette and sucked in a lungful. "So just how much did the good Mr. Coffrett's sanction cost y'all?"

Limberleg raised an eyebrow. "I never talk business with strangers."

The drifter smirked. "Oh, I don't think we're strangers." He put out a hand without standing up. "I'm Jack." Limberleg extended his own without moving so the drifter had to reach to shake it. "Nice gloves."

Vorticelt gave a chuckle like a short bark. Willoughby Acquetus folded his arms across his chest and twitched a grin in Argonault's direction.

"They're hardly rare," Limberleg said coldly.

"Don't suppose that makes each and every pair any less . . . special." He pulled on his cigarette, pale eyes glittering. "So what's a town like this cost?"

"Are you in the market?"

"Always curious."

"Sorry to disappoint. We're only visiting."

The drifter who called himself Jack smoked silently, watching Limberleg as if there was more to be discussed. The doctor brushed a spot of ash from his glove but said nothing. Behind him, Argonault and Acquetus stood like bodyguards. At last the drifter stubbed out his cigarette and rose.

"Nice talking to you." He lifted the lantern.

Thaddeus Argonault spoke up. "Why were you waiting for us?"

Limberleg's eyes narrowed. "What does it—"

"I'd like to hear the man speak." Argonault looked

at the drifter again. "How did you know we were coming here?"

Jack opened the little door on the lantern and blew on whatever was inside so that a brighter glow spilled from the holes punched in the tin. "Like to tell you, but I'm afraid I never discuss business with strangers, either."

Limberleg waited until Jack was out of earshot before whirling on Argonault. "Why in the name of—"

Argonault put a huge hand up. "Find. Our. Wheel," he snarled.

He stomped off, disappearing into the deeps of the medicine show. The remaining Paragons followed. Limberleg turned with his gloved hands in his pockets and watched the tin lantern with its odd pattern of light move away down the road into town.

"I know who you are," he said quietly. Then Jake Limberleg shuddered.

TWELVE

Limberleg's Ginger-Angelica Bitters

Mama's not coming today, either?" Natalie kicked a stone as she hiked along between her father and Charlie. She'd woken up in a bad mood, stiff and sore from hours of trying to master the red bicycle the afternoon before. The revelations about the pedals she'd had on Limberleg's blue Chesterlane hadn't quite solved the problem—or rather, they'd solved the *pedal* problem, only to reveal how many other difficulties were still standing in the way of an easy, effortless bicycle ride. If such a thing was possible on the red Chesterlane at all, she thought grumpily.

"Your mother's tired." It was Saturday morning, and her father looked tired, too. "If Dr. Limberleg asks, I'm still looking for the right size wheel," he said to Charlie. "Don't mention the telegraph machine if you can help it."

"The telegraph?" Natalie repeated as they left Mr. Minks

to turn onto Heartwood Street toward the fair. "Dad had a telegram yesterday. Is that what he's talking about? What was it?"

Charlie shook his head. "Someone broke into the general store last night," he said quietly.

"A *robbery?*"

"Shhh!" Charlie hissed. "Seems the thief got himself tangled in the Central Exchange wires. Mr. Tilden heard the noise, came down from upstairs, and scared the thief off, but Central's wrecked. The telephone lines and the telegraph machine are out of commission."

"So Dad's helping fix them."

"Yeah, and Dad doesn't want Dr. Limberleg to think he isn't paying attention to the wheel problem, but the Central Exchange *is* more important."

A nostrum fair, it turned out, was very similar to a technological medicine show: frying foods, syrupy sugar smells, penny amusements. Bursts of odd, discordant music from the One-Man Band. Sudden appearances and disappearances of the harlequin in its costume of velvet triangles and bells, capering and somersaulting and then vanishing in a flash of tarnish and motley.

The primary difference that morning was the bright signs all over the lot: COMPLIMENTARY CONSULTATIONS, they shouted, with arrows to guide potential patients to the correct tents. FREE DIAGNOSES!

A clash of horns and frantic banjo picking erupted

somewhere behind the main stage. The curtain zipped aside, and Dr. Limberleg strode out. "Welcome to your very good health!"

The applause was a little more ready this morning—by now everyone knew the Pinnacle flu had stopped menacing the town down the road, and that these so-called Paragons might have had something to do with it.

"Hey." Ryan and Alfred strolled up, pockets rattling with pennies, and Miranda predictably in tow. "Think they've got different films today?"

"This morning," Limberleg announced, "we welcome you to our nostrum fair, the greatest collection of technologies in medicine and purveyor of the most advanced panaceas and curatives currently available in these United States!"

More applause. Dr. Limberleg's frock coat swirled as he stepped aside to reintroduce the four Paragons. They were dressed much the same as yesterday, although Alpheus Nervine had thrown a patched velvet musketeer tunic over his overalls, so the rapier and boots looked a little less out of place.

"Herr Doktor Thaddeus Argonault! Sir Willoughby Acquetus! Dr. Paracelsus Vorticelt and the Chevalier Alpheus Nervine! Yesterday we presented the specialties of Phrenology, Hydrotherapy, Magnetism, and Amber Therapy! Today we invite you to experience in person the full benefits of these techniques!"

A raucous bleating of instruments passed for a fanfare. Dr. Limberleg waited with a slightly exasperated look for it to stop.

"For those who would like to be cured," he announced after the last squeak had died out, "our practice shall be conducted thus. Myself and Herr Doktor Argonault shall perform complimentary diagnoses in the Phrenology Pavilion and in the Consultation Wagon at the center of the fair. Quinn?"

The harlequin stood up from where it had been sitting on the stairs and disappeared behind the stage, only to emerge a moment later with a huge ladder. The top swung in lazy arcs as the harlequin struggled to keep the ladder vertical.

PLUNK. It stood the ladder upright in the dirt midway between the stage and the nearest pavilion and let go. The ladder stayed in place, as if balanced entirely on its own in thin air. Then the harlequin scrambled up the rungs, apparently unaware that it was bound to fall over at any moment.

"What the . . ." Alfred muttered.

When it reached the top, amid gasps from the crowd below, the harlequin stepped off the last rung into midair. It dropped about a foot but didn't fall.

"The wires," Natalie whispered. "The ladder's leaning against one of those wires up there."

And so it was. The harlequin sprinted a few feet down the almost-invisible wire, like a squirrel running along a branch. With a little tinkle of bells it began a series of tumbles and cartwheels, finishing with both little hands raised over its head in victory.

Then a dissonant burst of fanfare caught it off-guard.

The harlequin's arms flailed as it teetered back and forth, back and forth, until, at the last minute, it managed to regain its balance. Its head snapped around to shoot what would've been a nasty look at the One-Man Band behind the stage—if its porcelain-masked face had been capable of any expression.

"Thank you, Quinn," Dr. Limberleg said over a final banjo chord. "Be good enough to show our guests where the Phrenology Pavilion is to be found?"

The harlequin bowed and took off running across the web of wires, high enough over the maze of tents that everyone in the audience could follow its progress to the center of the fair. It somersaulted into a neat turn where one wire intersected with another, then cartwheeled the length of that wire only to leap onto a third and take that one halfway before diving for a fourth. Then it whistled and pointed straight down.

"And my Consultation Wagon?"

The little figure leaped nimbly across two more wires and whistled again.

"From there, ladies and gentlemen, it will be our pleasure to direct you, should you choose to heed our counsel, to the best course of treatment: with Sir Willoughby Acquetus in the Hydrotherapy Tent . . ."

The harlequin executed a series of backsprings across three parallel wires to the southernmost side of the fair.

". . . the Magnetism Tent and Dr. Paracelsus Vorticelt . . ."

A speedy pirouette, then the harlequin walked on its hands to the area Natalie and Alfred had explored the day before.

". . . or with Chevalier Alpheus Nervine in the Amber Therapy Tent!"

After several minutes of gamboling, the harlequin reached the last wire, which connected to the center pole of the Amber Therapy Tent itself, the largest and most elaborate structure on the lot. It was so tall that even from where she stood near the stage at the entrance, Natalie could see the harlequin as it crept higher and higher.

At last it spun to face the audience and flipped backwards off the wire to land nimbly amid a collective gasp atop the slender flagpole that stood at the top of the tent.

"Of course," Dr. Limberleg announced, "for most of you, your medical journey will bring you straight back here . . ."

The little tumbler leaped into motion again, crossing the fair at an unbelievable speed, springing from wire to wire as if it were no more difficult than running across solid ground, sprinting across straightaways and changing directions so fast that Natalie could barely make out the wire under its feet before it had abandoned that one for another.

"It looks like it's running on thin air," Ryan said.

"That's impossible." But Natalie gave up trying to spot the wires. It was just happening too fast.

". . . straight back here," Dr. Limberleg repeated, "to the Dispensary."

And suddenly the harlequin stopped dead above the front of a closed-up tent to the left of the stage. It swung its arms once, twice, and jumped, catching hold of a blank shingle at the front of the tent on its way down. The shingle flipped over, revealing the word DISPENSARY in flaking gold paint.

Dr. Limberleg flourished his hat as the crowd applauded. "The Amazing Quinn, ladies and gentlemen!"

The harlequin let go of the shingle, dropped softly to the ground, and pulled a cord. The flaps of the tent opened to reveal yet another thin, pale man behind the metal counter. He lifted his chin off his chest and raised a hand to wave. Behind him, neat rows of bottles and jars stood on bright metal shelves.

"May I present Mr. Dalliot." Dr. Limberleg descended the stairs and crossed to the Dispensary to shake hands with the pale man. "And if this fair is the flower of scientific medicine, may I present the nectar: Dr. Jake Limberleg's own patented panaceas!" Another flourish as he swept his hand out to indicate the rows of bottles lining the shelves behind Mr. Dalliot. "And, ladies and gentlemen, with every purchase, we will include a one-of-a-kind gift!"

"Let's go," Ryan muttered. "He's just going to talk about medicine now."

"Don't you want to know what they're giving away?" Natalie asked as the man called Dalliot lined up bottles on the counter.

"Probably a tea set or a quilt or something stupid. Let's go to the film tent." But Natalie held up a hand. "What?" Ryan whispered.

"Don't know." Something about this needled her, although she couldn't put a finger on it. She pushed forward through the crowd until she could see the patent medicines more clearly and try to make out their names. They were predictably strange, like the lot down at the general store—a collection of words Natalie didn't know all jumbled up together like fairy-tale spells: Vorticelt's Aqua Magnetica, Galvanic Amber Salve du Chevalier, Peruvian Apple Catarrh Compound, and Zedoary-Cassilago Household Soap.

There were about fifteen different kinds of bottles and jars in all, but Natalie's eyes kept coming back to a round, green one in the middle. Thanks to the shape, its label was hardest to read.

"Jake Limberleg's Ginger-Angelica Bitters," she read out loud. Why did that particular bottle demand her attention?

"Natalie!" Alfred whined.

"Can we go now?" Ryan grumbled. "I don't need to hear about pimple soap and cough syrup."

But that bottle . . . reluctantly, Natalie allowed herself to be hauled away from the lecture into the deeps of the fair.

"This is the wrong way," Miranda insisted half an hour later. "We've been past here three times."

"Don't be stupid." Alfred turned to glare at Ryan. "I thought you said you *remembered*."

"It was here yesterday!"

"It wasn't," Miranda interjected. "It was on the other side. If you'd just listen to me . . ."

They wandered farther. A shadow passed overhead: the Amazing Quinn on the wires.

"Is anyone ready to let me try now?" Miranda asked once they'd passed the Phrenology Pavilion three times.

Without waiting for an answer, she turned left between a booth containing a baseball toss and another that smelled like burned sugar.

They emerged onto a familiar corridor. Natalie paused to glance into the silk-topped box that contained the torso of Phemonoe, the Libyan Sibyl, but the waxwork woman sat composed and still, eyes closed, as they passed.

"Hey, look at that!" Alfred jogged ahead to the Cabinet of Curiosities to peer into the glass case beside the entrance. "It's a different one!"

The automaton shaped like the strolling One-Man Band had been replaced by a whole setup: two little vertical poles secured by thread stood about two feet apart from each other. A piece of wire stretched between them, and a tiny, velvet-suited harlequin cartwheeled slowly from one side to the other. At the end it turned smartly and pirouetted back to the other side.

"Wow, that's something," Ryan said. "What's that, a machine?"

"An automaton," said a grown-up voice. Dr. Limberleg stood behind them polishing his spectacles. "Of course, Miss Minks knows quite a lot about automata," he said. "How is yours coming along? The charming little flyer."

"Fine." Natalie hesitated. She didn't particularly want to have a conversation with Dr. Limberleg or spend extra time with his uncanny automatons. On the other hand, the idea of *not* asking the question on the tip of her tongue was just as aggravating.

"Dr. Limberleg?" He paused in the act of walking away. "Um. What makes it go?" She gave the little harlequin a closer look just to be sure she hadn't mistaken the key for clever decoration. "I mean, how do you wind the clockwork up?"

"It isn't clockwork." He smiled a little. It was the kind of smile she often got from an adult who didn't know her well, right before he gave her an answer he didn't think she'd understand. But there was something else in it, too; something wary.

"It is," said Dr. Limberleg, "a perpetual motion machine."

"What does 'perpetual' mean?"

"It means everlasting," said the doctor, smirking a little. "It means that this automaton doesn't *have* to be wound. It will go on forever, all on its own."

Lesson learned: never, ever admit (to this man at least) that she didn't know the meaning of any word, ever again. "That's impossible. Nothing goes forever all on its own."

"And who, if you please, told you that?"

"My dad."

Dr. Limberleg's smirk curled. "I hate to crush two misconceptions in one day, but parents have been known to be wrong before. Even, I would imagine, yours."

Behind her, Ryan, Alfred, and Miranda exchanged worried looks.

Natalie opened her mouth to set him straight, but Dr. Limberleg spoke first. "That automaton will carry on, now that it has been set into motion, forever—or at least, close enough to forever that none of us could possibly tell the difference—unless something stops it by force."

"No." Natalie shook her head. Why it mattered so much to prove him wrong, she didn't know, but the idea of that little tumbler going on forever made her feel uncomfortable, anxious, even a little sick. No bit of machinery, no matter how subtle and complex, could do what he claimed this one could. "Machines don't work like that."

"You could watch and see," Dr. Limberleg said carelessly, "but waiting for it to wind down would be a dreadful waste of time."

All four kids turned immediately to stare at the automaton. Natalie willed it to slow, however imperceptibly. She tried to measure the little delay between cartwheels, to watch for some hesitation as it changed direction at the end of the wire. . . .

"Poor Natalie."

She looked up at him with narrowed eyes. But Dr. Limberleg wasn't looking at her. He, too, was watching the automaton.

"You're lucky, really," he said. "Most people are much older when they discover their world isn't the place they thought it was. By then . . . sometimes . . . it's too late."

Natalie stared at him for a moment, so perplexed by the look on his face and the words he had just spoken that she simply stood there, eyebrows furrowed over her nose. Then something occurred to her.

"I'm not saying I believe you," she said, "but if all that's true, how do you start it in the first place?"

The strange look faded slowly. One eyebrow lifted over the top of Dr. Limberleg's blue-lensed glasses. "Are you sure you want to know?" Then he turned and stalked off with a swish of his coat.

"I hate when people say things like that." Natalie put her hands in her pockets so that her friends wouldn't see them shaking.

"Hey, Natalie." Alfred watched the doctor walk away, then pointed toward a wagon that stood at the end of a dead-end path. Dr. Limberleg ushered an older man up the stairs and inside. A little line of people clustered at the foot of the steps, with Natalie's brother unmistakable in the middle of it. "Isn't that Charlie?"

"What's that, anyway?" Ryan muttered. "I could've sworn the film tent was there yesterday."

"*For the fifteenth time*, if someone would just listen to me, the film tent's—"

"It's Dr. Limberleg's wagon," Natalie interrupted. "Remember the presentation? The bald man, Argonault, has the Phrenology Pavilion, and Dr. Limberleg takes patients in a wagon."

"So what's Charlie got that he has to see a doctor for?" Alfred asked.

"Nothing I know of." She jogged to her brother's side. "Charlie, what are you doing?"

Charlie jumped as if he'd been caught with his hand in the cookie jar. "Nothing. It's free, remember? Just for fun."

The door to the wagon opened, and Natalie's neighbor, Mr. Carlton, descended the stairs. He looked a little bit pale.

"Just a moment, my dear sir." Dr. Limberleg appeared in the doorway behind him, brandishing a small card on which he scrawled something with a fountain pen. He slid it into Mr. Carlton's hand. "Mr. Dalliot can see that filled for you. Next guest, please!"

Dr. Limberleg stepped aside to let a woman pass into the wagon. His eyes met Natalie's. He frowned and swung the door shut.

"Charlie, don't. I don't like this."

"Nattie, it's just for a grin," he protested. "Look, nobody's taking it seriously."

Nobody in *line* was, as they chatted with one another and in general tried to act like they were there only for novelty's sake, but Mr. Carlton had seemed a little rattled. Sure enough, the woman who'd been next in line almost tripped coming back down the stairs in her haste to get to the next phase of her treatment, whatever it was. She clutched her prescription card in both hands like something precious or miraculous—or both.

Natalie glanced over her shoulder at her trio of friends. Ryan, Alfred, and Miranda shifted uncomfortably, not sure whether to stay and wait for Natalie or tactfully disappear. After a minute's silent debate, the boys, with Miranda in tow, wandered around the side of the wagon to where there was just enough shade for the three of them to look as if they simply wanted to get out of the sun for a little while.

The line inched forward as another patient climbed the steps.

"Come on, Charlie. This is boring. You'll be waiting forever." The patient reappeared, and another stepped inside to take his place. The line wasn't taking forever at all. In fact, how could any doctor work so quickly? "We're going back to see what's in the Cabinet of Curiosities," Natalie said a little desperately. "That'll be more fun than just having some doctor try and sell you pills. There's nothing wrong with you, anyway!"

Natalie didn't realize how subdued the little line of customers had gotten until her voice, high and distressed, pierced the quiet.

"Charlie." She tugged frantically at her brother's arm. Everything about this felt wrong.

The man in front of them disappeared into the wagon. Charlie was next. Natalie fidgeted. Too quickly, the door opened again.

"You recall where to find the Magnetism Tent, don't you?" Dr. Limberleg's eyes fell on Natalie again and narrowed as he spoke to the departing patient.

This was it. She turned her face up to Charlie. "Please." People were staring at her, and she blushed at the childish fear she heard in her own voice, but Charlie just patted her shoulder with a smile that was probably supposed to be comforting, and climbed the steps.

Dr. Limberleg gave her a smile, too, another of his thin, unfunny ones, as he shut the door.

For long minutes—much longer, it seemed, than anyone else's consultation had taken—Natalie waited. The people in line shuffled.

The door opened and Charlie stumbled down the steps. Natalie sprang after him, her friends hurrying behind at a little distance.

"What is it?" Natalie demanded. "What did he say? What's in there?" Wordlessly Charlie showed her the prescription, a rectangle of heavy paper punched with a series of little holes on one side.

"Limberleg's Ginger-Angelica Bitters," she read. Only because she'd spent so long staring at a bottle labeled with these same words could she decipher Dr. Limberleg's spidery scrawl. "What's it for? Charlie?"

"For when I get the shakes."

"But you almost never get the shakes anymore."

"Why get them at all?"

Natalie's friends trailed her as she followed Charlie all the way to the front of the fair. The Dispensary looked as if it had seen good business already; the shelves were a little less crowded and Mr. Dalliot seemed to be exhausted. The second the customer he was helping left the counter, his chin dropped to his chest, one hand still resting on the cash register keys. Not for the first time, Natalie wondered how Limberleg had found so many people who looked just like one another to work there.

Charlie stepped up. "Um, hi."

Dalliot blinked once and raised his chin again. "Prescription?" Charlie put the card into his outstretched hand, and the dispenser, giving it only the briefest of looks, slid it into his breast pocket. He paused, then swiveled and reached for a bottle. "Dr. Limberleg's Ginger-Angelica Bitters," he intoned. "Two dollars and fifty cents."

Two dollars and fifty cents? All four kids gasped in disgust as Charlie slid his money across the counter.

"Charlie, that's—" The glare he gave her made Natalie bite down on the words *a whole lot of money*.

"Here," he muttered. "You can have this, Natalie. I don't want it."

He put something in her hands and then he was gone, sprinting toward home.

Natalie looked down at her clasped hands. The thing Charlie had given her was cold and irregular and, in places, round. Her friends gathered around as she opened her hands, one finger at a time, until at last there it was. Natalie felt all the breath go out of her.

"What is it?" Miranda asked.

"The free prize, obviously," Ryan said. "Because Charlie bought medicine."

Only Alfred noticed the look on Natalie's face. "It's pretty swell, Natalie," he said with forced cheer.

"I guess."

In her cupped hands she held a model of a bicycle and rider. She could see tiny gears, a mechanism of some sort that suggested it was more than just a model—that it was, in fact, mechanical. An automaton.

"Looks a little like you, doesn't it?" Miranda said.

"I don't think so." But the little figure in painted over-alls was definitely a girl. And the bicycle . . . it had two close-set wheels, the front one a bit bigger than the back. It was decked with springs. Even the shade of red was almost the same as Natalie's. *Please, please let there be a key*, she thought desperately. She turned it over and over, examining it as closely as she could with three kids leaning over her blocking the sun.

But try as she might, she could see no place to wind it.

THIRTEEN

Confidence

B Y THE END OF THE FIRST DAY of the nostrum fair,
something had happened to Arcane. It had become a town
of believers. Everyone who'd given it a try, it seemed, had
undergone an intuitive diagnosis and had miraculous,
almost instantaneous results. Natalie quickly tired of hearing her neighbors talking about the miracles of the nostrum fair as she walked through town toward the general
store, pulling the red enameled Chesterlane Eidolon alongside her. The only reaction Natalie had to Dr. Limberleg
and his fair was a fierce wish to get her own bicycle working, if only to show Dr. Limberleg that he didn't know
everything.

At the Central Exchange at the back of the general store, her father was hard at work on the telegraph
machine. As she passed the left-hand counter, Natalie
glanced at the shelf of medicine bottles on the wall, and

the new sign that read WE SELL PATENT MEDICINES BUT DO NOT ENDORSE THEM.

"Hi, Nattie. Have a good time at the fair today?"

"No," Natalie said sourly. "Charlie bought medicine, even though he doesn't need any." She leaned on Mrs. Tilden's desk and stood watching Mr. Minks fiddle with the telegraph. "Dad, can you look at something for me?"

He wiped his hands clean and straightened. "Sure. Got a scrape?"

"No." From the pocket of her overalls, Natalie produced the little bicyclist.

"Well, that's something! Looks a little like someone I know." He chuckled. "It sort of looks like your Chesterlane, too, doesn't it?"

"Yeah, I guess." She wasn't about to say out loud that she almost thought, despite the fact that it had been Charlie's free prize, that Limberleg had intended it for her. As if somehow he knew she hadn't figured out how to ride her own bicycle, and wanted to rub it in. "It seems like it's mechanical, right? Supposed to do something, I mean."

"Hmm." He turned it over in his hands just as Natalie had. "Sure does. So where's she wind up?"

"Can't figure it out. Dr. Limberleg has another automaton that he says doesn't need to be wound at all. A . . . *perpetual motion* machine."

"Not possible. It might not wind with a key, but something has to start it up, and get it going again when it slows down. Some kind of a force has to act on it."

"Then winding a key is like using a force."

"Exactly. People have been trying to find a way to create perpetual motion for as long as they've been building machines, but no one ever succeeds because the idea goes against the laws of physics. You need to apply force, whether it's with a key or an engine or what have you, to keep a machine going."

"That's what I told him," she said in exasperation, "and he said I was wrong."

"Of course you're not wrong! My Natalie, wrong about machines?"

"Well," she said, trying not to burst with pride, "I didn't believe him, anyway."

Natalie proceeded to get good and scraped up in Smith Lane for the next hour as she tried again to apply the practice she'd gotten on Limberleg's generator bicycle to her own. When she finally gave up and limped around the corner of the livery stable to head home for supper, the world's fastest bicycle remained untamed.

She heard the smirk in George Sills's voice before she saw his face.

"What's the matter, Natalie?" He stood at the end of the alley flanked by two laughing friends, blocking the way to Bard Street. "Daddy take off the baby wheels a few years too early?"

Heat rose on Natalie's cheeks as her heart sank; the blush spread like fire across her face. There was no mistaking it. He knew.

George shoved past his sidekicks. "Or maybe you just like bruises. Is that it?"

The push he gave her wasn't hard enough to leave a bruise, but whether by accident or not he caught her necklace in his fingers and, after a sharp, quick pain from the cord cutting into her neck, Natalie felt it snap. The little sprocket she wore like a charm fell in the dirt.

The older boys laughed as Natalie scrambled to pick it up. George cracked his knuckles unpleasantly. She looked up at him in disbelief. Was he really going to hit her right there, in plain view of anyone who happened to pass in the street? He couldn't be that stupid. . . . But he was looking at the bicycle, the fastest in the world, the beautiful one her father had built just for her. The one she could not simply jump on to escape.

"You know what I think," George said. "I think that bicycle's too big for you."

He was going to take her bicycle. The anger welled up like blood in a cut, flooding her brain. The fact that he certainly wouldn't be able to ride it either didn't even matter.

She took a step forward. She would fight. She would kick and hit so it would take all three of them to steal it from her, and then she would chase, she would run after it until her legs gave out. . . .

Then from somewhere in the street beyond George and his friends, Natalie heard music: she would not have known it was a guitar if she hadn't already witnessed with her own eyes and ears what a guitar could do in truly gifted hands.

She faced George Sills. He was no demon. What could he do, really? Forcing the answer (*He can take my bicycle, the fastest bicycle, my dad's bicycle, isn't that enough?*) from her mind, she willed the uncertainty to drain out of her eyes and let the space fill up with something else.

Confidence.

It was different from facing Mrs. Byron; there was something to lose here, something real she needed to defend. The other boys made noise, but Natalie didn't hear. She held her ground, her wide, bright eyes staring into George Sills's taunting ones.

He's no demon, she thought. *He's just a kid. He's tall and he's mean, but he's a kid like me. That's all.*

A few feet away, George hesitated. He flexed his fist, brought it halfway up, and changed his mind. "Can't even ride it," he sneered, and shoved a hand out to grab the handlebars. The fast motion made her want to flinch, but she didn't, and she didn't let go.

His lip curled in a sneer, and he shook the bicycle. Natalie forced herself not to look away. Why didn't he just take it? He could've pulled it right out of her hands.

He could have, but he didn't. *Because it was working.*

As if he had heard her thoughts, George gave the bicycle one last shove, hard enough to almost topple her, and retreated. "Can't even ride it."

His friends waited, suddenly quiet. George stamped between them and back into the street. The other two followed, shooting curious glances over their shoulders at Natalie as they went.

When they were out of sight, Natalie followed the music around the corner to where Old Tom Guyot leaned against the wall of the stable. "It worked!"

"I heard," he said with a big grin. "And no damage done?"

"Nothing hurt but my necklace." She held out the dusty little sprocket. "Guess I lost the string."

Tom rooted in one pocket with a weathered hand. "Here, darlin'. See how this'll do."

Natalie took the length of string and looped it through the center. It was heavy and not quite white. "What's this?"

"Busted guitar string, real old. An 'E,' prob'ly. Bust a lot of Es, playing like I do. Catgut." He grinned. "Gotta give it a good knot so's it'll stay tied."

Wordlessly she handed it back and watched as Tom carefully knotted the string with his arthritic fingers. He dropped the necklace ceremoniously over her head.

Maybe, just maybe this was one of the guitar strings that had beaten the Devil! In any case, it had been on Tom's guitar. It was special, and now it was hers.

Confidence surging through her, she swung her leg over the bicycle seat. This was it. This was the day. She put a foot on one pedal and kicked off, and landed in the dirt three feet away.

The stars were out by the time Natalie trudged home, but the light spilling from the barn told her that her dad was home and still hadn't called it a day.

She heard Charlie's voice first. "I'm telling you, it's uncanny! I don't know how it works, but it works! Everyone in town's talking about it."

Natalie leaned the Chesterlane against the wall and squatted just outside the big doors, listening.

Her father's voice drifted out quieter from up in the loft. "They're hucksters. They have dozens of tricks to make you think they're legitimate."

Natalie felt in her pocket for the little bicycle Charlie had handed her at the fair and inched closer.

"Dad, I tried it. I didn't tell him anything, but he knew. What if they can do something for—"

Tiny handlebars and pedals dug into Natalie's palm.

You shouldn't have done it, Charlie, she thought. *I don't know why not, but I'm right—I'm sure of it.*

"No. Doc said not to worry until he gets back and finishes the tests."

"What if he's gone longer than—"

"Charlie—"

"Dad, what if there's an answer, and we don't find it because we don't try everything?" Her brother's voice broke into a strange little choking noise. There was a long pause from inside, then Charlie again: "Would you just . . . just go yourself, then? If you still think it's a sham, I won't say a thing; I won't bring it up again. But if he changes your mind . . ."

The little bicycle snapped in her palm. Natalie wrenched her hand from her pocket as if she'd been bitten and flung the broken pieces of the toy into the weeds by the barn.

She backed away from the shop doors and made for the house. Whatever they were talking about, she didn't want to hear any more.

A hush sat curled like a cat in the Minkses' front parlor. Natalie frowned in the doorway. "Mama?" Where were the clanging, the dropped pots, the knocked-over books, the sounds of her mother?

She searched the house, picking up speed as she raced from room to room. Kitchen: empty. Parlor: empty. Dining room: empty.

But there was a noise, soft and repetitive, from somewhere on the floor above.

Snick-thump. Snick-thump. Snick-thump.

Natalie took the stairs two at a time, stumbled and fell headlong at the top, then flung herself into her parents' bedroom. She collapsed against the doorjamb in relief.

Her mother was asleep, a record skipping softly on the Victrola. *Snick-thump.* Natalie tiptoed across the room, reached into the big mahogany cabinet, and lifted the needle. The skipping stopped.

She was halfway down the stairs again when a nagging thought crept into her head. She hadn't seen her mother out of bed in a long time.

Her father's footsteps were quieter than usual in the hall. He put a hand on her shoulder and guided her gently down the stairs. "Let's make supper ourselves tonight, what do you say?"

Halfway down the staircase, something inside Natalie started to click into place: a realization, something she half knew but didn't want to know. There was a question she should ask her father, a question he would answer if she asked it now, because he would never lie to his daughter. She felt the question take shape, felt it rise to her lips, felt her heart prepare for the answer she already knew would break it.

On the last step she opened her mouth, but even as she spoke the words, she was running, sprinting out the door and off the porch, tearing hell-for-leather away, anywhere, so long as her father couldn't hear the question and she couldn't hear the answer.

The night cooled her face. She listened to the sounds of clinking crockery in her neighbors' kitchens and the little shivery songs of katydids and crickets. She heard the creak of carriage wheels and the whickering of horses, the whisper of warm breezes through cornfields, the padding of her feet in the dust, snippets of conversation as voices carried in the night. Summer sounds; normal sounds. Natalie shuddered and ran faster, listening for the noises of ordinary things. She ran until her face was dry again and for a little while longer, she forgot.

When she had gone as far as her legs would carry her, Natalie stopped and wandered back past the general store. It was late for the store to still be open, but hushed voices drifted out of the screen door. She remembered the failed robbery the night before and stopped to listen in the shadows where the stairs rose to meet the porch.

"Is it worth our asking him?" The voice was unmistakably Mr. Tilden's.

"I doubt it." That might have been Mr. Swifte, the blacksmith. "He doesn't do anything without his reasons, and he doesn't explain his reasons to anyone."

"But is it worth our asking anyhow?" (Mr. Tilden.)

"I should have thought anything would be worth trying." (Mr. Finch, the pharmacist.)

Then, after a moment's pause came Mr. Swifte's reply: "Asking, in itself, might carry its own . . . risks."

Natalie scowled. How did asking a question carry a risk? And what were they all doing there, anyhow?

"What's the issue here?" Natalie wasn't sure whose voice that was. "They seem harmless enough. Their medicines even seem to work."

"Every once in a while, Maliverny, your caution looks like cowardice," said Mr. Tilden. So the unknown voice belonged to the saloonkeeper.

"Not everything has to fall to us!" Maliverny snapped. It sounded like a fight was about to break out. To Natalie's surprise, the next voice was Tom Guyot's.

"If Simon Coffrett ain't sitting out there in his big house waiting for us to ring his bell, I'll run for mayor."

After that, nobody spoke for a while. She heard a sound that might've been Tom's fingers drumming on the tin guitar, and a shuffling noise that immediately made her think of nervous Mr. Finch moving his feet. Then the screen door swung open.

Natalie squeezed under the stairs as fast footsteps strode across the old wooden porch and down into the street. Mr. Maliverny stopped close enough that she held her breath. He mumbled angrily to himself as he fumbled with a cigarette, but before he could light it, heavier feet sounded on the porch—probably Mr. Swifte, who always walked heavily, as if each footfall were the landing of a hammer. Maliverny shoved the unlit cigarette back in his pocket and strode away.

Dark hobnailed boots descended the steps, and the blacksmith also strode down the street into the night. After Lester Finch and Old Tom Guyot had made their own exits, Natalie sat in the shadows under the stairs and thought hard.

What did they want to ask Simon Coffrett about? And what could possibly be risky about the bespectacled man who lived in the mansion?

Then Natalie remembered the two bizarre flashes that had come to her like memories: Mr. Coffrett walking to the center of the Old Village, seeing the town's dreadful past as clearly as Natalie saw the present, and Mr. Coffrett inexplicably plunging in sorrow and pain from a terrible height.

You think you're dead, Mr. Coffrett.

It had never occurred to Natalie to be afraid of Simon Coffrett, but as she remembered the way he had smiled, unsurprised, at the phrenologist's final, bizarre pronouncement, she was frightened.

The tents of the nostrum fair cast odd, flapping shadows by the light of the round bulbs strung from the roofs. Dr. Limberleg, cigarette smoldering in his gloved fingers, watched his last patient leave the Dispensary to head for home. The thin man called Dalliot slumped slowly on his stool, one hand still on the register and chin descending to his chest as if he were falling gently into sleep. From the deepening shadows between the tents, Vorticelt, Acquetus, and Nervine came to join Argonault near the stage.

"The mechanic is still looking for a wheel," Limberleg said without turning.

Vorticelt adjusted his spectacles. "How long?"

"His son says he'll build one, if necessary, but it will take time."

"We shouldn't have started dispensing yet."

Dr. Limberleg regarded Vorticelt, face harsh. "I am so tired of you behaving as though setting up shop here was my idea. The *rule* was my idea, Vorticelt. Two hundred miles or a hundred years in between stops, that's what I said, back in the days when the gingerfoot was the world's best game to you four!" He took a deep pull on the cigarette. "Well, we broke the rule. It was going to happen sooner or later. There's nothing for that now. If necessary, we'll take a wheel off another wagon."

"I think the better idea is to get the mechanic moving a little faster."

"Is anyone else at all concerned about the way that girl of his turns up everywhere?" Limberleg muttered.

"If you don't like it, do something about it," Nervine snapped, "but we need to be able to *move!*"

Dr. Limberleg took a last pull on the cigarette and flicked

it away. "Two hands can only do so much, gentlemen." He turned on his heel and stalked into the maze of tents.

Deeper into the fair, a soft noise made Limberleg pause on the steps of his wagon. He turned and squinted into the dark alley between the booths, but the sound of rattling tin did not repeat itself.

FOURTEEN

The Collector of Hands

THE NEXT MORNING, Natalie was up and out the door before anyone else in the Minkses' house woke. Barely twenty minutes after that, she was crawling into an old watering trough hidden by an overgrown hawthorn just outside the still-sleeping village of tents in the lot. It was perfect. She peered through the branches and waited for the nostrum fair to wake.

She nodded off once or twice before figures began stirring among the tents. One of the doctors—it looked like Nervine, with his spiky gray hair—moved here and there, putting placards on easels. Another untied the flaps of the Dispensary (had that pale man called Dalliot slept in the tent all night? How odd).

Little by little, the nostrum fair came to life. Natalie picked out each of the four Paragons as they prepared to open for business. But the one she really wanted to spot was Dr. Limberleg, and he was nowhere to be seen.

"What are you doing?"

Natalie jerked upright, smacking her head on a low branch so hard her eyes teared up. Miranda Porter's face swam into view.

Miranda crawled into the trough while Natalie blinked and rubbed her head. "Just having a look before it opens." Had she fallen asleep again? The street was full of people now, all headed for the fair. "Did anyone see you?"

"I don't think so," Miranda said. "Why are you hiding in here?"

Of all the people Natalie would've picked to help her with her mission today, Miranda was low on the list. Before she could decide how to answer, Vorticelt, Acquetus, Argonault, and Nervine filed up the stairs to the stage and took their places on either side of the painted curtain.

"I'll explain in a minute. Come on, and don't make a spectacle."

Natalie scrambled out of the trough and crept along the edge of the crowd with Miranda close on her heels, until they were only a few yards from the main path into the fair.

"My dear ladies and gentlemen!" came the sharp showman's cry. There was no time for hesitation.

"Come on." Natalie broke for the path as the curtain on the stage swept aside. She heard Dr. Limberleg's voice boom once more—"Welcome to your very good health!"—as she and Miranda turned the first corner and the crowd disappeared from view behind the Dispensary.

Natalie paused to get her bearings. "What's going on?" Miranda demanded.

"Are you going to be a coward about this? Because if you are, you can go back right now. I don't need your help."

Miranda's habitual dubious look froze on its way across her face. "I'm not a coward." Then, before the new, wounded look could fully take shape, "Help with what?"

"Sneaking into Dr. Limberleg's wagon." She decided on the left fork and took a step.

"Natalie, no!"

She rounded on Miranda, mouth open and finger up in warning, but before the first word could escape, Miranda pointed to the right.

"It's this way, I'm sure of it."

A strange vibrating over their heads made both girls look up. "Get back," Natalie whispered. They flattened themselves against the nearest tent as the blurred shape of the Amazing Quinn passed overhead. "He's showing them where all the tents are. We have to hurry."

It was much harder to find the wagon today than it had been to stumble on it by accident yesterday. They took a wrong turn, then another, and had to hide behind a placard on an easel as the harlequin zipped overhead again. Finally, they turned a corner and there it was: Dr. Limberleg's wagon, tucked into a dead end near the middle of the fair, and not a minute too late. Voices began to drift toward them through the tents.

"Better hurry." Miranda glanced over her shoulder. "Can't be far behind us."

They ran the last few yards to the foot of the little staircase.

"I'll stand guard," Miranda offered. "No one'll see me if I squeeze behind the wagon. I'll knock once on the back wall if he shows up before you come out, so you can hide."

"Okay." Natalie took a deep breath, sprinted up to the door, turned the handle, and slipped inside. Then she turned to face the room she had entered and clapped a hand over her mouth to keep the screech in.

In the gaslight and what morning sun filtered through the heavy curtains, startling shapes began to resolve themselves into familiar objects. Seeing them clearly didn't make her like them any better. In fact, some she liked even less—the ceramic head on the carved table, for instance. The strange chair, like a dentist's, in the corner. The collection of skulls in the glass-fronted cabinet. The things in jars that lined the shelves. The hands.

Natalie let her arms fall to her sides and rotated slowly. The room looked like a museum, chock-full of . . . of *things*.

Some of it, like the skulls in neat lines in their cabinet, had tags or labels. The odd shapes of exotic plants hung from hooks. Collections of knickknacks she didn't even know how to describe clustered on every horizontal surface. A fat, stuffed bird with a toucan's beak and stubby legs stood half in shadow on the floor, peering out from under a table.

Some of it made sense. The ceramic head with its eerie half-formed face and bare scalp marked out in a grid like Argonault's tattooed bald pate, for instance; she had seen other heads like this in the phrenology pavilion. The skulls, too . . . maybe they were like examples, something to make comparisons to. The half-reclined chair, with its elaborate, scoop-shaped headrest, would allow someone to relax his or her neck but still give a doctor access to the entire skull.

Perhaps the hands were phrenology things, too, since Dr. Limberleg had to touch a person's head to read it. The more Natalie looked around, however, the less that seemed to be the point.

The hands were everywhere. Wooden hands, marble and stone and crystal hands, many, many hands made of materials Natalie couldn't identify. They lurked. They crept out from behind jars. Some, palms-up, held bottles. They touched books, papers, oddities, as if they had been placed here and there to keep other things where they belonged. They held every conceivable posture and infested every surface, every cabinet, like mice in a pantry—except these were cold and dead and unmoving.

But even the hands weren't as unsettling as the automata.

She had expected to see more like the miniature harlequin and tiny One-Man Band, but the size of Limberleg's collection was unnerving. The clockwork things outnumbered even the hands: paired dancers and ugly-faced monkeys with fiddles or harps, finches in cages, a girl at a loom, a farmer with a pig on his knee, a spindly golden tree with a skeletal bird poised above a beetle. They had nappy fur and elaborate costumes. Moth-eaten antiques stood beside bright new tin or aluminum relations. Their rigid limbs stood frozen in awkward, half-completed gestures.

None of them seemed to have keys.

The most elaborate automaton was tucked into a corner half hidden by the examination chair: it was a clockwork man nearly two feet tall standing in a booth on a platform under a finely crafted little tree. He wore an old-fashioned frock coat and blue-lensed glasses. Strands of red and gray hair stuck out from under his top hat. It was a perfect replica of Dr. Limberleg, down to the long-fingered hands in ivory-colored gloves that he held out over four large flowerpots. One of the pots canted backwards, as if the toy had wound down in the act of raising or lowering it, and underneath it a smaller clockwork figure in floppy boots and a velvet musketeer doublet sat cross-legged. Gray, spiky hair stood up all over its little head: a tiny, miniature Chevalier Alpheus Nervine. It grinned ghoulishly over a pair of brass cymbals.

It was that particular automaton that started moving first.

She thought her nerves were playing tricks on her when the cymbals began slowly inching together until they connected and the first tinny *ping* sounded. The automaton's arms parted again, little by little, until they stretched as wide as they could go, and then began swinging back in, just a bit quicker this time.

Impossible. Natalie's heart began to pound.

The room looked like a museum, chock-full of . . . of *things*.

Ping.

It sped up a bit more, as if the motion had warmed its gears. *Ping . . . ping . . . ping, ping, ping . . .*

The second pot tilted slowly back, revealing another cross-legged automaton underneath. This one wore a long black robe like a judge's and a tiny white periwig on its head. It brought a mechanical arm down on the drum in its lap.

Tap . . . tap . . . tap, tap, tap, tap . . .

She backed away as the next pot lifted. The third automaton's glass eyes were covered by tiny silver lenses, but it seemed to stare nonetheless as it played short little whistles on a thin white flute. By the time the fourth pot lifted, the automaton under it was already moving. The cello in its lap emitted an otherworldly whine.

Its head was bald, with a dark grid drawn on the scalp, just like that of Thaddeus Argonault, the Paragon of Phrenology.

Natalie screamed.

As if cued by her voice, the rest of the automata in the wagon lurched into gear-grinding motion. Dancers whirled. The pig on the farmer's lap began to squeal. The gold beetle waved its little legs in the air with an ugly clicking noise, trying in vain to escape the skeletal bird before its beak descended.

She grabbed the closest one, a little barking dog with a wagging tail, in a half-formed attempt to silence it. *Find the key; turn it faster,* she thought. *Make it run down quick.*

There was no key.

She turned it over frantically as bristles rose on its back (*How on earth does that work?*) until she realized that while she was trying to stop one machine among dozens, she was losing precious seconds. She sprang for the door and touched the handle at the same moment Miranda's frantic knocking on the back wall began.

Natalie pressed her eye to the keyhole just in time to see Dr. Jake Limberleg, leading a column of patients, turn the corner into view. Too late.

She had to find a place to hide.

A table with a low-hanging brocade cloth covering it? Too obvious. There was one other door in the wagon, but given the uncanny collection in the main room, what awful things might be hidden out of view behind a closed door? Plus, to get to it she'd have to pass the tableau of miniature Paragons, and nothing was going to make her go any closer to those things.

Natalie's hands began to shake.

There.

The cabinet was low and looked deep enough for a small girl. She flung one door open, shoved its contents out of the way, and crawled inside. In the act of pulling the door shut, she froze.

One of the cross-legged automata from under the pots was on the floor in front of the platform.

It was still moving.

The little clockwork image of Nervine dragged itself across the wagon on the arms that had been clapping cymbals a moment before, its legs stretched out uselessly behind it. Of course, Natalie thought absurdly. Why would its lower half be mechanized? It only needed its upper body to play its instrument. She laughed crazily for just a second, then choked as she realized what the little Nervine was doing.

It was coming toward her.

She heard footsteps on the wagon stairs. *The automaton would show Dr. Limberleg where she was.*

There was no time for panic. Natalie sprang out of the cabinet, grabbed the thing from the floor, and dived back inside just in time to swing the door shut, leaving a tiny crack to peer through. The wagon door opened, and Alpheus Nervine, the full-size one, stepped inside.

He winced at the cacophony. Instantly, the automata, including the one in her arms, stopped moving and fell silent.

She saw his eyes dart around, and held her breath. In a moment they would fall on her hiding place.

But they didn't. Nervine disappeared, and ten horrible seconds passed—she counted each one—before Dr. Limberleg entered with a dramatic sweep of his arm, followed by his first patient: Miss Tillerman, Natalie's schoolteacher.

"Have a seat, dear lady." Dr. Limberleg cast his eyes about the wagon as Miss Tillerman eyed the odd chair. They swept over the cabinet . . . hesitated . . .

"Makes me think of having teeth pulled."

His eyes snapped back to his patient as she settled into the chair. "What a dreadful thought, madam! Put it out of your head immediately. If you don't, I shall know."

He positioned the ceramic head on a table beside the chair, then put his pale-gloved fingers on her temples and drew her head back so that the very base of her skull rested on the scoop. "All ready, then? You may close your eyes if you like. It will only take a moment." Dr. Limberleg waited until her eyes drifted shut, then unbuttoned the closures at the wrists of his gloves and began to peel one of them off.

Natalie's heart beat out of rhythm once, then again. She squinted. It had to be her eyes.

He tugged the leather fingers one by one and pulled the glove inch by inch off his hand.

It wasn't her eyes. It had to be a trick of the light.

The glove took too long to slide off his fingers; they seemed to stretch as it came off, as if the pale ivory leather had been holding them in.

It wasn't a trick of the light. Something was very, very wrong.

Dr. Limberleg finished with the first glove and began on the second. Natalie jammed her knuckles into her mouth and bit down hard. Slow horror began at her toes and slid up inside the bones of her legs, making them ache to kick out of the cabinet and flee into the safety of the world outside this wagon.

The second glove dropped on the table beside the first. Limberleg flexed his hands in the open air with a little sigh of pleasure. Natalie had never seen anything like them before, but she knew what they were. She closed her eyes and gasped silently for air in the musty cabinet.

The elongated fingers had too many joints, like spiders'

legs. They had no real skin, just a horny covering like a snail's shell. And in place of knuckles, little gears and cogs showed through as if their workings had, over long years—perhaps long centuries—worn painfully through to the surface.

Demon hands.

When she thought she could breathe again, Natalie put her eye back to the crack between the doors, hoping that she had seen only some medical oddity, some stretched specimen from his collection of hands or a pair of particularly horrible automata *shaped* like hands . . . that she had made a simple, dreadful mistake.

She looked, saw the monstrous hands, then saw something even worse. Through the crack in the cabinet door, Dr. Limberleg's eyes met hers.

He knew she was there.

"Now . . ." he said quietly, eyes still on Natalie in her hiding place, "let us begin."

For a moment, Natalie had forgotten about Miss Tillerman in the chair. Dr. Limberleg lowered his hands to her head and put his spidery fingers on her scalp. He touched her head for a minute with those abnormally long fingers, pausing once to glance at the illustrated head for reference. Then he drew his fingers out of her hair and slipped the gloves back on, compressing his fingers down to normal length as he buttoned the leather over his wrists.

"My dear lady, how long have you been experiencing these fainting spells?"

"Why, since I was sixteen!"

He pointed at a square on the ceramic head. "Inflammation of a lobe in this quadrant. Lodestone therapy would give you relief. There will be no discomfort, I assure you."

There was some discussion of the treatment, and a referral to Paracelsus Vorticelt. Dr. Limberleg helped the teacher out of the chair and down the stairs, then faced the cabinet and spoke quietly from the doorway.

"I know where you are, and I think I know *who* you are. Just remember this about what you see in this room: *No one will believe you.*"

Yes, they will, she thought fiercely. *My family will; I can always count on them.*

The next patient stepped inside. It began all over again. And again, and again, and again.

A parade of people filed through the wagon, and each time one sat down, Dr. Limberleg peeled the gloves off his demon hands and put them to the patient's head. After a moment he named the malady that had tortured him or her for days or months or years, and pronounced a cure. Judging from the patients' responses, it seemed that some of them had never discussed these illnesses before, not even with Doc Fitzwater.

Trapped in her cabinet-prison, watching the unbearable ritual over and over, Natalie began to understand. He wasn't reading their heads. He was reading their *minds*.

So at a crossroads somewhere who-knew-when, Jake Limberleg had met the Devil and made a trade . . . and, just as her mother had told her, the Devil had taken a down payment on his soul. Natalie thought uncomfortably about the collection of carved hands scattered throughout the room. Why had he surrounded himself with so many reminders of something so horrible?

Afternoon came. Patients continued to come and go. Natalie clutched the automaton like a doll and rocked in the cabinet.

"Aahh." Limberleg's little sigh was so faint, Natalie almost missed it. She pressed her eye back to the door.

The person who stepped into the wagon next was her father.

"My dear Mr. Minks. How is my wheel coming along?"

"Found one this morning that might fit. I'll bring it by later." Mr. Minks looked at the chair and laughed uncomfortably. "My son, Charlie . . ."

"Of course. The fellow with the tremors, wasn't he? How is he feeling today?"

"He thinks your tonic . . . he suggested . . ."

"Sit, please. Imagine that I am something innocuous like a barber."

Natalie opened her mouth to yell, but Dr. Limberleg shot her a warning look that made her jaws snap shut again. She squeezed the automaton so tightly she felt the sawdust and gears in its little torso grind together.

Gloves . . . stretching fingers . . . she clenched her eyes closed, but the tears squeezed out anyway. Couldn't he tell, didn't he know those weren't human hands? Couldn't he feel the spiders' legs on his scalp and understand they were in the pay of the Devil?

Eyes still shut, Natalie didn't see Dr. Limberleg's smile widen. She didn't see him pull the gloves back on. What made her look again was his voice, all mock-sorrow and dripping with acid concern.

"My dear sir," he said. "My dear sir, I am so sorry."

This wasn't the voice he had used for Miss Tillerman, or even Mrs. Anderson, who had broken down in sobs when Dr. Limberleg had correctly guessed that she couldn't have children. This was a voice you used for something else entirely.

Dr. Limberleg spoke quietly. "Bring her here. There are treatments, we can help. Bring her now. Dr. Acquetus can drive you."

Her father nodded miserably and rose. He stumbled out the door and down the stairs. Natalie sat back numbly and tried to remember how to think.

What had Dr. Limberleg seen when he probed into her father's mind?

Bring her here. Not Natalie, clearly. Dr. Limberleg knew right where Natalie was, after all.

It fell together with terrible precision, a series of images that made awful sense when she lined them up side by side. She had known it already, Natalie realized; she had just avoided thinking directly about it. She had avoided lining those clues up, because there was only one conclusion to draw from them.

Doc saying to her father: *Nothing to worry about.* Her father telling her mother at breakfast that Mr. Finch would wire Doc Fitzwater at a moment's notice. Her mother being suddenly very, very tired. The near fall down the stairs and the ever-present *vitamins*, which must not have been vitamins at all but pills that weren't working. Charlie begging her father to come here in case there was . . . what had he said? *What if there's an answer, and we don't find it because we don't try everything?*

Her mother was sick. Terribly, horribly sick. Then she heard Dr. Limberleg's voice, that strange tone. *My dear sir, I am so sorry.*

Not just sick.

Why hadn't they told Natalie?

She forgot about Dr. Limberleg, forgot about Nervine and his claw hammer, Argonault with his tattooed head, and all the rest of them, and plunged blindly, furiously out of the wagon after her father.

She shoved past Limberleg and the next patient, already on his way up the stairs, and sprawled headlong to the ground just in time to see her father turn the corner. Natalie shot to her feet and sprinted after him.

But the second she had rounded the corner out of view of the patients in line, the Amazing Quinn dropped from the overhead wires to land directly in her path. The harlequin tilted its head and stared at her through the white mask of its expressionless face. Natalie skidded to a halt—it was all she could do to keep from running headlong into the small figure. Its eyes blinked with a soft click. Natalie hesitated only a moment before coiling to sprint again, ready to kick and flail to get past the harlequin if she had to. Then a hand grasped her elbow, arresting her flight before she could take a single step.

She looked down and saw a bone-pale glove. With his other hand, Dr. Limberleg plucked away the automaton she hadn't realized she was still holding, and tucked it under his arm. "Your father will be back shortly, my dear Miss Minks. Dr. Nervine will take you to the Amber Therapy Tent. You may wait there."

FIFTEEN

Amber Therapy

NATALIE only half registered Alpheus Nervine's cold grip on her shoulder. A shaking hand took hers, and she dimly recognized the voice that said, "I'm going, too," as Miranda's.

"Don't look so grim," Nervine muttered, taking hold of the back of her overalls to keep her from running. "You're about to see a marvel of science."

He propelled them into the far deeps of the fair, farther than Natalie and her friends had explored. "Where are we going?" Miranda whispered.

"Don't you remember?" Natalie said dully. "Amber Therapy. All the way at the back. The tallest tent."

The fair seemed to stretch and widen as they wound their way through it, or else Nervine was taking the most circuitous route among the pavilions. At last he pushed Natalie and Miranda through the flaps of the huge tent. He hustled them past a front room full of placards and pamphlets and unidentifiable gadgets and flung open a curtain at the back. Natalie's jaw fell open. In the middle of the tent was the strangest, most amazing apparatus she had ever seen.

She had dragged Alfred around for more than an hour hoping to find this thing, the brass-wheeled vehicle that she had last seen peeking out from under dark oilcloth before Nervine had chased her away. Now that she stood before it, Natalie just wanted to run.

It was a giant, shining room of glass and brass, mounted on tires: two small and two taller than Natalie—a cross between Cinderella's pumpkin coach and a greenhouse on wheels. The whole contraption, roof, walls, floor, and all, appeared to have been pieced together from panes of glass in different sizes, the bulk of them shaped like the diamonds in a pack of cards. The glass panes had the thick, speckled look of old windows, most with air bubbles and some with a distinct bottle-green tint.

The domed roof was faceted like the top of a jewel, with a spire where all the brass fittings between the panes came together like the filaments of a tarnished gold spider web. Along the edges of the convex roof, curlicues of brass like vines or serpents were cast in slithering designs. The pattern was repeated in the door, which had only tiny panes of glass embedded in intricate, endlessly repeating whorls of metal.

The thick glass and the small panes that made up the walls fractured everything inside the chamber so that Natalie had to concentrate to figure out what she was looking at. The first object she could make sense of was a table upholstered in leather with brass rivets. Leather straps finished with big heavy buckles hung from the sides.

She bit her lip. Was that where they would put her mother?

There were other things in the glass room as well: a cabinet like a bookcase with windows enclosing each shelf held a battery of switches and huge bulbs shaped like sideways tears. A black, barrel-shaped machine with a hand crank sat on a tall, narrow table. Over all of these, cords and wires draped like creepers, linking one awful piece to the next and all coming together up inside the roof under the spire. At the center of the room, another collection of wires and belts came up through a hole in the floor, some connecting to the cabinet, others to the thing with the crank, and some rising straight up to join the wires under the spire.

"What is it?" Miranda whispered.

"The Amber Therapy Chamber," Nervine said.

Natalie's eyes flicked back to the table with its ominous straps. "You're going to put my *mother* in there?"

"It's a very advanced treatment," Nervine said carelessly. He hauled Natalie along as he strode up to the giant thing and whipped an oilcloth cover off of a bulky apparatus attached to one side between the wheels. There a pale man in a brown suit sat on the seat of a frame connecting the smaller rear wheel and the larger front one, hunched over a pair of handlebars as if he was asleep. His feet rested on pedals connected to the front wheel.

"Wake up," Nervine said, whacking him on the back with his free fist. The pale man coughed hollowly and straightened. All in all, it looked like he was sitting on a strangely oversize, stretched-out, high-wheeler bicycle. Then Natalie spotted the braces holding the wheels off the ground, and the collection of belts and pistons half-hidden underneath the chamber, which presumably hooked up to the cables coming up through the floor: it was some kind of generator, just like the one that ran the electric lights outside.

Nervine yanked Natalie around the other side of the giant chamber and uncovered a second, nearly identical man snoozing on another high-wheeler mechanism. The Paragon of Amber Therapy thumped him as well. "You, too. Wake up."

Now Nervine tilted his head to listen: the sound of approaching voices from outside the tent drifted in. "All right, come on. Back here." He yanked Natalie and Miranda behind a folding screen that partitioned off a little consultation area with a desk and chair from the rest of the tent.

The voices grew louder and became recognizable: Natalie's father, asking questions about the treatment, Limberleg giving clipped answers. Natalie heard the curtain swish and squirmed in Nervine's grip until she could just barely see around the edge of the screen that hid them. Four figures followed Limberleg in: Ted Minks and Charlie, with Natalie's mother between them, and Paracelsus Vorticelt bringing up the rear.

"Dad, no!" Nervine, still holding tight to her overalls, clapped a hand over her mouth before she could get the words out. "Dad! Charlie! *Mama!*" But no one could hear her muffled shouts. Miranda tried to bolt and ran straight into Paracelsus Vorticelt as he came around the screen.

Now Nervine handed Natalie off to Vorticelt. The Paragon of Magnetism held the girls, one under each arm and with his cold palms clamped over their mouths, as Nervine strode to where Natalie's family waited. The Paragon of Amber Therapy lifted Mrs. Minks as though she were a child and carried her up the tarnished stairs into the Amber Therapy Chamber, where, distorted almost beyond recognition by the thick old glass, he laid her on the leather table. Splintered into a sharp-edged monster by the green diamond-shaped panes, Nervine secured those thick straps around her; he placed a leather cap on her head, and suddenly the overhanging wires were connected to her as well.

Vorticelt let go of Natalie and Miranda now, and both girls sprinted out from behind the screen. "A mild electric current, very gentle," Dr. Limberleg was saying to Mr. Minks and Charlie. "Nothing to be concerned about, although I can see that Natalie there is very upset."

"Natalie?" Her father looked over, surprised.

She stopped a few feet away and looked from him to her brother to her mother, strapped into the giant glass chamber, and back to her father again. She didn't know whether she wanted to kick him for not telling her or hit him for putting her mother in that horrid box. In the end she flung herself into his arms.

"Dad, don't let them! Something horrible . . . I don't know what, but I saw—I saw—"

But Dr. Limberleg sprang up the stairs to close the door, and then it was too late. "All in readiness," he called, and inside the box Nervine rolled up his sleeves and took hold of the hand crank.

"I'm so sorry I didn't tell you, Nattie. It wasn't fair; I should have—"

"No, Daddy, listen—listen, please, *listen*—"

"Natalie," Charlie interrupted, "calm down—"

She whirled on her brother. "You can shut up. Why didn't you tell me?" Then to her father again: "Daddy, his hands! *Look at his hands!*"

Dr. Limberleg's voice cut through her pleas. "Start it up, Dr. Nervine. Dr. Vorticelt, kindly power up the generators." Unable to stop herself, Natalie turned to look.

It took mere moments. At a tap from Paracelsus Vorticelt's stick, the two men on the bicycles began to pedal. Inside, with Nervine's hand rotating the crank, the black barrel began to spin, slowly at first, then faster and faster as the gray-haired doctor's arm whirled, reaching speeds Natalie couldn't believe. On the bookcase, the bulbs began to glow with light that splintered and broke as it tried to escape through the chamber's hundreds of little glass panes. Weird greenish shadows emerged. And somewhere in the middle of it all, completing the circuit, was Natalie's mother, strapped to the table.

Natalie looked up at her father. His face was drawn tight, as though he was trying to force it not to show whatever he was feeling. He noticed Natalie's stare and put a quaking hand on her shoulder.

A live spark jumped off the black-barreled dynamo, then another. Suddenly the glass compartment was full of light, dozens, *hundreds* of live sparks leaping from the bulbs or coursing along the wires. Outside the chamber, the nearer of the two brown-suited men began to shake in his seat, feet still driving away at the high-wheeler's pedals. The low, chattering sound Natalie could just make out under the sizzle of the sparks might have been his teeth rattling.

Alpheus Nervine's arm kept going. His lips peeled back from his teeth in a grimace of exertion that stretched wider and wider, made horrifying by the jagged panes. Strange, irregular patches of darkness bloomed in the wake of the chaotic sparks. Tiny fizzes like bolts of lightning leaped from the spire on the roof and skated across the canvas above. Miranda hissed something about the tent catching fire. In a sudden burst of electricity, Natalie saw Nervine's skull through his skin, clear as day despite the warped glass.

Then she saw her mother's.

Charlie put his hand over his mouth and fled the tent, stumbling over his own feet. Miranda stepped a little closer to Natalie and clutched her hand. Mr. Minks's hand tightened on her shoulder. On the stairs of the Amber Therapy Chamber, Jake Limberleg watched them move closer together, then turned back to watch the patient inside.

It was awful. It wouldn't stop. It looked as though Nervine himself would have to keel over before the ordeal could end, and his arm moved as if powered by an engine of its own. Just when Natalie thought he must collapse, Nervine shouted from inside, "Vorticelt!" His voice was a distorted echo.

The Paragon of Magnetism strode forward, yanked the closest brown-suited man off his seat, and climbed up onto the high-wheeler himself. Vorticelt began pedaling feverishly, much faster than the thin man had managed, spinning the wheels at inconceivable speeds as the previous rider slouched into the shadows at the periphery of the tent, jaw still chattering as if he, too, was in the grip of the terrible current.

Natalie's mother seemed trapped inside a light bulb; her thin body was like the little wire inside the glass that glowed when you turned on a lamp and burned until it broke.

How long could she withstand this much electricity?

The fragmented light pouring from the chamber grew brighter and brighter as Vorticelt and Nervine forced the dynamo to greater and greater output. Natalie fought to keep her eyes open, but in the end she had to squeeze them shut and could only watch the sparks dance from behind her closed eyelids.

Finally, finally the light in the tent began to flicker and dim. She opened her eyes and saw her mother's body shake once, violently. Then it was over.

Nervine let go of the crank, clutching what must've been an aching arm, and the dynamo whirled to a stop. On the high-wheeler, Vorticelt slumped, propping his legs up on a pair of hooks above the pedals while the bicycle's wheels spun to stillness. On the other side, the remaining brown-suited man tumbled right off of his cycle, teeth clicking maniacally, and fell out of view behind the chamber.

When the sparks along the wires died, Dr. Limberleg himself opened the door, wincing for a moment as if the handle was scorching to the touch. He stepped in and unbuckled the straps. He put a hand to his patient's cheek. He slid an arm under her thin shoulders.

Mrs. Minks sat up.

In a quick motion altogether unlike the weak manner in which she'd moved for the last two days, she swung her legs off the table, looked down at her family, and gave them a confused smile, twisted by the glass.

Dr. Limberleg escorted her down the stairs and stepped aside.

"Mama?" Natalie asked in a shaking voice. "Are you all right?" And without waiting for an answer she flung herself into her mother's arms only a second before her father did the same. Charlie, who had been lurking at the entrance to the tent, came running to join them. Miranda fidgeted a few paces away, looking relieved and concerned at the same time.

"Well, what on earth is all this?" Annie asked, looking around. "I must've been out cold." Her voice was strong, bright as a bell.

Dr. Limberleg observed their reunion with clinical detachment until Mr. Minks disengaged himself. "What can I do to thank you, Doctor?"

Dr. Limberleg shook his hand. "Just find me a wheel, my dear fellow."

Natalie's father nodded weakly. "You'll have it before midnight, I promise."

"That would be a great relief," Limberleg said.

Strange things can happen at a crossroads, and if the crossroads is just outside of a town, sometimes strange things will happen in the town, too.

An itinerant medicine show, for instance, might change someone's life with a roomful of sparks, as it did for Natalie's mother. But celebration had to wait; Dr. Limberleg had been promised a wheel by midnight.

Natalie could not share in her family's joy. Her mother would understand what those awful hands meant . . . but Natalie couldn't bring herself to tell her. She sat at the kitchen table watching her mother sail around the kitchen with her much-abused *Boston Cook Book* open under one arm, measuring flour from a tin, taking eggs from the bowl in the icebox. As if she weren't just going to burn the cake in the end. As if nothing had happened. Certainly as if she hadn't been all but electrocuted less than two hours ago. As if it were just any other Sunday afternoon.

"Natalie?"

She flinched and looked guiltily up at her mother. "Yes?"

"What kind shall we have? Neapolitan? Sponge Cake? Orange Cake?" Mrs. Minks's smile faltered a little as she waited for the answer. "I think I have cocoa if you'd like chocolate."

"Oh. Chocolate." Natalie tried to look cheerful. It was hard, so very hard to do.

Her family, the family she'd thought she could always count on, had failed her. Her brilliant father had not been able to see evil when it had been right in front of him. Her mother had gotten sick and hadn't trusted Natalie enough to tell her. And Charlie, who ought to have told her even if no one else had, because what else did you have big brothers for . . . well, she just wanted to thrash him on principle.

So instead of staying in the kitchen stealing sips of coffee while Mrs. Minks baked a cake she was destined to burn, Natalie mumbled something and slipped out onto the front porch. The red Chesterlane leaned against the steps. She frowned, considering her choices: sit in the kitchen wondering how to talk to her mother about Dr. Limberleg's demon hands, or try and fail yet again to ride that stupid bicycle?

In the end, she chose the bicycle. Even making another failed attempt at riding it seemed easier than sticking around here trying to make sense of what had happened.

She headed toward her usual practicing spot, but when she got to Smith Lane Natalie found she didn't want to stop. She kept on walking, meandering aimlessly through town wishing she were riding, until she found herself turning off of Bard Street and onto Heartwood at the corner where the old water tower stood. Instead of following the road all the way back to the medicine show, however, she turned onto a much older lane that broke away from it and headed out of Arcane and toward the old forest to the southwest.

Cobblestones older than the town itself rounded up out of the dust under her tires. A faded street sign hung on a splintered post at the junction. Natalie squinted up at it. She'd passed this sign a hundred times, but it hung at an angle that made it impossible to read unless you were actually on the cobbled lane, headed for the huge house at the end. COFFRETFONCE, it said: the name of Simon Coffrett's family estate.

What on earth made me come this way? she wondered. After all she'd seen and heard in the last couple of days, it was hard to say whether it seemed a good idea to keep walking toward Mr. Coffrett's house or not.

The only mansion in Arcane sat at the top of the town's only hill. Even considering its size, it didn't look like any other house she had ever seen. It was built of stone and was surrounded by oak trees gnarled into odd shapes by unimaginable age. Tall, thin dormer windows and leaning chimneys of crumbling brick broke through the leaves here and there in unexpected places, so that it was difficult to see exactly where the huge house ended and the trees began.

The cobbled road led her patiently out of town and up the hill, lined on both sides by low stone walls and twisted black bushes with red flowers like twists of crepe paper. The bushes coiled along the walls like ivy, even working their way through holes between the rocks in some places. The mansion in its grove loomed ahead. She bent to smell one of the delicate red flowers, and tried to remember what it was Tom and Mr. Finch had said about Mr. Coffrett. He had rented the empty lot to the hucksters. They had wanted to ask him something about that.

The flower smelled like perfume and paper. Natalie remembered that the question they wanted to ask had carried some risk. It had to be more than a simple *why*.

A breeze pushed at her back. Underneath her nose, the flower rustled and fluttered upward into her face. Natalie stumbled away and watched as first one, then four small red butterflies lifted from the branch and circled her head, sending off whiffs of sweetness and dust with each swipe of their wings, a faded-sunshine smell a little like her mother's cosmetics. She stared in wonder as more and more of them rose into flight, a red cloud that left nothing but a bare skeleton of dead bramble below it.

The little wind reached the oaks, sending up a rustle that didn't sound like moving leaves, and Natalie thought, *This place is a dream.* The butterflies that smelled like flowers flitted around her, and she remembered Thaddeus Argonault at the fair, talking about how Mr. Coffrett couldn't distinguish dreams from reality.

She also remembered that the last time she'd thought about Mr. Coffrett and what the phrenologist had said about him, back when she'd been listening to the whispered conference at the general store, she had been afraid.

The butterflies resettled on the branches creeping along beside the road. They were once again indistinguishable from papery flowers, and Natalie was back on a perfectly normal road to a house she'd walked *past* if not *to* every other day of her life.

She leaned her bicycle against the first of the ancient oak trees and looked up as another breeze set them in motion. A collection of wind chimes on the lower branches clacked and clinked. Not one appeared to match another. Farther up, in among the leaves, larger shapes with wide, white wings moved: huge birds that shuffled and settled and looked down at her as if she were a trespasser. Natalie followed a slate path through the oaks to the front porch and found Simon Coffrett standing in the open doorway. Waiting, just as Tom said he would be, for someone to come by.

SIXTEEN

Jumper

"HELLO, NATALIE," Mr. Coffrett said, swinging his spectacles by one earpiece in his hand. He looked different in the shadows of the oaks. How old was he, anyway? She didn't even know what he did for a living. Maybe, since he lived in that enormous house, he had money hidden away and didn't need to work.

"Hi, Mr. Coffrett." She stopped at the bottom of the porch stairs. It was much cooler in the shade of the giant trees. "Sorry to bother you."

"I was just having tea." He nodded to where a ceramic tea service sat on a wrought-iron table a little ways down the porch. "You can join me if you like." There were already two thin china cups beside the teapot, and a little sugar bowl and pitcher. Simon Coffrett walked over, lifted the pot, and poured one cup, then the other. "I don't get many visitors. It helps to be optimistic."

She climbed the steps and crossed hesitantly to the table. "I don't know if I should. Have tea." Natalie sat and looked at the teacup. "You're sort of strange." The second it was out of her mouth she felt her face go red. "I mean . . . I meant . . ."

Simon Coffrett burst into laughter. "From the mouths of babes . . ." He laughed so hard, Natalie couldn't stay embarrassed. "I know what you meant," he said finally. "You meant to say that I'm sort of a stranger, but I think in the end you spoke just exactly the truth, neither more nor less." He pushed the sugar bowl across the table. "Go ahead. I am strange, but my tea is safe. Try two lumps."

Embarrassment forgotten, Natalie looked thoughtfully at the ageless man on the other side of the table stirring his tea with a silver spoon, the man she'd seen tumbling through the atmosphere and walking amid the ghosts of the past. After a moment, she reached for the sugar bowl.

"So are you selling bees today, or jewelry?" Simon Coffrett said at last. "Or did you just have nowhere else to go for tea?"

Another wind set the great birds in the trees moving. Natalie tried to see them clearly. "Is it all right if I ask you a question, Mr. Coffrett?"

"They're albatrosses. Sea birds."

"*Sea* birds?" Momentarily distracted, Natalie frowned up at the big wings in the oak branches. "But there's no water around here. Not for miles, and definitely no sea."

Across the table, Simon Coffrett smiled into his teacup. "There are stranger things in this town than sea birds,

Natalie, but I suppose you've noticed that. And I don't suppose that was the question you were going to ask."

"No." The wind chimes slowed as the breeze died down. Natalie watched the pieces, shards of painted porcelain and metal hanging on lengths of red string, go still. She hesitated. Only a day ago, Mr. Swifte had said that certain questions carried a risk. How could you tell which ones?

Moreover, it was hard to look at Mr. Coffrett. His spectacles reflected the fractured light coming through the oak leaves and made it hard to see his eyes. The overall effect was almost the opposite of looking at Paracelsus Vorticelt; Mr. Coffrett's face seemed not to want her to look too closely at it.

Confidence, she thought. *Just like Tom said*. "I wanted to ask you," Natalie said carefully, turning the cup around in her fingers, "about Dr. Limberleg and the medicine show." Simon Coffrett waited for her to continue. "They treated my mother, and I don't like them, and I don't understand it all."

"They . . . they treated your mother?" He looked away into the trees where the albatrosses shuffled on their branches. "I expected more of him."

"Who?" *Concentrate, be confident . . .* but it was no good, wouldn't work. She couldn't talk to him if she couldn't *look* at him, for goodness' sake. Why couldn't she look at him?

"Your father." Anger, real anger, infused his words.

"My *father?*"

For a moment Mr. Coffrett just drummed his fingers on the table. It reminded Natalie of the way her mother sometimes tapped her foot when she was angry and trying to control it. For some reason, the idea of Mr. Coffrett being angry was a little unnerving.

He ceased drumming and folded his hands. "So they treated your mother," Mr. Coffrett said, conversational now. "What made you come to me to ask about them?"

"Because . . ." Frustrated, she tried to decide how to answer. She couldn't make her eyes stay on his face. What on earth had he meant about her father, and what would he say if she admitted she had heard Tom Guyot and the others talking about him?

Behind his spectacles Simon Coffrett seemed to be watching her carefully. "Was there more to that, or just . . . because?"

"You rented the lot to Dr. Limberleg."

"Yes."

"Well, did he . . . did they . . . did you know what . . . he . . . is?"

"What, exactly, is he, Natalie?"

Her hands tightened on the cup in front of her. "Something wicked. I don't know." Simon Coffrett said nothing. "Tell me something! Anything! Will my mother be all right? And my brother? Will they leave, Limberleg and all of them? Will they go? What will happen then?"

Mr. Coffrett leaned back and sighed. A long moment passed as he stared out, looking neither right nor left, just as he had when Natalie had seen him in the strange moment at the crossroads, purposefully ignoring the crowd of staggering figures that weren't really there. "You think I'm in a position to answer all that?" he asked quietly.

Across the table, Simon Coffrett smiled into his teacup.

"Well . . . you see things," Natalie said before she could help herself.

"*I beg your pardon?*"

Natalie shrank in her chair. No going back now. "Don't . . . don't you? Things that happened? So . . . can't you see what *will* happen, too?"

Mr. Coffrett leaned in now as if he was looking at her closely, but there was no anger in the gesture. "Natalie, have you . . . have you seen things, too?"

"I saw you falling," she whispered. "I saw you at Trader's Mill."

"So it's started already." He nodded and sat back. Natalie frowned, utterly confused, but before she could speak a word, Mr. Coffrett asked, "What else have you seen?"

"I saw . . . his hands," Natalie whispered. "I can't stop seeing Dr. Limberleg's hands."

"Hands are skin and bone, mostly. Some are human; some are not. They're still only hands." He hesitated, and tapped his fingers on the tabletop again for a second or two. "I see things, Natalie, but it isn't as simple as seeing the future and the past. I'm not a fortuneteller. I can't tell you what's going to happen. I can't help you with that."

"But—"

"One more question, Natalie. Ask me one simple question."

You do not question me properly. You must begin at the beginning. That's what the sibyl in her glass case had said in reply to Natalie's question the day before yesterday. "Why did you rent them the lot?"

He poured himself another cup of tea, added a lump of sugar, and swirled it all together with his spoon. "I rented the lot to Jake Limberleg because all great works begin with small first steps."

"Great works?"

"Much depends on those small steps, Natalie, but they're like puzzle pieces." Simon Coffrett watched the albatrosses shift in the deformed oak trees. "You can't see the picture until they're all in place."

Natalie sat in silence for a moment, then spoke up. "Unless you already know what the picture's supposed to be."

"Natalie, listen very closely to me for a minute." He took off his spectacles. It was like a blow, like taking the lampshade away from a too-bright light bulb. His eyes were different from before. Blinding. Dizziness hit Natalie like a baseball to the head, and once again, just like the day she'd fallen on Main Street, she saw multiple Simon Coffretts splinter away from the one who spoke to her, moving around him like photographic negatives.

"Listen," he said. It took effort, so much effort; the spectral-Simons dodging around the real one seemed to be speaking, too. Natalie forced herself to focus on the true Mr. Coffrett, the one staring at her with blazing eyes.

"Only the most rare and valuable things are ever given free," he was saying. "Most things cost something you can give up, but they aren't worth anything—not really, not in the end. But *some* things . . . some have to be given free, because if you had to put a price on them, their true value would be too great for any one person to afford. Do you understand?"

She nodded fiercely, not because she understood but because she was a little afraid of how seriously he was talking. She blinked her eyes hard until the dizziness went away and the spectral-Simons merged back into one.

"I'm telling you this, Natalie, because when you ask a question, you must consider that the answer might cost you, and you must be sure that what you ask is worth the price." Those bright-burning eyes refused to let her go. "And you should remember that, too, when someone asks something of you."

"That I should make it cost them something?"

"That it might have cost them already."

"What does . . ." Cold tea sloshed over the rim as she set the cup down without looking and missed the saucer. She was suddenly very afraid. "What does this cost? All I asked so far?"

"Courage. And tea." He closed his eyes and replaced his spectacles. Right away, Natalie's eyes slid off him again. "Now. Have you any other questions before you go?"

She tried one more time to look him in the face. *Concentrate*. "What are the great works?"

"You want to see what the puzzle looks like." He nodded. "Some people start with the pieces at the edges, but if I were you, I'd go straight to the center. I suspect you'll find you have a gift for putting the pieces in the right places."

They clearly weren't talking about real puzzles. "I don't know what that means," Natalie protested.

Simon Coffrett smiled again, a little sadly. "I know." Natalie waited, thinking there must be more, that he couldn't possibly think that was any kind of answer. But he only picked up his teacup and took another sip. Infuriating.

"I don't mean to be rude, Mr. Coffrett," she said at last, "but what are you talking about?" He looked up and blinked. She pushed on. "This sounds like important stuff, and you must want me to get something from it. . . ." Secret meetings at the general store, great works, puzzles . . . why couldn't people just say what they meant? A thought occurred, hazy but with a sense of rightness to it. "Am . . . am I supposed to do something?"

His expression softened a touch. "You have a place in it. Possibly *the* place. But there's a great deal that isn't for me to tell you."

"Who, then?"

"It's for your mother to tell you. This is as simply as I can put it without . . . without doing any damage. Arcane is in the path of a storm. It's survived this kind of thing before, but only by a hair's breadth. This time . . ." Mr. Coffrett pushed his spectacles higher on his nose and leaned toward her again. "What happens this time is likely to be entirely up to you."

Natalie stared across the table for what seemed like ages, but Mr. Coffrett just looked steadily at her until she couldn't take it anymore.

"*Me?*"

"You."

"*Why?*"

He sighed. "Because I'm not sure Annie will be ready to do what needs doing. She isn't well."

"Mama? But . . . but she's better now!" Mr. Coffrett said nothing. The silence made Natalie feel like screaming. She held on to the edge of the table to stop her hands from shaking. "But *why?*"

"Because you are who you are. You're your mother's daughter. Because of the things you can see."

"The things I—you mean—*that doesn't make any sense!*" Now she had plenty of good questions, so many she could barely think, they were coming at her so thick and fast. She opened her mouth to start slinging them at him, but before she could get the first word out, he shook his head with finality.

"Natalie, it's not my place. When I step out of my place, it does no good for anybody."

There was no way she was walking away with that being the final word. "At least tell me . . . well, can you say what kind of storm's coming, at least?"

He considered. For just a minute Natalie thought she saw a strange reflection in his spectacles. She glanced over her shoulder, certain she had seen something flicker blue over his eyes, but there was nothing behind her but oaks, chimes, and albatrosses. When she turned back, the reflection, if it had been there at all, was gone.

"A firestorm," Mr. Coffrett said. "And that, I think, is all I can safely say."

Natalie pushed her cup away numbly and stood up. "Thank you for the tea, Mr. Coffrett."

"My pleasure. Come by anytime."

Metal and ceramic clinked tunelessly as she descended

the steps and took hold of her bicycle again. All those chimes. On impulse she turned back toward the man on the porch.

"What are all the chimes for?"

"You could say they were gifts." His voice sounded strangely flat. "People have always tied them in these trees." Another breeze slid among the branches, as if the chimes themselves had something to add to the conversation.

"Mr. Coffrett? Do you really think you're dead?" It came out whisper-quiet, mostly because Natalie wasn't sure she really wanted to know the answer.

Simon Coffrett smiled. "Don't tell me you doubt our esteemed phrenologists, Natalie."

"But why?"

A single red butterfly flew past her into the shade of the oaks. Mr. Coffrett followed its flight until it landed before him on the teapot. "A poet named Rilke wrote a line I like very much." He put out a finger and the little insect climbed onto it without hesitation. "He said that angels often do not know whether they walk among the living or the dead."

He watched the butterfly climb from finger to finger. His smile faded into a different, stranger expression, but it was one Natalie had seen before. For just a moment she remembered again the image of Simon Coffrett falling through the air with that same incomprehensible look on his face. She screwed up her courage one last time and asked, "Mr. Coffrett? What does . . . what does *jumper* mean?"

"It means someone who jumps." His mouth curled again briefly at Natalie's expression of disappointment. "I think you want to know, What does it mean that *I* am a jumper."

Natalie nodded. Simon sighed as the butterfly took off again and flitted back into the sunlight beyond the stand of oaks. "Once, long ago, I had two friends who quarreled. I knew they would want me to take a side, so before either had a chance to ask, I jumped off a cliff to get away from the argument." A deeper sadness came over his face. "If I had taken a side, I might have stopped the quarrel, but I didn't. My friends fought each other to the death while I ran away."

She stared at him. "Your friends . . . fought to the death while you jumped off a cliff? How could they do that? And you jumped off a cliff *and you're still standing here now?*" Nothing about this story made sense. "You're not telling me the truth, are you?"

Simon Coffrett frowned thoughtfully. "Well, I suppose it is a little more complicated than that. Let me try again." He paused for a sip of tea. "I was on a bridge over a gorge miles wide and miles deep. Two locomotives were speeding toward me from either side, bound to collide with each other in the middle. I jumped off the bridge to escape." He added another lump of sugar to his cup and stirred it, that same deep sadness creeping across his face again. "I might have stopped the engines somehow, but instead I ran away. The wreckage was terrible."

It was the strangest thing. It didn't have the feel of a

lie, but still it didn't sound right, and it certainly didn't make any more sense than the first story. Again, Natalie shook her head. "Mr. Coffrett, how could you have stopped two locomotives from crashing? And how could you survive jumping into a gorge miles deep?"

He considered. "All right. The truth is that I was on a battlefield, Natalie, high in the mountains. I stood between two armies about to charge at each other, knowing that if something didn't stop them, the battle would end in total disaster, chaos, uncounted loss of lives. I fled the field. I might have negotiated a truce, or stopped the first bullet, or done something—anything—to change the outcome. But instead I ran. I jumped off the mountain, and instead of changing everything, I changed nothing."

Natalie shook her head. This felt closer somehow, more right, and yet still there was something wrong with the explanation, something missing. "But still, Mr. Coffrett, how can one person stop an army? *Two* armies? And how could you survive jumping off a mountain? How could you survive any of the things you've told me?"

Mr. Coffrett's eyebrows came together over his spectacled eyes. "How do you know I survived?"

Natalie opened her mouth, closed it again, frowned. If he had to ask, then *Because you're sitting right there and I can see you* couldn't possibly be the right answer.

You think you're dead, Mr. Coffrett.

Another breeze shook the wind chimes. Natalie shivered. Simon Coffrett sipped his tea, his eyebrows still furrowed in a way that made him look as if he was thinking hard about something and might actually have forgotten she was there.

In the end, there was nothing for her to do but turn around and walk back into town. She decided Mr. Coffrett needed company for tea more often, if only to learn to have normal conversations with people.

When she reached Heartwood, Natalie leaned her bicycle against the Coffretfonce signpost and hauled herself to a seat on the stone wall. Simon Coffrett's strange warnings made no more sense here than they had in the oak grove, but they clearly had something to do with her mother. Mr. Coffrett had suggested that the town was in danger and Mrs. Minks had a role to play that she might not be ready for. But if Natalie's mother had something to do, why wouldn't she be ready? True, she'd been sick, but whatever sort of grim powers he'd used, Dr. Limberleg had cured her. She was stronger now than she'd been before. She'd actually been singing in the kitchen when Natalie had left.

On the other hand, Simon Coffrett had been disappointed that Mr. Minks had taken her to Limberleg for treatment. More than disappointed. Furious. What did he know that the rest of them didn't?

One thing was for sure: it wouldn't do any good to go back and ask. Simon had made it clear that for one reason or another, he couldn't say any more than he did. Which left one option. Natalie hopped down from the stone wall, grabbed the bicycle, and stalked back toward home.

She could smell the cake before she even got past the

bicycle shop. It didn't smell burned at all, which somehow made her nerves jangle even worse. The evidence that things still weren't right, if she'd needed any further evidence than her own gut feeling and Simon Coffrett's anger, was that perfect chocolate cake cooling in the wire-fronted cabinet beside the kitchen door.

She gave the cabinet and the cake inside it a wide berth and a dubious glance as she slipped inside.

In the kitchen, Mrs. Minks was sitting at the table chewing her thumbnail and flipping through an issue of *Life*. She brightened. "Nattie! Almost time to ice the cake!" She got up quickly, bumping the table as she did and upsetting her mug of coffee, so that it spattered across the cover of the magazine.

Natalie frowned as her mother muttered a word she probably hadn't meant to use and leaped for a dishtowel to mop up the spill. Mrs. Minks was always clumsy, but given the perfect cake, the nail biting, the distracted flipping of pages . . . *She's nervous*, Natalie realized. *She knows something's up.*

Lowering herself cautiously into the opposite chair, Natalie waited for her mother to finish her distracted cleanup of the table and sit again. Instead, Mrs. Minks fluttered around the kitchen like a moth, flipping through her cookbook, collecting butter from the bowl in the icebox and peering into the chipped jug of sweet milk. "Want chocolate frosting? Or I have some almond extract. I may even have hazelnuts if we want them on top."

"Mama?" Natalie said at last, staring at the coffee-stained

magazine as she worked up her nerve. "Can you stop for a minute? I have a question."

The clatter of a tin hitting the countertop made her look up sharply. White powdered sugar spilled in a soft landslide into the sink. Mrs. Minks stared at the upended sugar tin, an overflowing measuring cup shaking in one hand. "Surely, sweetheart. Of course."

Something was going on for certain.

Mrs. Minks set down the measuring cup, dusted her hands on the dishtowel, turned her back on the mess on the counter, and sat across from Natalie. "What's on your mind?"

They looked at each other for a long minute. "I went to see Mr. Coffrett," Natalie began, fidgeting with her fingers under the table, out of view. How was she going to ask this question?

It would mean admitting that she knew the treatment had been a mistake. It would mean acknowledging that her father and Charlie had done something wrong. It would mean telling her mother, if she didn't already know, that as good as she was feeling now, there was still something very, very bad about it all, even though Natalie didn't understand what, precisely, that very bad thing was. It would mean demanding to know whatever it was that Mrs. Minks knew and had, for some reason, chosen not to share with her.

She looked at Mrs. Minks, and Mrs. Minks looked back. If such a thing was possible, it looked like she was even more nervous than her daughter was. Natalie had the distinct impression her mother was fidgeting under the table, too.

"Natalie?"

She couldn't do it. It was cowardly, but she simply couldn't do it. The second Natalie realized she truly couldn't bring herself to tell her mother what she knew about Limberleg and ask why Simon was angry at her father for letting the treatment happen, she felt a huge pressure slide from her shoulders. But here they were, and the first words had already been spoken, so she had to ask something. Natalie thought fast.

"I asked Mr. Coffrett what a jumper was, and he told me three different things." The words came out in a tremendous rush. "I thought you might know which one was true."

Mrs. Minks's shoulders relaxed, as if she'd been holding her breath. She looked at Natalie closely. "You want to know about Simon Coffrett. Is that really what . . . well, okay."

The terrible tension drained from the room; they were back on safer territory. The relief was cold comfort, though; Natalie knew she had backed away from something important. Everything in her said that she should've stood her ground.

Meanwhile, Mrs. Minks sipped at the remaining coffee in her mug. "I can only tell you what I know, but if what Simon told you is anything like what my mother told me when I was younger, I don't think you'll be any happier with the explanation I'm about to give you. What my mother told me was that Simon Coffrett once lived in a very great city, high in the mountains. The city had a colony nestled in the valleys below, and the mayor and his second-in-command quarreled. . . ." She paused for another sip of coffee, thinking hard. "Isn't that funny? I can't remember."

Again Natalie felt the stirrings of dread. For her mother not to remember a story . . .

Mrs. Minks scratched her head. "Wait . . . yes. There was a great event, a ball or an exhibition or something like that, and . . . yes. Yes, I remember now. The quarrel was this: who would take precedence at the dinner? The lieutenant mayor officially outranked the governor of the colony, but the mayor announced that at the dinner and from then on, the colonial governor would be second in precedence and the lieutenant mayor third."

"That seems like a kind of stupid quarrel."

"Well, it was, but you have to remember that in the olden days, precedence and rank and things like that were terribly important. In this case, it was enough to divide the city and the thousands and thousands of people in it. The lieutenant mayor refused to take the third seat at the state dinner, so the mayor accused him of treason and told him he had to leave the city and never return. But the lieutenant mayor was very much loved by the citizens, and many of them thought the mayor was being terribly unfair. Half of them sided with the lieutenant, the other half with the mayor and the colonial governor."

"Did it start a battle?" Natalie asked, thinking of Simon Coffrett's third explanation.

Mrs. Minks nodded. "It was a truly terrible battle, and in the end, the lieutenant mayor lost, and he and all those who supported him were exiled from the city. But before the battle even started, a number of the citizens fled. Some were afraid their city would be torn apart, leaving no survivors at all; others simply didn't want to fight over something they felt wasn't worth the lives that would be lost."

"They were the jumpers? Why were they called that?"

Mrs. Minks paused to remember again. "Because to escape without being seen by supporters of either the mayor or his lieutenant, they couldn't leave through the city gates. They had to make their way down a mountain pass, a gorge so steep and treacherous it had always been said in the city that the only way down was to jump, but it would surely be a jump to the death."

Natalie waited, but this appeared to be the end of the story. "So . . . is that true, or not?"

"Well, like anything, I suppose it could be a little bit true and a little bit false. . . ." Mrs. Minks hesitated. "But to tell you the truth, Natalie, I always had the feeling that your grandma made that one up for the sake of having an answer. She could never tell me where the city was, or when it happened—which never made sense to me because as far as I know, Simon Coffrett has always lived here, and his family before that, I suppose, back to the days when nearly everything all the way to Pinnacle was part of the Coffrett family estate. And certainly no city in Missouri ever had any kind of colony, so whatever happened, it didn't happen here."

Mrs. Minks stood and began sweeping up the spilled sugar on the counter. "There is, however, a very similar story to that one that your grandma also liked to tell, and when I was younger I figured she sort of . . . well . . . adapted it to Simon Coffrett."

"Huh," Natalie said. From the look on Mrs. Minks's face, she seemed to expect that Natalie would know the story she meant. Natalie had no idea, but she didn't feel like starting another story right now when she still had to figure out what was going on down at the medicine show. She nodded seriously.

Mrs. Minks winked, and began to whip together the cake frosting in a yellowware mixing bowl. "I'm impressed that you had the courage to ask Simon Coffrett about that, but . . . where did you hear the word *jumper* in the first place?"

"Mr. Coffrett volunteered for the phrenology demonstration," Natalie said carefully. "I think I heard it there." Trying not to squirm under her mother's scrutiny, she slid off her chair. "I'm supposed to meet Miranda," she said as casually as she could manage. "See you later."

If she couldn't bring herself to ask her mother any hard questions, there was still one more place to go to try to find some answers. Natalie trotted alongside the Chesterlane down the middle of Bard Street until she got to the general store, then took a right on Sanctuary Street, which cut between the saloon and the old Methodist church, and sprinted half a block to a blue house with a wide porch. She banged unceremoniously on the door. While she was waiting for someone to answer, Natalie realized there was another problem with the story her grandma had told her mother.

The story implied that Simon Coffrett himself had been around a lot longer than was possible. Natalie had no idea how old he was, but he certainly wasn't an old man. How could he have fled a battle "in the olden days," long enough ago that Natalie's grandmother had to come up with a story about his escape to tell her own daughter? How could Mr. Coffrett have been old enough to have made a difference in the battle if he had stayed?

Just then a small hand opened the door. Miranda Porter peered through the screen.

"I have to go back to the nostrum fair," Natalie said simply. "Want to come?"

SEVENTEEN

Jasper Bellinspire's Bargain

A T THE END OF HEARTWOOD STREET, the strings of dusty round bulbs blinked to life along the roofs of the nostrum fair's tents, a little out of place in the early evening sky. On the stage, the Paragons were setting up some kind of apparatus for a demonstration.

Natalie tucked her bicycle against the old trough under the hawthorn, and the girls edged around the accumulating audience, trying to stay out of sight of the four men with their strange machinery. Miranda had needed no convincing to come along; she told Natalie that when she had run home after the episode in the Amber Therapy Tent, she had found her own mother in the kitchen, scrubbing her hands obsessively with a cake of Limberleg's household soap. By the time Natalie knocked on the front door, Mrs. Porter still hadn't stopped washing.

"But I don't understand what we're trying to find out,"

Miranda said as they paused beside a placard on an easel.

Natalie examined the schedule of events and gave a little shudder. "Look. Amber Therapy demonstration, seven till eight." She frowned up at the stage where Alpheus Nervine was beginning to set up a selection of pieces from the brass and glass chamber: the leather-covered table, the glass-fronted case with all the light bulbs, the crank-handled box that had helped to power the whole thing, which sat on a small wrought-iron table. "It must be nearly six-thirty. We can do a lot of searching in an hour and a half."

"But what are we looking for?"

Well, that was the question, wasn't it? "The reason Mr. Coffrett is upset with my father. Some idea of what my mother's supposed to do that she might not be well enough for. Anything that tells us what those Paragons and Limberleg are really up to." She bit her lip and watched Nervine attach some wires to the bookcase full of light bulbs and switches. "Let's start at the back."

Miranda led the way; Natalie had been too upset to pay attention to the route Nervine used to take them there earlier that day. Too quickly, it loomed in their path, throwing immense shadows across the surrounding booths: the Amber Therapy Tent. Natalie and Miranda slipped inside.

Natalie barely remembered the room they now stood in, a sort of antechamber they must have passed through on their way to the main part of the tent where the Amber Therapy machine was. One side was given over to a collection of electric apparatuses, assorted batteries and cables connected to weirdly shaped light bulbs, and all kinds of things—from boxes to an old round tub—sprouting wires and electrodes. The other side of the tent had a consultation desk flanked by placards on easels announcing THE FAME AND CREDENTIALS OF THE CHEVALIER ALPHEUS NERVINE and GRAND CORRESPONDENCES: THE INFLUENCE OF THE CHEVALIER ON THE MEDICINE OF THE MODERN ERA.

"I'll look through all this stuff on the placards," Miranda said. "You know more about mechanical things, so you take that junk over there, okay?"

Natalie picked up a heavy muslin belt connected to a pair of electrodes, then dropped it unceremoniously as an image of her mother strapped into the chamber in the tent beyond flickered through her mind. "I don't know anything about electricity, though. Can I help with the placards, too?"

If Miranda heard the desperate note in her voice, she didn't say anything about it.

What were they possibly going to find in here? Alpheus Nervine's "credentials" looked like the certificates they gave out when you graduated from one grade to the next in school. His "grand correspondences" were a bunch of letters and envelopes from faraway places, mostly illegible thanks to the supremely messy cursive writing most adults seemed to favor. About the only words you could really read were the names on the envelopes: Pulvermacher, Addison, Abrams, Sanche, Bellinspire . . .

Now, that was interesting.

The envelopes glued alongside the letters on the placard were all from different people and were addressed to Monsieur le Chevalier Alpheus Nervine at various addresses that ended with "Paris, France." All except one, stuck near the bottom, which was addressed to a Dr. Jasper E. Bellinspire, Oxford, England. It had been sent from somewhere in Connecticut. Natalie squinted at the signature. *Your loving mother*, it said.

Very interesting. Apart from the trouble she had believing anyone would write anything loving to Alpheus Nervine, this letter was clearly addressed to someone else. So why on earth was it here?

"Miranda. Look at this."

Over her shoulder, Miranda scanned the letter. "Who's Jasper E. Bellinspire?"

The letter itself was uninterestingly comprised of updates from someone's home, sentences like *Your sisters miss you and your father sends his love* . . . nothing about modern medical techniques or electricity or anything. If it hadn't been posted up for anyone who walked in to read, Natalie would have felt as if she were looking at a boring page out of somebody's diary.

"Maybe it got stuck up there by mistake," Miranda hazarded.

Natalie frowned. That vague, persistent buzzing started up in her ears and at the back of her tongue; the dizzy feeling that made her want to shake her head returned. *Not again.* She swallowed thickly. "Don't you think somebody'd have noticed? This has to have been glued there for years."

"I guess." Miranda hesitated. "Do you want to take a look in the . . . the other room?"

Natalie looked at the curtained entrance to the main space of the pavilion, where the Amber Therapy Chamber stood. Her hands started to shake, and she clasped them together to hold them still. "I don't . . . I don't want to, Miranda."

The girls jumped as the curtain swung open behind them, but it was only a cluster of older boys exploring the tents, laughing and blustering as they went straight for the big room that held the chamber itself. Natalie swallowed her reluctance and nodded to Miranda—there was nothing like a bunch of loud boys to provide a distraction in case somebody appeared wanting to know what they were up to. With Miranda at her shoulder, Natalie caught the swishing curtain after the last of the bigger kids ducked through.

There was the giant chamber, darkly gleaming. One of Limberleg's seemingly endless staff of identical brown-suited men sat on the nearer bicycle, lecturing the boys on some point of Amber Therapy. Natalie shook her head, drowning for a moment in memories of Mrs. Minks, her skeleton showing through her skin as electricity coursed through her. "I can't."

"It's okay, Natalie. Anyway, we've already been in there . . . once," Miranda whispered. "Might as well check all four of those doctors' tents, right? We can always come back."

Natalie couldn't stop thinking about Jasper Bellinspire's letter as she followed Miranda through the nostrum fair to the Phrenology Pavilion, where another pale man in a brown suit was dozing in his chair among Argonault's collection of labeled and grid-marked heads.

Miranda strolled casually to the curtains at the back of the pavilion and slipped through to the enclosed tent beyond. Natalie wandered through the heads more slowly, reading the dates written on labels on each ceramic neck, glancing at the words in each compartment. Causality, amativeness, temperance . . .

"Natalie." Miranda leaned through the curtain and waved her hand.

If she hadn't already been inside Dr. Limberleg's wagon, Natalie would have had to swallow a screech. She decided she needed to start giving Miranda, who hadn't made a peep, more credit.

The Phrenology Pavilion was lined with floor-to-ceiling shelves crammed full of grinning human skulls. Natalie examined the closest shelf: *Specimen 46-a, a classic example of the character of a serial murderer*, read the label beneath the first skull in the line. Little numbered red pegs glued to the dome of the skull corresponded to a short list of dangerous characteristics printed on the label below.

"Over here," Miranda hissed. She stood beside a table piled with charts. "Look at this."

The chart she held out was old and heavily creased, as if it had once been folded quite small. At first glance it looked like a particularly misshapen skull drawn in faded colors. Then Natalie saw lighter lines in the background, so faded they were almost undetectable. There was something familiar about the shape they formed, so faint she could barely make it out.

The curious vertigo punched into the back of her head,

and Natalie knew from the sudden grasp of Miranda's hand on her arm that she had nearly fallen over.

"You okay?"

"Fine."

Miranda eyed her cautiously for a moment, then turned back to the chart and traced with one finger the lines Natalie had thought were so familiar. "See? It's not a phrenology drawing at all. It's a *map*."

And not just any map; it was definitely the United States. If there had ever been any road names or places written in, they had long faded away; only the heavier lines that looked as though they'd been drawn on later with ink were clear.

"What do you think?" Miranda tapped one of the ink lines. "Is this a travel route?"

"Could be." It was hard to tell exactly, but one of the lines passed through the place where Natalie thought Arcane ought to be. On the whole, though, the map looked like a memento rather than anything anyone would use.

"Maybe it isn't important, but it was kind of like that letter you found. It just—"

"Didn't belong," Natalie finished, giving the map one last searching look. "So, we have a letter and a map."

Natalie tucked the map back into the stack of charts, and they crept out of the tent. The shadows had lengthened and grown darker. But in the sky over the front of the nostrum fair, strange lights flickered: the Amber Therapy presentation was under way.

"Do you think anyone volunteered, like they did at

the Phrenology one?" Natalie asked as they stopped at the Magnetism Tent. It was a horrible thought to consider.

Through the antechamber and into the tent . . . another strange medicine, another strange apparatus. Natalie stopped just inside the curtain and threw her hands into the air, staring helplessly at a giant oval steel tub surrounded by threadbare chairs. The tub held about a dozen or so corked bottles arranged under a foot or so of water, and a quantity of iron rods that rose upright out of the water at regular intervals. "I don't even know what—I mean, what on earth is that?"

A closer look didn't help; on examination it still looked like a tub, a bunch of bottles, and a few metal sticks. "I give up," Miranda mumbled, glancing around the tent. "There's nothing else *in* here."

But there was one other thing. In a corner, another collection of rods stood in an elaborate umbrella stand. Most of them were narrow, pale metal wands like the one Vorticelt carried for a walking stick. One was not.

Feeling the beginnings of the vertigo starting again, Natalie reached for the odd one out, a very old cane made of light wood with a slight crook at the top.

"This is it," she whispered. Then she crumpled.

The thunk of her head hitting the ground brought her back to consciousness at the same moment that Miranda reached her side. "Are you okay?" She let Miranda help her to her feet and looked woozily at the cane in her hand. The unsteady, giddy rush in her head was coalescing, forming flashes like the ones you got from looking too long at the sun. Almost pictures, just like before.

"We should get out of here," Miranda said worriedly. Natalie shook her head to clear it, then nodded in agreement. The motion sent the flashes skittering across the back of her eyes. The sensation of *almost there* was overwhelming, but she put the cane back and let Miranda lead her from the tent.

Folding screens partitioned off four little spaces inside Sir Willoughby Acquetus's Hydrotherapy Tent. Natalie and Miranda wandered through each one, looking for the thing that was out of place, but the rooms were pretty much all the same: each had a big bathing tub, a chair, and a little table equipped with a pile of what looked like ordinary bedsheets folded up next to a water jug and a basin with a sponge.

"Anything?" Miranda asked as they wandered back to the front part of the tent, where Acquetus had his desk and chair. Natalie shook her head.

She stopped and looked hard at the desk. Nothing strange on top, just some notepads, a pen, a little lamp. Nothing odd about the doctor's bag by the chair—it was an ordinary, pebbly old Gladstone bag just like Doc Fitzwater's . . .

And there it was, the pricking behind her eyes, the sudden dizzy swoosh that made her grab for the edge of the desk so she wouldn't fall into it. Dimly, she heard Miranda hiss her name, felt Miranda grab for her waist to hold her upright.

Natalie opened her eyes and looked at the leather bag at her feet. Embossed in gold near the clasp were the letters J. E. B. None of the Paragons had those initials.

Jasper E. Bellinspire.

"Come on," Miranda insisted. "We have to go. I'll take you to Mr. Finch; he'll know what's wrong."

Who was this Bellinspire person? The dizziness faded, but the flashes were now so close to real pictures that meant something. . . . Natalie shook off Miranda's hands and pressed her fists into her eyes. A letter, a map, a cane, a bag . . .

"I'm almost there . . . I can almost . . ."

"No, no, we have to leave. You're sick! Something's wrong!"

Natalie shook her head again, harder. "There's still something to find." She opened her eyes and forced them to focus on her friend. "What time is it?"

"I don't have a watch! Don't you see? Something's happening to you. *We have to leave!*"

Natalie stumbled out of the tent with Miranda following a step behind, pleading under her breath and looking frantically around—maybe for an adult to try to talk sense into Natalie. But it seemed everyone, customers and hucksters alike, was still attending the Amber Therapy presentation.

"We have one more place to look," Natalie insisted. They turned a corner into a familiar, dead-end alley. "There."

The inside of Dr. Limberleg's wagon was no less unsettling the second time around, and the sensation of vertigo was already starting. Somewhere in Limberleg's uncanny collection, a clue was hiding . . . maybe the *last* clue to the dizzy puzzle that was sending off sparks behind her eyes. Leaving Miranda staring, disconcerted, at a particularly withered hand under a glass dome, Natalie looked around the crowded wagon for a hint.

She glanced over the grisly examination chair and, behind it, the big clockwork tableau with the replica of Limberleg and the four miniature Paragons under their pots. The first flowerpot was canted back just enough for her to see the tiny Nervine doll back in its place, cymbals spread wide. Just beyond that was the door she hadn't tried last time.

Suddenly her skull was abuzz, and she could feel her insides spinning harder than ever. Willing herself not to pass out again, forcing herself to stay upright, Natalie crossed the wagon and opened the door.

The tiny room had one window at the end, covered with stiff curtains. Natalie waited for her eyes to adjust to the darkness in between the strange flashes in her head that were coming faster and faster now. A camp bed sat in one corner, made up with a thin pillow and a threadbare blanket. A lantern hung on a hook over a table next to the bed. Something small and rectangular sat on the table. A little book, maybe.

There was nothing else in the room.

Natalie frowned and peered under the table, under the bed, but nothing crouched in wait in any of the dark corners. With all the grim things in the outer room, why did this one look like a prison cell?

"Anything?" Miranda whispered from the next room. Natalie shook her head, swallowed queasily, and reached for the thing on the table. Before she could touch it, though, Miranda sprinted past her through the door and slammed it shut.

In the next room, a pair of miniature cymbals came together with a tinny *ping!*

Not again.

Miranda shoved the curtain over the window aside and peered out. "Someone's coming," she hissed. "We have to hide!"

"No, no. . . ." Natalie shook her head frantically. "He'll find us. He found me before. Can we get out the window?"

"There's no time to leave, he'll see us!" Miranda glanced around the room, looking for a hiding place.

"He'll know," Natalie whispered. "The automata will—" A sound in the next room made her bite down on her tongue. The outer door was opening. While Miranda examined the lock on the window, Natalie pressed her eye to the keyhole of the inner door and peered into the main room.

The figure creeping in wasn't Limberleg. The coat was longer, heavier. And the man wasn't wearing Limberleg's tall, old-fashioned hat, but a battered felt one. The real give-away, though, was the soft rattling sound that Natalie heard just a moment before she saw the old punched-tin lantern the man carried on a pole over his shoulder.

"It's that fellow," she whispered. "That one with the lantern. What's he doing here?"

Through the keyhole, Natalie watched as the green-eyed drifter strolled around the wagon, examining Dr. Limberleg's freakish collections. He squatted beside the setup with the miniature Paragons under their pots as the cymbal player continued its hollow clashing.

How long until his curiosity made him open the inner door?

Tap, tap, tap. The next pot must've tilted back.

Behind her, Miranda fumbled with the latch. "Almost got it."

The thin tooting of a flute joined the cymbal and the drums. The drifter sat back and chuckled as next the cello began to whine. Then, as the rest of the room burst into cacophony, he rose, set his lantern aside, and settled himself in Limberleg's examination chair, as calmly as if he were waiting in someone's parlor for coffee after dinner.

"Miranda," Natalie whispered, "get down. I think someone else is coming!"

In the other room the noise of the automata died suddenly as the door opened and Jake Limberleg stepped into the wagon. "Hmm," he said softly, as if it didn't surprise him at all to find a stranger waiting for him.

"You don't know who I am," the drifter said.

Limberleg raised an eyebrow. "I believe you introduced yourself as Jack."

"You know my name," the drifter replied, crossing his feet comfortably, "but do you know who you're talking to?"

"I do, actually." Limberleg cast an offhand look at the lantern where it leaned against the wall, glowing faintly. "Yes, of course I know who you are. It wasn't that complex a puzzle."

Eye to the keyhole, Natalie felt the dizzy oddness for just a moment. The lantern? How could that be significant?

"Then you know why I'm here," the drifter said.

The doctor lowered himself into an armchair. "Actually, *Jack*, I haven't got a clue. Except that you seem to enjoy poking your way into business you have no part of."

Jack grinned widely. "I came to make you an offer."

"I cannot imagine," Limberleg retorted, "what you think you could possibly have to offer me."

"Well, I can see how a distinguished fellow like yourself might think he had everything." Even Natalie could hear the sarcasm in the drifter's words, but Limberleg ignored it. He adjusted his blue-lensed spectacles expressionlessly. "For a start," the drifter continued, "how 'bout an end to the wandering?"

"Actually, as far as I can see, that's the *only* thing you've got to offer," Limberleg said, "and from the look of that"— he jerked his chin at the lantern—"I'd say you haven't even got that chip to bargain with. At least not yet."

"Matter of time. Only waiting till I find just the right place, that's all."

"There's nothing in it for me." Limberleg leaned back, fingers templed under his chin. "Absolutely nothing."

In the room behind her, a soft scrape told Natalie that Miranda had the window latch unfastened. She flinched. In the next room the two men stared silently at each other. Neither appeared to have heard the noise.

When the drifter called Jack spoke again, his voice was cold and quiet. "There's no other way out for you."

"Out?" Limberleg repeated. "There'd be a tremendously simple way out, actually, if I wanted it. When it's time, I have plenty of choices."

Natalie frowned. What on earth were they talking about?

"Plenty of choices you'll never make," the drifter scoffed. "You have too much conscience."

Sitting regally in his chair, Limberleg stiffened.

"Let me guess. You can control this lot"—Jack waved a hand around the room—"the fair, your medicines, maybe the Paragons—but just barely, only because they're bound to you. Now, if it was me, the thing I'd be worried about— if I had ever been a man of conscience, which I seem to recall you were, once upon a time—is this: what happens to them when . . . if . . . something happens to you? Will they keep going?"

The drifter kept on smiling, but his grin took on an unpleasant quality. Limberleg sat as still as one of his sculpted hands, his fingers clutching the arms of his chair.

"And, since I think we both know the answer to that," Jack continued, "what kind of damage will they do when there's nothing keeping them in line? Nothing, no one, holding them back?"

He nodded toward the door Natalie crouched behind. She tensed, ready to spring for Miranda and the window, but Jack wasn't looking at her, and as far as Natalie could remember, there was only one other thing he could be looking at by the door: the set of miniature clockwork Paragons under their tilted-back pots.

Across the room, Limberleg sat as if turned to stone. "Won't be my concern."

"You'll never take the easy way out, Limberleg." The drifter jiggled his foot, as if the conversation was beginning to annoy him. "You know it. But I can give you a haven. If there's no more wandering through towns full of innocent people, think how much less you'll have to worry about."

"What makes you think you have any way of countering the Devil's claim?" Limberleg said after a long moment.

"Simple matter of defection. The rules of the road allow for that," Jack replied breezily. "Only, when those rules were written, there were just two sides to choose from, and defecting to Saint Peter's side ain't some simple matter any old conjurer can manage; comes with too many strings attached for Beelzebub to have to worry about losing anybody thataway." He shrugged and pointed at the lantern. "But there's three choices now. That coal says I'm a force of my own, and I don't require a lily-white soul from my compadres, just a willing spirit. I invite you, Jake Limberleg, to come join me under my banner."

"If all I wanted was another kind of hell, I have my own direct line." Limberleg rose stiffly and opened the door. "I have a demonstration to finish. Good evening."

The drifter sat for a moment, considering Limberleg from the examination chair. "All right, then." He got to his feet, collected his lantern and carpetbag, and strolled to the door. Limberleg watched him from the doorway for a moment, then disappeared down the steps himself.

The door slammed shut, and Natalie and Miranda were alone in the wagon again.

Natalie sat back from the keyhole. "Huh." Then, "They're gone."

"Did you find anything?" Miranda asked. "Before that man came in?"

"No," Natalie muttered. She reached for the rectangle on the bedside table. It was the only thing she hadn't had a chance to look at, but it didn't seem like anything special. The second her fingers touched it, however, she felt a jolt like an electrical shock.

It was red, leatherbound, and hinged at one side, with a little brass hook holding the other side shut. She knelt on the floor, just in case she fainted again, and lifted the hook. The two halves fell open in her palm to reveal two picture frames.

"Um, Natalie?" Miranda said. Natalie ignored her.

The images inside were grainy and faded, daguerrotypes older than any pictures Natalie had ever seen. As she tilted the frame into the scant light for a better look at the five faces staring out, a pale little thing the size of her index finger tumbled to the floor. She groped absently for it as she examined the images.

On one side were a man and a woman in old-fashioned styles, probably from all the way back before the War Between the States. They stood arm in arm, unsmiling. On the other side, two girls, maybe six and twelve, sat in wooden armchairs on either side of a baby in a cradle.

There was something about those faces . . . it was odd to see people looking out so stiffly, but Natalie knew that people back then had to stand still a long time for the camera. On the floor, Natalie's roaming fingers connected with a narrow, brittle object. She grabbed the fallen thing and held it up to the shaft of dusty light from the window. It was a bone, the size of a large toothpick with one knobby end. She set it quickly back on the table.

The feeling came on suddenly, piercing the wave of dizziness and settling in its place . . . like something forgotten but just on the tip of the tongue . . . something just out of reach . . .

A letter, a map, a cane, a bag . . . a frame and a bone . . .

Natalie lifted the frame again, positioning it under the window so that the light fell on the faces of the man and woman on the left. There was something important here, something other than the rigid faces composed for the camera—what was it?

"Natalie!" Miranda said, louder.

Tilting the frame for a closer look at the three children, Natalie noticed a detail she had missed before. That feeling of *something* just out of reach hit her even harder, driving away the last of the vertigo and nausea so suddenly, it was as if it had never happened. Natalie lurched to her feet, shoved aside the curtain, and held the frame up into the light.

The children's eyes were closed.

A letter, a map, a bag, a cane . . . a daguerrotype of three children, their eyes closed in a picture you had to hold so still to take . . . a bone . . .

It happened so quickly, so completely. It was like looking at the works of a machine, following one piece to the next, and seeing it all come together. Like the way a chaos of puzzle pieces finally reveal a picture that makes sense.

As if recalling a memory of her own, she knew who Jasper E. Bellinspire was. And she knew the children's eyes were closed because they were dead when the picture was taken.

Natalie sat down hard against the wall, clutching the frame in her shaking fingers as she ignored Miranda's insistent voice.

The sensation was like standing at the place where waking becomes sleep. She closed her eyes, and the tale unfolded, dreamlike but as familiar as any bedtime story, as if she were remembering rather than piecing it together from the clues in the room. She knew with complete and utter conviction— although she had no idea how she knew, except for the clues like street signs pointing the way—that it was true.

In the next room, a pair of tiny cymbals came together with a metallic *ping!*

He had been a young doctor, just finished with his studies at Oxford. But when he came back, there was no place for him in the small New England town where his family lived, so he bought a horse and a wagon, kissed his mother goodbye, shook hands with his father, hugged his little sisters. He drove through the country, setting bones and delivering babies, treating people outside cities and towns with no doctor of their own.

The lines on the map crawled like dead branches, crossing and re-crossing one another to form that gridlike route. Natalie leaned her head against the wall of the wagon as an image of the young Dr. Bellinspire strode through her mind, favoring one knee and leaning heavily on the cane that now stood among the wands in Vorticelt's tent. She saw him as clearly as she'd seen Simon Coffrett walk into the Old Village.

Ping.

The Dr. Bellinspire in her vision stopped his wagon at a farm. As he limped toward the door, another man left the farmhouse with an old-fashioned box camera on a wooden tripod slung over one shoulder. The photographer tipped his hat and climbed into his own wagon.

Inside the house, people were crying. The doctor was too late. Illness had taken the family's youngest child. After he had seen the red in her eyes that told him her throat had closed up and choked her to death, Dr. Bellinspire noticed the girl wore her finest little frock. They had dressed her for the photographer, even though she had been dead for a whole day, because it would be the only picture of the child they would ever have.

That had been the beginning.

In the months that followed, Dr. Bellinspire chased the illness around the countryside in his one-horse wagon. It moved from farm to farm, town to one-horse town ahead of him, as if the sickness itself knew it was being hunted. It took children without mercy, choking them with invisible fingers. Bellinspire drove his horse until froth flecked its hide and its eyes were almost as red as the dead children's eyes, but still he could not catch up.

In every household he found children dressed in their finest clothes. In every home he found photographs. The photographer was chasing the illness, too.

Ping!

Natalie ignored Miranda's tugging fingers and looked at the hinged frame still clasped in her hands. Parents on one side, trying to hold the tears back until the image was fixed; children on the other, eyes closed as if they had fallen peacefully asleep in their best Sunday duds.

After a while, the young doctor began to think that if he could only catch up to the photographer, he would catch up to the illness. In one home, while staring numbly at a picture in which the only surviving child sat, haunted, beside his dead twin and holding his dead infant sister, it occurred to the exhausted Dr. Bellinspire that if he could *stop* the photographer, he might be able to stop the illness as well.

Autumn became winter. Bellinspire traced more inked roads on his map, limped into house after house to find death and its likeness waiting in the parlor. Twice he thought he saw the photographer's wagon on the long road ahead. On one occasion Bellinspire thought he saw the man carrying his boxy camera out of a house. He leaped down from the wagon and threw the stranger against the wall, but it was only a man with a crate of apples on his shoulder.

There were whispers from the old women that the sickness was the Devil's work for sure, and that it would take the Devil's work to put a stop to it. In one house, the doctor staggered into the kitchen, unable to take the silence and sadness that filled the spaces between the sounds of coffee cups on saucers in the parlor. "What do I do?" he whispered.

The cook looked up from the kettle on the stove. She took a battered tin off a high, dark shelf and came to sit beside him at the table. "I've been saving this, Doctor," she said, and opened the tin. Inside was a single white bone. "It's yours if you want it."

The doctor stared, uncomprehending, at the thing in the tin. "What is it?"

"It came from a black cat. It's the bone that floated upriver, and it's what you use to call the Devil. Take it to the crossroads and bury it."

Dr. Bellinspire didn't believe in the Devil, but when he undressed for bed in the wagon that night, he found the bone in his waistcoat pocket. He couldn't remember putting it there.

Ping!

Natalie opened her eyes and discovered that her own fingers were absently turning the bone as she imagined it in Bellinspire's hands. She closed her eyes, and the vision washed over her again.

At last, in December, the twin trails of the photographer and the choking illness went as cold as the bleak skies overhead. For two weeks, the young doctor treated living children and adults who still remembered how to smile. Christmas was coming.

Bellinspire drove home to Connecticut. In the back of his wagon was a brand-new velocipede, a boneshaker even older than Natalie's grandfather's, bought in Philadelphia for one of his sisters.

The young doctor was out of the wagon almost before

it had rolled to a stop. "I'm home," he called, stepping into the foyer and unwinding his scarf. Then his eyes fell on the sideboard in the hall.

Bellinspire didn't hear himself scream, nor did he hear the footsteps pounding down the stairs toward him, nor the voices that shouted his name. He didn't feel his father pick him up from where he had fallen, or his mother wrap her arms around him tight, so tight . . . as if by force she could hold on to him, her only remaining child.

On the sideboard, surrounded by cut flowers like a relic in a shrine, was a hinged frame bound in red morocco leather. On one side, his mother and father, faces drawn tight. On the other side, his three sisters, the two eldest seated on either side of the baby in her cradle. Something wet trickled down Natalie's cheeks.

All three girls' eyes were closed.

The rest of it seemed inevitable: Jasper Bellinspire finding his way to a crossroads somewhere, burying the bone from the battered old tin, and waiting in the freezing midwinter night, arms wrapped around his stiffening legs, for someone to come. The sound of hooves on the ice-cold road. The creak of a wooden wagon as it rolled to a stop. Bellinspire looked up.

It was the photographer.

Ping, ping, ping, ping, ping, ping . . .

"Natalie, *come on!*"

"You," Bellinspire snarled. He threw himself at the other man, dragged him to the ground, and began to beat his head against the frostbitten earth. He screamed horrible things, accused the photographer of bringing the sickness onto his sisters. He put his hands around the photographer's neck and squeezed, the way the sickness had squeezed the throats of the dead children.

No, no, no . . . Natalie shook her head, eyes closed tight. Miranda was pulling her by one arm now, but she barely felt it. She tried to make the vision stop, but the imagined Dr. Bellinspire's hands only tightened around the photographer's throat.

Don't think about it. Get out of this room, out of this wagon, don't think about it, go home! Natalie tried to stand up, tried to focus on Miranda's terrified face, tried to listen to what she was saying. *Think about bicycles. Think about something,* anything *else.* She slipped back to her knees, hands over her eyes. Miranda wailed. In the next room, the sounds of a miniature drum joined the tiny clashing cymbals.

After a while, the photographer stopped fighting back. Bellinspire's screams died in his throat. He staggered upright and looked down, sick horror rising in his throat—and in Natalie's, too.

The photographer lay dead at Dr. Bellinspire's feet.

Suddenly, a dark shadow flung itself onto the ground before him: Bellinspire's own shadow, cast as a blaze of blue flame spiraled into the air at his back. A voice spoke, low and grim. "This is how you attempt to save lives?"

Hot red shame rising on his face and in his heart, Bellinspire turned toward the voice. The shame turned to icy fear. The man standing silhouetted in the flames looked exactly like the man the doctor had just murdered.

Bellinspire spun to look at the place where the photographer's body had been only seconds before. It was gone, with no traces of a struggle in the frost to mark what had happened. He turned back to the man before the fire. "Who are you?"

Short, high bursts from a little flute only dimly registered in Natalie's consciousness.

The man with the photographer's face curled his lips into a grin. "I'm the one who can give you the means to make the difference you really want to make." His mouth formed a dreadful smile. "I'm the one you called."

"Did I—is the photographer dead?"

The horrible smile flickered in the freezing light. "You murdered a phantom. An illusion, nothing more. But that doesn't make the murder you committed any less real to me."

The miniature Argonault's cello began to wail. A cold, cold sadness crawled up Natalie's insides as the two men made their terrible bargain to the awful music of the four automata. A shaking Miranda grabbed Natalie by the straps of her overalls, but she didn't feel it.

It took so much effort to try to block out Bellinspire's misery, to try not to feel his terror and sorrow—but it was too strong. It was sick-making, violent . . . and then the deal was done, and the doctor held out his hands.

Natalie scrambled to her feet and felt blindly for the doorway, still unaware that Miranda was trying to drag her from the room, too. *I don't want to see this, I know what's coming. . . .*

But the man at the fire merely held out a pair of gloves

the color of the frostbitten earth. Bellinspire pulled them on and flexed his fingers.

A cacophony of sound vaulted Natalie abruptly out of the trance to find herself being hauled through the wagon. The entire army of automata had burst into frenzied alarm again.

"*Move!*" Miranda screamed.

They plunged through the door, then half-ran, half-tumbled down the stairs to the ground. Miranda yanked Natalie sideways and shoved her into a tiny passage between the wagon and the tent beside it only moments before Thaddeus Argonault sprinted past.

Natalie tried to pay attention as they zigzagged through the meandering crowds of people now fanning out from the Amber Therapy demonstration. Miranda was shouting something at her again, but even as they ran, the real world around her faded once more into that frozen crossroads of so long ago.

From thin air, the devil with the photographer's face conjured a crate the size of a doghouse. Whatever was inside, Natalie couldn't see it, not even as the story shifted forward and Bellinspire, alone on another road in bleak daylight, pried it open with a crowbar.

"*Move your feet, Natalie!*"

The story flashed forward again and the doctor sat in his wagon, the leg that made him limp propped up on the edge of the open crate. Whatever had been inside it was gone, and now the doctor's gloved hands clasped a tiny vial of ordinary-looking liquid. Bellinspire lifted the vial to his mouth and drank.

He swung his leg down and, using both hands, forced it to bend at the knee. Then he bent it again, back and forth, back and forth, without using his hands. It bent as normally and naturally as Natalie's own undamaged knees did. Bellinspire leaped to his feet, and Natalie felt fear turn to joy as something loosened in the young doctor's chest. He strode to the wagon's door, stronger than he had ever felt in his life. Whatever had been in the vial, whatever had been in the crate that he had used to make it, worked.

"Here. Sit."

Natalie dropped to the ground hard, her shoulders banging against a wall with a thud.

The last things she saw before the story-memory faded away completely were the four men standing in the sunlight when Bellinspire opened the wagon's door.

"Well?" said Paracelsus Vorticelt.

Bellinspire smiled his first genuine smile in a year and tossed the cane he no longer needed to Vorticelt. "You're right. I shan't require this any longer." He trotted easily down the stairs. "Very well, fellows. I'm ready to do something good at last."

All that joy—Natalie could feel it bursting the seams of Bellinspire's heart as he began making silent plans to heal the world, practically dancing as he walked around to the front of the wagon on his wonderfully agile knee.

She could also see what Jasper Bellinspire could not: the little smile that curled the mouth of the man with the spiky gray hair, a smile that would take the cheer off a bluebird. There was something going on that the four men knew about and the doctor did not.

"Well, let's get a move on, limber leg," said Alpheus Nervine.

Then everything went black.

"We warned you she was there the first time. You could've dealt with her then. Why did you let her stay?"

On the other side of the heavy curtain, people were still applauding the Amber Therapy demonstration. Faced with Paracelsus Vorticelt, Willoughby Acquetus, and the just-returned Thaddeus Argonault standing in various poses of anger inside the tent that made up the backstage area, Dr. Limberleg halted so abruptly that the curtain swished closed on his coattails, only to have Alpheus Nervine shove past him a bit more roughly than was probably necessary on his way off the stage.

He opened his mouth to reply just as the One-Man Band, standing in a corner of the tent, burst into a violent fanfare.

Limberleg turned to shoot the Band a scathing look. Behind the metal mouthpieces that hung in its face, the One-Man Band gave him an innocent smile.

"There was no alternative," Limberleg said when the cacophony ended. He shouldered between Acquetus and Vorticelt to a little table where a pitcher stood with a few tin cups, and poured himself some water. "She would have made a scene."

"Well, that's easy. Should have killed her."

Limberleg turned to find the leather-clad drifter called Jack silhouetted in the door of the tent. His pale eyes, rimmed by webworks of lines, glowed like a cat's.

"What are *you* doing here?" Limberleg demanded.

"He's right, Jake."

Now Limberleg set his cup down hard on the table and spun to glare at Alpheus Nervine. "*What?*"

"The man's right," Nervine repeated calmly.

Limberleg jabbed a gloved finger at Jack. "Get out of here, you crazy bastard!"

"*I'm* crazy?" Jack chuckled and lit a cigarette. "Damn, they don't make jokes with that kind of funny where I come from."

"Why didn't you just kill her?" Nervine asked, enunciating crisply.

"We'll discuss my decisions once someone gets that raggedy malingerer out of here!" Limberleg took a step toward the drifter, gesturing with the tin cup, so that drops flew out of it like flecks of spit. "I've heard your offer and declined. You have no right to involve yourself in my affairs. *Get out!*"

"What offer?" Paracelsus Vorticelt asked, adjusting his mirrored spectacles.

Jack and Limberleg looked at each other. The drifter gave a twitch of a smile. Limberleg's eyes narrowed behind his blue lenses. "I've declined," Limberleg said again, deadly quiet.

"Seems like this fellow might want to hear about it, though," Jack said casually.

A silence stretched over the tent. It was not a friendly silence.

"It doesn't matter." Limberleg's fingers clutched the handle of the tin cup so hard that it bent, taking the shape of his knuckles. "They are bound to my decision."

The silence, swept aside for a moment, flowed back in to fill the spaces between Jake Limberleg, the Paragons, and the drifter called Jack.

"'Course, you're right," Jack said at last. "As I understand it, they're bound to you—and your decisions—as long as you live."

The drifter took a deep pull on his cigarette and picked up the lantern at his feet. "So long, gentlemen." The canvas swished closed behind him.

Jake Limberleg exhaled a deep breath and poured himself another cup of water. His gloved hand shook.

"Interesting," Paracelsus Vorticelt said.

"Jake," Nervine said, "I would like to know why you didn't just kill the girl."

Limberleg stared at him for a moment, then muttered something that made the spike-haired Paragon put a hand to his ear sarcastically. "*What* was that, Jake?"

"The oath, *Alpheus*," Dr. Limberleg snapped. "I said, because of the oath: 'First, do no harm.'"

Behind Nervine, Vorticelt broke into terrible laughter. "Did he just quote the Hippocratic oath at you, Alpheus?"

"Why yes, my dear Paracelsus, I believe he did."

"I don't like your tone," Limberleg said through clenched teeth.

Vorticelt stopped laughing and stepped past Nervine to face Dr. Limberleg, whipping off his mercury-colored spectacles to bring the full weight of his dreadful, black-eyed glare to bear on the other man. Limberleg flinched.

"Don't you? All right, then. We'll have our wheel by midnight, the grateful mechanic says. What next, *master?* What orders from the doctor, whose will we are bound to ... at least as long as he lives? Something's strange in this town. What's your plan, *Doctor?*"

Limberleg held the Paragon of Magnetism's awful stare for a long, long minute. Behind Vorticelt the others moved restlessly, like prowling animals.

"We have some hours left before the gingerfoot begins to surface," Limberleg said, eyes flicking from one restive Paragon to the next.

In the corner, the One-Man Band stirred, sending up a nerve-racking rustle of noise with every twitch.

"And your instructions?" Vorticelt demanded. The others leaned inward like housecats toward a cornered creature.

Jake Limberleg drew himself up to his full six-and-a-half feet of height and eyed the Paragons, one by one. One by one, they stopped prowling and came to stand before him.

"My *instructions*," Limberleg said at last, "are these: we have some hours left. We have many, many people left to treat." The four Paragons exchanged a series of impossible-to-read glances. Limberleg nodded, as if he had heard an unspoken question. "Sell it all. We'll have our wheel." He smiled grimly. "Burn the lot."

An air of cruel satisfaction settled over the Paragons. It was an old hucksters' phrase, one Limberleg had never spoken before. It was an order to take the town for everything it had. It meant, *Don't concern yourselves with what they think of us afterward*. It meant they could never pass through this place again.

It also meant there would probably be nothing remaining of Arcane when they left.

EIGHTEEN

Burning the Lot

B Y THE TIME NATALIE RECOVERED and felt well enough to tell Miranda what she'd seen, the crickets were out, along with the earliest stars . . . and Natalie was pretty sure bruises were already coming up where she had fallen against the back wall of Ogle's Stable.

"But how do you know all that?" Miranda insisted.

"Keep your voice down," Natalie mumbled. Nobody could sneak up on them in Smith Lane without their knowing it, and Miranda really wasn't talking all that loudly, but Natalie had no answer for the very good question her friend had just asked and needed to buy some time.

"The things we found," she said, finally. It was a lame answer even to her ears. "They obviously didn't belong. That's all it was."

"Okaaay," Miranda said, her voice trailing off in that way that instantly tells you someone doesn't mean what she's saying at *all*. "Natalie, you told me way too many details to get from just that stuff."

No denying that. Natalie sighed. "I don't know." Dully, because Miranda was going to rip her apart for saying it, she admitted, "It just came to me. I saw it. I've seen other things, too." Let Miranda laugh, if she thought having all that stuff flood your brain was funny. After passing out at least three times in less than an hour, remembering almost nothing of their flight from the fair . . . heck, just after what she'd *seen*, Natalie thought she could be forgiven for not having a perfect explanation for it all.

But there was no doubt or scorn on Miranda's face. She was watching Natalie with something closer to curiosity. Fearful curiosity, perhaps, but curiosity nonetheless. "I don't understand," she said quietly, but it was different from any other time Natalie had heard her say those words. Usually, Natalie knew she really meant, *Shut up* or *Knock it off*. But this time she seemed to mean, *Go on*. Impossibly, Miranda believed her.

"Do you think you were reading his mind?"

What a horrible thought. The awful image of Limberleg reaching into his patients' minds without their knowing it was still so fresh—had she done the same thing? Sneaked into someone's memories without his permission? Been inside a damned man's head, unwelcome and unable to get out?

"I don't think so. Because . . ." Because it was a horrible possibility, but that wasn't enough. Natalie thought hard. ". . . because there were things missing—things I couldn't figure out or I couldn't see. But he would have known them. Limberleg, I mean. If I was reading his mind, wouldn't I see everything?"

Miranda nodded as if that made perfect sense and put her chin on her knees. "That must've been really weird."

What was really weird was Miranda Porter, who made a hobby of acting as if she thought Natalie didn't know what she was talking about, accepting at face value all the absurd statements Natalie had just made. There had to be a catch.

"It *was*, really . . . I couldn't . . ." Natalie's eyes began to prickle. Why? Why tears, on top of it all? She swiped a fist across her eyes and tried to hold her voice steady. "I couldn't make it stop." Natalie leaned her head back against the wall, looking straight up and willing her eyes not to overflow.

"I'm sorry," Miranda said simply.

"Thanks."

Miranda smoothed her dress over her knees. "Just keep your weird mind-reading thing out of my head, is all," she said primly.

Natalie snorted out a laugh so unexpected she almost choked on it.

"I mean it," Miranda retorted.

They sat in silence for a while. "Miranda," Natalie said at last. "That drifter, Jack—I feel like I know him from someplace."

"Well, I don't see how you could," Miranda said. "Other than seeing him around town, I mean. But Dr. Limberleg knew who he was, didn't he? The drifter said so."

Natalie nodded but didn't say anything. There was something, something she ought to remember; she was certain of it. Something that had jarred her memory when the drifter had talked about finding just the right place. Something, too, when he'd said what he did about defection. To *defect* was to change sides in a battle, and the drifter had claimed that there used to be two options and now there were three. *That coal says I'm a force of my own*, he'd said. Why did that seem so significant?

After a moment, Miranda got to her feet. "Let's go get a soda. Then I have to go check on my mother, okay?"

Natalie groaned inwardly, realizing she would have to go back to the fair for the Chesterlane before she went home herself. She'd been in such a state when Miranda had dragged her out that neither of them had remembered the red bicycle tucked under the hawthorn. "I'm okay. You should go home."

"Well, I will, but I want a soda first, if that's okay with you," Miranda said in the snotty tone Natalie was used to hearing. It was strangely comforting.

They trooped back out to Bard Street and up the stairs of the general store. It was late, but the lights were on and the front door was still open, so the girls trooped inside to find Mr. Tilden and Mr. Finch standing at the back of the store near the Central Exchange. They turned to look at Natalie so sharply that she stopped in her tracks. A thin sheet of paper shook in the grocer's hand.

"Hey, did my dad get the telegraph working?" Natalie asked.

Neither of the two men answered. Instead, Mrs. Tilden, whom Natalie hadn't even noticed, rose from the desk where she ran Central. She came forward and put her hands on Natalie's shoulders. When she spoke, her voice was soft, serious, terrifying.

"Natalie, is it true what Mr. Finch says? That this Limberleg fellow . . . treated your mother?"

Like a punch to the stomach, Simon Coffrett's words came back to her: *I expected more of him . . . your father . . .*

"Is it true?" Mrs. Tilden asked again.

Natalie felt sick. She wanted to lie. She wanted it so badly she actually tried. She looked Mrs. Tilden in the face, tried to look truthful and confident. "No."

It didn't work. "Oh, Natalie," Mrs. Tilden said, her face falling into something worse than sadness. "Oh, Natalie."

That was it, absolutely the last straw. Natalie pulled out of Mrs. Tilden's hands and stamped her foot in a fury, making the old floorboards shake. Behind the counter along the left-hand wall, the patent medicine sign fell and shattered.

"What is it?" Natalie tried to keep her voice even, but every bit of her was trembling. "Someone has to tell me. *Someone has to tell me what's going on!*" Her voice rose into something unnatural, not quite a scream. "I know it's bad that—that they—and I tried to figure it out on my own— we went back there—we looked—we found things—something happened to me!"

Now she was crying freely. Miranda came to put an arm over Natalie's shoulder, and Mrs. Tilden silently bent to put her arms around her, too. The grocer and the pharmacist looked each other, then at Natalie, both of them stunned and uncomfortable. "If you don't tell me what's happening to me . . . and to my mother, I'll . . . I'll . . ." But there was nothing she could really do, so Natalie just stood red-faced and stiff in Mrs. Tilden's arms and waited for the sobs to subside.

"I'll check on Annie," the grocer's wife said after a moment. She gave Natalie a last squeeze and swept out the door.

"I wish I could explain everything," Mr. Tilden said after a moment. "I really do."

Natalie nodded, gulping air. "But you can't. I know." She looked at the glass shards from the smashed sign on the floor and sighed. "I'll get that, I guess."

As she started picking up the glass behind the counter, the grocer and the pharmacist turned to speak with each other in quiet voices. "We've got to tell everyone," Mr. Finch said.

"Mr. Tilden?" Miranda said.

"The fair's closed," Mr. Tilden muttered. "The damage is done. How are we going to get them to believe a word we say?"

"Mr. Tilden!" This time Miranda's voice had an unmistakable edge of panic to it. Behind the counter, the sign's broken frame in her hands, Natalie stiffened.

"It doesn't matter. People have bottles of that stuff in their homes now. We have to move fast," Mr. Finch snapped.

"*Mr. Tilden!*"

The bell over the door jingled. Mr. Tilden inhaled sharply and stepped around the counter fast. He shoved Natalie roughly underneath it and dropped the paper he'd been holding in her lap.

"Yes, sir, can I help you?"

"One of my colleagues is expecting a wire." The voice was Alpheus Nervine's.

"No wires, sir, just as I told you," Mr. Tilden said. "Still broken. Nothing yesterday, nothing today." He nudged Natalie with his foot once, then again.

"That's odd. I thought for sure you gents would have it up and running by now."

"Nope." This time Mr. Tilden nudged her hard. She tucked the paper in her mouth and began crawling beneath the counter toward the back of the store. What was going on?

"You're positive? It's a very important wire. Would've been from . . . what's that town just down the road? *Pinnacle.* Maybe you mistook our wire for someone else's. Let me have a look at your book."

Natalie scooted along the length of the counter to the far end near the Central Exchange and ducked around back into the aisle just as Nervine stepped behind the counter to examine Mr. Tilden's ledger. Farther down the aisle, near the soda fountain, Mr. Finch put a hand behind his back and beckoned.

Natalie pressed up against the counter and crawled on all fours toward Mr. Finch and the petrified Miranda. If

Nervine came back around, he would spot her, if not trip over her. If anyone came up the porch stairs to the front door, they'd see her plain as day, crawling down the center aisle like an idiot, and probably loudly inquire as to why.

And, incidentally, she thought wildly as she listened to Nervine flipping pages in the ledger, why *was* she crawling down the center aisle of the general store with what seemed to be a secret message of some sort in her mouth? For sure she didn't want to see Nervine ever again, but surely she didn't have to hide from him here in the general store.

"Well," announced Mr. Finch, "guess I'll be going. Come by the pharmacy later for coffee, Ed." Nervine, bent over the ledger, ignored him. The pharmacist strolled down the aisle until he caught up with Natalie. "Miss Porter, let's go have a look at that splinter now." He shoved open the door for Natalie and Miranda to duck outside.

"Tear that wire up," he whispered. "Don't let any of them see it. I'm going to make sure Mr. Tilden's all right."

Natalie shoved the paper into her pocket and dashed down the stairs with Miranda at her heels. By unspoken agreement they sprinted until they reached Miranda's house on Sanctuary Street. Natalie dropped onto the bottom step, head in her hands.

Minutes passed. Too exhausted to cry anymore, unable to think, she stared miserably at the patch of dirt between her shoes. Miranda stood silently at her side. Then another pair of shoes stepped into view, toe-to-toe with her own.

Old Tom Guyot looked down at her. "Natalie? Y'all right, darlin'?"

She handed over the crumpled telegram. "I think Mr. Tilden is in trouble. Mr. Finch said to tear this up before anyone saw it."

Tom scowled as he read. "It's from Doc Fitzwater. *Pinnacle flu ended but citizens demonstrating new symptoms, beginning with inability to walk. Symptoms may be connected to merchandise sold by itinerants; do not make purchases from itinerant salesman until samples are tested. Doc.*"

"Itinerants?"

"Traveling folk. Limberleg and his lot, no doubt. Looks to me like a lot of folks are in trouble, Natalie," Tom said. "Maybe everyone who took that tonic of theirs."

Miranda sprinted wordlessly up the stairs and through the front door. Inside Natalie could hear faint voices— Miranda pleading, trying to convince her mother to stop scrubbing her hands.

The blood drained out of Natalie's face. "Tom . . . Charlie took that medicine . . . and they did something to Mama, too. . . ."

Tom's face went ashen. *"Your mama?"*

She swallowed. "I saw his hands, Tom. Dad wouldn't listen. Dr. Limberleg told me no one would believe me. What do I do?"

Down the street she saw Argonault, his bald head unmistakable even at a distance, even in the dark, knock on someone's door a few houses down from the Porters'. After a moment, he lifted the box at his feet—shining bottles peeked out the top—and followed the woman inside.

"They're going door to door," Tom whispered. "They'll have the whole town in their bottles by nightfall."

"We've got to tell them! We have to tell them all!" She took a step, ready to start shouting to the entire street, and then remembered the way everyone in town had come to believe in the medicines. The looks of hope on Charlie's and her father's faces as they carried Natalie's mother into the Amber Therapy Tent. Her heart sank.

"They won't believe us, will they?"

Tom looked sadly at her. "Maybe not, if they want to believe Limberleg more." He lowered himself onto the step and closed his eyes for a minute. "You say you saw his hands? Do you know what that means?"

"Demon hands. It means he lost his soul." She looked up sharply. "How did you know?"

"Knew from the minute I saw him," Tom said quietly. "Those old gloves of his."

"Well, if the medicine's what makes people sick, there's got to be a cure," Natalie said desperately, twisting the guitar string at her neck nervously around one finger. "We'll find it. If we can't stop them from taking the medicine, we'll find the antidote."

"Darlin', do you really think what's in those bottles is some kind of *medicine?* This town's been drinking some kind of . . . some kind of demon brew."

"So there's nothing? *Nothing* to stop it?"

"Only one man can tell us, and I guess we better ask him while his . . . *colleagues* are out and about on business." He got shakily to his feet and swung his guitar over his shoulder. "Let's go find us Dr. Limberleg."

NINETEEN

First, Do No Harm

THE VILLAGE OF TENTS was silent. The strings of light bulbs cast long shadows across the lot as Natalie and Old Tom came to stand before the entrance to the deserted nostrum fair.

"I hope I remember how to get to Dr. Limberleg's wagon," Natalie whispered.

A quiet voice answered, but it wasn't Tom's. "I remember how." Natalie turned to find Miranda standing nearby. Her eyes were bloodshot from crying.

"She still won't stop?" Natalie asked quietly.

Miranda shook her head tightly and glanced from Natalie to Tom and back. "I know the way. I'll stand guard again."

"All right, then," Natalie said. They started into the maze, two thirteen-year-old girls and an immeasurably ancient man.

"Where is everybody?" Natalie asked. "The Paragons are in town going door to door, but what about all those folks who work here in the pavilions, the fellow in the Dispensary, the One-Man Band?"

"Dunno," Tom said. "Maybe they turned in early." He didn't sound like he thought that was likely.

True to her word, Miranda navigated the dark alleys between the tents and pavilions. She hesitated only once, when they reached the corridor where the sibyl stood guard in her glass case. As Miranda debated left, right, or center, Natalie fished in her pocket and fed a coin into the box. She turned the crank and leaned close to the brass grille over the trumpet's mouth.

"I know who Limberleg is," Natalie whispered, "but I don't know *what* he is. I don't know how to stand up to him. And you're probably on his side, but he told you to answer my question once, so maybe you'll do it again. What is Jake Limblerleg?"

She whispered a low chuckle into the trumpet. The sibyl inhaled, straightened, looked at Natalie with an unreadable expression. She tapped her wax fingers and selected a card.

Natalie plucked the card from behind the little brass door and held it up into the scant light of the old bulbs. *He is not spirit, for he exists. Nor is he matter, as you understand it.*

Miranda tapped her shoulder. "You ready, Natalie?"

Natalie shoved the card in her pocket. "I guess."

Two more turns and then there they were, somewhere

near the center of the maze of tents, facing the dead end and Limberleg's wagon.

"If I see anything I'll yell," Miranda said, looking nervously back the way they'd come.

"Ready?" Tom asked quietly. Natalie nodded and slipped her hand into his.

The door swung inward before they could touch it. Dr. Jake Limberleg stood on the threshold.

"Well," he said, eyeing the three of them, "come in."

"I can't . . . I'll just . . ." Miranda stammered.

"Don't be silly. You can look out quite as well from inside," Limberleg said carelessly. "Sit there, pull aside the curtain."

Tom took off his battered hat and followed the doctor in as if he'd just received a social invitation. Miranda trailed in after Tom and climbed nervously onto a little stool by the window. She stood on tiptoe and peered around the curtain. Natalie entered last, and glanced at the four automata under the miniature Limberleg's outstretched hands.

"Yes," the doctor said, seating himself in the examination chair, "they will know you've come. I suggest you don't waste your time."

"Why did you invite us in?" Tom asked.

"Because you would've come in anyhow, and because my four will be back, and because Natalie's father is at this very moment replacing my missing wheel. He's a good man, your father," he said to Natalie, a horrible twist to his mouth. "Would've traded his soul to keep your family together."

How dare he! Tom put a hand on Natalie's shoulder to stop her from lunging at him.

Dr. Limberleg smiled thinly. "Mind your task, young lady," he said mildly to Miranda, who had turned to see what the fuss was about.

"How long until the symptoms start?" Tom asked.

"Aahh. Your good doctor must've finally managed a wire from Pinnacle." He interlaced his gloved fingers and rolled his eyes upward. "By midnight, I should think, the gingerfoot will be showing."

"Gingerfoot?"

"Called after the first elixir I patented. Jake Limberleg's Ginger-Angelica Bitters!"

"That's what you sold to Charlie," Natalie hissed.

He laughed, a horrible, humorless laugh. "Yes, of course, *Charlie.* I've given it to hundreds of people, that and dozens of other panaceas. The gingerfoot doesn't come only from the ginger bitters. It doesn't matter what I sell. That's why your mother will get the gingerfoot, too, and everyone else, no matter what their treatment was. Young lady, keep your eyes out that window!"

Miranda glanced at her friend briefly before obeying. Tom squeezed Natalie's hand. She forced herself to stand still.

"It begins as a difficulty with balance, then hardship with walking." He ticked the symptoms off on his gloved fingers. *Those hands* . . . Natalie tried to find someplace else to look. "It becomes an inability to make one leg work separately from the other. Then a violent shaking, as if from deep within the bones. A lack of sensation, an utter deadness, spreads upward from the toes. At the end, people drag themselves on their forearms, and then they lose use of those as well."

Dr. Limberleg leaned back in the chair, tapping his fingers on the armrests. "When the malady has run its course, it leaves the sufferer trapped, suspended in a shell of a body that does not recognize a controlling mind. It might or might not move, but if it does, it does not move on any command the soul inside it gives."

"Then what?" Natalie demanded. "You just leave them there to die wherever they fall?"

"*I* am long gone by then," Limberleg said. "But no, I do not imagine they simply lie there and die. The darker spirits of this world can always find uses for human puppets. I suspect only the stronger ones wind up dead—the ones who fight too much against the things that try to take them over when they have truly lost all control. If they cannot be manipulated, they are likely left to die. And I have run into some poor creatures in sanitariums that I suspect were too strong to give in totally but not quite strong enough to fight the demons off." His face became a mask of distaste. "They go mad with the struggle. They are never the same again."

"And the rest?" Tom asked.

Limberleg shrugged. "The struggles between the dark and the light have gone on since long before my time. The commanders change; the battle does not. I don't know what becomes of the weaker victims of the gingerfoot. But

I know they disappear, and I know the Devil and his like prefer not to kill. They do not waste materiel that might someday prove to be useful."

"Like your hands, you mean," Natalie said coldly.

He smiled that thin smile again, but his fingers stilled.

"Oh, no, Natalie, it's not like that at all." His lips twisted, revealing teeth. "I can do anything I want with these hands, so long as it's wicked." He looked at Tom. "I know what you are, old man. Want to see them?" He leaned forward in the chair, templing his fingers together on his knees. "Want to see what you almost won?"

"No, but I'm real curious about something else." Tom grinned back. "Why don't you tell me what you got out of the deal, Jake?"

For a moment the pearly smile flickered. "What I got." His hands moved back to the arms of the chair and flexed, sending two little hairline cracks along the grain in the wood. "What I *got?*"

The corners of Dr. Limberleg's mouth inched upward toward his ears as his smile transformed bit by bit into something wider, crueler. "I *found* the crossroads. I *offered* my soul, I offered it up on a big silver plate, and I asked for the ability to cure *any disease on earth!*" The last four words came out like projectiles, lifting Jake Limberleg half out of his chair as they burst forth.

"So sit there and judge me for it, but that was my evil, selfish wish," Limberleg spat. "I wanted to be a healer! I thought the knowledge was worth one man's soul. I thought that was a fair trade, a sacrifice worth making. My soul, to save other people's lives!"

Limberleg paused and took a ragged breath. When he spoke again, his voice was even, deadly.

"So he took my hands and gave me new ones that had the capability mine lacked, the capability to make cures out of whatever they touched. He gave me four mechanical demons, the Paragons. All I had to do was start up those bloody miserable little effigies"—he pointed to the automata under the flowerpots—"then give each of the Four a possession of mine to bind them to me, and they would serve me, build my traveling fair, do my 'good work' forever. Perfect perpetual motion machines, all of them. And then, to fill the void I would make by curing every earthly disease I encountered, he cursed me with a malady from Hell! I can heal anything, treat anything, but with every remedy comes a new disease: the gingerfoot, the one thing that cannot be cured."

"But your leg," Natalie protested. "You tested it!"

If it surprised Limberleg to find that Natalie knew that, he didn't show it. "Would've spoiled things if I'd gotten sick from one of my own cures, you see. I might not have gone through with it." His hands twitched and balled into fists on the arms of his chair. "It's possible I wasn't always a monster."

Natalie shook her head, unable to take her eyes from the little cymbal player. The setup, four small figures under flowerpots, Limberleg under a tree . . . one of those unbidden images appeared in her head, and she saw the doctor taking them, one by one, from the crate she'd seen before and dusting away a film of sawdust before arranging them in their little tableau.

Lights flickered behind her eyes, white flashes like fluffs of popping corn in a skillet. She shook her head and forced herself to focus on what was happening now. "Perpetual motion isn't real," she said with effort.

"Machines require force, is that what your *daddy* says, Natalie?" Limberleg snarled. "Did he talk to you about physics? All things come to rest? Well, it happens that there are forces in the world that don't answer to physics, just like there are sicknesses that don't answer to science."

Behind him, the Alpheus Nervine automaton began to move, its arms swinging slowly toward one another. Natalie flinched, but Tom squeezed her hand again.

"I've tried to control them! I've tried to find a way!" Limberleg raised his bone-colored gloves and flexed his fingers angrily. "The gears in my hands, the gears in all those things out in the nostrum fair—oh, there's a force working on them, sure enough, but after all these years it still doesn't answer to me!"

Ping.

Natalie glanced sideways at Tom, then at Miranda, who wasn't even pretending to look out the window anymore.

"*I tried!*" He flung one hand out, gesturing around at the collection of automata in the wagon. "I obtained all these, took them apart and put them together, tried to figure out the clockwork, to find something, anything that would help me control the others. . . ." *Ping.* "And each time I did, each time I rebuilt one of the perfectly normal automata in my collection, when I wound it again the key would fall out but they would keep on moving, just like the Four and Dalliot and Quinn and the rest. All out of my control and under the power of something else!" *Ping!*

Limberleg reached with a shaking hand into his pocket for a cigarette. "I couldn't stop what I'd set in motion, but I tried to set rules. No visiting towns within two hundred miles of each other, for at least a hundred years. I convinced the Four we'd be found out if we weren't careful, but really it was to stop them from tearing up every single village we passed through, every farmhouse, every home. I thought it was possible we'd hurt fewer people."

He fumbled with a match, but it refused to catch on the matchbox. "You don't understand how they are. You don't know what they're capable of." *Ping!* "Young lady, if you are going to be a lookout, for goodness' sake, will you *pay attention to what you are doing!*"

Ping! . . . Ping, ping, ping, ping!

He turned to stare over his shoulder at the little tableau in the corner as the second pot lifted and the drummer shaped like Acquetus began to swing his arms.

"I told you they would come," he said.

Natalie flung herself at him. "How do you stop the gingerfoot?"

"You can't." Limberleg ran a gloved hand through his wild red and gray hair. It parted for his fingers like seaweed waving in a current. Behind him, the third pot tilted back and the little flute player started its reedy piping.

[311]

"You can't," he said again as the fourth pot began to cant backwards, revealing a tiny, bald Argonault. The miserable strings began to wail.

He twisted his mouth into another one of his thin, humorless smiles and looked at Tom. "You should thank me, old man, for putting this town out of its misery. There are worse ways to die. I know what else walks your roads around here, and the gingerfoot is definitely the better way to go."

Tom frowned. "What's that mean, you old liar?" For the first time, he actually sounded unnerved.

"There has to be a way!" Natalie insisted.

"I tell you, there isn't." He raised a hand. "It's been set into motion, and now it will continue on its own, unendingly."

"Perpetual motion," she whispered. Limberleg nodded with a humorless smile.

Tom put a hand on her shoulder. "We got to get out of here, Natalie. They're coming, and *he* ain't gonna tell us anyhow. Ain't a single reason why he would."

Natalie put her shaking hands in her pockets. In the left one, she found the cards the waxwork fortuneteller had given her on the first day of the fair.

All things are either good or bad by comparison, the sibyl had said. Natalie hadn't quite known what to make of that. Compared to Jake Limberleg, obviously lots of people were good, or at least *better*. Maybe Phemonoe had only meant what the doctor had just said to Tom: that there were also lots of worse things out there in the world.

But it could mean something else, too.

Hadn't he told the sibyl to answer Natalie? Hadn't he invited them into his wagon only minutes ago? Hadn't he come up with rules to try to keep the Paragons under control?

Maybe the sibyl had meant for Natalie to understand that nothing and nobody was all bad or all good. Maybe, just maybe, as frightening as Jake Limberleg was, he still had some good in him.

"Yes, he will," Natalie said slowly, raising her eyes to look at the doctor who sat glowering back at her. "I think he will."

But Natalie didn't know if she really believed it, or what to believe at all—if anything could be counted on ever again, or whether her whole world was really as twisted and strange a place as the last three days seemed to make it out to be.

Everything had changed.

Even her brilliant father, her mother who loved to explain things, her brother . . . she couldn't count on any of them, not right now, not at this moment, not facing the man with the demon hands in his wagon full of clockwork.

Even I've changed, she realized. And maybe, just maybe, it was okay that she couldn't count on her family right now.

They'll have to count on me.

The automata burst into motion around them. Tom pressed his hands to his ears as though his head would explode. Miranda cried out but forced herself to keep her eyes on the alley. Jake Limberleg exhaled a slow, tired sigh. Suddenly he looked much older.

Tom tugged at Natalie's arm. "Come on!"

"No." She stood beside the chair and, struggling to ignore the cacophony, she looked Jake Limberleg straight in the eyes.

She forced all the anger to drain from her face, all the fury and fear, and made herself believe she could fill the empty space with confidence, the way Old Tom Guyot had taught her.

It was hard. This wasn't Mrs. Byron, or George Sills, or even strange Mr. Coffrett. This was a man who'd trafficked with the Devil, who'd commanded demons, who'd let evil walk beside him for a very long time. His hands were not his own, and who knew if he had any kind of a soul left at all.

But, when it came down to it, Jake Limberleg still wasn't a demon himself. No matter what kind of man he was, no matter what the sibyl said about matter and spirit, he was still just a man. Long, long ago, he might even have been a good man. He had once wanted to do good things in the world. That had to count a little, at least.

Limberleg's eyes narrowed, and suspicion lanced his features. Natalie wanted to look away, wanted more than anything to flee with Tom and Miranda, to escape these awful, clicking clockwork nightmares . . . to get far, far away from those awful hands. . . .

Hands are skin and bone, mostly. Some are human; some are not. They're still only hands.

Natalie pushed the memory of the demon hands down into the deepest, darkest cabinet of her mind and locked the door. She forced herself to think of the young doctor Bellinspire whose story had come to her in the cell-like room next door, and she slid her small hand into Jake Limberleg's leather-clad palm.

Tension speared through the doctor and fought battles on his face. The sounds of gears and moving limbs vaulted to a fever pitch, but there was silence in the space between the two of them. The silence stretched. And then something happened.

"First," he murmured, *do no harm*." Jake Limberleg smiled. It was a real smile, a gentle smile. There was hope in it.

"There might be a way," he whispered, so quietly Natalie had to lean close to hear. "But you'll only have one chance."

Then, abruptly, his fingers twitched. He jerked his hand away and stared down at it with something awful waking on his face. He leaped to his feet.

For a moment Limberleg had forgotten that the hands weren't his.

"Natalie"—his fingers flew over the buttons at his wrist—"you've got to destroy the Four. They are his instruments—his devices. . . ." His face went red, then drained dead white as he tried to force the hands still, but they flicked the buttons open easily and began peeling back the leather. "If you can find a way to break them, you might break what they've—get out," he snarled, fighting to keep the gloves where they were, with hands that would not obey him. "Get out! Take those with you!" He kicked a foot at the four automata, still wringing awful noises from their tiny instruments, as the seams of the leather fingers began to split.

But Natalie could only stare at the things emerging from the ruined gloves. At the window, Miranda whimpered, but kept her eyes on the path outside.

The gloves fell to the floor. The demon hands reached up for Jake Limberleg's throat.

"Natalie, go!" She barely heard him shouting to her, so mesmerized was she by those horrible fingers of bone and sinew and calcified gear. Then Tom's voice shook her out of her stupor: "Natalie!"

Tom reached for Limberleg's wrists, trying to pull the demon hands away. "Are you crazy, old man?" Limberleg howled, flailing a foot at Tom to keep him back. "Natalie! *Move!*"

She ducked past the struggling Jake Limberleg to sweep the automata up in her arms. "Then what? Jake! *Then what?*"

"Go to—" The first spidery hand closed around his neck, and then the next, the too-long fingers wrapping with horrid ease all the way around his throat. Limberleg flung his body sideways, backwards, anywhere he could, but there was no stopping those uncanny hands as they began to squeeze. He grunted something that might have been an order or a plea.

"*No!*" she screamed.

Then Tom grabbed her around the waist and flung her outside, where she landed next to a trembling Miranda Porter. Tom stumbled down the stairs after them.

"No," Natalie sobbed. "He tried to help us—he tried to—we can't leave him! We have to save him!"

The wagon shook.

"Natalie, we got to save the town," Tom said shortly. "We got to save your mama, honey. We got to do that first. Old Jake wanted us to undo what he did. You saw he wanted us to do that, didn't you? Because you made him see, Natalie. You made him believe he could still do good. Now we got to go. They're coming for us. We got to get out of the fair!"

Fair, not fair . . . Natalie allowed herself to be drawn, sobbing, away from the quaking wagon. It wasn't fair. But Tom was right.

"This way," Miranda said shakily, running toward the end of the alley. Natalie followed blindly. They turned left, right, then left between tents and booths and dark pavilions. . . . Miranda stopped short and turned. She looked confused. "Should've gone right."

They backtracked and went the opposite way. "Are you sure?" Natalie asked. Silly question. How could anyone be sure of anything in this place?

Miranda stopped in her tracks but didn't answer. She looked straight up.

"Did you see that?" she whispered.

"What?" Tom asked.

"It saw us, I'm sure," Miranda said softly. "It knows where we are." Natalie's stomach lurched. She stared up at the thin, dark lines stretched like a web overhead.

Then they heard it: a soft jingle of bells.

"It'll lead the Paragons right to us!" Natalie hissed. "Run!"

"No, wait," Miranda said. "We can cut through here."

Natalie followed her gaze up to the sign over the entrance to the tent that Miranda was ducking into: CABINET OF CURIOSITIES. She took a breath and followed Tom and Miranda into the darkness.

Tom lowered the canvas carefully back into place behind them so it wouldn't give them away. With a little snap, a spark flicked to life between his fingers. The tiny light of the match reflected off a dozen smooth surfaces.

"What is this place?" Miranda whispered.

"Looks like some kind of odd museum," Tom said, glancing into the nearest display case. "Got a skull with horns in here."

"What are we going to do with these?" Natalie asked. Her voice sounded so much thinner and shakier than usual. The clockwork figures in her arms were making her feel sick to her stomach. She didn't know whether it was from nerves or from the simple fact of being so close to machines that didn't answer to the laws of life.

"Not sure, darlin'. Break 'em somehow."

"How do we break machines that can go on forever?" Miranda's voice whispered.

Natalie licked her lips. "That day we saw the miniature

She took a breath and followed Tom and Miranda into the darkness.

harlequin, Dr. Limberleg said it would go on until something stopped it by force. So maybe they can be stopped . . . but how on earth can we . . . when the thing that's moving them is . . . is . . . the Devil?"

"Well, that's something, anyway," Tom said. "We know at least one force that can act on 'em." He looked doubtful, but it might only have been the shadows from the light of the match on his lined cheeks.

They fell into single file with Tom in the lead, lighting one match after another. The aisles between the cases were narrow enough that they caught glimpses of their contents in the flares of light.

A twisted little tree bent under the weight of flickering light bulbs rather than fruit. A miniature castle made entirely of glittering sewing needles. A collection of butterflies and moths on pins with wings that looked like carnival masks. A display of four stuffed and mounted cats: a tabby, a ginger, a black, and a Siamese . . . each with a pair of furry wings sprouting from just behind its front limbs. One case held a perfect model of the fair, complete with tiny bottles and strings of minute light bulbs. The miniature One-Man Band and harlequin were both there, moving about the little walkways, along with Mr. Dalliot in the Dispensary and the army of Dalliot look-alikes who seemed to run everything else.

Natalie stopped short at a display on a table. "Tom?" He lit a fresh match and raised it to illuminate a grouping of pictures labeled THE TRAVELS OF DR. LIMBERLEG AND COMPANY.

"I know that place." Natalie stared at a framed daguerreotype. It looked different with whole buildings rather than crumbling façades, but it was unmistakably a picture of the crossroads outside Arcane.

With a sudden lurch, it all came together: the telegraph, the diary, Natalie tripping over the squat, round green bottle at the dusty junction. The string of words on the label, and on the prescription card, and spoken like an incantation in a wagon full of clockwork. The round, green bottle in Charlie's hand. The staggering, illusory figures that had surrounded Simon Coffrett as Natalie had seen him stride through the Old Village in her strange vision days before.

"*And the ones who could still walk flung themselves about like the clumsiest of machines,*" Natalie whispered. "The gingerfoot! That's what happened to the Old Village. Remember what he said? You can't balance, can't walk . . . you drag yourself around, just like that old diary said—"

"But how can it have been going on so long?" Miranda protested. "You said that was before the war, and that's—"

"Shhh," Tom whispered. Somewhere in the darkness overhead and outside, they heard bells. The match went out in Tom's fingers. He lit another with a snap and a sizzle. "That old Quinn's looking for us. Got to keep moving."

They pushed on among bizarre and ghostly shapes in gloomy cases: flowers that seemed to have been turned to stone, jars of fireflies blinking strange colors, a shimmering miniature of a house that disappeared and reappeared at different angles as they walked past, a live toad and the ancient rock it was found inside, and pictures made of feathers, and scales, and bones.

Tom was down to his last match when they stopped to carefully draw aside the canvas flap at the back of the tent. They peered out onto the deserted path and up at the silent web above. The moonlit wires seemed to be spun from silver.

"Quiet, now," Tom whispered, "and stick close to the tents."

The second they stepped back into the night, the automata in Natalie's arms began to move. She winced and clutched them closer.

They're trying to give us away, she realized. *They want the harlequin to find us.*

She kept one eye on the wires as she followed Tom and Miranda, thinking perhaps she would see something, a vibration, *anything* that might give some warning of the Amazing Quinn's approach. But they shone still and silent overhead.

"I think the entrance should be right up ahead," Miranda whispered, creeping forward to peer around a corner. "Just up to the—"

Then she backed up frantically, stumbled, and landed in the dirt. "Go!" She hauled herself to her feet and hissed, "It's coming!"

They backtracked as quickly as they could. Natalie glanced over her shoulder as they scrambled away; no sign of the little harlequin, no sound to give it away. How far behind was it?

"Where—"

A dark shadow flitted overhead, across the alley they had just left, with the softest jingle of bells. Natalie bit her tongue and brought Miranda and Tom to a quiet halt. Had it heard them?

The shadow stopped dead. Its head swiveled, and the dead white of the porcelain face caught a shaft of moonlight. A soft click as it blinked, the polished surfaces behind the eyeholes disappearing and then reappearing.

No one breathed.

Then the Amazing Quinn gave a short hiss. Its little body shifted on the wires.

"Run!" Natalie screamed.

Hauling Tom between them as best they could, the girls broke into a sprawling race for the nearest pavilion, knocking over placards and easels as they flung themselves inside. Bells overhead jingled. Something dropped onto the canvas roof.

"We can't outrun it," Tom panted. "Not with you dragging me along."

"We can run through the tents. Change direction," Natalie argued. "It doesn't matter if we make it to the road; all we need to do is get out of this fair. We can lose it in the cornfields if we come out the wrong way."

They crept through the pavilion and out the opposite side just as the harlequin swung itself through the entrance. In the open air they ran again, half pulling, half carrying the quietly protesting Tom.

A snarl of fury from inside told them the Amazing Quinn was not happy to find them gone. The second they heard its bells approaching in the night, they plunged into another tent. Natalie smacked into a pedestal; Tom caught the giant glass light bulb that tumbled from it just in time to keep it from smashing. Miranda untied the flaps at another corner for them to sneak out again.

They hurried through the shadows, then ducked into another pavilion, changed directions, and tiptoed out a different side. There was no further sound different from the Amazing Quinn.

On the other hand, they were now completely lost. There were still booths, pavilions, wagons on all sides. No sign of the entrance, no sign of the open fields that surrounded the lot.

"I think . . ." Miranda hesitated and turned to survey the dark canvas around them. "Maybe this way?"

At that moment the harlequin dropped to the ground, landing between Natalie and Miranda. Glaring out at them from eyes like ghastly pits under bristly false eyelashes, it hissed again through its pink painted curve of smile.

Miranda screamed and backed away; the harlequin bounded after. Old Tom stepped up to shield her. Natalie took a hesitant step forward, but a warning look from Tom stopped her in her tracks.

The harlequin stopped, too. It tilted its head and stared at Tom, then at Miranda behind him. Then something in its posture changed. It swiveled its head slowly to look at Natalie, black eyes shining behind that expressionless white porcelain face. In her arms the automata shifted, as if they were reaching for Quinn.

She didn't have to be told to run. The harlequin lunged after her.

She sprinted and dodged, not caring which twists and turns she took in the maze of tents. Bells jingled overhead; the harlequin had taken to the wires again.

Her feet kicked up dust and slid on old straw. The things in her arms stirred restlessly. The Amazing Quinn raced alongside and above on a wire parallel to her path. Natalie glanced up, and out of the corner of her eye she saw it pivot and gather itself to jump—just as a break in the tents opened right underneath it. She pitched herself into the little passage. The harlequin sailed just over her head, so close that one of its bells yanked out a few strands of her hair, and tumbled into the dust with a soft crunching sound.

Left again, right and through a tent, another right, left, right . . . her ankles hurt from turning in the straw. Somehow, she managed to keep just ahead of the harlequin as it raced through the air on the wires. Every time she thought she must be getting close to a way out of the fair, the Amazing Quinn appeared in her path, forcing her to scramble back the way she'd come. It was hard to hear the soft ringing of the tarnished bells that told her where it was over her own breathing.

She gained a second every time it had to change direction to stay on her trail, and lost four each time she found herself on a path that ran parallel to (or worse, underneath) one of the lines. But they were next to impossible to see in the dark without the harlequin flying along them, at which point it was better not to look.

Just run. As long as she couldn't *see* it, it couldn't be close enough to jump.

At least, she hoped not.

Abruptly, Natalie realized she couldn't hear the bells anymore. Was that possible? She glanced up again as she ducked around a corner. No shadows above. She slowed, squeezed up against the canvas, and held her breath. Her heart pounded in her ears, her lungs throbbed, but no ghastly bells jingled on the wires.

She couldn't possibly have lost it, could she? There was no way she had outrun it—

From behind her a pair of hands clapped onto her arm and over her mouth and dragged her back through a flap of canvas. Natalie tried to scream.

Miranda's face popped into a sliver of dim light, finger over her lips. "It's us," Tom whispered as he released Natalie. "Where'd the harlequin go?"

"I don't know. I think I lost it."

Miranda shook her head. "I followed it—both of you—for a while, but I lost it a couple of minutes ago not far from here. You came along the same way afterward. It must've stopped following you before that."

Natalie sank to the ground and gulped air. "What now?"

"We're not far from the front, Miranda reckons," Tom said. "We can make a run for it when you catch your breath."

"I'm ready." Her lungs were burning, but if she waited any longer she would have to think about the pain in her legs. She gripped the four automata more tightly. "Let's go."

Miranda peered out and looked up and down the lane. "All clear."

One by one they crept into the night: Miranda navigating, Natalie in the middle with her uncanny burden, and Tom bringing up the rear. Miranda was right; they were back in familiar territory, not far from the Magnetism Tent.

The wires overhead were silent.

"Look!" Tom whispered as they rounded one last corner to find the entrance to the fair only a few yards away. "All we gotta do now is go quick."

The girls saw it at the same time. Natalie grabbed Tom's arm to stop him from ambling out into the open, and Miranda pointed to where a dark shape sat hunched and still like a vulture on a dead branch, balanced on the wire directly over the exit.

"Come on," Miranda said. "We'll cut along the side and go through the field."

Tom shook his head. "Ain't time to be foolin' around anymore. Time's running out. I'll go first, and while he's wastin' his time with me, you two run, fast as you can go."

"So it can attack you instead of us?" Natalie demanded. "It could kill you! We don't know what it might do."

"Anyhow," Miranda said shakily, "if any of us is going to be the distraction, it's got to be somebody who can run."

"Miranda, darlin', the idea ain't that I'm gonna try and get away," Tom said gently. "You and Natalie got to do that part."

Before they could protest any further, the crouching figure straightened, craned its neck, and scurried away, over the wires and out of sight. Natalie squinted in the direction of its gaze and felt as if she had swallowed a stone.

"There." She pointed out toward the road beyond the fair, where four bobbing lights glowed in the fists of four figures walking shoulder to shoulder toward the entrance to the lot. "It wasn't waiting for us. It was waiting for *them.*"

TWENTY

Gingerfoot

THEY CARRIED LAMPS that illuminated their twisted, angry faces: Acquetus, Vorticelt, Argonault, and Nervine, each looking less like a man and more like a nightmare the closer he got. In Natalie's arms the automaton-doubles thrashed wildly as she, Miranda, and Tom walked out of the fair to stand under the banner at the entrance. From here they could run, perhaps even get away . . . but one thing was certain.

There would be no standing up to these creatures.

"Natalie," Tom said, "might be we got only one chance to do this. Got to get it right the first time, or not at all."

Natalie nodded, not daring to look away from the things coming toward them. In her arms the figures struggled more violently. How were they going to sort through all the pieces they'd found out over the last hours, to say nothing of the days since the medicine show had pulled into Arcane, before the full-size versions of these horrid machines bore down on them?

Pieces.

As Natalie stared ahead, the swinging lamps in the hands of the advancing Four became the sun reflecting off metal chimes as she remembered Simon Coffrett's words for the second time that night. *Some people start with the pieces at the edges, he had said, but if I were you, I'd go straight to the center.* And then, the sibyl: *You must begin at the beginning.*

"We've got to go to the crossroads." As soon as she said it, she knew it was true. "That's where we can end it right. We'll fight fire with fire. The Devil started them up; the Devil can shut them down."

Tom nodded. "But you got to go quick, Natalie. Make the Four follow you."

"Me?" She froze, eyes wide. "But . . . but you're coming, too, aren't you?"

Now he laughed. "How, darlin'?"

"I'll—I'll go with you," Miranda whispered, worrying the hem of her dress in one shaking hand.

"Ain't time. Ain't time but for one. Natalie, you got to move!"

Natalie whipped her head back and forth. *No, no, no . . .*

"Yes, darlin'. Get on that thing and get going." Tom nodded at the bicycle, leaning where she'd left it against the trough under the shrub. "But you got to make it fly, Natalie. You got to outpace the Devil's boys tonight."

She heard herself protesting and hated it, hated that

she was arguing—but he *knew*, didn't he? Tom had *seen* her try and fail over and over and over! She was thirteen, the daughter of a bicycle mechanic, and she couldn't ride this bicycle. It fought her; it threw her; it hated her.

"Natalie," Tom interrupted, speaking gently but firmly, "you got to race the demons and win, and then you gotta demand to talk to their boss."

His fist opened between them. In his palm the strange coin glinted, uneven edges catching the flickering lantern light.

"Take this and tell him I want my favor, and don't you let him give you any trouble about it. The favor travels with the coin, or it wouldn't have kept turning up again every time I tried to throw it away. But keep a tight hold on it, Natalie. Ain't nothing it would like better than to turn up in my hand just when you need it in yours."

He tipped it into her palm. A sudden cold burned her skin so that she ached to shove it deep into the pocket of her overalls.

"Now you got to, Natalie. You got to try. They're counting on you, everyone." Beside Tom, Miranda stood, wide-eyed, shifting her weight and unable to speak.

The swinging lamps were close enough that they could see clumsy moths bumping around the glass. She could see the grid on Argonault's head, could feel Vorticelt's black-pit eyes searching for purchase on her soul. Natalie ran to the red Chesterlane Eidolon, shoved the automata into the basket on the back of the frame, and buckled it shut. She steadied the bicycle, trapping the Devil's coin between her left palm and the handlebar. *They're counting on me.*

On Limberleg's Chesterlane, she had figured out how to pedal better, and Natalie thought she might even have figured out part of the steering. If she could get up onto the red bicycle, get going, get up some speed . . . if she could do that, she might just have a chance. She hadn't figured out how to do any of those things yet, but there was no more time. If she was going to do any good for anybody, she was going to have to get the Chesterlane working for her, boneshaker tendencies and all.

"Go!" Tom yelled, and Natalie was running, racing alongside the bicycle—then throwing one foot at the whirling pedal, missing, stumbling, and picking up speed again. *Remember where the pedals are*, she thought to herself. She ran, kicked off the ground to get her foot on one pedal, swung the other foot—*whoosh*—over the saddle, and suddenly she was churning her feet, pedaling, flying over the dirt road. The bicycle listed, and Natalie leaned away from the tilt. It righted itself effortlessly. Behind her she heard Miranda give a shout of triumph.

She was riding, really riding.

Natalie let out a scream of joy, of relief, of escape as she swooped past the Four with their lamps. Her triumphant shout became a laugh at their stunned faces as she zoomed away down Heartwood Street toward the center of town.

"Look at that Natalie go," Tom said. "Good girl." He allowed himself a rusty chuckle as the Four broke into a run toward the fair.

"Tom," Miranda said, clutching at his sleeve, "they're still coming!"

"They won't want nothing with us. It's Natalie who's got what they want, and they can't afford to let her get away." He sighed and turned away from the four angry Paragons and called into the dark. "All right, now, you old buckra, show your face."

The Four sprinted right past them and disappeared into the dark of the fair with the Amazing Quinn zipping across the wires overhead. Miranda ducked behind Tom, but the old guitar player only shouted again into the night.

"Come on out, I say! It's time!"

Miranda squinted. "Who are you talking—"

"Don't tease." The voice that came out of the shadows was tired. "I'm old. I don't know how to joke anymore."

"Well, that ain't true. I heard you laugh good and hard just the other day." Tom smiled at the creature—half railway hobo and half dead man—all wrapped up in a threadbare suit, who hobbled into the dim light that spilled from the fair. Miranda's eyes opened wide.

"It felt good to laugh," said Chester Teufels.

"Well, old conjurer," Tom said, clapping him on the shoulder, "it might be that this child's ready to settle things up."

"Mr. Teufels?" Miranda stared at the little old man. "*You're* the demon?" She turned to Tom. "The demon who wanted you to choose your favor? He's the one who followed you around for so many years like a . . . like a *lawyer*, Natalie said?"

Mr. Teufels frowned at her and looked down at his rumpled suit. "I clean up just fine, young lady, when I want to."

Natalie saw the first victim of the gingerfoot before she reached the water tower at the corner of Heartwood and Bard. She spotted him the second she switched on the chrome light between the bicycle's handlebars: Tyler Marsh, the groom who worked at Ogle's Livery Stable, dragging himself along by kicking one leg awkwardly out in front of him, and then kicking the second after it. Even in the bright glow from the bicycle's lamp, it was impossible to tell whether the expression on his face was pain or frustration before he passed out of view.

For just a moment, almost overcome with fear at the sight of what the gingerfoot was capable of, Natalie thought about turning left, away from the crossroads and toward home. She pictured the big light over the doors of the bicycle shop glowing. Just beyond that, the windows of her house would be flickering warmly, the porch smelling of the miraculously unburned chocolate cake. What if she just stopped there? Her father would be able to break these pathetic little machines. Her father would . . .

If she went home, she would find her mother and her brother with the gingerfoot.

The thought made her sway on the bicycle, and for a moment her feet fumbled on the pedals almost as if she had it, too, this horrible sickness that made you forget how your limbs were meant to move.

She pictured her brother, flailing in the middle of the

street like Tyler Marsh. For all she knew, even her father, made a believer by his wife's quick recovery, might have taken something. What if he had gone suddenly immobile in his workshop with a wrench dangling uselessly in his fingers? She imagined her mother, stricken suddenly in the middle of cooking supper, unable to save even a single pork chop as they burned on the stove. Like a Victrola record played to the end and forgotten, the needle skipping endlessly, helplessly, against the spindle.

Her mother, reduced to a human-shaped machine, helpless and haunted—it was this image that finally jerked Natalie back to herself. She forced her body straight and her legs into rhythm.

They were counting on her.

There was only one way to do this. She couldn't lose her lead, not now, when she still had so far to go. She put all thoughts of home out of her mind, steered for the center of town, and kept pedaling.

Tyler Marsh had it better than the next one she passed: Miss Tillerman, who at first looked merely drunk as she stood wobbling in the middle of Bard Street. Then Natalie realized with a twinge that Miss Tillerman couldn't move. She had lost control of her body completely, like clockwork winding down, helpless until someone took pity and wound it again.

When she saw the third one as she zipped between the general store and the saloon, she almost lost control of the bicycle and nearly ran the poor soul over. It was a woman, and Natalie almost didn't see her because she was dragging herself across the street on her belly.

It was horribly familiar, that image, and it only took Natalie a second to understand why. It was the same way the little Nervine automaton had dragged itself across the floor of Dr. Limberleg's wagon. *It might or might not move,* Limberleg had said when he described the gingerfoot's effect on a body, *but if it does, it does not move on any command the soul inside it gives.*

The townspeople were turning into automata, without gears or keys, but automata nonetheless. Puppets. She shuddered.

Then the line of pearl buttons down the woman's back caught the light, and Natalie recognized the thing in the dirt as Mrs. Byron. Tears reflected wetly on the old woman's face as she dug reluctant hands into the ground—trying to move her own body or trying to hold it still, Natalie couldn't tell. *I should stop. I should help her get where she's going,* she thought miserably. In her basket, the miniature Paragons shifted restlessly. Natalie kept pedaling.

She passed others. She forced herself onward.

It had just begun to feel possible that she might reach the crossroads without incident when a sudden swoop of wind made her glance over her shoulder. She almost lost control of the bicycle again.

The Four were coming.

Behind her, at the far end of the street, a mass of sparks barreled down the road. It was something halfway between a greenhouse and a light bulb that cast strange, fractured light through old, bubble-pocked glass panes; frantic light that glinted on big brass wheels.

They were chasing her in the Amber Therapy Chamber, propelled by those huge high-wheelers. They were gaining fast.

Flapping canvas and splintered stakes marked the route the Amber Therapy Chamber had cut through the fair. Jack the drifter ambled down the center of it with the air of a man strolling along a broad country lane, light leaking through the punched-tin lantern over his shoulder and carpetbag swinging jauntily in one fist. He inhaled with gusto, as if taking in sea breezes rather than dust and the smell of cold frying grease.

Somewhere near the middle he stopped to examine something partly hidden under a pile of collapsed canvas. After a moment's study he lifted a section of fallen tent and shoved open the door underneath.

He picked his way into the wagon, treading carefully through the clutter on the floor: a jumble of mechanical toys, shattered ceramic fingers, and cogs and flywheels from smashed antique engines. When his pale eyes had adjusted to the dark, he saw what he had come looking for on the far side of the room, mostly hidden under a toppled dentist's chair: a pair of scuffed shoes at the end of two half-buried legs.

Natalie cycled harder, legs spinning so fast she could barely keep them on their pedals. Behind her, the glass room made strange noises as it cut through the night. She ventured another glance.

They had already cut her lead in half, plunging forward in the Amber Therapy Chamber as if it were some kind of nightmarish motorcar. Now she could see it more clearly: Acquetus and Argonault sat on the pedaling apparatuses on either side, the same ones that had powered the circuit when her mother was inside the box. This time Vorticelt turned the hand crank to generate the frightful current coursing through what looked like a thin gray body in a light brown suit—though it was difficult to tell through the thick, discolored glass.

A few moments later, the Four in their glass coach had halved the distance again. Natalie saw Nervine now, crouching on the convex, faceted roof of the chamber, clinging to the brass spire at the top with one hand even as the little lightning bolts shot out of it. The other hand was raised, pointing at her, and sparks flew from his fingers and the spiky ends of his gray hair, making his angry face garish and horrible as he shouted at his colleagues below, urging them on, demanding that they pedal faster, drive the dynamo harder. The little harlequin skittered across the dome, clinging to the brass between the glass panes, then hanging from the curling metal that hung like ivy from the roof edge, now perching for a moment at the very top of the spire like a lookout. The sparking light flashed briefly across its porcelain face, illuminating a webwork of cracks on the surface from when it had tried and failed to catch her with a flying leap.

Natalie pedaled harder. The next time she hazarded a glance, she saw the man in the brown suit give off a shower of sparks that flitted along the wires hanging over his head. It would kill him, she thought miserably, but then she saw his skeleton show through his skin with the next electric surge. Even through those thick, greenish panes she could see that the skeleton was nothing but a mess of gears and chains.

An image of Vorticelt unloading a cart full of old bicycles and coffin-sized crates flashed through her mind . . . a dozen such crates full of thin, pale men in identical brown suits. Natalie shook off the memory. She forced her legs, willed them to fly.

The glass chamber was less than ten yards behind her and closing fast; the crossroads was still at least a mile away. Natalie felt something shift in the basket and reached back to whack her palm on the lid as the half-destroyed buildings on the outskirts of the Old Village began to pass by in the dark.

Then sparks showered down onto her arms; the chamber loomed over her. It drew up alongside the Chesterlane, and Acquetus reached out from his seat, his fingers grazing her collar as his legs pedaled faster than was humanly possible. She flung an elbow back and connected with his arm out of sheer dumb luck.

Three quarters of a mile to go, maybe more.

She felt fingers swipe her shoulder, and more motion in the basket. Panic began to swell in her stomach. She could not outpace them.

Fingers again, this time on the top of her head, trying to catch in her hair. Natalie swerved, silently willing the

Behind her, the glass room made strange noises
as it cut through the night.

bicycle to stay upright and biting her lip as she felt a hank of hair tear from her scalp. Out of the corner of her eye she saw the harlequin balancing at the edge of the roof, its small form curled like a cat ready to pounce, holding itself steady as the chamber bounced over the uneven road. It caught her eye. Then the Amazing Quinn actually *smiled*, its painted mask cracking at the lips as the pink mouth formed a ghastly grin full of menace and crumbling porcelain.

It was about to jump.

Jack squatted beside the upended chair and addressed the body beneath it.

"Told you, didn't I? Didn't I say you had this place measured wrong?" He lifted the chair easily with one hand and tossed it aside. It collided with a cabinet full of specimens, sending glass shards and skull fragments spilling everywhere. "Didn't I say that?"

Jake Limberleg's lifeless body sprawled, twisted. His arms lay at strange, improbable angles from his body. His face was mostly covered by a fallen shutter, but the part that could be seen was the same ashy ivory as his gloves . . . except for the purple choke marks around his throat. His mouth was twisted in pain.

"Sorry to see you go this way, lad," the drifter muttered. "Wish we could've come to see eye to eye."

He stepped across the corpse and reached for the four little flowerpots in the corner. One by one he flipped them over. His easy grin faded, pale eyes hardening into jagged chunks of emerald.

The clockwork Paragons, of course, were gone.

Jack hissed, a snarl of fury through clenched teeth. He snatched up the one remaining figure: the doctor whose miniature hands in their pearly gloves had stretched over the pots as if conducting the Four with their instruments.

Jake Limberleg's body—his actual body—flung itself upright from under the rubble.

The drifter screamed and fell over backwards. The doctor, or anyhow his hands, with their many-jointed, gear-knuckled digits protruding from the ragged seams of his leather gloves, grabbed for him, arms flailing in from odd, disconnected directions. His lips snarled over broken teeth. His eyes bulged, sightless and red.

Jack scrambled back on his elbows through the wreckage. The demon hands dragged Limberleg's body across the floor after him. Its cracked teeth parted, and a string of strangled noises barely recognizable as words slid out through the contorted lips.

"That . . . is . . . not . . . for . . . you!"

Suddenly, there was nowhere else for Jack to go. The chair, cabinet, and wall slammed up against his back, one after another. Limberleg's gruesome corpse leaned over him, its twitching fingers inches away from his face.

"That . . . is . . . not . . . for . . . you!"

Jack held very still. "Why . . . why not?"

The wagon door opened. Simon Coffrett stood on the threshold.

"Because he cannot be forced to defect. Even the dead may choose."

Jack opened his mouth, but before he could speak, Simon stepped forward and plucked the clockwork doctor out of his hands. As the drifter reached instinctively for what had been taken from him, Simon Coffrett turned to the thing that had been Jake Limberleg.

"Choose," he demanded.

For the briefest of moments, the dead, red eyes of the man who had once been Dr. Jasper Bellinspire flashed with gratitude.

"The choice is made," Simon Coffrett said. "Sorry, Jack." A column of blue flame spurted like a fountain from his palm. At the center of the column, the automaton in the shape of Jake Limberleg burned.

Then Limberleg's body crumpled face-first to the floor, once again lifeless and still.

The drifter scrambled out of the way. Simon shook from his hand all that remained of the automaton: a pile of hot ash and a few pieces of clockwork that bounced and rolled away to join the rest of the debris.

"Some things can't be stolen, and you aren't the only one who can parley with defectors."

The drifter grinned. "I wondered just how he worked a deal with you, jumper." Then his smile vanished. "How did you know my name?"

"I've been walking a lot longer than you have. I see more than you do, I hear more than you do, and I've had enough time to lose the arrogance I suspect you're stuck with." Simon stepped back out of the wagon and into the darkened fair. "You were right about one thing, though:

Limberleg didn't have the measure of this place. Thing is, Jack, I don't think you do, either. Get out of my town. Go do your recruiting someplace else."

Jack's eyes narrowed to knife-edge slits. "*Your* town?"

Against the gloom of the fair, Simon Coffrett turned to face the drifter. Without any change in the light, he seemed suddenly to stand out, distinct, from the murk and shadow behind him. As if someone had drawn around the outline of him, toe to crown, with a black charcoal pencil, or colored the rest of the world in an extra layer of shading that made Simon somehow not brighter but *clearer* by contrast.

"My. Town." Simon pronounced the words like bullets. He smiled, a grin that hinted at a snarl.

Jack grinned back, a gash of tooth and ire that twisted his face into something monstrous, and pitched his response in the same warning tone. "For now."

"Forever." Simon turned toward the entrance of the fair.

"Don't you dare," the drifter snarled, "turn your back on me! *Do you know who I am?*" Tense with fury, he launched himself to the door of the wrecked wagon and gripped the frame so hard his hands splintered the painted wood. "If you know who I am, jumper, you should be afraid. Or maybe you've just learned how to hide it. *You should be in fear!*"

Simon dusted the last of the ash from his palm as he stalked away. "Get out of there, if you don't want to burn with it."

@ @ @

Natalie watched the harlequin as she sped through the Old Village. The bells reflected the sparks in strange fits of light as it balanced at the curlicued edge of the glass chamber, waiting for the moment to jump. How could she possibly fight it off? Heavy, hot fear crept up her throat.

Dad would not be proud if I died on a bicycle, she thought.

The harlequin crouched, about to leap.

There!

A patch of empty blackness opened up to her right. Natalie swerved, straight off the road and into the narrow space between two ruined houses. She flung a hand out in front of her and slapped off the electric lamp, then turned the bicycle again and rode parallel to the road, behind the row of houses. The steering was coming easier now; instead of seeming just wildly temperamental, the hinged frame of the Chesterlane was actually starting to feel responsive to the smallest suggestion Natalie gave it.

In the sudden dark, she hit a patch of loose stone. The wheels shook and slid, sending pebbles flying and raising clouds of dirt she could taste but not see, rattling her teeth and shaking her hands so hard they numbed on the handlebars. But somehow, the bicycle stayed upright.

From the road, the violent light of the Amber Therapy Chamber threw horrible silhouettes through the skeletal houses. Natalie burst in and out of dark patches, dodging rubble and crumbling foundations. She stayed as close as she could to the wreckage so she wouldn't get too near the old riverbed that lay somewhere in the darkness to her right.

Nervine cursed. She could see him over the derelict rooftops, clinging to the flashing dome as it barreled along on its parallel course. Natalie grinned; they had to slow down the chamber so as not to lose her in the dark, and Nervine was *furious*.

Then she saw something else moving in the alternating patches of darkness and light, and her smile disappeared.

It raced along the sagging lines of the old roofs and rafters between Natalie and the glittering glass box, swinging from what was left of the eaves of one house to a windowsill on the next as easily as if there were silver wires connecting it all. Almost as if it were capable of moving across the night air itself.

The giant glass chamber couldn't leave the road, but the harlequin could.

Instinctively Natalie veered right, farther away, desperate to put herself out of range of any of the Amazing Quinn's acrobatics, and this time she overdid it. Almost immediately she felt the ground slope and the bicycle list dangerously. A shower of stones slid out from under her wheels.

For a crazed, desperate moment, she imagined that she was back in the alley where she'd tried and failed for so long to master this bicycle. She longed to fall gracelessly against the wall of the stable, and for a moment she felt herself sway . . .

Put out a hand and the stable wall will be there to break your fall, she thought, clamping her eyes shut. She hit a pile of rubble head-on but miraculously failed to lose her balance. *Just fall, and open your eyes, and you'll be home, and this will all go away.*

Her legs pedaled furiously as ever, but her right palm let go of its handle, and Natalie reached sideways, wishing with all her heart for the tumble and the bruises and the familiar alley to wake up to. . . . She listed a little farther, and one wheel slid . . .

Natalie righted herself with a lurch. It was so natural, it didn't even seem like a conscious decision. It was almost as if the Chesterlane was now as determined that she should stay upright as it had previously been to throw her off.

And then suddenly for a moment she was airborne, clearing a decaying back porch thanks to a timber that formed a ramp just big enough and high enough to help her over. She landed effortlessly, sturdy and sure, and for a moment forgot the predicament she was in. It used to be like this to ride—no obstacle stood in your way, no mere geographical inconveniences could hold you back. Pedal hard enough, and you might just leave the ground, like Wilbur and Orville. You might fall, but sometimes, oh, so rarely, sometimes, you flew.

Natalie was finished with falling.

She glanced over at the remnants of the buildings and picked out the harlequin's outline, nearly level with her and gaining ground. Up ahead was the big, wide façade of Trader's Mill's old livery stable. If the harlequin got there ahead of her, she would have to pass right underneath it to make the left that would get her back to the crossroads. She would be an easy target.

Half dead from exhaustion, Natalie gave the bicycle one last good push, one more shot to show her what it could do.

"Come on," she hissed through clenched teeth, "the only way now's to outrun them all."

The red bicycle surged ahead, with Natalie's aching knees and numb feet pedaling on.

On the road, the glass box fell back again, Nervine's curses ringing through the night. The harlequin hurled itself through the air onto the livery stable roof, all but flying, bent on a collision course with the place the bicycle would have to be. . . .

At the last possible minute, Natalie pitched the bicycle hard to the left, aiming for what she hoped was a sliver of an opening in the façade of the stable. Gravel and dirt exploded from under the wheels as she passed over the ground where the building used to be. She screamed and flung up her hands to protect her face from the crash in case she was wrong . . . and burst almost gracefully through the stable doorway to arrive back on the road mere yards from the junction.

She spun to a neat stop and turned just in time to see the harlequin, utterly confused by her emergence through the façade rather than around the corner where it had plotted its interception. It floundered in midair like a fish out of water, limbs waving uselessly as it smacked through the last remaining panes in the window of the general store in a spray of broken glass and shards of bone-white porcelain. The Four in their flickering electric machine were still a full twenty yards away.

She lifted her left hand carefully away from the handlebar, slowly so that the precious thing in her palm couldn't tumble out and disappear into the dust and darkness. The coin was still there, pressed into her skin. Natalie took the first full breath she'd drawn in what seemed like a week, and faced the crossroads.

A horrific sight awaited Simon Coffrett at the entrance to the fair. In the streets beyond, figures lurched and staggered. Some crawled.

By the old watering trough under the hawthorn near the front of the lot, a cluster of adults and one girl waited.

"What have you done?" demanded Mr. Swifte, towering over everyone else.

Simon curled his fingers around the smudges of ash in his palm. "Wait and see."

"I'll have you know Natalie Minks is on her way to the crossroads," Tom Guyot said quietly. "If anything happens to that girl, Simon, I'll be knocking on your door."

Simon Coffrett smiled a terrible, sad smile that made even Tom's heart sink. "Everything is going to happen to that girl, Tom. You know as well as I do. It isn't anything I have the power to stop."

Old Tom didn't answer, only turned and struck off after Natalie's tire marks. Chester Teufels emerged from the shadows and fell into step beside him as he walked.

"Why?" Everyone turned to look at Miranda Porter as she stepped timidly to the front of the little group. "What's going to happen to Natalie?"

"Ah, Miranda.... So much, I can't see the extent of it. This is . . .." Simon waved a hand as if to dismiss the fair, the gingerfoot, and whatever was happening to Natalie on her way to the crossroads as so much nothing.

"But *why?*"

"Because the place at the center is hers by birthright. You know what a birthright is? It's an inheritance." He glanced up at the people behind her: Edgar Tilden, Lester Finch, Christopher Swifte, Wiley Maliverny . . . the dozens of townspeople lurching and helpless in the streets of Arcane. "You all know what that means. Dr. Fitzwater knew it weeks ago. Annie Minks was sick before this mess began. Natalie has begun to *see*. The *phantasmata* are already passing to her. It will be her fight, and make no mistake, *this* is not even the beginning of the fight I mean."

"If she makes it through tonight," Mr. Tilden said coldly. "There's no birthright to guarantee that."

"No, there isn't. That depends entirely on her. But this much is certain: *things are in motion*."

"She'll do it," Tom shouted from a little ways down the road. "And not because of any old birthright! Ain't nobody braver in this town than that girl!"

"Wait and see," Simon murmured.

If there was anything Natalie didn't feel at that moment, it was brave. In fact, she thought she might be sick.

A little blue-flamed fire burned where the two roads met. She swung down from the bicycle. A man she had never seen before stepped forward. The crickets stopped singing suddenly, as if they had never existed in the first place. Natalie knew she was looking at the Devil.

"Hello, Natalie Minks."

Her own name, spoken in that voice, made Natalie stop dead in her tracks. Goose flesh spread over her sweaty skin in cold waves, making her shiver hard. She didn't look up, only reached her shaking hand to unbuckle the basket in which she had imprisoned the automata. Her heart pounded; she hadn't spared a thought for them since turning off the road. What if they had fallen out? What if they had gotten away?

"That's a charming bicycle."

The clockwork things moved restlessly as she took them out. *One . . . two . . . three . . . four . . .*

"And it certainly does get some speed."

The Amber Therapy Chamber came to a screeching stop a few yards from the fire. Jagged shadows cast by the sparking chamber and the blue fire painted the crossroads in even odder shapes. Natalie held the clockwork figures tight. This wasn't going to be easy. Fear lumbered up and down her spine. She forced herself to remember why she was here. *To save Mama. To save Charlie. To save everyone.*

"Would you like to have the fastest bicycle there is? Ever will be?" The Devil smiled charmingly, blue flames reflecting in his eyes and making them disappear. "Let me have that bicycle, let me have one little spin about on it. When you take it back from me, it will fly."

One by one the Four climbed down from the glass chamber. The automata lurched in her arms. It was not that she had any desire to agree to what the creature across the flames was offering, but she didn't know how to begin to refuse. For a moment she could only think that this was unfair, that she was just a little girl, that no one could expect a little girl to stand up to the Devil.

Then, for a moment, she forgot the Devil was there. If anyone else had called her *just a little girl*, she would've given them an earful.

Something that had been fluttering in her chest grew strong, and something that had been very, very tight loosened just a little.

When I get home, she decided, *I'll tell Mama what happened, and it will make a great story.*

The man on the other side of the flames held up a hand as he waited for her answer. The Four stopped in their tracks, eyeing Natalie with loathing.

"It already flies," Natalie said, because when she got home and told her mother the story, she wanted to have said something brave. "I flew here, didn't you see?"

The creature across the fire didn't like being ignored, but he liked being talked back to by a thirteen-year-old girl even less. When he spoke again, the voice came from right beside her and bore a new, harsh tone.

"Do you know who I am?"

Gripping the spiky miniature Nervine and tiny sharp-eyed Vorticelt under one arm; the periwigged Acquetus and bald, tattooed Argonault under the other; and Old Tom's coin tight in one fist, Natalie looked up at last and felt her eyes glance off the figure in front of her like a stone skipping over water. The fear was thick in her belly. *Look him in the face, like Tom*, she begged herself. *Be brave like Tom.*

"I know who you are," she said. *Look up.*

He came to stand between Natalie and the blue fire. "Who am I, then?"

"You are the collector of hands," Natalie said, because it sounded like the kind of thing a brave girl in a good story would say, and because she didn't feel brave at all. "You are the gambler of souls. You are the gingerfoot, and you are evil. You can do anything at all, as long as it's wicked." *Look up.* . . . Even the voice in her head sounded small and weak and afraid.

The Devil looked down at her, blue fire flickering behind him. The Four waited, just outside the circle of the flames. Natalie's heart beat slow and cold. The small voice in her head urging her to be brave was crying. In a moment she would be frozen, like Miss Tillerman, caught by the gingerfoot and powerless. Helplessly, still holding the coin tightly, and with the miniature Four clutched under her arms, Natalie put a hand up awkwardly to where the sprocket hung from the guitar string around her neck and twined it in her fingers.

Then, without a clue as to where it came from, she heard the music. It was Tom's music, music you would never have known could come from a guitar if you hadn't seen it for yourself.

Natalie raised her eyes to the Devil and met his stare. *Oh* . . .

"I know who you are, and I know why you're here." The gaze was like Vorticelt's, only much, much worse. It was sick-making, dizzy, terrible. It hurt her head and her heart, and made her voice feel thick on her tongue, but she forced herself to go on. "You aren't here for me. You owe a favor to Tom Guyot, and I'm here to tell you what that favor is." She swallowed hard. "Undo the gingerfoot. All of it. Everything back the way it was."

A moment's still silence stretched between them.

"Everything?" the Devil asked quietly.

Suddenly, those eyes she had worked so hard to look into were her mother's eyes, and her peripheral vision swam so that for an instant the Devil was gone and Natalie saw her mama, thin and pale in her bed. The music so much like Tom's came to an end as if it had been nothing more than a recording, and Natalie heard that horrible skipping again . . . *snick-thump, snick-thump, snick-thump.*

"Mama," she choked.

No one had told her what made her mother sick, or how serious it was. She didn't know what it would mean if she said yes now: *Yes, put everything back, even my mother, back the way she was, too.* She did know what it would mean if she backed down. She thought of Mrs. Byron in the road, dragging the weight of her useless body with her forearms until those became useless, too. Natalie couldn't let her mother be turned into a puppet. Even if she wasn't really sure what the alternative was.

But how could she stand up to this thing?

Mrs. Minks's voice spoke in Natalie's memory, telling

the story of Tom Guyot, his tin guitar, and the human hands he was born with. *If this was the last song they would all play together, they'd better make it a song worth dying for.*

She frowned, forcing herself to stare until her mother's eyes dissolved back into the Devil's face.

I'll make this a story worth dying for, she thought fervently. *If it's the last one Mama hears, I'll make it the best story there ever was. And I'll make it home to tell her, too.*

Heart pounding in her chest, Natalie Minks stepped around the Devil to the blue flames and, one by one, tossed the automata in.

The little group gasped as the tattered fair burst into flames behind Simon Coffrett. Simon turned slowly and watched as blue fire climbed the canvas. Overhead, the wires snapped, whipcracks lashing in anger at the night.

"Wait and see," he whispered. He turned to face the others. "Go. People will need help." He nodded to indicate the staggering figures in the town beyond.

Miranda would remember that sight for the rest of her life: the fair burning behind Simon Coffrett, his eyes invisible behind the blue-flame reflections in his spectacles . . . even though the burning fair was at his back, and his glasses should have reflected the town instead.

The minute she realized that, she turned and ran.

"No!" snarled Alpheus Nervine as the last miniature Paragon disappeared into the flames. He leaped at Natalie, only to be caught like a bee in a jar as a pillar of indigo fire spat up

from beneath his feet, then the feet of each of his companions, encompassing them and cutting off their screeching
voices so suddenly that Natalie shivered.

She put her fists on her hips so they would stop shaking
and faced the Devil again. She knew he was angry; it made
her bones ache to hold his stare, but she forced herself not
to look away.

"Pay up," she said, and held the coin out.

The man-shaped creature by the fire clenched his fists.
Natalie knew better than to look at them.

"That Tom," the Devil spat at last, his words coming
out in a furious rush, "is a bigger botheration than any three
Apostles put together. I had better never again encounter
him in this world or any other, and for the record, I don't
want to see you again, either. Ever!"

He pointed a long, spidery finger at the Four burning
slowly in their flaming columns, then pointed another over
Natalie's shoulder. She heard a rustle of bells and turned to
see the harlequin freeze in midair not three feet from where
she stood. Half of its ruined face was crazed into numberless
cracks, but the other half was missing whole pieces; the eye
on that side was smashed shut, and the gaps where the porcelain had fallen away emitted curls of steam. Its broken mouth
howled. Tiny glass shards on its velvet suit sparkled blue in
the firelight. Natalie had no idea where it had leaped from.

"My debt is clear," the Devil snarled.

He flung one hand into the air between them. The
coin flared with a cold little flame in Natalie's hand. Without thinking she let go, and it spun out of her fingers and

into the Devil's. For a second Natalie saw a face, a real human face at the end of one of the fingers lit by the flame as he curled his awful fist around the burning coin. She thought she saw it wink at her.

Then it was all gone—the Devil, the Four, the harlequin, the coin, and the chamber—leaving Natalie Minks standing on one side of a perfectly normal, dying campfire. Side by side across the fire from where she stood sat Chester Teufels in his threadbare suit and Old Tom Guyot with his guitar on his knee. Tom picked out a tune with his crown cap pick. In the darkness beyond the flicker of the flames, the crickets began to chirp softly again.

"You told the Devil to pay up," Chester Teufels said, and burst into uncontrollable laughter. He wiped a tear out of his eye. "That's funny. Brave . . . but funny."

"Yup," Tom said, slapping the strings with the flat of his hand—*one, two, three, four*—so that the guitar itself seemed to be applauding. "More than brave. Bravest thing I ever saw."

Chester Teufels scratched his scalp. "Suppose I can get on my way, now the matter of that debt's all taken care of," he said, glancing around in all directions, plainly without a clue as to where his way might have gotten to after all these years.

"You got four perfectly good roads right here," Tom said.

Chester nodded, then, "Tell you what. I'd sure like to hear you play one more time before I go."

"Got a particular tune in mind?"

Natalie came around the fire to sit down between them. Suddenly she was tired, so tired she had to concentrate hard on what they were saying.

"Let me think." Chester looked younger in the firelight. The deep-scored lines on his face seemed to smooth away as he gave Tom a wide grin and Natalie a conspiratorial elbow in the ribs. "The one you played last time you were here. One more time, I'd like to hear that, if I get to choose."

Natalie looked back and forth between them, running her fingers over the old E string around her neck as her eyelids started to droop. Why had she ever thought Chester Teufels looked like an old man? she wondered sleepily. Up close you could tell he was no older than her father. Or was it only the firelight?

Old Tom strummed a chord. "All right." He smiled, looking up at the sky as his fingers drummed on the guitar. "Let's see if I can recall how that song goes."

"Sure you can," Chester said. "Those old hands of yours'll remember for sure."

"You know," Tom said, "I just bet they will."

TWENTY-ONE

Crossroads

STRANGE THINGS CAN HAPPEN at a crossroads; this much surely we have come to expect.

Doc Fitzwater had lived in Arcane since he'd come into the world, and he also knew to expect oddities where the roads outside of town came together. Sometimes, though, the specifics still surprised him, even after all the long decades of his life. Like finding Natalie Minks curled up by the burned-out, years-old circle of an old campfire in the middle of the Old Village before the sun had even come up.

On the other hand, given the wire he'd gotten late the evening before, maybe it wasn't so strange after all.

He stopped the Winton and climbed out, leaning on his alligator cane. "Natalie? What are you doing out here, all by yourself?"

"Dr. Fitzwater?" Natalie rubbed her eyes and squinted through the gray dawn at Doc, the dusty motorcar, and the cold ash on her fingers. There was no sign of Tom Guyot or Chester Teufels. "What are *you* doing here?" she mumbled. Then she sat bolt upright. *Mama. Charlie.*

The car was pointing toward Arcane, so Doc was probably just passing through the Old Village on his way back home. He wouldn't know yet whether her mother and brother had recovered, but if the sick people in the other town had gotten better . . . "Is everyone all right?" Natalie demanded. "What happened in Pinnacle?"

"Well, it's the funniest thing," Doc muttered, helping her lift the bicycle into the back of the motorcar. "Last night, it . . ." He paused and gave Natalie a shrewd look as she hopped into the seat beside him. "Things got strange, Natalie. Not to scare you, but things got strange over there. Then last night it all just—"

"Went back to normal? Did everything go back to normal?" She sounded desperate even to her own ears, but she didn't care.

"Well, for lack of a better way to put it, yes. The strangeness sort of . . . stopped. That, and Mr. Tilden sent me a wire about some shenanigans going on over here, in some of which your name figured quite prominently. So I decided to head right back home. Don't know how I managed to stay awake. Suffice to say, it was a long night."

Natalie's breath came out in a rush as the Winton chugged into motion, and she nearly stood up and started dancing on the burgundy leather seat. Instead, she twined the guitar-string necklace through her fingers and, for a moment, thought she heard the sounds of music from somewhere far, far away.

As they drove toward Arcane, the crumbling houses dwindled and were replaced by open fields of wildflowers and brambly hedges, vague twisty shapes that took form slowly as the sky warmed.

"Doc," Natalie said after a long silence, "is my mother going to . . . is she . . . is she going to be okay?"

Doc Fitzwater shot her a glance that, three days ago, would've made her sink through the seat. Today, however, she just looked back at him and waited for his answer. He sighed.

"Your mother's very sick, Natalie. If I tried to deny it, I'd have to lie. But your mother's very strong, too. Furthermore, if *I* had to be very sick, *I'd* want me for my doctor, not to sound my own trumpet. So that's two things in her favor. And then she's got your dad, and you, and Charlie to care for her while she needs it, so there's three more good things to help her on her way back to health. But Natalie, your mama's health aside, it's time you and she sat down and had a very serious talk."

No fooling. First Mr. Swifte, then Simon Coffrett, now Doc. . . . Clearly, Natalie was owed some explanations about something, and ordinarily she would have put all her energy into pestering answers out of her traveling companion. But she couldn't worry about that yet, not while the most important question in the world still hadn't been answered.

"Is she going to get better, then?"

Instead of answering, Doc Fitzwater gave her a searching look, one that seemed to read on her face all of the events of the last days. "Only magic illnesses have magic cures, Natalie. Only hucksters make promises nature can't be made to keep. But I have every hope."

Natalie thought about that for a moment. She nodded.

"Drive faster, Doc. I know for a fact this old motorcar can make thirty-five miles an hour, and I gotta get home and tell my mother a story."

"Thirty-five? That a fact?"

"That's a fact. My dad said so."

Doc smiled sideways at her, one eyebrow raised over the monocle glinting in the sun as the motorcar accelerated. "Well, then."

The Winton chugged down the road toward Arcane. "Hang around the crossroads long enough, Miss Minks," said Doc Fitzwater after a while, with a look that was probably meant to be scary, "and they say you might get to meet Old Scratch."

Natalie smiled, flicking the string around her neck with a thumbnail so it made tiny twanging sounds that only she could hear.

"Really," she said.

Doc Fitzwater stopped the Winton in front of the Minkses' house so Natalie could hop out. Her feet stumbled on the running board, as if they wanted to climb back up into the car even as she was trying to climb down.

Together they lowered the Chesterfield to the street. Natalie glanced up to find Doc watching her with an expression too close to sympathy for her liking. He took the monocle away from his eye and smiled. "Go on, Nattie. Say your good mornings and tell your mama and your dad I'll be along shortly. And remember, you're part of the good medicine."

Natalie stood at the front door until Doc's car had puttered on its way, then pushed it open as quietly as she could. Inside, the house was silent.

She sank onto the bottom stair, steeling herself for the climb upstairs. For the disappointment.

When Natalie had last seen her mother, she had been well, recovered from whatever awful thing had been making her so sick, planning some kind of elaborate frosting for that stupid cake. She would be sick again now, which was better than what Limberleg's medicine would've done in the end . . . but still. She would be sick, and there was no getting around that.

Natalie rose and put a hand on the banister to steady herself. But before she could take her first step, a sound— the soft shifting of hesitant feet in the kitchen—made her turn.

"Natalie," her mother said.

A tide of strange emotions poured through her as she stared at her mother, pale and nervous in the doorway. Relief, anger, love, dread. . . . Natalie held tight to the banister and concentrated on the grain of the wood under her fingers. Whatever other malady she was suffering, Mrs. Minks clearly did not have the gingerfoot. It had worked, all Natalie had done.

Now what?

Natalie wanted to run into her arms and throw a tan-
trum at the same time, to demand to know why her mother
hadn't told her she was sick, and to be told what was really
going on. Unable to decide which to do first, she settled on
walking to the kitchen table and sitting down while she
thought it over. The kitchen smelled of coffee, and from
the number of rings on the table, it looked like her mother
had been awake for a while. Waiting for her.

Mrs. Minks stood in the doorway, eyeing Natalie
warily. "Your dad and Charlie went out looking for you.
Are you all right?"

"I'm okay," Natalie said, and then, as lightly as she
could manage, "You?"

Her mother nodded with an expression of relief and
made a beeline for the coffeepot to refill her cup. *No*, Natalie
thought, *I didn't mean to pretend nothing's wrong. That's not
fair.* And yet she still couldn't bring herself to throw a tan-
trum. Where on earth would she start, anyway? *Maybe I could
just ask another time*, she thought briefly. Just as quickly as
she had the idea, though, she shook her head and dismissed
it. The time for that kind of behavior was over.

Some questions cost things, and for sure the can of
worms she was about to open was going to be a very costly
one. On the other hand, after all she'd been through, Natalie
decided she was done with being afraid to ask the questions
she needed to know the answers to. She took a deep breath.

"Something happened to me at the fair." It was as good
a place to begin as any. "It's happened to me a couple of
times, actually, and nobody wants to tell me what it means.

I saw—I knew—things there was no way for me to know. Everyone said to ask you . . . about it."

At the sink, Mrs. Minks paused in pouring coffee. Her shoulders did something shivery, and then she was still. She reached for another cup and poured coffee into that, and then she added a sugar cube, a slosh of cream, and a little jot of rum to each. At last, she carried both cups to the table, set one in front of Natalie, and sat down.

Natalie picked hers up in both palms, blew on the surface, and watched her mother through the steam as she took a sip.

"My grandmother called those moments the *phantasmata*," Mrs. Minks said at last. "Seeing—or at least knowing—a story there's no way you should know. That's how I know all the stories I've told you about Arcane. Someday you'll know them all, too. The phantasmata are a gift of memory. They're a way for a whole town to survive through just one person. One storyteller."

"How?" Natalie frowned. "Mama, why would one person have to know everything?"

Mrs. Minks looked out the window for a long moment. "There are some places in the world that are . . . different . . . from others. Where strange things happen. For reasons I don't even really understand, the crossroads outside of Arcane is a place of power, and thanks to that, all the towns built near it have always been in a kind of danger. Someone has to have the job of remembering the stories of the town, to keep them alive in memory, even if the town itself doesn't last."

For just a moment, Natalie felt the vertigo starting in her throat again. She swallowed it back. "Like the last time Dr. Limberleg was here?" Her mother nodded. "So, the woman who survived the last time," Natalie said slowly, "the one from Trader's Mill who married the judge in the diary . . . ?"

"Yes. She was an ancestor of ours. She couldn't save the town, but because she survived, the stories survived. Arcane almost didn't make it this time. But you saved it. If you hadn't—and if I hadn't made it through . . ." Natalie's mother shook her head and rubbed a trembling hand over her pale face. "We can talk more about it another time. Right now . . . I'm just . . . I need to sleep."

Any other time, Natalie would've pestered and insisted on hearing more about this amazing, wild claim. How could it be true? How could anyone know the stories of an entire town? Inherit the knowledge just like that, the way you inherited blue eyes or freckles?

But her mother looked so tired. Deep, purple shadows rimmed her eyes. "There will be plenty of time to explain it all later," Mrs. Minks said quietly.

"Really?" Natalie asked in a very small voice.

Her mother looked up. Something in her expression made Natalie sadder than she'd ever felt before. A moment's silence stretched between them.

If she could face the Devil, she could ask her mother a question. Even if the idea of knowing the answer was a little scary. Natalie took another deep breath and said, voice shaking, "Mama, can you please tell me how sick you are, really?"

She had to force the words out; it was as if they were stuck to the roof of her mouth and did not want to be spoken. But then the question was there, alive in the space between them, and nothing could take it back.

Her mother looked at the tabletop. "Natalie, we aren't sure what it is. That's—you have to believe me, that's the only reason we didn't tell you. Because . . . because it's"— her mother's voice caught—"because it's very scary when you know something's wrong but you don't know what it is. When you don't have a name for it."

"I'm not a baby," Natalie whispered. "I'm not afraid of things just because I don't know what they're *called*." But a nagging little part of her knew that wasn't entirely true.

Across the table, Mrs. Minks nodded. "I know you're not, sweetheart. But I am. This time. I needed to be able to explain it to you, and to do that I would have to understand it myself."

"You told Charlie."

"No, I didn't," her mother said in a rush, "I didn't; I promise. Charlie's the first one who thought I should see Doc Fitzwater."

That made Natalie's face burn. "Charlie noticed *first?*" Mortifyingly, tears began to prickle in her eyes and she stood up to turn away so her mother wouldn't see. "Charlie doesn't notice *anything!* Why didn't I—why didn't—"

Mrs. Minks came around the table, and Natalie reached blindly into her arms. As if Natalie weighed nothing, her mother lifted her and held her close. "It isn't your fault. It isn't. You couldn't have known. Charlie saw me faint, and the last time he saw me faint was when I was pregnant with you. He thought I was going to have another baby." She made a noise like a laugh and a sniffle all at once. "He was really excited, Natalie, because—because you turned out to be such a terrific kid."

Natalie hugged her mother as tightly as she could. "But, Mama, Doc Fitzwater said it might be okay, so maybe you just need to rest a little longer."

Mrs. Minks set her down and stooped beside Natalie, her face suddenly very, very serious.

"I promise I'll tell you if I find out anything different, Natalie. Okay? Can you trust me, even though I didn't tell you before?"

It wasn't the answer she wanted. Natalie rubbed the backs of her hands across her eyes until all the tears were gone. It took a long time, because as soon as she brushed some away, more kept on coming.

"Yes," she said when her eyes stopped blurring. Her mother looked at her carefully, closely, as if that one word might turn out to be a lie. "Yes, Mama," Natalie said again.

She climbed back into her chair and picked up her coffee cup. She took a long, shaky sip that emptied the mug, and held it out.

"Can I have more rum this time, please?"

For the first time in what seemed like weeks, Natalie's mother smiled. It was a real smile, at last. "Don't think for a minute this is going to be how you get your coffee from now on."

@ @ @

Two cups of coffee but very little conversation later, Natalie's mother went to bed and Natalie went to sit on the porch steps. It was too quiet in the house.

In the distance, a thin veil of smoke hung over what could only be Simon Coffrett's lot. Natalie shaded her eyes and gazed around the sunlit town so full of strange things and strange stories. It seemed as if the town she knew from her mother's stories and the town she had lived in all her life had finally fused into one Arcane: the real Arcane that had been waiting to come to life for Natalie all along.

As she sat there listening to her town stirring awake, the drifter with the pale green eyes strolled down the center of the street, carpetbag in one hand and faintly glowing lantern slung over his shoulder on its pole. He spotted her sitting on her porch and touched his knuckles to his forehead in a little salute.

The dizziness hit so abruptly, Natalie put a hand down on the porch floor to keep from reeling. In that moment, she knew why he seemed so familiar.

Remember, her mother had said, *the one where Jack's so awful even the Devil's a little scared of him and won't let him into Hell? So he has to wander the earth with a coal of hellfire looking for his own place?*

Clever Jack, the man who'd won three wishes from an angel and used them to foil the Devil so badly he wasn't allowed into Heaven or Hell, was strolling through Arcane before her eyes.

Jack was wandering in search of his place, an afterlife

of his own where he would rule. He had come to Arcane trying to recruit souls for whenever—wherever—he finally found it. *I can give you a haven*, he'd said to Limberleg. At long last, that strange, strange conversation overheard in Limberleg's wagon made perfect sense.

He stopped before the porch and reached up to adjust the wide felt hat shading his pale eyes. "Morning."

"Morning." Natalie made her mouth into the shape of a smile. "Your name's Jack, isn't it?"

His eyes narrowed for just a moment. Then he nodded and adjusted the bag in his hand again. His smile was curious. She wondered if maybe hers wasn't very convincing.

"You leaving town?" Natalie asked casually.

He looked over his shoulder, toward the crossroads he had passed through on his way to Arcane. "Just passing through. Lots of country out there."

For a moment, it was almost as if they were normal people having a normal conversation, and Natalie wondered if she was just tired and confused after all she'd seen and heard over the last few days. No one said *all* the stories her mother had told her had to be true.

Then Jack took the pole from his shoulder, opened the lantern that hung from it, and blew on whatever burned inside, making it glow a little brighter for a moment.

"It's pretty bright out today already," Natalie said, eyes on the lantern.

Jack's eyes glinted, surrounded by webs of crinkling lines in his otherwise smooth, youngish face. "Now, I think you know it ain't lit for light."

"Your name's Jack, isn't it?"

Natalie nodded. No point in lying.

"Anyhow," Jack said, "it's a nice town, this one. The kind of place a fellow could imagine making his own."

He tilted his head, and she could tell he was watching to see if she'd rise to the challenge he'd just flung in her face.

"I don't think you'd better plan on that, actually," she said at last.

His smile stretched even wider across his teeth. "Honey girl, if you know the stories, you know I don't lose."

"Yes, that's true," Natalie said thoughtfully. "But it's a funny thing about those stories, Jack. It's always you against someone mean or arrogant or just plain stupid." She smiled back at him. It was a real smile. One with confidence. "I'm not any of those things."

Jack considered her for a moment, very seriously. "I think that's the truth, all right." He raised his knuckles to his hat brim again. "See you around, kid. Maybe."

Natalie watched him until he was just a tiny fleck of motion disappearing over the horizon. Then she skipped down the steps, grabbed the handlebars of the red bicycle, and took a running start down the street.

One foot on the pedal, then the other, and the world rolled away beneath her tires. Natalie turned her face up to the sun and flew.

KATE MILFORD lives in Brooklyn, New York. She has written for stage and screen, and is a regular travel columnist at www.nagspeake.com.

This is her first book. To find out more about Kate and her work, visit www.clockworkfoundry.com.